HEALED
THROUGH
the Power *of*
LOVE

Rosanna Almonte

CLAY BRIDGES
PRESS

Healed through the Power of Love

Published by Clay Bridges in Houston, TX
www.claybridgespress.com

ISBN 978-1-953300-99-7 (paperback)
ISBN 978-1-953300-98-0 (ebook)

Special Sales: Most Clay Bridges titles are available in special quantity discounts. Custom imprinting or excerpting can also be done to fit special needs. For standard bulk orders, go to www.claybridgesbulk.com. For specialty press or large orders, contact Clay Bridges at info@ claybridgespress.com.

Table of Contents

Trust in the LORD with all your heart
and lean not on your own understanding;
in all your ways submit to him,
and he will make your paths straight.

—Prov. 3:5–6

Dedication

First and foremost, I dedicate this book to the Almighty God. I wrote it to exalt, glorify, and honor Him. As His Word says in Psalm 37:4, "Take delight in the LORD, and he will give you the desires of your heart." The Lord blessed me with the desire I've had since I was 14 years old to become a published author. I rewrote this novel numerous times as I tried to find a niche for my writing within the genres. My family dearly termed it "the never-ending book." After I accepted the Lord as my Savior and as my life molded and transformed to follow His lead, the goal and purpose of my book changed. With the Lord as my guide, I converted my book into a Christian fiction novel that highlights our struggles as Christians. Following the Lord's path, accepting His will, letting go of ties to the past, and having unshakable faith are a process. Our Lord never gives us more than we can handle and never forsakes us, yet with each challenge we choose either His path or our own. The ongoing process we experience as we live a life with Him, in Him, and through Him awakens us to His truth that what we consider impossible is possible. It is through the Lord's guidance that our heart's desire becomes reality.

I dedicate this book to you, the reader. Here are my prayers for you as you read this book:

- That you will know our Lord is real, merciful, and powerful, and that His grace is unending.
- That you will see that He is a living God who is always with you through all circumstances.
- That it is solely through Him that we can achieve peace, joy, and an abundant life.
- That you will recognize that adversities are part of a growing process the Lord uses to transform us, mold us, and give us victory.
- That you will trust in the Lord completely and allow Him to bless you with so much more than you dreamed or imagined.

- That in the worst adversities, He glorifies Himself, and you will always attain something good.
- That you will accept His plans and purpose in your life as greater than your own and will exalt, honor, and glorify Him.

May you delight in this expression of my love and adoration for my Heavenly Father with the same joy I wrote it.

Prologue

"You have to take care of yourself. Forgetting your medication, not eating, getting depressed, and hiding from your family are bad habits."

"I'm not hiding," Yasmin asserted, pressing speaker on the cordless. "Dad's demand was clear. He doesn't want to see me again—he hates me."

"That's such a strong word," Ani said in a gentle tone. "I'll continue praying so God can provide discernment."

"I need it," Yasmin admitted. Propping up the pillows on the arm of the sofa, she sat up.

"You were reborn," Ani reminded her. "You began a new life, and now you're part of His family—past sins forgotten and forgiven. You can be at peace, Yasmin, and feel secure that He is always with you and will help you in all circumstances and situations."

Yasmin nodded. She had attended church with Ani for almost a year. Each sermon stirred a growing desire for meaning and stability. The week before, she had stood with a dozen or so parishioners in front of the pastor and professed John 3:16: "For God so loved the world that he gave his one and only Son, that whoever believes in him shall not perish but have eternal life." She realized that He would become her life, priority, and focus.

Tears of happiness had trailed down Yasmin's cheeks as she sat next to Ani, the congregation clapping with exhilaration and joy that would overwhelm her for days. She felt revived and peaceful. She could sleep again, and her migraines had ceased as spontaneously as they had begun.

But as the week progressed, the anxiety resurfaced. She recalled in detail the pastor's sermon topic. His discourse was based on Proverbs 4:23, and those words were still fresh in her mind: "Above all else, guard your heart, for everything you do flows from it." He stressed that it was essential to guard your heart from resentment, grudges, and unforgiveness.

How to do that perturbed her.

She was aware that her heart was crammed with regret, dread, and remorse. Was it possible to break free from the painful experiences she tried in vain to forget? What about the secret she vowed never to reveal, the secret she pushed as deeply as she could into the depths of her heart?

"Yasmin?"

"Yes," she replied hoarsely, blinking several times to clear her vision.

"Saying what you're going to do and even planning it are useless without action."

Yasmin was silent. That week, she suppressed her qualms about her family and focused on analyzing why the pastor's words stirred up so much unease.

"For over a month," Ani continued as Yasmin remained silent, "you've mentioned recurrent dreams about your parents, a feeling that something's wrong, fears that someone in your family might be ill. Why haven't you gone to see them? What are you waiting for?"

"I . . ." Yasmin began but hesitated. Her failed attempts were nothing to boast about. She would not admit that she had been unable to follow through. She had driven past the building several times, parked, and walked slowly to the entrance. She'd stood motionless by the doors, her heart beating fiercely. Lacking the courage to enter, she had rushed back to her car each time.

"He helps us in all situations," Ani added.

Yasmin heard many testimonies from parishioners confirming that. Some were healed of all types of illnesses—even cancer. Others shared that their wives, husbands, and family members had overcome addictions, given up drinking, and stopped abusive behaviors. Their lives were transformed.

Would her testimony be similar?

"Why are you so anxious? He is your companion," Ani reassured Yasmin as if reading her thoughts.

"Yes." She knew that but still felt uneasy. She prayed for peace and tranquility.

"Don't think about it anymore," Ani urged.

"I promise."

"Go see them." Ani cut her off and then changed the subject. "What's happening tonight? Ismenia mentioned you weren't feeling well. A migraine again? That's a sign you're upset and stressed over the issue with your family."

"I'm taking the medication as indicated and *resting*." She emphasized the last word to appease Ani's concerns. "The pain is dull now."

Rushing in and out of stores with Ismenia from morning to mid-afternoon to buy an outfit and some last-minute items had caused her headache to become stronger. Ani's question reminded her that she had to refill her container. She kept the prescription bottle on the bureau since it was too large and bulky to carry in her purse.

"You're going to a club with a migraine?" Ani marveled.

"I'll be fine." Yasmin refused to disappoint Ismenia. They had spent months planning every detail of their outing for that night. Although she'd been tempted to cancel when Ismenia confided that Nestor would join them, she would keep her promise and tag along. She would disregard her ill sentiments over the possibility of another reconciliation between Ismenia and Nestor. She would have preferred to celebrate with Ismenia as they'd originally planned, just the two of them. She disliked being around Nestor.

"You'll go even if you shouldn't," Ani said. "I wish you'd take that same attitude and resolve the situation with your parents."

"I will." Yasmin tried to sound convincing but wasn't sure she had succeeded.

"You won't be alone. Remember, the Lord is always with you. Rest, and take your meds. I'll see you later."

Placing the receiver in place, Yasmin lay down. Hopefully, Ismenia and Nestor would not stay in the club until the wee hours. The next day, regardless of how she felt or how many hours she slept, she would visit her parents. She would arrive when her mother, Carmen, was walking to church. She doubted that her mother's preference to attend Mass on Sunday mornings at 10:00 had changed. She considered it best to speak to her mother first before meeting with her father.

Walking to the bedroom, Yasmin poured several pills into the small container. Placing the rest of the medication on the bureau, she gazed toward the bed. The items she had bought were still in bags. The dress she purchased wasn't her style. She never wore anything that exposed her shoulders or back. She wished she hadn't mentioned the outfit she chose for that night or allowed Ismenia to convince her to get a new one. Ismenia was blunt, insisting that wearing a black pantsuit was old-fashioned, unattractive, and too conservative. Yasmin disagreed and was still debating if she would wear the dress, the pantsuit, or another outfit.

Returning to the sofa, she lay down, hugging the pillow.

The mere thought of facing her father made Yasmin shiver involuntarily. She had shared little with Ani about what occurred that horrid day. She felt ashamed of her father's unwarranted aggression and was still unable to fathom her mother's reaction.

It was another scar she needed to mend and then let go.

Resting her head on the pillow, she recalled what had happened. The images seemed so real, and she felt like she was reliving the experience.

She surprised her mother by dropping by after work. They cried and hugged each other. Carmen kept asking if she was there to stay. Reluctant to admit her objective, Yasmin merely smiled in response, leery of her father's reaction when he arrived and saw her.

Sitting in her favorite spot at the dining room table, Yasmin grinned. It was the best seat to see everything in both the living room and the kitchen and see who entered or left the apartment. She watched with delight as her mother returned to the kitchen and moved about, humming happily while preparing a plate for her. Carmen's wavy black hair was shoulder length, but she always tied it back in a bun and rarely wore it loose except on special occasions. Her eyebrows were rounded and her coffee-brown eyes intense. With a fixed stare, Carmen could make anyone freeze and tremble inwardly. But that evening her eyes shone with glee. She was jubilant. Carmen was thrilled that Yasmin was visiting her.

Yasmin smiled, amused by her mother's attire. Carmen wore a floral print robe with short sleeves, front pockets, and snap buttons on the front. She had an assortment of similar styles that she wore daily. It reminded Yasmin of her grandmother in the Dominican Republic who not only wore robes at home but also to go shopping and about town. Her mother followed the custom at home but always dressed up when she went out.

The aroma of stewed beans, white rice, and fried chicken permeated the apartment, awakening Yasmin's appetite. Dreading the outcome of her impromptu visit, she had fasted for days. Surprisingly, she now felt at ease, thrilled to be home. She waited with anticipation to savor the tasty meal her mother had prepared. Yasmin's smile widened as she remembered arriving home from school to a warm delicious meal and then doing homework and chores.

Her appetite, serenity, and sense of belonging vanished, however, as her father unlocked the front door. Face-to-face with him, Yasmin stared, motionless. Her father had a full beard with patches of gray, and his cinnamon skin appeared much darker as if he'd recently traveled to the tropics. Roberto's mahogany eyes flared up dangerously as he slammed the door shut with such force that the floor shook.

Yasmin's mouth became dry, and her heart thundered loudly. She shrank back involuntarily, pressing her back against the chair. Her gaze fixed on him, she cringed. The sneer on his thin lips became more profound as he came near her. She jumped back, knocking the chair down as Roberto reached for her with his massive granite hands.

"Roberto!" Carmen cried out nervously, placing the plate of food on the kitchen counter along with the glass of apple juice she had in her hand. "What are you doing?" Carmen asked, stepping in front of Yasmin.

"Get out of the way," Roberto commanded menacingly and gestured with his hand for her to move aside. Carmen cowered, giving him just enough room to pass and watching as he grabbed Yasmin's arm just above the elbow.

"You are not welcome here," he growled ferociously, glaring down at Yasmin.

"No, Roberto, no, no," Carmen cried.

Yasmin sobbed quietly and allowed herself to be dragged out of the place she once called home.

"Please," Carmen begged, frantically following Roberto.

He tightened his grip on Yasmin's arm. "Don't come back!"

He opened the door and flung Yasmin out of the apartment. She caught a glimpse of her mother sobbing and heard her yell, "Stop! Stop!" Then Roberto shut the door with such force that it sounded like an explosion. Stumbling in the hallway, Yasmin crashed into a wall and fell into a sitting position on the dingy floor.

The taste of blood filled her mouth as a sharp pain shot through her temples. She gasped aloud, placed her hands on the sides of her head, and applied pressure to alleviate the pain. Crying softly, she sat and listened to the shrill voices inside the apartment. Their argument was clearly audible despite the closed door.

Remembering was painful. Tears were useless. And as much as she wanted to control herself, sobbing was inevitable whenever she recalled how vicious her father was.

Help me forget, Lord, Yasmin murmured to herself as she stumbled off the couch and headed to the kitchen. She poured herself a glass of juice and returned to the living room. Taking several sips of the juice, she curled into a corner of the sofa. Recalling how that horrid evening ended, Yasmin closed her eyes and prayed aloud, *Lord, help me calm down. Give me peace.*

Yasmin sat on the floor for a while and then stood up, gathering strength after being flung out of her parents' apartment like trash. She leaned against the wall near their door, sobbing quietly. The shouting match between her parents seemed endless. The argument ended with her father's ultimatum: "If she ever sets foot in this apartment and I find out, I'll leave. And I won't return."

His words felt as if someone had punched her in the gut. She fell limply on her knees and covered her face with both hands. When the tears subsided and she regained her composure, her first instinct was to run down the stairs and out of the building to oblivion. Instead, she stood up and knocked softly. Her purse with her money and ID was still on the sofa.

The door opened, and her mother stood there, eyes bloodshot, face contorted with regret and anguish.

"Your . . ." Carmen cleared her throat and then spoke hoarsely. ". . . father needs time. He'll forgive you . . . eventually."

Yasmin felt as if she'd been shoved into a bottomless pit. She had a horrid sensation of falling and then crashing on a surface, her life and hopes shattered.

"You never apologized and never admitted your mistake," Carmen continued hoarsely. "Roberto will calm down in a few days. Call, and speak to him. Ask for forgiveness. Then he'll allow you to visit and maybe move in later." Carmen hugged Yasmin tightly, tapped a kiss on her forehead, and handed her the purse.

Yasmin bolted out of the building as if distancing herself from the area would alleviate the desolation she felt. She was unaware of her surroundings, oblivious to traffic lights, cars approaching, or the people cluttered in front of buildings, on corners, and on the stoop. She stopped abruptly, her chest blazing with unbearable pain. Slowly, the coughing and panting for air diminished. Gazing around, she realized she was near the entrance to the train station.

She staggered into the train, tears still trickling down her cheeks, and slumped into a seat near the door. People standing and sitting near her were staring. No one asked what was wrong or why she was crying. She didn't care. If her own family rejected her and had no pity, why should anyone else?

Yasmin cleared her throat and wiped her cheeks.

It had happened a year after the dreadful incident with Manuel. And now, five years later, she still felt apprehensive and uneasy about facing her father.

"Coward!" she scolded herself. She had procrastinated enough. Ani was right. She needed to confirm if her dreams and gut feelings were a warning or a premonition.

Chapter 1

Orlando glanced from one side of the block to the other. The funeral parlor was in a commercial area in Washington Heights. A variety of businesses were lined up on both sides of the street. From where he stood, he could see a children's store and a pharmacy, and past that was a bodega with large bins of tropical fruits and vegetables stacked on a downward slope. Across the street were a Spanish restaurant, another bodega, a liquor store, and a barber shop where a merengue was playing full blast.

The intense humidity was no deterrent for being outside. The streets were piled with people clustered together in small groups, shopping, walking, and playing dominoes. He could hear the laughter of the players as they slammed the tiles loudly on the wooden table and their dissonant voices as they sang the verses of the merengue.

Orlando glanced at his watch. It was three hours before the wake would end. He was optimistic and believed Yasmin would find out that Roberto had passed away and would join the family to pay her last respects.

Yasmin's absence and silence distressed Carmen. She had shared her fear with Orlando that Yasmin might not attend the wake or the burial, and she was also worried that something may have happened to her. Orlando disagreed and assured her that Yasmin would attend. He had no tangible reason to say that. He couldn't understand the rationale or certainty of his gut feeling, much less explain it. He anticipated Yasmin's arrival and was looking forward to seeing her.

He heard boisterous laughter and whistling and then turned to see what the racket was about. He saw four men standing in front of the restaurant, and a young woman was rushing past them. She stopped at the corner to wait for the light.

Orlando studied the slender woman as she approached. She looked elegant in a black lace dress that outlined her hourglass figure. The short length exposed her shapely legs. Silver-strapped sandals matched the clutch that hung from her shoulders. Her brown curls bounced lightly over her bare back and arms as she moved forward.

Aware he was staring, she refused to acknowledge him and walked past him as if he didn't exist, her gaze straight ahead.

"Yasmin," he called, certain it was her.

Stopping, she looked at him and studied him from the corners of her eyes. Then she recognized him. Orlando was her brother's closest friend and ally in mischief. Tall, well built, with light skin, he was dressed all in black—a blazer jacket, with a crew neck T-shirt, jeans, and shoes. The look was casual but presentable.

Strolling over to him reluctantly, Yasmin tilted her head slightly and faced him. His chestnut-brown eyes shone with approval, and his broad smile expressed delight, which surprised her as did his change in appearance. His jet-black hair was slightly longer on top and combed back. The fade haircut and goatee made his face look thinner and accented his square jawline.

"Orlando?" she said his name in greeting. Her cheeks turned red, and he was aware that she had scrutinized his features.

He nodded, his smile turning to a grin. Her grief didn't diminish her beauty. She wore a hint of makeup and plum lipstick that made her tanned skin look a shade darker. Physically, she looked the same, although much thinner. He guessed she was two sizes smaller than when he'd last seen her. He wondered if she had a health condition. Was that the reason she'd stayed away? Or was there another cause? "I'm sorry about your father," he uttered, the words sounding empty and inappropriate.

Yasmin had promised herself she would remain in control of her emotions, but she burst into tears. Covering her face with her hands, she wept quietly. Her father had been ill for more than a month, but her family had made no attempt to contact her.

Orlando embraced her. She rested her head on his chest. He wanted to alleviate her grief and comfort her and tried to think of something meaningful to say. Nothing occurred to him that would sound genuine, so he decided against it. Patting her back gently, he waited for her to calm down.

Yasmin stepped back. Her head lowered, she patted her face dry with a tissue. Glancing toward the funeral parlor, she wasn't sure what angered her most—breaking her promise not to cry or willingly nestling in Orlando's arms.

She distanced herself. The scent of his cologne lingered. Dismissing her angst, she focused on the stark reason that had brought her there. "Why didn't Raul or Isabel notify me?"

Her question puzzled Orlando. When Roberto's condition deteriorated, Carmen had demanded that Raul contact her. Orlando had accompanied Raul to the only address they had for her. But the people who lived there had no idea who Yasmin was or who had resided in the apartment before they moved in. It was ridiculous for Yasmin to assume her family could contact her when they didn't know where she was.

"Without your current address or phone number?" Orlando asked.

"You're well versed," Yasmin complained sourly, crossing her arms. "You're Raul's close friend."

Her sarcastic tone and the scowl amused Orlando. "I don't see how one thing relates to the other."

"Who lied and said I knew Dad was sick, that he passed away, and that I didn't care?"

Orlando understood why she was outraged and cross. He was convinced she had met with Maria or Luisa. They were the only ones foolish enough to generate and repeat that false comment.

"That's how you're dressed to come to Dad's wake?" a familiar voice asked.

Orlando and Yasmin turned simultaneously to see Raul. As he walked toward them, Orlando scanned Yasmin from head to toe. Her attire, although inappropriate for a wake, was not offensive or vulgar. It was evident that she was going out that night and had just been informed of her father's death.

For a moment, Yasmin froze. Raul looked like a younger version of their father—dark skin, brown curly hair, shaved beard. His mahogany eyes flared dangerously. His thin lips curled down, the acrid grimace identical to their father's.

"I rushed over," she began, her voice trembling.

"Not interested in your excuses," Raul interrupted, stopping directly in front of her. "You wasted your time coming here."

Yasmin shook her head. "I won't leave until I see Dad."

"Dad?" Raul repeated. "The word sounds dirty coming from your mouth. Go to your party. Celebrate that he's gone."

"No," she replied defiantly.

"Let her go inside for a few minutes," Orlando urged, although he knew it was useless to attempt to persuade Raul. Aware a crowd was forming around them and that people walking by were stopping to see what was happening, Orlando just wanted to end the spectacle.

"How long have you been away?" Raul pretended he hadn't heard Orlando's comment and ignored the crowd that surrounded them. "Five years? Did you care about how we were? Did you know if Ma was all right?" He gestured for her to stay quiet by lifting his hand and holding his palm inches from her face. "Keep pretending we don't exist."

"I'll leave after I see him," Yasmin insisted.

Raul grabbed her arm and flung her aside like a rag doll. Skipping several steps, Orlando caught her as she stumbled backward and helped her regain her balance. He whispered emphatically, "Stop provoking him."

Yasmin tapped Orlando's hand so he would release her and then gazed at him, eyes lit with anger. Regardless of what Raul said or did, she was determined to go inside the funeral parlor.

The resolve Orlando read in her mannerism outraged him. It was apparent that Yasmin had forgotten Raul's volatile temper. Confronting Raul was the equivalent of striking a match and throwing it on gas.

Orlando stood strategically in front of Yasmin and faced Raul. From his peripheral vision, he saw Yasmin move forward but gestured with his hand for her to stay behind him. She shook her head but stayed where he directed. Orlando was convinced that if Raul tried to strike Yasmin, he could prevent it. "Violence won't solve anything," Orlando persuaded. "Let Yasmin see Roberto. Then she can leave."

"No," Raul said, glaring at Yasmin. "You don't deserve to see him. I'm going to make sure you don't."

"I'm not leaving," Yasmin emphasized each word as she attempted to move forward. Turning, Orlando whispered, "Stop instigating him," and gestured with his arm for her to stay where she was.

"Move, Orlando." Raul stepped forward menacingly.

Orlando purposely stood in front of Yasmin. Gazing over his shoulder, he noticed her apprehension and was glad she had listened and stayed where he requested.

Raul lifted his chin and gazed down at Orlando as if they were opponents in a boxing ring. "I'm going to make sure she leaves."

"You know Carmen would disapprove," Orlando reminded him.

For a moment, Raul's expression softened, but then he shook his head. "She's not going to see him."

"Raul," a female voice shouted from behind the crowd.

Orlando saw Josefa walk through the cluster of people. Raul turned around to face her. "What?" he demanded in a loud, harsh tone.

Taking advantage of the distraction, Yasmin stood next to Orlando and studied the woman who had joined them. Yasmin guessed the woman was in her 30s. She was dressed in a black, sleeveless dress that fit like a glove over her pear-shaped body. She wore no makeup, and her long, ink-black hair was combed neatly and tied into a ponytail. She looked as if she had been crying for a long time. There were red blotches over her cheeks, and her eyes were swollen and puffy. Yasmin wondered who she was. Was she one of her father's distant relatives? A close friend? A colleague?

Yasmin glanced at Orlando who appeared relaxed and calm as if the confrontation between him and Raul had not occurred. In contrast, Raul was livid.

"Are you related to us?" Yasmin asked the woman.

"If you'd been around, you'd know," Raul commented sourly.

"Josefa Arias." She embraced Yasmin affectionately. "I've heard so much about you."

Yasmin lowered her head. What did Josefa know? What had she been told about the situation that caused her to leave home?

Orlando noticed the hue on Yasmin's cheeks and her nervous smile. Her reaction piqued his curiosity. What was she embarrassed about?

"I'm glad you're here." Josefa hugged her again and glanced at Raul. "The manager has the itemized bill you wanted, Raul. He's waiting for you in the office."

"I'll speak to him when I'm ready."

"Your decision, Raul," Josefa replied, unaffected by his curt tone. Turning to Yasmin, she said, "I wanted you to see your father before . . ." she took a deep breath, ". . . the burial."

"Why?" Raul asked her.

12

"Yasmin is part of the family, Raul."

"No, she isn't," he corrected. "She's not welcome here or at home."

"In the funeral parlor, I decide," Josefa pointed out. "I'll escort her inside."

Raul gave Josefa a long, hard look and then gazed at Yasmin. "I don't want to see you here when I return." Without waiting for a reply from either, he spoke to Orlando. "I need something strong to calm down. Joining me?"

Orlando had been waiting for Raul to go to a nearby restaurant where they planned to have something to eat and a few beers. Yasmin's arrival had altered his plans. Concerned that Isabel might mirror the scenario with Raul, he decided to stay. "I'll meet you there."

"Make sure she leaves, or I'll escort her out myself," Raul warned and then ran across the street.

* * *

Yasmin muttered a silent prayer. *I need You with me. I need Your strength.* She was grateful that Josefa had rescued her from Raul's wrath.

Arias was Josefa's last name. Was it possible that she was Raul's wife? If they were married, the way he'd treated her was unacceptable. His tone and attitude were belittling. Why would Josefa tolerate such blatant disrespect?

What was she thinking? Yasmin rebuked herself. Whatever happened between Raul and Josefa shouldn't concern her. She was glad Josefa had intervened. Otherwise she would still be arguing with Raul or leaving.

Her thoughts scattered when Josefa stopped walking. Lifting her gaze, she surveyed the room. Every seat was occupied. From where they stood, she saw the open casket. Her eyes swelled with tears. She still couldn't believe her father was dead. They would never see or speak to one another again. She had wasted a lot of time by fearing what would happen if she visited. She could have seen him alive and perhaps asked his forgiveness and reconciled their differences.

Tears trickled down her cheeks as Josefa led her forward. An active drum roll boomed in her ears. Sweat beads formed on her forehead, her mouth became dry, and her lungs felt empty and devoid of air. She inhaled through her nose and exhaled slowly through her mouth.

"It's all right," Josefa whispered.

Yasmin realized she was clinging desperately to Josefa's hand as they reached the casket and only hesitantly let go. She had no recollection when she had grabbed hold of it. She stood frozen in place. Josefa squeezed her hand, reassuring her. Lifting her gaze, Yasmin blinked several times to clear her vision and then saw the casket a few paces away.

Where was her mother? Why hadn't she rushed to embrace her and console her? Lethargically, she glanced back. She didn't recognize the older couple who sat on the sofa in front of the casket or any of the other faces in the seats on the first row. Why wasn't her mother there? Where was Isabel? Horrid scenarios overwhelmed her.

Yasmin felt Josefa grasp her shoulders firmly and lead her forward. She knew she was standing in front of the casket when they stopped. She kept her eyes shut tightly as she lowered her head. *Give me strength*, she prayed. Roberto appeared to be sleeping. The vicious expression Yasmin was accustomed to had become mellow. He seemed calm, at peace.

Her hands trembled as she caressed his face. She expected him to sit up, recognize her, and demand that she leave immediately.

"What happened wasn't my fault," Yasmin muttered inaudibly. Her hopes of reconciliation would be buried with him. He would never know the truth.

Resting her head on her father's hard chest, Yasmin sobbed. She felt someone take hold of her shoulders and gently pull her away from the casket. Covering her face with both hands, Yasmin rested her head on the offered shoulder, grateful that someone had noted her pain and offered empathy.

The barrel chest and masculine scent roused her from her stupor. Lifting her head, she looked up and saw Orlando's face through a mist.

"Why did you bring her here?" Yasmin turned toward the familiar voice. "Isabel?" Yasmin gasped. The black dress draped loosely over her sister's body. Her curvy shape had dwindled to bones. Her blonde hair was combed back into a bun, and her face was ashen. Dark circles accented her red, swollen eyes. Isabel looked ravaged. Yasmin's initial instinct was to embrace her and share her pain, grief, and loss. But she hesitated.

Isabel was glaring at Yasmin with antipathy. "You brought Yasmin?" she said to Orlando. "Escort her out." Her scorn echoed Raul's.

"I came alone," Yasmin corrected, wondering where Josefa had gone and when Orlando had taken her place.

CHAPTER 1

* * *

Orlando blocked Yasmin's path, determined to restrain her if necessary. After literally carrying her out of the funeral parlor and forcing her to walk beside him, he would not allow her to return to the wake.

Yasmin looked up at him, her coffee-brown eyes spurting fire. "First Raul and now you?" she yelled.

"I was trying to persuade him to let you in," Orlando responded.

A smirk formed on her lips. "Did Raul listen to you?"

The cause of her amusement was unclear to him. Instead of lashing out, she should have been grateful that he'd gotten her out of the immediate vicinity.

"A routine for you and your family," he noted.

She stared at him with such enmity that he burst into laughter. "The glare—another family trait."

Crossing her arms, Yasmin turned away and stood with her back to him. Hadn't he seen what happened? She had reacted swiftly and struck Isabel in the face before Isabel could hit her. Instantly, Orlando had stepped in front of her as a group of women surrounded Isabel. As Orlando carried Yasmin out, Isabel shouted profanities.

"You struck first," Orlando pointed out, admiring her graceful figure—the dainty waist, curved hips, and well-formed legs. He liked the way her curls caressed her lightly tanned skin as she moved about restlessly.

Yasmin turned around. "Should I have stood there?"

Orlando frowned. It seemed she'd forgotten how Raul reacted before Josefa intervened. Envisioning what Raul would have done if he had arrived when Yasmin struck Isabel, he grimaced. "Raul won't care about that."

The concerned expression surprised Yasmin as did his insistence on protecting her. "Why do you care?" she asked.

"Just trying to help," Orlando said, peeved by her sarcasm.

"Raul's closest friend," Yasmin complained with disgust, "the one he shares all his secrets with—is that someone worthy of my trust?"

"Trusting me is irrelevant," Orlando shrugged. "You saw your father."

"For five minutes or less?" Yasmin spat out.

"Eight, maybe ten."

Yasmin sighed aloud with resignation. "Who is Josefa?"

"Your stepmother. The widow."

15

"My what?" Yasmin cried out.

"Wife of your father. The deceased," Orlando clarified.

"No." She shook her head and stared at him, wide-eyed. Was it possible that all the time she had stayed away to avoid causing a separation between her parents had been in vain?

"Mami and Dad got divorced? Why? When?"

Orlando realized her questions weren't directed at him. She was speaking her thoughts aloud, expressing her disbelief. "Ask Carmen when you see her," he said.

"Why wasn't Mami at the wake? Is she sick?"

"Speak to Carmen." He decided not to mention Carmen's health. He feared Yasmin would rush to the apartment to see her. He dreaded what might ensue if Raul and Isabel arrived while she was there.

"Mami is not the widow?" Yasmin asked, still dazed by the news. Nothing made sense. Her father was dead, and her mother wasn't at the wake. Raul refused to allow her into the funeral parlor. Isabel wanted to physically assault her in front of all the guests just paces from where their father's corpse lay.

It was bizarre—incomprehensible. Without meaning to, she burst into tears.

Orlando embraced her. Nestling her head on his chest, Yasmin sobbed inaudibly. He placed his hands gingerly on her back and held her, careful not to press her body against his.

"Sorry," she said, her voice barely audible.

"Apology unnecessary," Orlando reassured her. He noted that Yasmin moved back, creating physical distance from him. Despite her distrust, he was there to help, to comfort her in any way possible.

"Josefa didn't want Mami there?" Yasmin asked, after clearing her throat.

"Carmen will explain. Remember, I'm the friend you can't trust." Orlando humored dryly.

"I'm sure you know all the gory details," Yasmin said.

A smirk formed on Orlando's lips. He was aware of the particulars. Gory was a matter of perspective.

"Raul and Isabel have no right to stop me from seeing Dad." Her shoulders slumped. She lowered her head and wiped her tears with the tips of her fingers.

Orlando wanted to stress that he agreed with her but reconsidered. She would doubt his sincerity and accuse him of lying. She would refuse to believe that he had gotten into many disputes with Raul for voicing his opposition and defending her. He agreed on one thing, though. She should have maintained contact with the family—at least with Carmen.

"What did you imagine would happen?" he asked. Was she so naïve that she expected to return without consequences?

She stared at him in silence. What difference did it make? Raul and Isabel were following her father's example—rejecting her.

"I'd like a response," he insisted.

"What I expected has nothing to do with Raul's and Isabel's reactions. Why ask? Do you agree with them that I didn't deserve to see my father?"

Orlando decided their conversation was over. His priority was dropping off the drinks his mother had asked him to contribute to his sister's anniversary. He also needed to get some rest. Since Roberto's hospitalization and death, he had been consumed with running errands with Raul, supervising the mechanic shop, and trying unsuccessfully to spend time with his mother before she traveled back to the Dominican Republic, which he suspected would be sooner than he preferred.

"Is your opinion different?" Yasmin reproached as he strolled away.

Orlando measured his pace, though he hoped she had enough sense to stay away from the funeral parlor. He suspected she would follow her instincts and go back. Despite her ungrateful attitude, he was prepared to restrain her if she attempted to go past him.

"Orlando."

Although tempted to stop, he continued walking.

"Orlando," she called again. "Please stop."

Reluctantly, he halted. It was rude—uncomfortable—to walk away, but he refused to waste more time discussing a situation he couldn't control.

Yasmin ran to him and looked up apologetically.

The guilt Orlando felt surprised him. She had rejected his help and insulted him, and now he felt remorse? Orlando smiled. It had been a long day, and he needed to rest. That would clear both his mind and his emotions.

"It's been a rough night," she admitted in a defeated tone, "and it's not finished yet."

"Still planning to go to the celebration?" Orlando asked.

"Oh God!" Yasmin exclaimed. Ismenia and Nestor had to be frantic. She'd rushed to the funeral parlor without contacting them. She hoped they had left without her, but she needed to make sure. "I need to contact Ismenia." Yasmin glanced around, looking for a phone booth. "No public phones," she said.

"You don't have a cell phone?" Orlando asked incredulously.

Yasmin shook her head. That was another thing Ani had encouraged her to do.

Laughing, Orlando handed Yasmin his cell phone. He watched her tap on the numbers. What was she going to celebrate? Why was she alone?

Yasmin walked back and forth impatiently as she waited for someone to answer.

"It's me, Ani," Orlando overheard her say. She strolled away as she spoke and stood with her back toward him.

"I was worried," Ani said with concern.

"I'm fine," Yasmin replied, regretting not contacting her before.

"They just left. Ismenia wanted to cancel. Nestor insisted. They were arguing as they went downstairs. I prayed they would calm down so she could enjoy her birthday."

Yasmin glanced at her watch. The club wasn't far from Ani's. When she arrived, they would either be inside or in front of the line. "I'll meet them there," she told Ani.

"Ismenia said you had the address."

"I do." She returned the cell phone to Orlando. "Thanks."

"You can make another call," Orlando urged, aware that Yasmin mentioned Ismenia but had spoken to Ani instead. "Need a ride?" he asked, as she turned to walk away.

She shook her head. "My car is parked in the next block. When is the burial?"

"Mind if I walk with you? I'll tell you the itinerary for tomorrow."

She smiled in response. He walked beside her.

* * *

"Are you staying?" Nestor asked, pointing to the entrance of the club. "A friend of mine is holding our place in line. He's not going to stand there all night. Make up your mind. I'll pay, and we can go into the club."

"I'll speak to Yasmin. Wait by the entrance," Ismenia urged.

"No," Nestor replied.

Ismenia gestured with her hand for Nestor to leave. He grumbled aloud and ambled slowly toward the club.

Yasmin questioned her reasoning. Her initial instinct was to go home. Ignoring it, she hastened to the club to apologize, inform them why she was late, and leave.

"Let's go inside and start celebrating," Ismenia declared, reaching for Yasmin's hand.

Envisioning the crowd, laughter, shrill voices, music, and couples dancing, Yasmin shook her head. She longed for solitude and silence. Sharing her misery served no purpose other than ruining Ismenia's birthday. Ismenia and Nestor could enjoy the night without her.

Ismenia gestured for Yasmin to follow her. "Why are you standing there with that depressed look?"

"I . . . can't stay," Yasmin said.

"You arrive two hours late just to say that?" Ismenia was furious.

"Ani told me you'd left already," Yasmin replied. Ironically, the one thing she wanted to avoid—to cause Ismenia grief on her birthday—was what she had done. "I didn't want you to spend the night waiting for me."

"Do what you want." Ismenia stormed past Nestor into the club.

Her eyes misty, Yasmin walked to the corner. Regret and feelings of guilt were useless. At least Ismenia knew she was not staying. Although initially she was upset over Nestor's joining them, the Lord ensured that Ismenia had someone else to celebrate with.

Stopping for the light, Yasmin sighed aloud.

"Miss, are you all right?"

Yasmin wiped the tears from her cheeks and turned to see who was speaking to her.

"You're Raul's sister." He seemed delighted with himself for recognizing her. "What happened?"

"Nothing," Yasmin replied, deducing he was one of Raul's many acquaintances. It was the only way he could associate her with her older brother. She tried to recall where they'd met. He was tall and had black hair and bronze skin. His light green eyes shone as brightly as his white teeth.

"Why are you upset?" he asked.

She remained silent and recalled that Raul introduced his friends all the time. It was his way to ensure they recognized them as his sisters.

Once they knew who they were, courting them was a mistake. It was also cause for a beating, with an added perk—they instantly became enemies.

"Raul in the club?"

She shook her head.

"I'm Angel." He extended his hand, introducing himself.

She nodded and kept her arms at her sides. Eager to be rid of him, she hastened her pace. He kept up with her. She noticed how he ogled her, his gaze absorbing every aspect of her attire and physique.

"Stay. We're celebrating Papo's birthday," he said.

His impertinence offended her. It was the way he stressed the name as if just hearing it would prompt her to accept his invitation. The camaraderie he used was unfounded. She had no idea who he was and intended to keep it that way.

"I'll pay your way and reserve a table. All drinks are on me."

Gritting her teeth, Yasmin stopped abruptly, unwilling to walk any farther alongside him. Wasn't her silence hint enough? She wanted him to leave her alone, and he was acting as if she would accept his invitation.

"I meant no disrespect." Angel apologized when he noticed the grim expression on her face.

Yasmin glanced back. Nestor was running toward her. She heard him yell her name several times. She sucked her teeth aloud as he approached her.

Angel waited beside her as if they were together. For the moment she dismissed that.

"Why didn't you stay where you were?" Nestor demanded. "You show up late to say you're not staying? Smart."

"You ran over here to tell me that?" she scoffed, refraining from voicing aloud that she had wanted to cancel after finding out he was joining them.

Angel tapped Nestor on the shoulder. "You interrupted our conversation."

Nestor lifted his chin and looked directly at him. "And what are you going to do about it?"

Unimpressed by Nestor's bravado, Yasmin walked away.

Chapter 2

Orlando slept soundly for several hours before waking abruptly. When he gazed at the clock, he got up, took a quick shower, donned the suit he chose to wear to the burial, and rushed out of the apartment. Mass was at 8:00 a.m., and afterward they would head to the cemetery.

It was drizzling when Orlando stepped outside the building, but it began to pour as he got in his car. After several attempts to start the car, Orlando leaned back against the driver's seat and watched the water splatter on the windshield. He'd planned to take the car to Raul's shop but got caught up helping Raul plan Roberto's wake and funeral and overlooked it.

Taking the umbrella from under the driver's seat, he walked to the corner and hailed a cab. He gazed out the window of the taxi as it sped down the street.

It was dreary weather to attend a burial. Orlando was exhausted. He'd been going to bed late, sleeping only a few hours, and then getting up early. He needed to rest before returning to work the next day, which might prove challenging. After going to the cemetery, he might be able to lie down for a while before heading to Clara's anniversary party. That seemed unlikely, though, given the weather and the long drive to the cemetery and back.

As his mother requested, he'd dropped off the beverages he'd purchased the night before. He left shortly after arriving and was glad Clara wasn't there. He wanted to avoid another quarrel. Clara was argumentative and constantly meddled in his affairs.

It was true that opposites attract. Clara's husband, Mario, was a thin, quiet man. Nothing swayed him one way or another. He kept his comments and opinions to himself, something Orlando appreciated, more so when Roberto's illness and passing revived the gossip about Yasmin's estrangement. Maria, Luisa, and even Isabel took unwarranted delight in soiling Yasmin's reputation more than it already was.

It was spiteful. None of them had any idea what happened, yet all of them spoke with absolute authority. Orlando was convinced that Yasmin was unaware Roberto was sick. She had not purposely stayed away and wasn't being vindictive, coldhearted, or indifferent as rumored. Her grief and pain were genuine, not that Raul or Isabel cared about that. The unnecessary scenes they provoked were hideous, and neither considered the misery it would cause Carmen.

As he'd anticipated, Yasmin attended the wake, and Carmen's prayers were answered. It was the work of the Lord. Josefa had shown up at the precise moment and intervened, and Yasmin was able to pay her last respects to her father. Orlando wished it hadn't been so brief and that Isabel and Raul could have been civil. Regardless of past events, Yasmin didn't deserve to be treated with such contempt.

He was convinced a lecture from Raul was forthcoming. Regardless of how Raul felt, Orlando had provided Yasmin with the itinerary for the burial, agreeing with Carmen that grieving required unity. Family problems could be addressed after the rituals ended. Both Raul and Isabel seemed oblivious to that. There was another critical issue they both ignored, or at least it appeared that way to him. That issue was Carmen's health.

Getting out of the taxi, Orlando saw Raul standing in front of the entrance to the church. The rain had dwindled to a drizzle. Looking up, he noted the dark clouds. His hopes of getting home early were unlikely, and the trip to the cemetery would be prolonged by the weather. He decided not to worry. If the burial didn't interfere with his plans for the evening, it didn't matter. Resting could be postponed.

He skipped several steps to join Raul.

"What's wrong with your cell? I called you several times last night and this morning."

"Uncharged." Orlando had put it on mute after the incident with Isabel and had forgotten to change it.

"Okay." Raul was skeptical. "When can we talk?"

"Anytime." Orlando anticipated having that conversation the night before when he returned to the funeral parlor after Yasmin left. Josefa was waiting for a taxi with her family and told him Raul had just driven away with Isabel.

"Where did you take Yasmin?" Raul asked.

"To her car," Orlando replied.

"Whatever she's doing must be profitable," Raul bantered with animosity.

"She's your sister," he reminded Raul, annoyed by the double meaning in his words.

"Finish your degree. Become an attorney," Raul mocked.

"I might," Orlando responded. His mother and Clara reverberated the same advice. He had completed his bachelor's degree and was enjoying his position as a paralegal. Researching cases, interviewing witnesses, gathering sufficient data to substantiate the innocence of their clients, and doing clerical work were challenging and time-consuming. Some cases required long hours and days of preparation before they went to trial, which forced him to work overtime and weekends when necessary. He reconsidered his goal of going to law school but had postponed it for the time being.

"You're defending the wrong client," Raul humored, smirking.

"Her case was never on trial," Orlando pointed out.

Raul taunted him by pretending they were discussing an authentic case. Orlando considered it as such and felt as if he were researching and compiling data to come up with sufficient evidence. Thus far, he had deduced from his analysis that significant details were missing to conduct a trial, much less provide a verdict. Most of the comments, descriptions, and explanations were misleading and based on rumors or supposition. The two significant witnesses and participants in the case, Yasmin and Manuel, never provided an account of what occurred. Roberto's testimony wasn't valid since his derogatory comments were based on emotion and lacked pertinent details and facts.

"Yasmin is guilty," Raul assured.

Orlando smiled. Since the incident, Raul's reaction and attitude had matched Roberto's. Neither was interested in justice or the truth.

"You came in a taxi? Where's your car?" Raul asked.

"Wouldn't start."

"Should I call one of the guys at the shop? Have them pick it up?"

Orlando handed him the keys. "It's parked in front of the building."

"If you don't mind snuggling with your ex, Maria, you can ride in my car."

Orlando regretted the meaningless interlude. Raul enjoyed teasing him, but Orlando ignored him. "I'm going with Mario. You're not going in the limousine with Josefa?"

"He is," Carmen said before Raul replied. Both turned simultaneously to face her. She was standing there wearing a white skirt suit with matching high heels and purse, holding one of the church's double doors ajar. Orlando noted that, like Yasmin, Carmen wore her curly hair loose and barely wore makeup. She had just a touch of pink lipstick and a dab of rouge on her cheeks. Mother and daughter preferred a natural, elegant look.

Orlando greeted Carmen with a hug. The sad expression and dispirited mood reminded him of Yasmin.

Carmen tapped a kiss on Orlando's cheek. "Both of you should wear suits more often. You look like honest, responsible men."

"We are," Raul boasted proudly, patting Orlando on the shoulder.

"Is that why none of the women you've been with take you seriously?" Carmen challenged.

Raul chuckled. "Not interested in being serious. Neither is Orlando." Orlando nodded.

"I spoke to Luisa last night," Carmen said. "She gave Yasmin the address of the funeral parlor. Did she go?"

Raul's mahogany eyes flared up as he exchanged glances with Orlando.

"You remind me of your father with that look, Raul," Carmen objected as she gazed from him to Orlando.

"Everything makes you suspicious, Ma."

"Instead of answering my question, you're looking at each other," she said, studying their features. "Did Yasmin go? You didn't answer."

Orlando allowed Raul to respond. It was obvious Raul and Isabel had decided not to mention it, a mistake they would regret.

"No," Raul replied. "Let's go in. Mass will begin soon."

Carmen shook her head, a distressed expression clouding her gaze. "Something must have happened to her."

"You're worried, and she's enjoying herself," Raul griped.

Orlando stood next to Raul and then turned away, allowing them to speak directly to one another. Raul spoke about Yasmin with conviction and confirmed it as if possessing ample proof. Her absence was like a blank sheet filled with question marks. No one knew what she had been doing, but that didn't stop Raul from creating innuendos and making false accusations.

"You saw her? Spoke to her? Heard something?" Carmen asked, staring at Raul as if he knew something but refused to tell her.

"Yasmin made her decision, Ma. She chose not to return."

"Who returned?" Luisa inquired, joining them. "Yasmin?"

"Why do you have the bad habit of getting into other people's conversations?" Raul asked, turning to her.

"Respect me," Luisa reproached.

"Apologize, Raul," Carmen scolded.

"Luisa knows I dislike *bochinche*."

"I don't gossip," Luisa corrected in a defensive tone. "It's all right." She placed her hand on Carmen's shoulders. "I ignore Raul's comments."

"Stop talking about what happens in our family," Raul warned Luisa.

"Stop being disrespectful and rude," Carmen reprimanded him.

Orlando withheld a smile. Although close friends, they were opposites. When he disliked someone or something, he was tactful about what he said. Raul blurted out any response without qualms.

"The Mass is going to start," Isabel called from the doorway.

Orlando followed them inside and stopped when he noticed a narrow doorway on the right side of the swinging doors. He had attended a wedding for a colleague there and recalled family and guests taking pictures from the balcony.

* * *

Yasmin gazed at her mother. Carmen was sitting next to Isabel on the front pew. How would she react if she saw her? Run to her? Embrace her? Then what? Would she denounce her, accuse her of not being there throughout her father's illness?

"Yasmin," said a male voice.

She looked toward the doorway and saw Orlando. She looked anxiously over his shoulder and then met his gaze.

"Best hiding place." He had anticipated finding her there.

"If it occurred to you . . ."

"Few people notice this church has a balcony," Orlando explained.

"Quiet." An elderly woman sitting two pews ahead of her gestured for them to be silent.

"Come," he whispered, taking her by the hand.

Yasmin followed him without hesitation. It felt strange to walk beside him with their hands woven warmly together. Orlando descended several steps and turned around. She stood facing him in the narrow passageway, her hand still in his. The scent of his cologne inundated the area. It was masculine but not overpowering. It suited his attire. He looked distinguished in his black suit, white shirt, and matching striped tie. He was very handsome, a realization that stunned and surprised her. Since her relationship with Manuel, she hadn't met anyone she considered attractive.

She lifted her gaze, and their eyes met. The amusement in his chestnut-brown eyes and his broad grin made her realize she was staring at him.

Her cheeks bright red, Yasmin slipped her hand out of his. Lowering her gaze, she focused on the buttons of his jacket.

He placed his hand under her chin and lifted her face gently with the tips of his fingers. "That's better," he said when they were face-to-face.

"Did you see me from downstairs?" She avoided his eyes.

"Relax. It was just a guess."

"Did you tell anyone?" she asked, stunned that he'd figured out where she was.

"I wouldn't do that," he replied. "The chaos yesterday was enough."

Yasmin disagreed. She was convinced Raul and Isabel would delight in causing her more grief and wouldn't hesitate to embarrass and humiliate her in front of her mother and everyone there.

"How do you feel?" he asked. Her face was pale and her eyes puffy. She looked tired, even ill.

"Mami is downstairs. She thinks I'm not here."

"Join her," he encouraged, doubting she would follow his suggestion.

"No." Leaning her head against the wall, Yasmin closed her eyes tightly. Her efforts to stop the tears failed.

"Carmen asked about you. She expected you to be here."

"I'm not going downstairs," she admitted hoarsely, refusing to take the handkerchief Orlando was handing her. She took out a stack of tissues from her purse and dabbed one at the corner of her eyes.

"Forget about Raul and Isabel," Orlando stressed, putting the handkerchief in the inside pocket of his jacket.

"No." Yasmin shook her head, unwilling to cause her mother more grief.

A female voice echoed throughout the church. The first reading had begun.

"We're missing the Mass," Yasmin said, turning to go up the stairs. She felt his fingers brush hers gently as he took her hand in his again. He skipped several steps and stood next to her. She tilted her head up to look at him.

"Planning to go to the cemetery?" he asked.

Yasmin felt his breath on her face as she nodded, aware that their lips were inches apart. She pressed her body against the wall to avoid physical contact.

"Give me directions." She tried to focus on the conversation and ignore the anxiety she felt being physically close to him. "Or let me follow," she paused to breathe, "you."

"My car didn't start this morning." Orlando moved down two steps. He wanted her to focus on what he was saying, not on his proximity. "I took a cab. If I don't go with you, I'm riding with my brother-in-law, Mario."

She pretended not to notice that he perceived her anxiety. "I can follow another car."

"What if you fall behind or get lost?" Orlando's tone indicated that she should know better than to even consider that.

The first reading ended. The second began. Glancing toward the pews, Yasmin frowned. She was there to listen to the Mass, not dispute how to get to the cemetery. "Fine," she conceded, acknowledging that it was more prudent to go with someone who knew the directions.

* * *

"It's strange that Yasmin didn't go to the funeral parlor. Luisa gave her the address," Carmen commented with concern.

Orlando pretended not to hear her.

Raul, Isabel, Clara, Mario, and Eva were still gathered around the grave. They seemed immersed in their conversation with no indication they were ready to leave. Orlando wanted to join Yasmin before it started pouring again.

"Yasmin would have gone to the wake."

27

"I'm sorry, Carmen, what did you say?" Facing her, Orlando spoke as if he had no clue what she was talking about. He disguised his discomfort behind a serene expression, although lying disturbed him. He wanted to confide that Yasmin was a short distance away. Involuntarily, he was part of Raul's and Isabel's deceit while also following Yasmin's mandate not to mention that she was there.

"After Luisa told Yasmin, she would have gone to the wake," Carmen insisted.

Orlando nodded. Carmen's perception of Yasmin's reaction was correct. She had an incredible sixth sense. It amazed him how she discerned whenever something was amiss.

"I'm sorry you're going through so much grief," he voiced his regret.

Carmen managed to smile despite the tears that filled her eyes. She patted him on the arm. "I apologize. You must be tired of hearing my complaints."

"I'm thankful that you trust me," he smiled. Carmen confided in Orlando, speaking freely about her concerns and worries. It was an added perk for being considered a member of the family. Like Raul, Orlando got the indignant glares, the rebukes, the lectures, and the warnings from Carmen. His presence was expected at all family events, holidays, and weekends.

Saturdays and Sundays, Carmen always served Orlando and Raul a delicious meal, along with a lecture. The theme varied depending on what Carmen dreamt, her intuitions, or the mischief she heard about. Unlike Raul who ignored everything Carmen said, Orlando learned from experience that her insight was keen. The warnings of situations they needed to avoid were on point most of the time. Carmen tended to exaggerate, but that did not diminish or negate the validity of her words.

"I worry about Yasmin. She's been away so long. Sometimes I think..." she wiped her tears, "...the worst."

The anguish in her voice nourished the remorse Orlando felt. "She might show up unexpectedly," he added.

"I've prayed for that every night." She paused and then whispered, "She will come home."

He nodded in agreement.

"We're going to Josefa's. Joining us, Ma?" Raul asked, standing next to Orlando and Carmen. Isabel placed her arm over Carmen's shoulder.

"We discussed that already," Carmen reminded him.

"Please, Mom," Isabel begged. "Just for a little while."

"I'm going home. I haven't been feeling well. I'm tired."

"Isabel will stay with you," Raul suggested.

Orlando stepped aside, waited in silence for their discussion to end.

Carmen shook her head. "Why do you contradict me?" she stressed. "It's your place to be there with Isabel and Yasmin. I'm not the widow."

"Why are you mentioning her?" Isabel asked.

"It's your father's funeral. The three of you are supposed to be there, tending to the guests, helping Josefa serve the food and beverages."

"It's just Isabel and me," Raul corrected.

"Yasmin is part of our family," Carmen pointed out sternly. "Go with Isabel to Josefa's," she ordered. "Stay until all the guests leave. Help clean up."

"I will," Raul agreed, begrudgingly. "First, I'll take you home."

Carmen nodded and got into the car.

"Joining us?" Raul asked.

"No," Orlando replied. "It's Clara's anniversary—seven years with Mario."

"That long with one person?" Raul laughed boisterously as he got in the driver's side.

Orlando walked to the van as Raul sped away. The way things were going, he would barely have sufficient time to shower and get dressed. Yasmin had to be wondering what was taking him so long. He'd parked her car a few blocks away from the cemetery and promised to return right away, which was a horrid exaggeration. It hadn't occurred to him that it would take so long for everyone to leave.

"Orlando wouldn't change his plans for a guy," he overheard Clara say as he reached the van.

Sliding the van door open, Orlando saw Clara sitting next to his mother, Eva, in the back of the van. It was the first time he'd seen Clara wearing glasses. Her face looked rounder with the square, full-rimmed style. It gave her a bookworm, studious look, which was deceptive. Clara rarely read, and she'd been an average student. She excelled at being intrusive, always a tattletale when they were growing up. She never gave up that horrendous habit.

Orlando gazed at his mother. Eva smiled thinly. Dressed in a black pantsuit with a white blouse, her long platinum straight hair framed her face. She was always elegant and polished, her makeup and dressing style impeccable. Clara opted to dress casually—no makeup and jeans with a T-shirt, blouse, or sweater. It was rare to see Clara dressed up.

Orlando smiled. Eva nodded in reply, the facial expression warning him that they needed to talk.

He faced forward. Despite Clara's habitual outburst, he understood their irritation. They had no clue how he had arrived and were appalled when he hopped into their van at the entrance to the cemetery. He provided no explanation despite the questioning looks and ignored Clara's sarcastic comments. He was grateful that Mario had seen him and stopped. It was drizzling when he reached the gate and pouring when he got into the van. He had left his umbrella in Yasmin's car. Without a ride, he would have been drenched. The distance from the entrance to the grave was more than a mile.

"How did you get here?" Clara demanded.

"We are not discussing that now," Eva said. She leaned forward so Orlando could see her face. His parents never argued or rebuked them in public. Unlike Clara, his mother remained calm. It was in the privacy of their home where thunder erupted and the reprimands were as certain as the punishment.

"You're too polite, Mom," Clara complained sourly. "You're seeing her."

"Who are you referring to?" Orlando looked at her.

Clara was churning with anger.

"Her," Clara replied, her tone indicating he knew exactly who she was talking about. "You disappeared without telling us you got a ride with someone else while we waited outside the church for nothing. Luisa told us Yasmin is back, that she was dressed to go dancing when they met near City College. She told Yasmin her father had passed away. Rumor is that you defended her, almost got in a fight with Raul, and then disappeared with Yasmin for hours." Clara emphasized the last two words. "You should've seen Maria's face when Luisa said the funeral parlor closed and you still hadn't returned."

Orlando kept smiling despite the ire he felt. Luisa's mouth was vile. She'd overheard rumors about what occurred and spoke as if she had witnessed it. He didn't care what Maria's reaction was.

"You almost fought with Raul?" Eva asked with concern.

"No, Mom. We had a disagreement. One of many," Orlando explained.

"It was serious." Clara contradicted him.

Orlando promised himself that he would have a conversation with Clara as soon as he could manage it. She was making the situation sound worse than it was, spouting unfounded fears.

"Don't listen to Clara, Mom." Orlando spoke calmly to dissipate her apprehension. The look of concern assured him she wasn't convinced. "Did you notice anything different in how Raul and I treated each other?"

Eva shook her head.

"Nothing happened. Clara knows Luisa loves to gossip. Why is she taking her lies seriously?"

Eva grunted aloud and looked away in silence.

"You're upset because Luisa told us the truth," Clara said.

"Her version," he replied, ending the conversation. Resting his head on the back of the seat, he closed his eyes.

* * *

Yasmin approached the grave with deliberate steps, the heels of her shoes sinking into the mud as she moved forward. Her heart thundered when she caught a glimpse of the flowers, yet she forced herself to proceed. She stopped at the edge of the grave. Unable to look down, she closed her eyes. After several deep breaths, she lowered her gaze slowly. The casket was submerged in a muddy hole. Water drops trickled off the three white roses on top of it. There should have been four. Since she was no longer considered part of the family, her rose was unnecessary.

"I don't know if you would have forgiven me. I'm sorry, Dad." Unable to utter another word, she wept.

"I love you," she continued when she regained control of her emotions. "I didn't want to hurt you or anyone in the family. I followed your command to stay away."

* * *

Orlando scrutinized Yasmin. She had insisted that he wait near the car, but he followed her and stood a few paces away. He worried how she might react in her emotional state. She was standing too close to the edge. She could slip or, worse, jump in.

Prepared to act if necessary, he waited patiently.

He recalled attending the burial of the mother of a close friend at work. The guy's sister seemed fine. She was calm throughout and spoke and greeted everyone who visited the funeral parlor without any signs of emotional duress.

It was when the casket was lowered into the grave and the flowers dropped inside that she became frantic. She screamed her mother's name and then leaped forward. Her husband and brother caught her and carried her away.

The incident was etched in his memory. He felt edgy and remained alert whenever he attended a burial.

* * *

She should have followed her intuition and Ani's and Ismenia's advice. Perhaps if she had, she would have seen her father alive and spoken to him. She would have had the opportunity to make up.

"Dad." Yasmin felt her heels digging into the mud and looked down. She was unaware of how close she was to the edge. She tried to move back and then slipped. Instantly, two arms encircled her waist, lifted her, and placed her on solid ground. Shaking violently, she turned around.

"Orlando." She clung to him, weeping.

Overwhelmed by sorrow, Yasmin succumbed to the desperation she felt. Feeling an unbearable pain in her chest, she gasped for air.

"Focus on your breathing," Orlando guided her. "That will help you calm down."

Yasmin did as he instructed. For a moment she was unaware of where she was. Slowly she became conscious of her surroundings. The scent of Orlando's cologne made her realize her head was nestled comfortably below his neck, her cheek resting on the smooth fabric of his jacket. She felt his hands on her back, one slightly below the other.

The comfort and serenity she felt in his arms puzzled and disturbed her. She shrank away from him and lowered her head. What was wrong with her? He knew the details of the incident with Manuel. He probably thought she was leading him on.

* * *

Orlando parked the car in front of the diner despite Yasmin's complaints. Begrudgingly, she walked alongside him and then sat across from him. Yasmin was silent as he studied the menu and then gave the waiter his order. At his insistence, Yasmin ordered coffee.

32

While they waited for the food, Orlando pretended to review the text messages and emails on his cell phone while studying her discretely. She was visibly distressed. Lost in thought, she blinked repeatedly to clear her vision. Orlando could tell she was restraining her emotions and struggling not to cry. He considered it best for her to weep. It was part of the grieving process and would help her heal.

Yasmin avoided eye contact. Stopping at the diner was a waste of time. She wanted to go home, to succumb to her intense desire to cry. A migraine had kept her awake all night, as did the recollections of the past. There would be no reconciliation with her father. She'd lost the opportunity to absolve herself. Manuel was to blame. He'd ruined her life, destroyed her relationship with her family, and caused her estrangement. Drained of energy and exhausted, she could only envision getting home, donning her pajamas, and lying down to cry.

The waiter placed the food before Orlando. "Sure you don't want to eat anything?" he asked, taking one of the fries and nibbling on it. "I don't mind sharing,"

Yasmin shook her head.

Hamburgers and fries weren't Orlando's favorite, but the meal would quench his appetite until later. He was looking forward to the feast his mother was preparing for Clara and Mario's anniversary that evening.

He watched with creased eyebrows as Yasmin took a pill from a small container and popped it in her mouth. She gulped it down with coffee.

"For a migraine," she replied, placing the mug on the table.

"Why are you taking medication without eating?"

"I don't want anything. Lost my appetite."

"Not wise to take any medication on an empty stomach."

Lifting her gaze, Yasmin glared at him. Without responding, she picked up the mug and sipped the coffee.

"What are you planning to do when you get home, Yaz?" He liked the shorter version and decided to call her that.

"Yasmin," she corrected.

"Answer?"

"Nothing." She would go home and cry herself to sleep. "Dad was healthy. When did he get sick?"

"His liver. He refused to follow doctor's orders. Wouldn't stop drinking." Wiping his mouth with a napkin, Orlando moved the plate to the side and leaned back casually. Finally, they were having a conversation.

"Mami insisted he stop, but he ignored her."

Orlando nodded in agreement. Roberto could have lived many more years. His reckless lifestyle prompted his death. "That's a family trait. No offense, Yaz."

"Yas-min." She said it slowly, emphasizing each syllable.

"Years without contacting your family. Why?"

She lowered her eyes and seemed to be studying her hands that were wrapped tightly around the mug. Leaning forward, Orlando placed the tips of his fingers under her chin and lifted her face gently.

Yasmin tapped his hand so he would remove it. "It wasn't intentional, although that's what you and my family assume."

"I assumed that?"

"You have a different opinion?" Yasmin asked suspiciously.

"Yeah."

She smiled skeptically. "You're Raul's friend."

"Meaning?" Orlando was intrigued by her supposition that his friendship with Raul was synonymous with sharing Raul's opinions and attitudes. "You're close to Ismenia. Each of you has your own personality." From what he recalled, they were opposites. Ismenia was outgoing, daring, and bold. Yasmin was timid and conservative. From his observation the evening before, she had also become self-conscious.

"True," Yasmin admitted, nodding. She wondered if she should divulge anything pertinent about herself. By choice, she never spoke about what happened or how she felt.

Orlando crossed his arms over his chest, signaling that he was waiting for her to reply.

"I . . . couldn't go back." Yasmin cleared her throat. "All Mami focused on and kept demanding after Dad threw me out was that I return home. Mami was oblivious to everything else. She ignored Dad's aggressive behavior and acted as if it was normal." Yasmin paused and dried her tears. "What Dad said about the incident with Manuel condemned me."

Orlando waited in silence. Yasmin stared at the mug before her, recalling the ghastly scene when her father burst into the room and lifted his arm to strike her. Manuel intervened to stop him, pushing him away. A fight ensued. It moved from the bedroom, through the hall, and into the living room. She ran after them, shouting for them to stop. Manuel headed toward the door, intent on leaving, when Roberto grabbed her by the shoulders. She screamed as he flung her toward Manuel who embraced her and led her out of the apartment. Sobbing, she walked alongside Manuel out of the building and to his car. She had no idea where he was taking her.

She straightened her shoulders, determined not to cry, and murmured the verse she'd memorized and kept repeating to herself. "Philippians 4:13: 'I can do all this through him who gives me strength.'"

"Yaz?"

She lifted her eyes and faced him.

He waited patiently, allowing her to talk at her leisure. Recalling it and talking about it were painful. Although it was the opportunity he'd longed for, to hear the actual details and compare them with Roberto's crude descriptions, he wasn't going to pressure her.

"I didn't want anyone to know I moved in with Ani," Yasmin continued. "Weeks later, when I got enough courage to call Mami to tell her where I was staying, Dad picked up the phone. He heard my voice and hung up. I called after several days. Mami insulted me and demanded I come back home." Yasmin paused. A pained expression masked her face. "I stopped calling. Mami never asked what occurred or how I felt."

"How did you feel?" Orlando asked. "What did you go through?" He wanted her to be specific.

"I stayed with Ani and moved with her to Queens. We had been living there almost a year when Ismenia broke up with Nestor and moved in with us. She was pregnant again. I considered moving back home and visited Mami."

Orlando recalled that Carmen was taken to the emergency room that night. Raul had mentioned how Yasmin popped up and caused a heated argument between Roberto and Carmen. Hours later, Carmen was rushed to the hospital and diagnosed with high blood pressure.

"We moved to Manhattan, the same apartment Ani lives in now," Yasmin marveled. "All those years I didn't visit Mami to avoid causing their separation."

"You think they got divorced because of you?" Orlando asked, astonished that she would voluntarily place that load on her shoulders.

"Dad threatened to leave Mami if I visited again."

"He was angry, Yaz. I doubt he meant that."

"Yasmin," she corrected firmly. "He did."

"I disagree." Orlando shook his head. "Discuss it with Carmen. Blaming yourself and worrying about it without knowing the facts are unneccessary."

Picking up the mug, Yasmin sipped the remainder of her coffee although it was cold. She sighed aloud.

Orlando leaned forward, reached for her hands, and held them in his. "Be optimistic."

Yasmin smiled thinly. Ani always said the same thing. Pulling her hands out of his, she stood up and grabbed her purse.

An idea occurred to him as they walked toward the exit. "Instead of going home, I can drop you off at Carmen's."

Yasmin's eyes lit up for a moment. The smile faded almost instantly. "Not if Raul and Isabel are there."

Orlando glanced at his watch. "They're at Josefa's." Carmen would be alone for a few more hours. He could drop off Yasmin, take a cab home, and head to Clara's anniversary after showering and getting dressed.

Yasmin smiled happily. "I was going to ask you when they weren't around so I could visit Mami. Thanks."

"Anytime," he replied, pleased by her change of mood.

Chapter 3

"Stop lying, Yasmin," Carmen yelled angrily.

"I went to the wake," she alleged in a firm tone. "I attended the Mass and went to the cemetery."

Carmen fixed her eyes steadily on her, the frown turning to a scowl.

Convincing her mother would be difficult. Yasmin tried to think of what to say to prove she was telling the truth. "Ask Orlando," she blurted out.

"Orlando?" Carmen repeated, aghast.

"He was there last night when I arrived. He drove me to the cemetery this morning."

Carmen stood abruptly. "I asked Orlando several times about you. He pretended he didn't hear me."

Yasmin recalled telling Orlando not to mention that she was at the cemetery and now realized that her request complicated the situation. "How can I convince you?" she asked, exasperated.

"Watch your tone," Carmen rebuked, lifting her arm as if to strike her.

Yasmin sat motionless. Her mother insisted on treating her as if she were a child. Carmen returned to where she'd been sitting. Yasmin kept a blank expression. When her parents scolded her as a child, she learned it was prudent to mask all emotion. Facial expressions and body language were considered disrespectful, an affront that made the punishment more severe.

Lowering her gaze, Yasmin stared at her hands clasped together on her lap and prayed inaudibly, *Lord, help me.* It occurred to her to describe what she saw. Lifting her head, Yasmin spoke eagerly. "You were sitting in the first pew on the right. You sat between Raul and Isabel. Next to her was Maria after Luisa. On the other side next to Raul was a couple, a skinny, tall man with his arm over the shoulders of a plump woman wearing glasses. Next to her was a very distinguished woman with gray hair, and then Orlando."

"*Dios mio!*" Carmen's eyes widened. "That woman was Eva, Orlando's mother. The couple was Clara, his sister, and Mario, his brother-in-law." Pausing, she lowered her brows. "Where were you? I didn't see you in the church."

"I was in the balcony."

"Why?" Carmen asked, disappointment and disapproval evident in her expression.

Yasmin gazed at her hands clasped tightly on her lap.

"Can you tell me where you met Luisa?" Carmen asked.

"Hundred thirty-ninth and Broadway, on my way to Ani's."

"I thought she bought a house in Queens."

"That was Ani's plan until the bridal shop closed. She couldn't afford the rent. A friend from church helped her get a two-bedroom apartment on Amsterdam Avenue across from City College. Now she works from home and is affiliated with several bridal shops that recommend clients if they want their dresses tailor-made." She paused and then added, "I'm sorry I didn't give you the new address or phone number."

"You lived with Ani temporarily and then got a place with Manuel?"

"I have my own apartment. I live alone," Yasmin replied, explaining in detail how she'd become an accountant and saved sufficient money to get her own place. A relationship with Manuel never materialized. She'd walked out on him the same day her father threw her out, and now she had no idea where he was.

"You live alone?" Carmen studied her face closely. "Are you saying that because we would never accept Manuel, not after he fought with your father? Raul and Orlando spent days trying to find where Manuel lived. They waited around your school to see if he would show up. They never found him. Nor did they see you," she added sarcastically.

Ismenia, who attended the same high school, mentioned that Raul and Orlando had shown up before and after school looking for Manuel. Yasmin shared her mother's sentiment—she was glad there had been no confrontation with Manuel. After witnessing his fight with her father, Yasmin never wanted to see another physical confrontation with a family member or anyone else.

Opening her purse, Yasmin took out her phone book and ripped out a page. She wrote her address and phone number on it and added Ani's information. Her mother could reach her at either place. "You can contact me always."

Carmen read the information, folded the paper, and shoved it into the pocket of her robe. "Having an address is no proof you live there or that you'll visit or call."

"I'll visit often," Yasmin assured her, determined to keep her promise.

"We'll see," Carmen said skeptically. "Can you explain the familiarity between Orlando and you?"

Yasmin disliked the double meaning she inferred. "Orlando was being . . ." she hesitated, searching for an appropriate word, ". . . helpful."

Carmen burst into laughter, "You don't think he wants something in return?"

Yasmin had heard similar comments when she was growing up and understood the warning. Despite that, she had trusted Manuel. Her first and only encounter with love had ensured that she would remain alone.

"Why didn't Orlando tell me the truth? Why the secrecy?" Carmen asked.

Yasmin doubted that providing details would alter Carmen's preconceived notions and opted not to respond.

"When we left the cemetery," Carmen continued, "Raul told me Orlando wasn't going to Josefa's. How long were you there? Where did you go afterward?"

"We . . . stopped . . . at a diner," Yasmin stammered.

"After?" Carmen scrutinized her face.

Her cheeks warm, Yasmin recalled the pastor's sermon. How could she safeguard her heart and forgive? The incident with Manuel had tarnished her life, and it was constantly used against her.

"I'm waiting," Carmen stressed in a curt tone.

"He left after driving me here," Yasmin replied.

Carmen leaned forward, placed her hand under Yasmin's chin, and lifted it so they faced each other. "The truth, Yasmin."

A burning sensation crept up, scorching Yasmin's throat. She kept her gaze fixed on her mother's icy stare. She regretted allowing Orlando to drive her to the cemetery.

They heard someone unlocking the door. Isabel entered.

Carmen stood abruptly and confronted her. "Why did you and Raul lie to me?"

* * *

Orlando watched Raul take a beer out of the refrigerator, drop the can opener on the dining room table, and stroll past him into the living room. He sat on the black leather couch. Orlando followed him, picked up the remote, and lowered the music. He sat on the chair opposite him.

"Who are you going out with?" Raul asked, eyeing Orlando from head to toe.

"Clara's anniversary," he replied. Partially dressed, he wore black jeans, matching shoes, and a white T-shirt. The plaid shirt he'd chosen was on top of the bed. "It's still early." Orlando gazed at his watch. He would leave within the hour.

"I'll make it brief," Raul promised. "I thought you understood how I felt about Yasmin going to the wake."

He nodded, holding the beer in his hand.

"You challenged my decision. I never contradict you in public, even if I don't agree." Raul took a gulp and set the beer down. "When family is involved, you accept my decisions."

"I didn't want the situation to escalate."

"I understand. Makes no difference. As soon as Yasmin went inside, she started trouble."

"Yasmin defended herself," Orlando noted.

"Caressing Dad's face? Lying on his chest? Crying? She's a hypocrite."

"I disagree," Orlando stressed.

"That's why you consoled her?"

"Yasmin was sobbing. Should I have ignored her like everyone else did?"

Raul took another gulp of beer and leaned forward. "After you led her out of the funeral parlor, she still needed to be comforted?"

Orlando disregarded the sarcastic tone. He hadn't expected Raul to show any remorse, concern, or empathy for Yasmin. "When she calmed down, we talked for a while."

"About?" Raul studied Orlando's features carefully.

"She wanted to know why Carmen wasn't at the wake."

40

"Yasmin was upset, crying uncontrollably, and she noticed that?" Raul asked with dismay. "Wow!" He finished his beer and placed the bottle on the floor. "If Yasmin cared about Ma, she wouldn't have stayed away so long."

"I agree with you." But unlike Raul, he understood Yasmin's perspective. It was true that Roberto had overreacted, and it was evident that Yasmin was afraid he would hurt her.

"And you continue to defend her," Raul added.

"I'm on the opposing team," he reminded him, smiling, "with Josefa and Carmen."

"I'm going to speak to Josefa. She shouldn't have intervened," Raul complained. "Is it clear that we discuss opinions after? Even if you disagree, you don't interfere."

"Agreed," Orlando replied.

Raul's cell phone rang. He looked at the number. "What, Isabel?" He listened and then sprang up. "Go with Ma in the ambulance. I'll meet you at the hospital. Tell Yasmin not to leave until I get there."

* * *

"I was visiting," Yasmin said, hoping the tremor in her voice was not evident.

"The result?"

She glanced in the direction Raul was pointing and stared at the entrance to the emergency room with disbelief. Why visiting her mother would end in a trip to the emergency room was beyond her understanding.

Raul placed his index finger on the center of her forehead and nudged her head back. "Leave. Now."

Rooted in place, Yasmin ignored the pressure he was exerting on her forehead. She considered slapping his hand or shoving him back, but she controlled herself. If he retaliated, she couldn't defend herself.

Looking briefly toward Orlando, her anger escalated. From his stance, the pretense was over. He kept a safe distance while waiting for Raul.

"What's wrong with Mami? Has she fainted like that before? Is she ill?" Yasmin said as she stepped back fearfully.

Raul remained where he was, staring down at her. "Ma doesn't need you. She has Isabel and me. Continue living as if we don't exist."

"No." She was determined to stay. She needed to find out why her mother collapsed and if she had a serious condition.

"Attempt to go into the hospital," Raul challenged.

Tears streaming down her cheeks, Yasmin felt helpless and trapped. Concentrating on her breathing, she composed herself, refusing to give Raul or Orlando the satisfaction of seeing her break down. Lifting her head, she straightened her shoulders and glared at Raul.

"Leave!" Raul ordered, shoving her back.

She stumbled but felt a firm grip take hold of her upper arm and straighten her up.

"Go," Orlando whispered. He turned away and gestured for Raul to follow him.

The distraught expression irritated her. Why was Orlando upset? Like Raul, he was insensitive. He pretended to be concerned about her when all he wanted was to pry and inform his buddy of everything she had said.

"We need to see how Carmen is doing, Raul," Orlando said, looking directly at her. "Yasmin is leaving."

"Is she?" Raul asked, stepping in front of her. "Are you?"

* * *

Restraining himself took effort. Somehow, he managed to move in the opposite direction without looking back.

Following Raul into the emergency room, Orlando scanned the crowded room and chose a seat in a corner. Dropping heavily onto the dingy, plastic chair, he sighed aloud. He'd kept his promise and watched Raul insult and mistreat Yasmin, who was aware of the change in his behavior. She had glared at him with angst, unaware of the self-control he had to muster or how disgusted he felt with himself.

Lifting his gaze, Orlando saw Raul standing near the guard by the entrance to the treatment area. Raul's pleased expression angered him. He agreed that no one should intrude on their family affairs or problems, but he never imagined how far Raul's enmity would go. Denying Yasmin access to the wake was vicious. Demanding that she stay away when Carmen was in the emergency room and insulting her with such spite were inhumane acts.

Leaning forward, Orlando rested his elbows on his knees, his head on the palms of his hands. He regretted not asking Yasmin for her phone number. They were together all morning and part of the afternoon, and it had never occurred to him.

Taking the liberty of calling Ani, whose number was now saved on his cell phone, was not an option. He wished Yasmin had his cell number so she could contact him—not that she would. If she doubted his sincerity before, her distrust now became concrete.

He felt his phone vibrate and read the number. "Yes, Mom," he replied.

"All the guests are here. We're waiting for you so we can serve dinner," Eva said.

"I'm in the emergency room with Raul waiting to find out if Carmen will be admitted. I'll leave as soon as I can."

There was a long pause. "Fine," Eva said dryly and hung up. He would explain what occurred and apologize to Clara and his mother when he arrived.

Isabel sat next to him. Orlando turned slightly and looked at her out of the corner of his eye. She seemed extremely pleased with herself. Although Raul blamed Yasmin, Orlando doubted that she was the culprit. He was convinced that Isabel had arrived while Yasmin was visiting and started an argument, and the scenario the night before had reoccurred.

It was his fault. He should've taken Yasmin home instead of suggesting she visit Carmen.

"Why do you defend Yasmin all the time?"

"What?" he asked.

"Is there a reason you're her protector? If Raul finds out, your friendship will end."

Orlando stood up and strolled away. He leaned against the wall near the exit, his back toward Isabel. Her comments and opinion were unimportant.

He gazed outside. It was pouring. People were running to and fro seeking shelter. He hoped Yasmin was home, wherever that was.

It was intriguing that she wore no rings. Her delicate fingers were unadorned. It might not be a sign that she was single, but most of the females he knew flaunted their engagement rings, wedding bands, or both with pride. It was odd that she had attended the wake and burial alone. Where was Manuel? Why had she spoken to Ani and not to him?

"Ma is asking for you, Orlando," Raul said.

"What did the doctor say?" Orlando was eager to know Carmen's condition.

"Ma asked for Yasmin," Raul continued, speaking without answering the question. "She was crying and talking about dying. She kept saying that her wish before passing away is for the family to be together. She wants Yasmin to be here." Raul frowned. "It upsets me when Ma talks like that."

"Did you speak to the doctor?" Orlando asked, rephrasing the question.

Raul nodded. "Blood pressure was high. She's at risk of a heart attack or stroke. Ma needs rest, medication as prescribed, and a low-sodium diet. Most important, she needs no stress."

"The three of you have to accommodate Carmen," Orlando advised.

"Ma's health is the priority," Raul admitted bitterly. "Yasmin wins."

* * *

Yasmin watched Ani place a cup of tea on the nightstand along with the small container in which she carried her medication. Ani was tall and heavyset with bronze skin, her smile warm, her laughter jovial, and her voice soft and mellow. Ani had offered her a home and provided security, solace, and affection when she was ostracized from her family.

"I'm sorry your father passed away, that you couldn't resolve things," Ani said. Sitting on the edge of the bed, Ani reached for Yasmin's hand and squeezed it gently. "Relax and rest or your symptoms will get worse."

Closing her eyes, Yasmin envisioned her mother in the emergency room. Tears trickled down her cheeks. She had no way of knowing if her mother had been admitted and no idea why she had lost consciousness.

Taking several tissues, Yasmin dried her tears and lay as still as possible. Each time she moved, her temples throbbed painfully. "Raul and Isabel treated me worse than Dad," she murmured, still unable to grasp the extent of their animosity. As she suspected, Isabel had ignored Carmen's presence and demanded that she leave. "Instead of following my instincts, I listened to Orlando. He suggested that I visit Mami, and I did."

"Orlando?" Ani asked, wide-eyed. "He and Raul are still friends? I like him. He seems decent, educated, and conscientious."

"*Seems* is the right word." Yasmin was sarcastic. "This morning he appeared concerned, but when Raul insulted me, he acted as if I didn't exist."

"There must be a reason for that."

44

"He's a hypocrite and a liar," Yasmin accused, placing her fingertips on her temples and applying pressure.

"You're angry with Orlando because?" Ani asked, still unsure why Yasmin was upset.

"I didn't ask for or want his help."

"Perhaps if he hadn't been there, the situation might have been worse."

Yasmin agreed but was still skeptical. What if her mother was right? What if Orlando wanted something in return?

"Mami already accused me of . . . being with him." Her voice trailed off. Her cheeks took on a reddish hue.

"If Carmen knew you, that wouldn't occur to her."

"He just drove me to the cemetery. After we stopped at a diner, he left me at Mami's place."

"Since Manuel, you've isolated yourself and refused to go out with anyone. It's odd that you went to the cemetery and then to a diner with Orlando."

Yasmin pressed her hands on her temples and closed her eyes. Mentioning Orlando to her mother and Ani had been an oversight. It wasn't a date. The circumstances prompted her decision. It wasn't voluntary or preplanned as her mother and Ani erroneously deduced. "I shouldn't have accepted his help," she voiced her thoughts aloud.

"Sometimes the Lord sends someone we don't expect or know to help us. Sounds to me like Orlando gave you the assistance you needed. The Lord wants us to show gratitude and be thankful."

Yasmin thought she would have been better off without any assistance from him. He and Raul probably still spent their meager earnings partying every weekend. They were avid dancers and frequented nightclubs, discotheques, and bars. They drank, picked up women, and got into childish fights. She doubted they had changed.

Yasmin grunted aloud. She would not see or speak to Orlando again.

"Remember, Yasmin, our Lord wants us to be humble. Drink the tea. I took these out of your purse." Ani handed her the small container. "I made soup. Would you like some? You shouldn't take pills on an empty stomach."

"Later." Yasmin forced herself to sit up, took one of the pills out, and popped it into her mouth. She drank enough tea to swallow the medication and then placed the container and cup back on the nightstand.

"Rest," Ani said, turning off the light and closing the door.

Yasmin lay motionless. It was the only way to stop the painful throbbing. She imagined Raul and Isabel by Carmen's bedside. "Lord, I want to see Mami again." She prayed.

* * *

"I have to stay until my blood pressure gets stable. I could be discharged tonight or tomorrow." Carmen pointed to the two pouches that hung next to a pole near her bed. She was being given the medication intravenously. "Orlando, I wanted to speak to you privately."

Orlando moved closer to the headboard. The suspicious stare and disapproving expression intrigued him. "Okay," he replied, a blank expression on his face.

"You knew Yasmin went to the wake, and you took her to the cemetery. When I asked, you didn't answer."

"I'm sorry, Carmen. I think it's best for Raul and Isabel to explain what happened."

Carmen studied his face in silence. "Why did she choose to go with you? Why did she sit alone in the balcony? It seems like she was hiding. From who?"

"Did you ask her?"

"I don't know my own daughter," Carmen admitted. "All these years I believed she was with Manuel. Now she claims she has her own apartment and never moved in with him, that she stayed with Ani until she moved out."

"Why would she lie?" he asked. Now he understood why she wore no ring and attended the last rites by herself.

"I didn't bring her up to move out on her own. She's supposed to get married and move in with her husband. That's the decent thing to do."

He smiled, although Carmen's expression was somber. What Carmen considered disgraceful was a sign that Yasmin was independent and financially stable.

"Yasmin also has a car." Carmen shook her head. "Where is she getting the money for all that? Supposedly, she continued her education, got a GED, took training in accounting, and works as a bookkeeper for some firm."

He was pleased to hear it. Yasmin had character and drive. Like Carmen, she was strong, determined, opinionated, and even critical.

"She could have gone to college and gotten a career if she hadn't ruined her life by getting involved with that horrid man," Carmen voiced with indignation. "Yasmin is so different, not like I brought her up to be."

"She works, has her own place, and pays her bills. She has sufficient financial stability to own a car." He was compelled to add that she accomplished all that without any support from her family, but he reconsidered. "Isn't that what every mother wants—for their daughter to be independent and self-sufficient?"

"I suppose if what Yasmin said is true, it's not as bad as I thought," Carmen admitted. "I never had financial freedom. Roberto supported me, and after the divorce, Raul is doing it."

Orlando nodded, pleased that he could enlighten Carmen and mend the miscommunication between her and Yasmin. "Sometimes things are different from how we perceive them."

"True." She looked directly at him, her eyes fixed on his. "You helped Yasmin and took her to the cemetery."

He nodded and smiled, although the double meaning of her words stung. Until that moment, he felt his integrity was intact. The possibility that he could be wrong disturbed him.

"Help, when done for the *right reasons*," she stressed the last two words, "is admirable."

"I agree." He noted her insinuation that his assistance sought some type of recompense. He maintained a calm, aloof expression. He'd done his best to make a horrific situation bearable for Yasmin.

"I didn't believe Yasmin when she told me she'd attended the Mass and went to the cemetery with you. How was that possible when you arrived alone? Where was she?" Carmen stopped as if recalling something and added, "When we left the cemetery, you got in the van with Eva, Clara, and Mario. How could you drive Yasmin back to the city and then to my place? Where was she? Where did you meet?"

He understood her confusion, but any attempt to explain would complicate the situation and arouse more suspicions. It was evident by her tone that she had misconstrued the situation.

"When you speak to Raul, Isabel, and Yasmin, you'll understand," Orlando explained. "If you still have questions, ask me, and I'll answer them."

"I'd prefer that you tell me now."

Orlando shook his head. "After discussing it with them, you'll understand."

47

"Why?" Carmen asked, alarmed.

"The doctor said you need to relax and stay calm," he reminded her.

"That's the recommendation, but I'm not sure how I can do that," Carmen said. "Orlando, please don't take my complaints seriously."

"Your concerns are legitimate," he assured her in a serious tone.

"If you ever decide to get married, she'll be very fortunate." Carmen smiled. "You're thoughtful and respectful."

"Marriage?" Orlando shook his head. Feeling at ease, he smiled, content that the conversation had taken on a lighter tone.

"Yes," Carmen assured. "When you find the right person, you'll look forward to getting into a serious relationship and having a family."

His smile widened. He led an active social life and had no intention of getting into a commitment. He enjoyed his freedom and was at liberty to delight in the company of many while committing to none.

* * *

Yasmin rushed through the living room. She noticed that the light was off in Ani's bedroom as she passed by. She hoped Ani had not been awakened by whoever was banging on the door without any regard for the time.

"Who?" she asked softly, her voice barely above a whisper.

"Is Yasmin there?"

Her hands trembled as she unlocked the door. Face-to-face with Raul, disturbing images assaulted her. Everything swirled around her and then turned black.

Raul caught her before she dropped to the floor and carried her into the kitchen. He set her carefully on a chair. Wetting a paper towel, he patted her face gently.

The cold water revived her. Alert, she gestured for Raul to stop and then watched as he threw the paper towel into the garbage and returned to stand before her.

"Mami," she murmured, covering her mouth with her hands.

"Ma's still in the hospital. The doctor gave her medication to lower her blood pressure."

Speechless, she stared at him, wide-eyed. Her heart beat so loudly that surely Ani could hear it on the other side of the wall.

"You think I would be this calm if anything happened to Ma?"

She studied his face. He looked miserable and cross, his usual demeanor. Placing her hands on her temples, she applied some pressure. "Was Mami admitted?"

"No." He stepped back and leaned against the sink. "You told Ma you weren't living with Ani and wrote two addresses on the paper. I wasted my time going to the first."

"You came just to verify the information I gave Mami?" she asked, unable to disguise her surprise.

"I already spoke to Isabel," he continued, ignoring her question. "The doctor said Ma needs rest and should be calm and not stressed, which means we're like this." He clasped his hands and held them before her.

"You think Mami is blind?" she asked, appalled by his assumption that their mother would be oblivious to their despicable charade.

"Convince her," he ordered.

"And you?" she asked.

He shrugged. "If having you around will make Ma feel better and keep her calm, then you'll be there."

Yasmin was silent.

"Understood?"

Yasmin met his icy stare. "Yes," she replied tersely. After mistreating her verbally and emotionally, he was there to impose his will as if she were a marionette.

"Don't upset Ma," he forewarned. "You have five minutes to get ready."

"Why?" she asked, stunned by his demands.

His cell phone rang. Answering, he spoke with concern. "Is Ma all right, Isabel?" He listened and smiled. "Great news! I'll go back to the hospital and pick you up." He sucked his teeth loudly after Isabel spoke to him again. "Don't contradict Ma if she wants to take a cab. I'll meet you at home." He put away his cell phone and faced Yasmin. "I'm taking you to Ma's."

"I'll drive," she said, delighted that she didn't have to put up with his presence more than necessary.

He swept past her and stopped by the doorway. "I'll be downstairs in my car. I'll be right behind you to make sure you go directly to Ma's. Hurry up, or I'll come back to take you downstairs personally." Unlocking the door, he exited and slammed it shut.

Yasmin staggered sluggishly into the bedroom. Raul was inconsiderate and obnoxious. She felt ashamed that she was related to him.

Ani entered the room, tying her robe as Yasmin was getting dressed. "I heard a man's voice."

"I'm sorry, Ani. I didn't want to wake you." If their voices hadn't awakened her, Raul's slamming the door had. He was too egocentric to care about anyone's feelings. Yasmin took a deep breath to calm herself. "Raul came to drag me to Mami's place."

"Is Carmen all right?"

"According to Raul, the doctor said it was her blood pressure. Mami wants to see me." She recalled praying, asking the Lord to help her see and be with her mother. *Thank you,* she said silently, gazing up.

Taking her purse, Yasmin faced Ani. "Where's Ismenia? Why isn't she here with the kids?" Yasmin meant to ask earlier but was too overwhelmed with her emotions and ailments.

"She arrived at 8:00 this morning," Ani explained. "She got upset when I suggested that if she and Nestor wanted to get back together they should move in, get married, and get their own place. She got furious, called Nestor, asked him to pick her up, and then packed her clothes. She woke the kids, dressed them, and left."

Yasmin frowned, feeling guilty for being engrossed in her own problems as if she were the only one going through hardship. "I'm sorry, Ani," she said and hugged her.

"I've been praying for you and Ismenia," Ani said. "The Lord knows what you need and will provide it. He is never late and always arrives at the precise time."

Ani's serene composure and affirmation inspired Yasmin. She longed to be calm, at ease, in peace, and ecstatic about the Lord and how He was transforming her life. Instead, she felt emotionally drained and weak.

"You'll be with Carmen, helping her recuperate," Ani said as she hugged her tightly.

"If Raul and Isabel let me."

"Who do you think brought Raul here to humble himself before you?" Ani marveled. "Need more proof that the Lord is in control?"

Chapter 4

Orlando debated the appropriateness of calling early in the morning. Unless it was an emergency, he avoided disturbing friends or family while they were sleeping or getting ready for work. Despite his reservations, he dialed Carmen's number and decided to call Raul if there was no reply.

If Carmen had been admitted, he could go during visiting hours. He might work through lunch, leave early, go to the hospital, and then stop by Clara's to see his mother. If time allowed, he might attend the first *rezos*. Josefa was following a Dominican Republic custom when a person died. For nine consecutive days, family and friends gathered to pray for the deceased. Although the tradition was practiced more often on the island, some people still adhered to the custom in New York.

A soft voice greeted Orlando.

"Yaz?"

"My name is Yasmin."

"Yaz sounds so much better, don't you agree?"

"To you."

"I'd like to continue calling you Yaz if you don't mind." Although she acted offended, Orlando sensed that she liked it.

"Fine," Yasmin agreed. She doubted they would see each other again and wasn't going to waste time fretting over that.

"How's Carmen?" Orlando asked.

"She's supposed to be sleeping," Yasmin said.

"Otherwise, she would be cooking and cleaning," Orlando jested.

"That's Mami."

"If you're staying to take care of her, you'll have to encourage her to stay in bed so she can rest."

"The boss hasn't given the orders."

The defiance he detected worried him. Yasmin was rebellious, and Raul was intolerant. "Please don't antagonize him."

She grunted inaudibly, annoyed by his bogus concern. "If I breathe too loud, he's barking."

"Avoid confrontations," Orlando advised, aware that Raul and Isabel would find fault in everything Yasmin did. "Focus on Carmen. She must be pleased that you're there."

"Maybe."

"I'm sure she is."

"Mami disapproves of everything I do. I doubt that changed overnight."

"That's the way Carmen is. Raul and I have been criticized, lectured, and yelled at countless times."

She laughed. "You deserved it."

"Sometimes. Carmen tends to exaggerate." He was tempted to add "like her daughter" but thought better of it.

"Yeah," she agreed. "She was trying to make you and Raul act civilized, which was useless."

He grinned. He would rectify Yasmin's misconception when and if they had the opportunity to talk for a prolonged time. "Raul there?"

"He's in the room talking to Isabel."

"*Rezos* begins tonight. Are you going?"

"I didn't think someone her age would follow that custom," Yasmin complained.

"Age has nothing to do with following the custom. I'll see you at Josefa's for the *rezos*."

"No, you'll see Raul and Isabel." Yasmin's plan was to go straight home. She wanted to avoid being anywhere with them.

"Speak to Carmen, and then decide."

"*Argue* is the word."

"Eventually you'll be able to talk calmly and confide in each other," he said.

"*You* are being thoughtful?"

"Yes," he replied. The double meaning of her words reminded him of his conversation with Carmen. He wondered if Yasmin realized how much she resembled her mother.

"Is that a trait your females recognize?" she sneered.

She was baiting him. He realized that talking with her required armor and a shield. Like Raul, she was on guard, her sword lifted to strike. "If I'm not compared to someone and my reputation isn't used against me, yeah. I prefer to be judged on my own merit," Orlando explained.

"I'm sure you and Raul earned your reputation based on what you did and continue doing—unlike mine that is based on appearances and false judgments."

"What are you referring to? Be specific." He wondered why she made that comment. He understood that her decisions had triggered the sour situation with her family. The events that led up to her estrangement weren't based on false perceptions or fabrication. They were real.

"I'll get Raul," Yasmin said.

"I'll see you at the *rezos*." If she had forgotten how Carmen imposed rules, she would be reminded soon enough.

* * *

Yasmin walked down the hall eager to make sure Carmen was still sleeping. Opening the door quietly, she smiled. After getting home in the wee hours, Carmen needed rest. Yasmin tiptoed to Isabel's bedroom to alert Raul that Orlando was on the phone. The door was partially open. She hesitated before entering.

"Why should Yasmin be the one to stay?" Isabel complained.

"I don't want any problems between the two of you, " Raul warned.

Yasmin glanced toward the living room. Should she tell Orlando that Raul wasn't available? Should she wait until Raul finished talking with Isabel, or should she interrupt? Unsure of what to do, she waited.

"Just because Mom is sick? She can come anytime."

"I told you what to do, Isabel." Raul sounded angry.

When Yasmin heard Raul's footsteps approaching, she pushed the door open.

"Orlando is on the phone." Without waiting for a reply, she returned to the living room.

"Raul will be right with you," she told Orlando. After placing the cordless on the dining room table, she turned on the television. Dropping heavily on the sofa, she glanced around. The décor had not changed. Two shelves of the étagère were crammed with souvenirs from celebrations her family had attended, along with knickknacks and family pictures. The ancient stereo with radio, record, and tape player gleamed as if it were brand-new. Below was the TV. On the bottom shelf was a stack of old albums, some with covers so worn out that the titles of the songs were illegible.

The sectional sofa curled around the living room directly in front of the étagère. The rocking chair was placed strategically near the dining room so her mother could watch television and face whoever sat on the sofa. Yasmin wasn't sure what was worse, the maroon color or the horrid plastic that covered it. Her mother insisted on covering all the furniture with plastic for durability. Yasmin grunted aloud. The one change that wasn't evident was that she no longer lived there.

She heard footsteps and then saw Raul pick up the phone. She purposely tuned him out. Whatever he and Orlando needed to discuss was of no interest to her. Her preference would have been to go back to bed. She felt horrible.

Exhausted from barely resting the night before, she feared falling sleep and not waking up on time to call the office. She needed to speak to her supervisor. She had three days of bereavement and decided to use some of her vacation time to take the entire week off.

"Leaving, Isabel?" Raul asked, placing the cordless on the telephone base.

Yasmin saw Isabel nod her head, glare at her, and then walk out of the apartment.

"Isabel won't stay because I'm here?" she asked Raul, facing him with a thin smile on her lips. She wasn't the only one objecting to his authority.

"Ma prefers to be with you." He walked toward the door and opened it. "Tell Ma I'll call her later. She needs to rest. Don't let her do any housework or cooking."

"Would you be able to stop her from doing that?"

"You're taking care of her." He stepped back into the apartment and held the door open with his hand so it wouldn't slam shut.

"Mami isn't going to stay in bed all day." She ignored the heated glare in his stare.

"Not interested in your explanations or smart replies," he said. "Make sure Ma gets the rest she needs."

She rolled her eyes, frowning. Raul's threats were as tiresome as his pathetic attempt at a father role. Neither impressed her.

* * *

54

"I thought you and Clara were closer." Eva lowered the volume on the television and sat across from Orlando on the love seat. "If she needed your help, I thought you'd comply."

"Although occasionally I don't appreciate Clara's comments or attitude, I'll provide whatever support she needs." Orlando was candid. He wanted to make sure his mother understood that his behavior was not a reflection of his feelings.

"Not sure what your definition of support is," Eva commented. "She needed you to attend and give priority to her anniversary. Had you been the one celebrating, you would have wanted her to be there to share your joy. You arrived after most of the guests left."

Orlando sat up straight. Convincing himself that he made the right decision by accompanying Raul to the hospital and staying until he spoke to Carmen was easy. He could justify his actions until he faced his mother. The weight of her words was like an anchor. Pinned under her disapproval, his excuses drowned.

"With Roberto's death, the funeral, the burial . . ." It was a weak defense but his only recourse.

"How did you get to the cemetery?" asked Eva. "I know you didn't ride with Raul. He told Mario you were going with us, that the mechanics were picking up your car. You had not mentioned it. Mario wanted to confirm, but you vanished. Even Raul asked where you were when the Mass began," Eva noted with disapproval. "You seemed very pleased when you returned halfway through the Mass."

Orlando maintained a blank expression. He'd learned at a young age that it was useless to deny his emotions or lie. By a mere look or the tone of his voice, his mother perceived his feelings.

"We waited, but you never showed up," she continued. "When we arrived, we saw you walking toward the entrance. I should have told Mario to keep driving just to see if you intended to walk to the burial site without an umbrella in the pouring rain."

It was what he had planned, and he was fortunate they arrived when they did. "It's complex."

"Raul's problems with his family shouldn't concern you."

"You taught me to defend my beliefs." He knew the death of a loved one, more so of a parent, was grueling for relatives and friends. Alone, it had to be devastating. If that wasn't enough, Yasmin had to confront the stark reality that Roberto had passed away before they made amends, a fact that, unlike Raul and Isabel, he refused to overlook. Their attitudes were ludicrous—unforgivable.

"Also that there are limits," Eva went on. "You're so involved that you don't recognize what's important in your own life. When did Raul's problems with his sister and Carmen's health take priority over your own family? Clara was upset. What was supposed to be a happy occasion became sour. Your decision made your priorities clear. I'm disappointed, Orlando."

He remained calm, although Eva's words were like an unexpected punch to the jaw. The pardon he'd expected would not be forthcoming. That realization felt like a second blow.

"I didn't want to take you or Clara for granted," he apologized. "It's been hectic. You arrived the same day Roberto died."

"I did," Eva nodded. "Raul is like a brother to you . . . *like*." She emphasized the word.

"Our friendship is solid." He was confident that they could overcome any problem. "Not every family is like ours. The bonds that tie a family together can break. Yasmin is suffering through that now."

"Yasmin." Eva's lips curled at the corners. "She must be very charming that you defend and protect her."

He shook his head. He understood her horrid plight and just wanted to be supportive.

"You almost got into a fight with Raul because of her."

"A disagreement. We've always had opposing views on the situation with Yasmin," he explained calmly.

"It escalated into a serious argument. How can you be sure it won't happen again?" Eva asked with concern.

"I'm going to let them settle their problems without interfering." Unintentionally, he sounded cross.

"At Raul's request." Eva discerned his indignation. "My advice: be tactful."

Walking over, Orlando sat next to her on the couch. "Mom, I don't want you worrying unnecessarily." He placed his arm over her shoulder and tapped a kiss on her cheek. "Raul has to deal with his family. I have to handle the issues with mine."

"Since I arrived, you've been involved in their lives and their problems, oblivious to your own family. You can't ignore that fact or take it for granted."

"I need to prioritize."

"And apologize to Clara. Let her know that what happens in her life matters to you."

Orlando agreed and nodded. "I won't allow that to happen again."

Eva smiled. "I expect you to speak to her soon."

"Promise."

Eva shook her head.

"Action." He repeated the word she'd told him dozens of times after scolding him. They had to practice what they preached; that was the mandate in their home. His parents had been good role models. They followed through on every promise they made. He admired that about them.

"Right," Eva nodded. "I spoke to your father before you arrived."

That was something else he'd postponed.

"He wants to speak to you. Call him." Eva's tone was soft although it was a reproach. "I'm leaving Friday."

Eva hadn't been in the city a week and was already returning to Santo Domingo. Without realizing it, Orlando had missed the opportunity to spend quality time with his mother. That disturbed him, as did the fact that he had no idea when they would see each other again. He had taken a week to address the issues of Roberto's wake and burial with Raul and would have to wait several months to request more vacation time.

"Your father misses me. I just came to sign the lease. I wouldn't want Clara and Mario to be evicted after they gave up their apartment to keep mine. You won't have to purchase my ticket," she added. "Clara already did."

"Why didn't she speak to me first?" Clara was not responsible for planning Eva's trips. He always planned for her arrival and departure. It gave him the flexibility of selecting a time frame that would not affect his work schedule. He could pick her up and take her to the airport at ease.

"You always purchase it; this time she did."

He disguised his irritation and forced a smile. His negligence had consequences. He disliked arriving late to work and even more so after he'd taken time off. "What time are you leaving?"

"My flight departs at 11:00 in the morning. Please don't get upset with Clara. She reserved what was available. You already took a week off. I'll take a cab to the airport."

Orlando smiled thinly. His mother had just finished lecturing him about priorities, and she expected him to let her take a cab?

"I've always done it. No reason to stop now," he said, determined to meet that same week with Clara to apologize and clarify some issues.

* * *

"That's how you're taking care of Mom?" Isabel yelled. "She's in the kitchen cooking while you're sleeping."

Yasmin glanced groggily at the empty space next to her. She had snuggled next to Carmen after calling the office and then fell asleep.

As Isabel exited the room grumbling and cursing aloud, Yasmin glanced at the clock—5:45 p.m. She had slept most of the day and had no idea when Carmen got up or Isabel arrived.

She sat up, and everything swirled around. Placing her hands on her temples, she remained motionless. She closed her eyes to steady herself and wanted to crawl back under the cover and continue resting.

She whispered a prayer. "Lord, make this horrible pain dull, and provide the energy I need to endure."

With measured steps, Yasmin staggered to the bathroom. The cold water revived her. Fully awake, she opened the medicine cabinet. Her mother also suffered from horrid migraines. Rummaging through the medications, she found her same prescription. She popped one of the pills in her mouth, scooped some water in her hand, and swallowed it. She had forgotten her medication at Ani's. It was still on the nightstand.

Yasmin studied her reflection in the mirror. Her face was pallid, and she looked worn down, depressed, and ill. She was still wearing the black pantsuit she'd worn the day before. Thankfully, it wasn't wrinkled. The extra clothes she kept at Ani's were inappropriate—too colorful. She had plenty of black outfits in her closet. She would go to her apartment, pack some clothes, and leave them at Ani's.

Yasmin scanned the room she had shared with Isabel. She suppressed the disturbing visions that surfaced. She wasn't the culprit as her family erroneously believed. "Please, help me forget," she prayed. She had pushed the hideous memory deep within her heart and vowed to never speak about it.

Taking several deep breaths, she calmed down, walked to the bureau she had as a child, and opened a drawer. She anticipated finding it empty, but her clothes were still there, intact. She grinned despite the sadness that overwhelmed her. She supposed that if she wasn't there, her father didn't care what she left behind.

She strolled toward her bed and touched the mint comforter with the tips of her fingers. It had been a gift from her father. She'd pestered him for months to buy it for her. Had been delighted when she unwrapped the gift. As she requested, she got the quilt, shams, accent pillows, and skirt. Her father had gone out of his way to buy everyone a Christmas gift—a rare, one-time event.

Roberto never remembered birthdays, holidays, or special celebrations. Yasmin was aware of her mother's indignation when their anniversary passed, unperceived by her husband. The hints her mother had provided were ignored. Frustrated and disillusioned, Carmen stopped giving clues. Their anniversary became as unimportant as the rest. Yasmin resented how Roberto had treated her mother. He never cared about her or took her wishes into consideration. Making Carmen happy seemed unimportant to him.

Yasmin studied Isabel's side of the room. It was unkempt—the bed still unmade, her pants, blouses, skirts, and stockings hanging over the headboard. A pile of clothes was bunched at the foot of the bed. Isabel never got around to putting away the clothes she wore. The drawers in her bureau were partially open with clothes spilling out. Carmen's rebukes, incessant quarrels, and punishments prompted no change.

Yasmin had kept her space immaculate. It was one of the many differences between them. Their interests, friends, and goals were also opposite. Yasmin loved going to school, studying, and being on the honor roll. Isabel struggled through high school and barely passed. Yasmin wanted a career, her own apartment, and financial stability. Isabel was content with a high school diploma and willing to work in a sewing factory and make minimum wage.

Yasmin and Isabel had no physical resemblance either. Isabel was light skinned with blonde, wavy hair. Raul, who had their father's dark brown skin tone, was the darkest of the three.

"This is my room," Isabel hollered.

Yasmin turned around and saw Isabel standing by the entrance. Before the incident with Manuel, Yasmin had also felt possessive about her side of the room.

"Excuse me." Yasmin gestured for Isabel to move out of her way, but Isabel remained motionless, daring Yasmin to remove her physically.

Stepping back, Yasmin crossed her arms and refused to get into another confrontation. If Isabel wasn't concerned about her mother's health, she was.

"Mom would allow you to stay," Isabel retorted, "but like Dad, Raul and I don't want you here."

Yasmin debated if she should respond. Her initial instinct was to remain silent, but the temptation to lash back was too strong. "I have my own apartment." She lifted her chin proudly. "I'm glad I don't have to stay here and be bullied and treated like a child by Raul."

"Yasmin Arias," Carmen called out her name. "Remember, Raul is your older brother, and you have to respect him."

Isabel stepped aside, grinning triumphantly.

Face-to-face with her mother, Yasmin felt her bravado deflate like a balloon stuck with a pin. She lowered her head and stared at the mud smeared on her shoes.

"Refusing to stay and not considering us family—you already chose that," Carmen said emphatically, handing her the tray. On it was a cup of tea, a teaspoon, and a pill on top of a folded napkin.

"Not purposely, Mami."

"No?" Carmen asked, incredulously.

Yasmin stared at the smoke that swirled out of the cup and evaporated, and she wished she could do the same.

"You wanted her to come back so you could serve her?" Isabel was furious.

"Yasmin is sick too," Carmen replied. "Take the medication, and you'll feel better."

"She should be serving you," Isabel said.

"You need to go to Josefa's," Carmen told Isabel. "Take a cab. You need to arrive early to help her prepare everything. Yasmin will join you later."

"Hasn't she embarrassed and humiliated our family enough?" Isabel asked. "Now we have to be with her at the *rezos*?"

"Yes," Carmen replied, pointing toward the door. "Go."

Isabel eyed Yasmin with antipathy, took her purse from the bed, and stormed out.

"Why are you so considerate to Josefa? Didn't she cause your divorce?" Yasmin asked, following Carmen to the kitchen. Placing the tray on the dining room table, Yasmin sat down and glanced anxiously toward the door, envisioning Roberto entering and rushing toward her.

"You're misinformed. Your father and I were divorced before he married Josefa."

Yasmin refocused on their conversation. "How long since you got legally separated?"

"Almost three years," Carmen replied.

Yasmin frowned. Her father hadn't waited long to find someone else. "And he's been married to Josefa for . . ."

". . . ten months," finished Carmen.

Yasmin visualized a timeline. If her calculations were correct, her parents got divorced either the same year she had visited or the beginning of the next year. The frown on her lips deepened.

"Why did you get divorced?" Yasmin asked, still unable to believe that her worst fears had materialized.

Carmen shrugged. "There are things about my relationship with your father I've never mentioned. Josefa was not the cause."

"Was I?" she asked. "I heard Dad's threat that if I ever visited again, he'd leave."

Carmen stared at her in silence, and then a knowing gleam shone in her eyes. "That's why you didn't visit or call?"

Speechless, Yasmin lowered her head. The reason seemed valid enough. She realized that after the incident with Manuel, everyone questioned what she did and perceived it as malicious.

"I'm speaking to you, Yasmin Arias."

She met the arctic glare.

"You will be cordial and respectful to Josefa," Carmen instructed with authority. "The reason I want the three of you to attend the *rezo* has nothing to do with Josefa. I expect you to attend every *rezo*," Carmen added, looking directly at Yasmin. "You'll join Raul and Isabel there."

* * *

"Yaz!" Orlando yelled, grabbing her by the shoulders and dragging her out of the way as the car sped past them. The sound of the horn echoed in his ears as Yasmin turned around and gazed up at him, startled.

Embracing her, he held her firmly in his arms and felt her trembling as she rested her head on his chest. His heart was drumming wildly, and he shook his head to dispel the horrid images of what could have occurred. He was thankful he reached her on time.

Orlando felt Yasmin stirring in his arms and studied her face as she moved back. Still petrified, she stared up at him and then looked toward the area where she had been standing. Facing him again, he noticed that her face was ashen, her eyes cloudy. She rested her head on his chest and shivered. Placing his hands on her back, he pressed her close to him. Thankfully, she was safe and unharmed, and he waited motionless for her to regain her composure.

"Okay?" he asked when she stepped back. Although still shaken up, she seemed calmer. "Your car?"

"It's parked . . . around . . . Mami's way," she stuttered, her voice quivering. "I was going to take a cab."

"I'm taking you home." Yasmin shook her head. "We're not discussing it," he said firmly. Placing his hand on her back to ensure she remained next to him, he hailed a taxi.

"Your address, Yaz?" he asked, getting in beside her. He repeated it aloud after she recited it and settled back, his arm over her shoulders. She rested her head on his chest, pressing her hands against her temples.

"Should we go to the hospital?" he asked and felt her head move from side to side. He decided that after taking her home, if he felt she needed medical attention, they would go to the emergency room.

She insisted on walking up the stairs. He would have carried her, but she refused. Still pale and listless, she appeared emotionally drained. Entering the apartment, he walked alongside her past the living room and into the bedroom. He watched her push the bedspread aside, take off her shoes, and sit down.

"Your medication?" he asked. She nodded and pointed to the bureau.

He handed her the prescription bottle, hastened to the kitchen to get a glass of juice, and returned to the bedroom. He waited as she placed the pill in her mouth and drank the juice. Taking the glass, he held it and waited until she lay down.

"Rest, Yaz." Turning off the light, he left the door partially open and walked quietly to the living room. Placing the glass on the coffee table, he took his jacket off and draped it over the arm of the sofa. He loosened his tie and sat down.

It distressed him to think about what could have happened if he hadn't arrived when he did. The thoughts and images were disturbing. Sighing aloud, he tried to relax. Yasmin was fine, just emotionally strung. After resting, she would recover.

Ironically, Orlando had been thinking about her as he walked toward Josefa's apartment building. He had also spoken to Carmen after he left Clara's apartment. He anticipated hearing that Yasmin had gone to the *rezos*, and after Carmen confirmed it, he hurried over there. As he reached the entrance of the building, Yasmin was dashing down the stoop toward the corner. He had run after her, convinced that another quarrel had ensued.

Her migraine had been a reaction to the emotional shock she had been through and the stress she'd endured at the *rezos*. She was impetuous and allowed the situation with her family, their crude comments, and their nasty attitudes to agitate her.

Now Orlando tiptoed to the bedroom and gazed inside. Yasmin was asleep. He returned to the sofa and lay down, resting his head on the palms of his hands. More at ease, he closed his eyes. He planned to stay until she woke up to verify that she was fully recuperated. Depending on the time, he might go home or directly to the office.

It was odd. When he embraced her, she huddled against him. Perhaps it was the need to feel comforted, the need to share her anguish and be consoled. Surprisingly, she felt right in his arms.

"What are you thinking?" he scolded himself aloud.

As he'd promised his mother, getting his priorities straight, being logical, and focusing on his family took precedence.

* * *

Entering the kitchen, Yasmin pulled back one of the dining room chairs and sat down. She'd had sufficient rest. Her headache was dull but bearable. Taking the medication regularly was supposed to control the symptoms, but the continuous stress sabotaged her efforts. She swayed emotionally from one extreme to the other. She experienced highs, despair, indignation, outrage, lows, shame, remorse, and dread. Crying all the time didn't help. Placing her elbows on the table, Yasmin rested her forehead on the palms of her hands.

"Yaz!"

"Oh God!" she gasped. She was always alone in the apartment, so it was eerie to hear a voice behind her.

"Sorry." Orlando squatted in front of her. "Didn't mean to frighten you."

"You did." Her heart raced uncontrollably. Her hands shook violently. She held them together tightly on her lap so Orlando wouldn't notice.

"You're too anxious," he said in a quiet tone, combing her hair back gently from the sides of her face so their eyes met. "That doesn't help your condition."

Shifting her gaze, she leaned back. Orlando reminded her of Ani who was always giving her advice on one topic or another. "What I need is to be more careful," Yasmin told him.

He stood up, a thin smile on his lips. "Glad I could help."

"Who knows what would have happened to me if you hadn't shown up?" She watched him walk to the other side of the table. Stopping, he looked at her. The anger she expected was nonexistent. He seemed unscathed by her remark.

He sat opposite her. "Running and escaping may seem like the only solution. Try to relax, Yaz. Find ways to distract yourself."

"That was the problem," she humored dryly, shifting sideways so they weren't facing each other. "I was too distracted."

"Not funny." He wasn't amused.

Instead of going home to rest and in order to avoid disappointing Carmen, Yasmin had gone directly to Josefa's. "I doubt I impressed anyone or proved with my actions that the death of my father was painful, or that I cared for him."

He shook his head, frowning.

"I rushed out when the *rezos* ended." She barely heard the prayers and was unaware of who was staring or pointing at her. Immediately after it ended, she got her purse and hastened out. Raul followed her, and when she stopped, he blocked her path.

"You ran out of the building and down the block as if someone was chasing you," Orlando noted.

"Raul insulted me," she said hoarsely. Raul's desire to hurt and demean her did not diminish the validity of his words—with his last breath, their father cursed the day she was born. Raul added that he felt the same. She ran out of Josefa's apartment building, blinded by tears and anguish.

Leaning forward, Orlando placed his fingers under her chin and lifted her head gently. "I'm sorry you went through that, Yaz."

"I prayed the situation with my family would work out."

He stood up, ripped a paper towel from the roll and handed it to her as he sat down. "Raul can be tough. We disagree on how he handles family issues."

Yasmin scrutinized Orlando's face. How could he lie and maintain such a calm demeanor? He seemed sincere, but she knew his reputation.

He and Raul couldn't be trusted. Her mother knew that. It was the reason she questioned Orlando's intentions.

"You're like Carmen," he said, "tough, resilient, with a razor-sharp tongue."

"Hope you're not bleeding too much from the cuts."

He wondered what caused her to become defensive and sarcastic. "Best to have a positive attitude."

"Do you charge per hour?"

"I'm serious, Yaz," he said coolly, annoyed by her dry humor.

"I take things too seriously. That's considered my worst habit."

"By?" he asked.

She avoided his eyes and purposely kept her face down. She disliked his demands for details and lengthy explanations. Rather than answer, she changed the subject. "It's weird that Josefa is following that custom."

"Yeah," he agreed, noting that she opted not to talk about herself. "Raul was upset. He thought she would only have a Mass. Instead, she decided to do the *rezo* for nine days and a *rezo* every month on the date Roberto passed away. The last *rezo* will be next year for the first anniversary."

"She's exaggerating." Yasmin had often accompanied her mother and Isabel when close friends or family members died. They followed the usual custom—nine days of prayers and a Mass on the first anniversary. Monthly *rezo* were rare; she had never attended any.

"Josefa is the widow. She decides."

Yasmin frowned. Did her mother expect her to attend all the *rezo*? It was another reason to pray for strength and endurance, to believe the Lord would resolve the situation and amaze her as Ani always affirmed.

"Where did you come from?" she asked. She wasn't sure what had surprised her more—the car almost striking her or his sudden appearance?

"I was visiting my mother," Orlando answered. "She's staying with my sister, Clara, who lives several blocks from Josefa."

"Eva?"

He was surprised that she recalled his mother's name and looked at her with lifted eyebrows.

"Mami told me your mother's name. To prove I attended the Mass, I made the mistake of mentioning I was at the church. She didn't believe me, so I told her who was sitting in the same row with her."

"Are you getting along?"

"No." Crossing her arms, Yasmin forced a smile. It was bizarre that they were sitting in her kitchen chatting amicably. Again, she was voluntarily spouting information about herself.

Pressing her lips together, she stared at her hands. Everything in her life was the opposite of what she wanted.

"Yaz?"

Straightening her shoulders, she lifted her chin. "I'm sorry you won't get much sleep before you go to work." His laughter surprised her. "Did I say something funny?"

"You're asking me to leave."

She lowered her gaze. He discerned precisely what she meant.

"I'm used to sleeping only a few hours before I go to work."

"I'm sure," she spat out, disgusted by his remark.

His calm demeanor irritated her. She watched him stand, push the chair in, and walk out of the room. Following him into the living room, she waited with crossed arms for him to put on his jacket.

She scrutinized him from head to toe. He was wearing a gray suit with a matching plaid shirt and tie. His shoes shone as if they were brand-new or recently polished. The attire suited him. She was tempted to ask what he did for a living but just grunted softly. The polished look was a sign he took his appearance seriously, which she deduced was to impress women.

"As difficult as it is to deal with your family, try to stay calm," Orlando said as he headed to the door.

"Great recommendation from Raul's best friend," she retorted angrily.

"We discussed that, right?" His tone implied there was no need to address that topic again. "You need to stop overreacting, Yaz."

"Go home, Orlando. I'm sure you have more important things to do than lecture me."

Chapter 5

Placing the file on the desk, Orlando dialed Raul's number. Yasmin hadn't told him outright what Raul said, nor did he need to hear it. What bothered him most was that if Yasmin had been severely hurt or hospitalized, Raul would have attributed the accident to something other than himself.

"Can I speak to Raul Arias?" he asked the secretary.

"Orlando?"

"Hi," he greeted her, surprised by her enthusiasm.

"Hopefully, I'll see you soon," she teased. "You've got my number. Call me."

"Okay," Orlando replied, although he had no intention of contacting her. Unlike Raul, he'd learned from his experience with Maria that getting involved with someone at work or close to the family caused constant problems. His office and home were sacred; he preferred not to use either location when he was involved with anyone. That made it easy to start a new romance without concerning himself with an impromptu visit at home or work. His apartment was a place to relax and enjoy his privacy.

"Worked overtime yesterday?" Raul asked.

"I was with my mom. She's traveling to Santo Domingo on Friday."

"Eva didn't stay long."

"She came for a few days to take care of some errands." He was still upset with Clara about purchasing the ticket and planned to speak to her that evening if his mother wasn't there.

"Josefa should be more organized," Raul continued. "First *rezos* and nothing was prepared. I had to go downstairs several times."

"She just became a widow. She's grieving." Orlando questioned what, if anything, would make Raul empathetic.

"I attend because of Ma. Josefa and Isabel need to prepare everything. Tonight I'll get there when the *rezos* begins or after," Raul laughed. "Guess what, defense attorney? I spoke to Ma this morning, and Yasmin wasn't there. Instead of going early to take care of Ma, she was with Manuel."

"She could be working," Orlando said, ignoring Raul's suppositions. If she hadn't gone to work, he hoped she had lain down after he left. Sleep and rest were the best way to control the migraines.

"Working?" Raul was skeptical. "Some consider it work."

Orlando was silent. Raul's gross view of Yasmin irritated him. Yasmin was reticent and secretive, unlike the secretary who was dating Raul and flirting with him when she knew they were friends. He had been in Yasmin's bedroom. They had been alone in her apartment. He had fallen asleep on her couch for a few hours. When they spoke in the kitchen, she focused solely on their conversation.

"Ma insists she has to attend the *rezos*," Raul declared. "Everyone is talking about her and about our family."

Orlando was convinced that Yasmin's behavior did not stir rumors. Luisa, Maria, and Isabel did the stirring. Not everyone who attended the *rezos* knew Yasmin or what had occurred. It infuriated Orlando that they purposely spread malicious rumors.

"I had your car picked up this morning. I'll check it later. Need another?" Raul asked.

"No." Unless he planned to do something special after work, he would use public transportation. It saved him time, money, and the hassle of trying to find parking.

"How are you going to impress the ladies?"

Orlando laughed. "Not necessary."

"Since Dad got sick and passed away, I haven't gone out. Papo invited me to join him along with a few of the guys at a new lounge in Inwood. We're going tonight if you want to join us."

"Yeah, going to Clara's after work. I'll meet you at Josefa's or at the lounge."

* * *

After Orlando left, Yasmin took her medication and lay on the sofa. She fell asleep and awoke several hours later. Sitting up, she gazed at the time—midday.

She considered calling Ismenia to find out if she was home. Fearing Ismenia would not reply, she decided to go in person. She showered, dressed, and left the apartment.

The walk to the train station in the sweltering heat was long. The train arrived as she was going down the stairs. By the time she got on the train, she was drenched. Sitting next to the doors, she enjoyed the cold air from the air-conditioning.

Ismenia's building was close to the train station, and the entrance was unlocked. Yasmin walked eagerly up the three flights of stairs. Hesitating before knocking, she muttered a silent prayer. *I admit I was wrong. You know my heart. I didn't want to hurt or exclude Ismenia.*

She knocked several times and waited. She turned to leave but stopped when she heard the locks opening.

Through the partially open door, she noticed that Ismenia was wearing pajamas—a gray tank top with matching boxers that exposed her lean legs. Her blonde, curly hair was disheveled, and she looked as though she had just woken up.

Yasmin slipped through the narrow space Ismenia provided and stood beside her. The hallway was dark as Yasmin followed Ismenia down the L-shaped corridor to the kitchen.

She glanced into the living room as she passed by. The furniture had been pushed to one side to accommodate a stack of boxes. Yasmin remembered Ismenia mentioning that Nestor's mother, Ramona, was moving permanently to the Dominican Republic. Ramona would be residing in the capital, Santo Domingo.

"Is Ramona taking the walls too?" Yasmin humored as they entered the kitchen.

"Probably," Ismenia replied with a scowl on her face as she stacked several bowls that were still filled halfway with milk and cereal. She dropped them loudly inside the sink on top of the pile of dirty dishes. Turning on the faucet, she sprinkled water over the bowls. She poured liquid soap over the sponge and then returned to the table to wipe up the spilled milk.

"Nestor never picks up after the kids," Ismenia complained as she rinsed the sponge. Returning to the table, she wiped it again and then flung the sponge from where she stood toward the sink. Dragging a chair back, she sat down and crossed her legs.

Yasmin surveyed the kitchen. Dirty pots and pans were stacked on the stove. She wanted to maintain a blank expression but failed. The greasy pots and dingy stove made her cringe. A row of used cups and glasses were cluttered on the counter next to the dish rack. She pressed her purse close to her chest and forced herself to remain still. The disarray, the filth, and the grime disturbed her. She always made sure her apartment was spotless and the kitchen gleaming, a habit Carmen had sternly enforced.

Ismenia cleared her throat loudly. "If you came to inspect the kitchen, you've seen how dirty it is. So you can leave."

Yasmin disregarded her comment and refocused her attention. "I'd like to see the kids. Are Ismael and Andres in the bedroom?"

"Nestor took them out. He's visiting a friend of the family with Ramona and picking up a package they're sending to relatives in Santo Domingo."

"You're traveling?" she asked, stunned by the news. "How long will you be away?"

Ismenia shrugged. "You look horrible. Who would find you attractive?"

"Someone might," she smiled widely. Orlando did; she was certain of that.

"You smile then frown. Why?"

Yasmin grimaced. The thought that Orlando liked her had resurfaced her mother's warnings about his intentions.

"Something else you want to keep secret?" Ismenia accused when she remained silent.

"Nothing worth mentioning." Yasmin preferred not to discuss it.

"Like your father passing away and not telling us you were late because you were at the wake?"

"I'm sorry."

"Is someone interested in you? Nestor mentioned you were talking to some guy and that they almost got in a fight."

"Why is Nestor getting involved? Correcting me?" Nestor needed to devote himself to his relationship with Ismenia and stop gallivanting with his friends.

"We waited two hours," Ismenia reminded her, sourly. "Who was the guy?"

"Raul's friend," Yasmin blurted out. "A snob. I'm glad I've never liked any of Raul's acquaintances or friends."

Ismenia laughed heartily. "How is Orlando?"

"I'm happy you and Ani are speaking to each other again." If Ismenia was mentioning Orlando, she and Ani had spoken about him.

Ismenia leaned forward eagerly. "Orlando drove your car and took you to the cemetery. What else?"

"Nothing." She could imagine what they would think if they knew he had been to her apartment.

"If you acted your age and enjoyed life, you wouldn't be sick, depressed, and hiding at Mom's place or yours."

"I should have explained why I was late. I didn't want to ruin the night for you."

"You did," Ismenia said. "Nestor kept complaining. We argued most of the night. I left him at the club. He took a cab and caught up with me as I was entering the building. He insisted we go to a restaurant. I agreed, so we went to the IHOP on one hundred twenty-fifth. The place was packed. That's why I got home in the morning. We didn't go to a motel like Mom thinks."

"Ani didn't mention that."

"I didn't bother to tell her," Ismenia sneered. "You probably thought the same thing."

Yasmin was silent, refusing to admit that the idea had occurred to her.

"You denied us the opportunity to grieve with you. That was our decision to make."

"Things happened so quickly," Yasmin began.

"Mom lectured me about being understanding," Ismenia said, "and told me to pray for both of us. She said to ask for insight and wisdom on making decisions and not allowing our emotions to control us. Mom wants me to be—what was the word?" She paused as if thinking. "Empathetic. Mom forgave you. I didn't."

Yasmin was silent. She watched Ismenia storm down the hall. "You know the way out," Ismenia yelled. Without waiting for a reply, Ismenia entered the bathroom and slammed the door.

The silence in the apartment wrapped itself tightly around Yasmin. She felt her chest constrict and opened her mouth to breathe. She stood near the dining room table, immobile for an indefinite time.

The sound of the shower spurred her into action. She rushed down the hall and out of the apartment. Her shoulders slumped and her eyes glossy, she exited the building, walked to the corner, and lifted her arm as a cab approached.

"Where?" the driver asked jovially.

Still unsure, Yasmin remained silent. Going to Ani's at that time of day without confirming that Ani was home wasn't wise. A call would have confirmed that. Accustomed to calling from her office or home, she abstained from purchasing a cell phone, a decision she needed to reconsider.

It was too early to visit her mother. She already felt wretched and couldn't stand being battered verbally for a prolonged time. Yasmin sighed aloud and then blurted out Carmen's address.

Leaning back, she closed her eyes. She yearned to be home under the covers, asleep and oblivious to everything. The driver had the radio on and sang along with the chorus, praising the Lord for his presence, deeds, and love.

Yasmin forced a thin smile as she exited the cab. She'd heard that song at church and had sung along emphatically with tears of joy and adoration clouding her eyes. She longed to feel the same; instead, she felt alone. Was God with her amid the pain and struggles that overwhelmed her?

There were no signs that her problems were being resolved. She was waiting, praying, and anticipating a signal or confirmation that the situation would change.

Yasmin entered the building and read the sign on the elevator door—
Out of order.

She glanced toward the entrance. Her car was parked several blocks away. Walking in the intense heat would be uncomfortable, though she could blast the air-conditioning as she drove home.

Home? Was that the right word for it? It was a decorated cubicle where she often felt alone, destitute, and trapped, the silence and solitude smothering her.

Deciding to stay, she trudged up the four flights of stairs. Out of breath, mouth dry, and her face dripping with sweat, she entered the apartment.

"Did you lose your job?" Carmen asked as Yasmin swept past her.

"No," Yasmin replied, placing her handbag on the dining room table. She walked to the kitchen, took the ice tray from the freezer, put several cubes into a glass, and filled it with water. She drank a full glass and then filled it again. After placing the ice tray and pitcher back in the fridge, she walked into the living room, glass in hand.

She sipped the water. The living room was cool and comfortable. She was tempted to curl up in the corner of the sofa. Instead, she placed a chair next to the rocker.

"Where's Isabel?" Yasmin asked, anticipating that Isabel had taken the day off to take care of Carmen and was either in the bedroom or doing an errand.

"Working. She took off several days last week after your father died and can't take any more days."

"I have a lot of vacation time accumulated," Yasmin said, "so I took this week off. Is she still working at the sewing factory?"

Carmen nodded. "She and Maria have been there for years. They complain about the pay but never try to get a better job. Isabel makes extra money on weekends helping Luisa with her catering business. I suppose what she earns at both jobs is enough."

"And Raul?"

"He owns a mechanic shop," Carmen smiled with pride.

Yasmin thought repairing cars was a hobby he'd overcome. When he was a toddler, he frequented a mechanic shop where a friend of their father worked. As he got older, he spent most of his time there. In high school, he worked there on weekends alongside the mechanics. It was his favorite pastime—and Orlando's too.

Had they become partners? When she spoke to Orlando that morning, he mentioned visiting his sister. It was unlikely that he would leave the mechanic shop, go home, shower, and get dressed in a suit just to visit family. His appearance spoke office job.

"Raul is doing well financially," Carmen shared. "Seems he'll never get serious, married, or have a family." She sighed aloud. "I wanted the three of you to have more productive, stable lives."

Yasmin placed the glass on the table. She had financial stability, but the other areas of her life were in disarray.

"Ani dropped by yesterday after you left for the *rezos*," Carmen informed her. "She told me you sleep over frequently," she added with disapproval. "Did you sleep there last night?"

"No," Yasmin replied. Her initial plan was to go to Ani's. But almost getting hit by a car had altered that idea. Until that moment, the severity of what could have happened eluded her. If Orlando hadn't arrived when he did . . .

Carmen leaned forward, "You look pale, Yasmin. The migraine again?"

"Yes," she lied.

"Ani mentioned that Ismenia moved in with Nestor again. She was calm as if it didn't bother her that they keep getting together," Carmen continued.

Yasmin nodded. Ani's attitude and reactions to conflict amazed her. Problems and challenges, regardless of how intense, didn't appear to affect her. She always seemed at ease, tranquil, and content. Late one night when she was staying over, she asked Ani why she took conflicts and problems so calmly. Ani quoted Proverbs 3:5: "Trust in the Lord with all your heart and lean not on your own understanding."

Yasmin yearned for a solid faith like Ani's. She wanted serenity, peace of mind, and joy, regardless of what her family did or said about her.

"She sounds so confident," Carmen marveled. "She told me she knows her prayers will be answered and that she's patient and at peace while waiting. All these years I prayed you'd return home and waited in vain for you to move back in."

Carmen's hopelessness reminded Yasmin of her own disbelief and doubts. Why was she questioning if the Lord was with her? Why was she incredulous about the work God was doing in her life? Why was she unhappy with His timing—as if He would act in her time and not His own? "Never late or early. Precise." Ani's words always redirected and refocused her and made her conscious of the kind of thinking, attitude, and life she should have. Immersed in her emotions, she overlooked the daily blessings she received.

"I hope Ismenia won't have a third child," Carmen went on.

Yasmin gazed at Carmen but didn't respond. Ismenia lived her life frivolously without inhibitions or regrets. She would have a third child without qualms.

"You were smart, Yasmin. You made sure you didn't conceive."

"That would have never happened," Yasmin assured her mother. The relationship they kept alluding to had never materialized.

"Never?" Carmen repeated, offended. "That word defines the deception of your life, Yasmin Arias."

Gazing at her hands, Yasmin recalled the pastor's sermon. Even if she wanted to forget, disregard what had occurred, and begin anew with a clean heart, every conversation with her family focused on the past.

"Raul said you were doing well or you wouldn't have stayed away so many years."

"You believed that?" Yasmin asked. Her mother constantly accused her of being deceitful, and Raul and Isabel were the ones who kept fabricating lies about her.

"What I believe matters to you?" Carmen asked with disbelief.

"Are Raul and Isabel reliable, honest, and truthful?"

"We're talking about you, Yasmin."

"They don't do anything wrong or make mistakes?"

"Speak to me in a respectful tone," Carmen warned, standing and lifting her hand. "I don't care how old you are, you'll lose some teeth."

Yasmin waited until Carmen sat down and then stood up and walked to the kitchen. Wetting a paper towel, she placed it on her forehead. The cold water was soothing and relaxed her somewhat. She looked out the window and smiled. The kids were screaming at the top of their lungs as they ran in and out of the sprinkler. Dropping the paper towel into the garbage, Yasmin dragged herself back to the inquest. The sweltering July heat was no comparison for the furnace of the living room.

"I spoke to Luisa last night," Carmen went on. "She told me you'd been rude."

"She called to tell you that?" Yasmin wondered, sitting down. "Why do I need to acknowledge her in any way? She's just looking for any excuse to gossip."

"Greeting people is social etiquette. And what you call an excuse to gossip is a conversation about what you do."

Yasmin lowered her eyebrows and asked, "Like what?"

"Didn't you rush out of the *rezos* to meet Orlando? I know he didn't attend the *rezos* and that you got together afterward."

When Yasmin ran out of the apartment building, she had been oblivious to everything and hadn't even stopped to make sure it was safe to cross the street. Thankfully, Orlando was there and saved her life. Despite her resolve to avoid him, he was the only one concerned about her and interested in her well-being.

"We met by coincidence as he was headed to Josefa's," Yasmin explained. "We talked for a while. Luisa must have seen us when she left the *rezos*." She wished Luisa had also seen what occurred, but it wouldn't have made a difference. Luisa revealed what was convenient.

"What do you have to say to each other?"

"Should I run when I see Orlando?" she asked wryly.

"You know his reputation."

"Why should that concern me?" she objected.

"Ever since you came back, you and Orlando have been together frequently."

Her mother made it sound as if it had been months. It was barely three days. "All we did was talk."

"It's my choice to believe it," Carmen pointed to herself. "What do you think he wants?"

Yasmin shrugged. She had already decided what course of action to take. His intentions, if he had any, were irrelevant.

* * *

"I'm glad Mom isn't here, Clara. I wanted to speak to you," Orlando told her. He followed her into the living room. Taking the remote, he lowered the volume on the television as he sat down on the sofa.

"The *novela* is almost finished." Clara gestured for him to wait.

"I need to speak to you, and you want to watch a soap opera?"

Clara turned off the television and faced him. "Any other requests before I sit?"

"Beer would be nice." He softened his tone.

"Soda or juice?" she said dryly, heading toward the kitchen.

"Soda with ice," Orlando called out, taking off his suit jacket and placing it on the arm of the sofa. The air conditioner was on, which was a great relief from the smothering heat outside. His shirt was damp just from walking from the train station to the building.

Sitting on the sofa, Orlando waited for Clara to return with his drink. He wanted to take advantage of Eva visiting a friend to talk privately with Clara. Eva had mentioned her plans when he called from the office.

"Since Mom arrived, you've been here only a few times." Clara handed him a glass of soda. "It's cold. Ice isn't necessary." She sat on the opposite side of the sofa, facing him.

Orlando drank most of the soda and then placed the glass on the coffee table. He gazed at his sister. Hair in a ponytail, she wore an oversized T-shirt, shorts, and flat sandals. Although hefty, her legs were muscular and defined.

Clara waited for Orlando to speak. He met her cool stare. Arms crossed, she waited in silence, a disgruntled expression on her face.

"I'd like to apologize for coming late to your anniversary," Orlando said hesitantly. "It was an important day for you. I needed to be here." Clara pressed her lips together but made no comment. "And for your information, I dropped by yesterday evening. You weren't here," he said. "Add that to your count."

"Won't make much difference," she noted. "Mom asked you to apologize?"

"She pointed out some things I need to reconsider, changes I need to make. Apologizing is the start of rearranging my priorities."

"Meaning?" Clara was unconvinced. "You're going to stop hanging out with Raul? You won't visit Carmen every weekend? Are you going to stop defending that . . ." Clara paused, ". . . Yasmin?"

"Has she done anything to you?" Orlando asked, annoyed by her demeaning tone. "You have no idea what really happened."

"You do?" Clara challenged.

"I'm not judging her, listening to, or believing gossip or ridiculous comments that have no basis."

Clara rolled her eyes. "Everybody is aware that *Yasmin*," she stressed the name, "was dumb enough to take her boyfriend home and get thrown out. Now that her father is dead, the indignity is forgotten, and she returns home."

"Let's focus on what I came to discuss."

"When it happened," Clara continued, ignoring his comment, "everywhere Raul went, you trailed after him. You forgot all the lectures Mom kept giving you because you were arriving at wee hours of the morning."

"Be specific," Orlando ordered, annoyed by her recollection of unimportant events.

"You were Raul's shadow, and now you're the same." She made a circle with her forefinger. "It's vicious."

"Anything else?" he asked, eager to move on to the topic he wanted to discuss.

"Everything that happens with Raul, Carmen, and their family is more important now that Yasmin is back. She's your concern."

"Your comments are worrying Mom. Stop talking to her about my personal affairs."

"What you mean is *conceal*." Clara was outraged. "Lie."

"The correct word is *discretion*. Whatever goes on with you and Mario, I'm not going to mention it to Mom. Give me the same courtesy. Mom thinks that if you need my help, you won't get it."

"Being with Raul, concerning yourself with Carmen's health, and meddling in Yasmin's problems are your priority." She paused, gave him a long, disapproving stare, and then continued. "Our family events are put aside. For Mario's sister's wedding, her baby's birth, and the christening, you weren't there. Most holidays and birthdays you stay a short time. On the day Mom arrived, you couldn't pick her up at the airport. You act like we're acquaintances. You don't make the effort to attend our celebrations."

Sliding close to Clara, Orlando placed his arm around her shoulder. Her complaints were legitimate. Clara's thorough description made him realize again that his family had taken second place.

"You can't blame Raul and Carmen for that. There are other reasons, Clara. It gets hectic at work. Also, there are issues—situations—that have nothing to do with them."

"You're the one not making us the priority." Clara was blunt.

He smiled sheepishly. "Guilty," he conceded. "Why tell Mom and not me? Why worry her?"

"Mom and I start talking and . . ."

"You said more than you should?" Orlando completed her thought.

"I'll be more careful," she promised, "but I haven't lied to Mom."

"Does Mom need to know? She's unhappy and upset. She'll tell Dad, and he'll be concerned. I don't want Mom or Dad worrying about us." He paused and added, "Don't mention the incident with Raul to her again."

Clara twisted her lips to the side, frowning.

"Don't repeat what you're told or what you hear from Maria, Luisa, or Isabel." He stressed.

"They didn't make it up." Clara noted.

"Not all of it."

Clara lifted her eyebrows.

He pretended not to notice her reaction. "I'll make sure to visit often and attend celebrations, and you'll be tactful."

She nodded.

"Where's Mario? Isn't he usually home at this time?"

"Working. The company is always changing his shift. Some weeks he works nights and others during the day. He's used to it, and I'm not," she admitted glumly. "Why do you defend her?"

"Her reputation is unwarranted."

"You're the only one who thinks that," Clara protested. "Be careful."

"You sound like Mom."

"Just a warning." She hugged him.

"You and Mom worry unnecessarily," Orlando reproached.

Clara shook her head. "You're being arrogant, Orlando. Not everyone is going to agree or see things from your perspective."

He nodded, although he disagreed. He didn't consider himself smug, vain, or patronizing. He wished his mother, Clara, Carmen, and even Yasmin would focus on what was real, not on erroneous perceptions.

* * *

Unable to endure Carmen's constant badgering, Yasmin insisted she had to meet Ani before going to the *rezos*—a lie she wished was true. At Ani's, she could be at peace. Instead, she drove to Josefa's, spent almost an hour looking for parking, and then purchased a coffee and sat in her car sipping it. The cool air and silence were a blessing.

Although Yasmin disliked being alone, the short time she'd sat in the car made her feel more at ease. She strolled the five blocks to the building. Once inside, she sat next to Josefa, oblivious of her surroundings. It was the only way she could withstand being the center of attention. Raul and Isabel made it obvious that she wasn't welcome, and everyone else followed their example. Josefa was always cordial and polite, which made her stay tolerable.

As she had the night before, she rushed out when the *rezos* ended. Raul was busy talking to some friends of Josefa's father who had attended the *rezos* for the first time. Isabel, Maria, and Luisa were chatting with some of the guests and enjoying the coffee, refreshments, and finger food. If they noticed she left, it wasn't obvious. That was a blessing. Content there had been no confrontations, she was eager to go home. She would follow her plans from the night before, pick up some clothes, and then spend the night at Ani's.

Orlando wasn't waiting for her in front of the building, and his absence was a reprieve. He was unaware of her predicament—the constant insinuations and rebukes that meeting with him caused.

"Yaz." She heard his voice as she reached the corner. Looking back, she gazed toward the building and then at Orlando. Although there was no sign of Luisa or Maria, they could appear at any moment.

As he approached her, Orlando wondered why she studied her surroundings with angst.

Yasmin stepped back to avoid physical contact. Lifting her hand, she wiggled her fingers to greet him.

Expecting to see Raul, Orlando glanced in the direction she was facing. He saw nothing out of the ordinary. The streets were empty.

Yasmin ran across the street as the light was about to change. She walked as fast as she could down the block and reluctantly stopped at the next corner. She continued walking briskly toward her car that was parked on the next block. Once she got out of that area, she could relax.

Orlando walked beside her, certain her desire to flee was prompted by another dispute with Raul or Isabel, if not both.

"Follow your usual routine, your plans for the night, Orlando," she urged, stopping next to her car. Not seeing Maria or Luisa was no confirmation that she hadn't been seen walking beside him or that her mother wouldn't hear about it.

"Who do you expect to see?" he asked, looking back and then facing her.

She rummaged through her purse looking for her car keys and giving herself time to organize her thoughts before speaking.

"Not safe to do that, Yaz. Take out your keys before you exit the building so you're ready to unlock the car and get in."

Inattentively, Yasmin nodded and pretended she was trying to find something else. She needed time to gather enough courage to voice her ultimatum. Facing Orlando, she tilted her head up and met his questioning gaze. "The few times we've seen each other caused . . ." She paused and then added quickly, ". . . comments."

"Did I hear you correctly?" he asked, unable to resist laughing. That's what she was concerned about? It amazed him that she allowed something so inconsequential to disturb her.

"You think it's funny?" she snapped, his smirk aggravating her.

"Running from a problem doesn't solve it." He placed his hand on her shoulder to stop her from getting into the car.

"No, it just gets me tired and out of breath."

"You need to be . . ."

"Everyone knows what I should do," she interrupted. "But I'm the one being insulted, criticized, and reprimanded by Mami constantly. I'm the one at the *rezos* being humiliated by my brother and sister as I pretend not to care. Except for Josefa, everyone there can't stand my presence."

"What does any of that have to do with me?"

She faced him, exasperated. Hadn't he been listening?

"Just because your family wants to believe the worst, don't expect me to run away each time I see you," Orlando argued. "I'm not going to stop talking to you or ignore you over unfounded accusations. I don't live by what other people say. Their opinions and comments don't affect my decisions."

"Yeah," she nodded. "A man who doesn't take any female seriously, discards them often, and changes them continuously wouldn't care what anyone says." Her tone made her disgust obvious. "That includes Eva? If she disapproved of something and told you, would you ignore her?"

"No, Yaz. I'd listen, analyze the situation, and make changes if necessary."

"That's you," she glared at him. "My situation is different. My family ruined my life."

"How?" he asked. Her comment was absurd. Her own actions triggered the unpleasant situation she was going through.

She turned away, opened the car door, and placed her purse on the driver's seat.

"Yaz," he called in a quiet tone and waited until she turned around. He lifted her face gently with the tips of his fingers. The mixture of anger and frustration in her eyes distressed him. "Be assertive," he said in a quiet tone.

She pushed his hand away and snapped her fingers. "Easy."

"No, Yaz, it isn't." He was candid. "Admit your actions caused the situation you're in, and stop being so sensitive and allowing what others think or say to affect you."

"What happened wasn't my fault." She crossed her arms defiantly as her cheeks burned red from outrage.

Her comment puzzled him. "Why didn't you go somewhere else?"

She shook her head. When she planned what to tell him, getting into a drawn-out argument didn't occur to her. "I'm going home. Maybe then I'll get enough energy to face Mami again tomorrow."

"Why visit every day? Take your medication, rest, and give yourself time to heal."

"Mami expects me," she replied, her tone indicating he should know that.

"Don't confuse responsibility with being a martyr."

"If I don't, Mami will think I won't come back. Raul will keep his promise of going to my place to harass me."

"Why worry about that? You will either satisfy them or you won't, and they'll complain and criticize you anyway. Do what's in here," he said as he pointed to his heart. "That's what counts."

"Finished?" she asked, tired of the conversation. "I'll put a check in the mail."

He stepped back so she could get in the car. He knew her sarcasm and snippy remarks were a defense mechanism. "Since you're going to ignore what I said, I'd like you to be clear, Yaz. What is it that you want me to do?"

Chapter 6

Orlando followed Raul to a table in the back of the restaurant and sat opposite him. Glancing at his watch, he frowned. It was 2:30 in the morning. When he got home, he would sleep a few hours before going to work. He wasn't always with a female, as Yasmin thought.

Raul studied Orlando's face as he sat down. "I could tell when you arrived at the lounge that you were upset."

"Nothing worth talking about," Orlando responded. He understood how Yasmin felt, but he was not the problem.

"But you're worried," Raul commented, a thin smile on his lips.

"I'm inundated with work from last week, and some things came up with Mom and Clara."

"Problems at work are endless. Family is the same. I thought it was an issue with one of your ladies. If it is, forget her."

"No issue." Orlando shook his head. It was odd. He was usually the one who moved on. If the request was made, he had already anticipated what might happen. He was prepared and sometimes eager and willing to go in another direction. Yasmin's decision had the opposite effect. He questioned her judgment and the logic of making a decision based on false rumors.

"Did you like the lounge?" Raul asked.

"It was okay." The small cubicle, decorated with palm trees and etched drawings of a tropical beach on the walls, was crammed with men drinking and ogling the waitresses. They paraded themselves in skimpy bikinis, their hips swaying rhythmically to bachata and merengue while they served the enthralled audience.

"Okay," Raul slapped him on the back, laughing boisterously. "We've been to worse, and you had no complaints. I'm going tomorrow night. You?"

"I'm spending as much time as I can with Mom before she travels."

"We can meet after."

Orlando shook his head. After stopping by Clara's, he wasn't sure what he would do. Seeing Yasmin would have been his preference, but he was unsure if he should meet her again.

"I'll go solo." Raul gestured for the waitress to come to the table. "I'm hungry! Take care of me," he hollered.

"Wait, Raul," the waitress waved from behind the counter.

"They always make you wait." Raul slapped his hand loudly on the table. "Angel got scared when I asked if he was with Yasmin."

"Had you asked me in the same tone, I would have too." Orlando grinned. Angel's face had become white as paper as he denied it emphatically and laughed nervously as if Raul were joking.

"Why is he telling me he saw Yasmin at some club?" Raul wondered. "I'm sure she frequents that as much as . . ."

"That didn't stop you from wanting to beat him up?" Orlando cut him off purposely. He disliked hearing demeaning remarks about Yasmin, a horrid habit that Raul thrived on.

"He likes Yasmin." Raul's tone voiced his disapproval.

Orlando got the same impression. He disliked Angel upon meeting him. Conceited and arrogant, Angel bragged incessantly about his intimate encounters. Mentioning to Raul that he had met Yasmin had been unwise. The smug expression disappeared when Raul glared at him.

"He asked Yasmin about me and thought I was in the club with her," Raul spat out. "I don't go out with my sisters, and I won't tolerate any guy who gets out of hand."

Orlando grinned. Raul acted as if some of the girls he was messing with didn't have brothers who might feel the same way toward him.

"Angel said he'd met her but didn't mention what else they did," Raul grimaced.

"Nothing," Orlando stated confidently, astonished that Yasmin had spoken to Angel. From his observations, Angel was too crude and too forward—traits Yasmin would find repulsive.

"Your client has a history," Raul sneered. "Forgot?"

"No law against talking to someone you meet in front of a club," Orlando commented. "Do you think Angel is foolish enough to hint that he and Yasmin had a fling—knowing your temper? I think he would have boasted about it to his friends, and you would have heard about it from one of the guys."

"Maybe he just said what he wanted me to know."

"He didn't say much. Ran off like the coward he is," Orlando stated and then grunted aloud.

Orlando deduced from Angel's comments that the conversation with Yasmin had been brief. If she'd accepted his advances, Angel's stance would have been haughty, his demeanor triumphant. Yasmin's reaction to Angel was probably acidic, her words razor-sharp. Yasmin could be standoffish, blunt, sarcastic, and succinct.

If she'd so desired, Orlando realized, Yasmin could have treated him the same way. When he asked her to be specific, to state her request, she drove off without answering—no snippy remarks—a sign that even if she refused to admit it, she liked his company.

* * *

Voices woke Yasmin. Lifting her head, she realized she had fallen asleep with the TV on. Instead of going to Ani's after speaking to Orlando, she had gone home. Although she longed for Ani's company and nurturing, she also knew her somber mood would provoke questions.

Drained of energy by her mother's constant accusations and discouraged by Orlando's lectures and incessant probing, she sought solitude, a place where her emotions required no explanations or reasons.

She had made herself comfortable on the couch, turned on the TV for company, and then cried herself to sleep. What prompted her tears eluded her—perhaps her mother's ridicule or her own lack of courage. She didn't understand what stopped her from being frank.

She was certain Orlando would be waiting for her after the *rezos* that night. Luisa had probably mentioned to Maria and Isabel that she saw her with Orlando. She would certainly spread the word. And everyone would assume the worst, just like her mother. She was certain that if Orlando attended the *rezos*, everyone there would examine her actions and gestures closely, misinterpreting and making false assumptions. Again, her reputation would be soiled.

"Will it ever end?" she asked, gazing up toward the ceiling. Ani would reply that she needed to wait confidently and trust that the Lord was working. But what she was experiencing and seeing gave no indication of His presence.

Going into the bedroom, she undressed, put on her robe, and went into the bathroom. She stood under the shower, letting the fine spray wash away the fatigue that oppressed her.

Later in the kitchen, she made coffee and sipped the brew slowly, revisiting her conversation with Orlando. Although she refused to admit it, his point was valid. Visiting her mother every day was not necessary. When she returned to work the following week, visiting on weekends was her only option. She'd taken the week off to spend quality time with her mother but had not anticipated so much strife. Carmen was relentless, her verbal attacks unwavering.

Yasmin glanced at the time—6:00 in the morning. She was tempted to call her supervisor and tell her she was willing to work half days. She decided to take advantage of the time she was off and use it more effectively. She would do some errands, take some outfits to the cleaners, and buy groceries. The next day she could do laundry.

She had to be wise. Spending an entire day with her mother and then going to the *rezos* was emotionally draining. Planning how long she'd visit was crucial if she wanted to stop being a martyr.

She laughed aloud. It wasn't humorous, nor had Orlando meant it to be. It bothered her that his comments and constant advice were accurate. He easily perceived her emotions, quirks, and gestures. He was attentive, questioning her directly on comments she blurted out.

Finishing her coffee, Yasmin washed the mug and then headed to her bedroom. She packed some clothes to leave at Ani's. That gave her the option of staying overnight or going home.

She decided not to fret. The *rezos* would end the following week and then she might see Orlando once a month if he attended. Her goal now was to gain her mother's trust. As Ani told her repeatedly, the One in control would make sure that happened.

* * *

"I knew you would keep your word," Eva exclaimed as she hugged Orlando. She placed her purse on the sofa. "Were you leaving?"

Although he was heading out, he shook his head. "Clara said you'd come later tonight. I was going to the *rezos* and planned to return after."

"I went to visit a friend at the hospital," Eva explained, embracing Clara.

"Should I serve you, Mom?" Clara tapped a kiss on her cheek.

"Not hungry. It's good to see the two of you together," she smiled. "I'd like to attend one of the *rezos* before leaving."

"We can go tonight or tomorrow," Orlando said.

"Today is best," Eva said. "I don't really like to go out the day before I travel. I like to pack all my stuff the night before."

"We have plenty of time to walk over and arrive when it begins," Orlando said. "Will you join us, Clara?"

"Yeah, I'll get ready." Clara headed to the bedroom.

"Sit." Eva patted the space next to her on the love seat. "I expect you to continue visiting Clara regularly. How's Carmen?"

"Fussing, cleaning, and cooking." Although she'd been taken to the emergency room for treatment, she wasn't following the directives of the doctors, just like Yasmin who took medications on an empty stomach. Neither took their health seriously and constantly stressed over trivial issues.

"Hard to rest when you're always active. Have you had more disagreements with Raul over Yasmin?"

He shook his head. "We have different opinions, but we get along. We went out last night."

"To a club? To drink, dance?" Eva asked, wide-eyed.

He nodded. "Yeah, to a lounge."

"During the nine days of prayers?"

"Raul is following Roberto's model. No matter who died, he always listened to music and drank after a wake or burial. He never attended *rezos*. He said that was for women."

"Raul's father wasn't a good example, but that's no excuse. Going to a club or lounge is acceptable for a friend or acquaintance, but for an immediate family member?" Eva shook her head.

"Raul doesn't concern himself with that," Orlando said. He respected Raul's decision, though he wouldn't have gone if it had been his own father.

"Everyone mourns differently. When a family member is gone, the time spent together is what's left—the good times shared and the memories."

"I doubt there are many of those. Roberto was a tough character. He was a harsh disciplinarian, though most of the time he was at Luisa's."

"That's sad. Must have been difficult for Carmen."

"It was. She suffered a lot." Orlando wondered if Yasmin had visited her mother that day and hoped she'd taken his advice to stay home, rest, and rethink her resolution. Carmen's accusations and criticism would not be altered by anything Yasmin did. He knew from experience that once Carmen set her mind to something, it solidified like cement.

* * *

Yasmin sighed with relief as she stepped out of the building and headed to the corner to hail a cab. At the *rezos*, Orlando had walked in with his mother and sister. When she saw Clara, Yasmin thought he'd brought a girlfriend but realized her mistake when Eva followed them. She recalled seeing both at the Mass and Carmen explaining who they were from her description of where they sat.

Eva was cordial, sophisticated, and well mannered—like Orlando. Yasmin liked her. There was no facial resemblance except their eyes. Eva's were just as inquisitive.

Clara didn't like Yasmin, not that Yasmin cared how she felt about her or why. Clara could join Luisa, Maria, and Isabel in the back row or stand next to Raul by the entrance and chime in when they began to criticize her.

Yasmin waved at a cab that was approaching. She got in and gave the driver instructions. Instead of driving, she opted to take public transportation to visit her mother, attend the *rezos*, and then take a cab home. Parking was limited in Josefa's area, and the available spaces were too far away.

As the taxi sped downtown on West Side Highway, Yasmin stared at the dark waters of the Hudson. She spent less time with Carmen that afternoon, but that didn't give her any reprieve. At the *rezos*, it was the same.

Raul's total disregard for her privacy was offensive. He made comments without caring who was listening. Isabel followed his lead, making derogatory remarks about Yasmin to the guests. Along with Luisa and Maria, they mocked her publicly. She was glad Maria and Luisa weren't there that night to humiliate and embarrass her in front of Eva and Orlando.

She sensed the disapproving stares of the guests and their reluctance to go near her during the rite of peace. She disguised her discomfort, unease, and embarrassment behind a calm expression and dared to smile thinly at some of the guests who gazed at her.

At least her prayers had been answered. What she'd considered impossible, she'd achieved. She had endured, felt at peace, and was content—feelings she hadn't experienced in a long time.

"I can do all this through him who gives me strength," she murmured. It was Philippians 4:13, the verse Ani repeated so many times.

* * *

"When you come back to New York, I'd like you to stay for two weeks or longer, if possible," Orlando told Eva. "We'll plan in advance, and I'll take a vacation. We'll go to a Broadway show, a concert, museums, and dinner. There are many places to tour in the city."

"I'm flattered." Eva placed her hand over his. "I pray you'll find the right woman."

"I haven't met anyone I consider worthy," he replied, convinced he'd stay single for many years.

"Sometimes we're unconscious of our feelings, but others see it in our behavior."

"You think I'm acting like I found someone and saying I haven't?" He recognized the knowing expression on her face, the look she always gave him when she made some keen observation he was not aware of.

Eva smiled. "She's much slimmer than I remember her."

"Yasmin?" he asked, pleased that she'd changed the subject. He wasn't interested in talking about serious relationships or marriage.

"She didn't look very comfortable."

"Raul and Isabel criticize and embarrass her in front of all the guests," Orlando added. He noticed how Raul kept glancing at Yasmin with obvious disapproval and overheard Isabel in the back criticizing how she was dressed. He studied her attire casually. She wore black capris and a white blouse, and her hair was combed back in a ponytail. There was a hint of face powder and radiant tinted lips. There was nothing to criticize, nothing improper.

"Although you told me you'll let them handle their issues," Eva reminded him, "you still get upset when you mention it. Your tone and facial expression change."

"Their behavior, their comments, and the way they treat Yasmin is unjustified. There's no need for scenes, arguments, or crude comments in public. Family issues should be private. Yasmin was indiscrete by error, coincidence, or bad luck. It doesn't matter. It's been five years, and they're acting like it just occurred."

"That also applies to you, Orlando."

"No." He shook his head, certain she was mistaken.

"When it occurred, you came home at wee hours of the morning. That semester, you failed most of your classes. You went late, cut classes, or didn't attend at all, supposedly looking for the guy she was found with. My prayers were answered. You didn't find him. I feared you'd ruin your future and end up in jail over a problem that didn't concern you." Eva paused and stared at him with evident concern. "I didn't understand it— until now."

"Why are you anxious, Mom?" He was unsure what Eva was referring to, what had made her so apprehensive.

"After many prayers, you got back into your studies. You took courses on evenings and weekends to graduate on time. You went out more often with Raul." She paused, the sad expression changing to a serene smile. "Are you and Yasmin together?"

"Yeah," Clara chimed in, handing Eva a mug with coffee. "Not that he'll admit it."

"Clara, I'd like to finish this conversation with Mom."

"Fine." Clara was indignant. "I'll go to my room and watch television. When you leave, I'll join Mom."

"You and I talk privately all the time, Clara. Orlando has the same privilege," Eva said in a calm tone, smiling. She took several sips from the mug.

"That's Orlando's choice," Clara retorted. "Nothing stopped him from visiting more often to speak to you," she said as she walked into the kitchen.

"True," Eva said, loud enough for Clara to hear. "He'll keep his promise and visit more often."

"Maybe," Clara shouted back.

"Actions," Eva reminded him, grinning.

Orlando nodded. Although they'd made a truce, Clara was still skeptical that he'd follow through. He understood why she felt that way. Reestablishing the trust he'd severed would take time. "I don't want Clara to get upset," he said. "We can continue talking tomorrow when I drop by after work."

Eva grinned and picked up her cell phone from the center table. "I want to speak to your dad and confirm that he has all the information on my flight."

"Clara," Orlando called. "Join us. Mom is calling Dad."

* * *

"Did Ismenia travel to Santo Domingo?" Yasmin asked, propping the pillows and lying down.

"Yesterday." Ani sat on the bed facing her. "She called this afternoon. We didn't talk much. She said Nestor left shortly after they arrived to visit some friends and still hadn't returned."

"I don't understand why Ismenia is with him again. Every time they travel over there, he disappears with his friends to go to resorts, bars, discotheques, and clubs. She keeps forgiving him and accepting it."

"When you don't forgive, you punish yourself."

"Forgive men like Nestor, Orlando, and Raul? They're selfish and have no regard for how much pain they cause."

"Forgiving is about you, not the other person, Yasmin," Ani clarified. "It gives you peace and tranquility. It frees you."

Yasmin grunted.

"Nestor cares for Ismenia but doesn't show it in the right way," Ani continued. "He gives her money and gifts. He takes her to expensive hotels, resorts, and restaurants. They're only part of his role in a relationship. Trust, respect, communication, commitment, and unity are also necessary."

"I doubt Ismenia cares about that."

"Like you, she doesn't listen. She uses her own judgment."

Yasmin's cheeks flushed, and she remained silent. She and Ismenia differed in their approaches to the situations they encountered. Ismenia was bold, made choices spontaneously, and was unconcerned about approval. Yasmin sought solitude, gave in to her emotions, and rarely followed her instincts.

"It is through God's help that we can change. Only He can renew our lives and heart," Ani went on.

Yasmin lowered her gaze. Restoring her life, the pain in her heart, and the acrid situation with her family would take a miracle. She felt as though she were going backward. She saw no progress.

"Change is a process," Ani continued. "Pray for guidance, Yasmin, so you can make decisions and take action in the appropriate time. Problems become more complicated if you ignore them or wait indefinitely. Be strong. Have courage."

Yasmin nodded. She was praying constantly. It seemed she kept adding things to the list and requesting the same things repeatedly.

"I don't think Nestor loves Ismenia." She refocused on the topic again. "He's not faithful, doesn't help her with the kids, and is inconsiderate."

"His behavior has nothing to do with how he feels, Yasmin. Unfortunately, sometimes there is an assumption that providing financially is enough."

"Dad was like that," Yasmin said. "I don't know if he was ever unfaithful. Mami never spoke to us about their relationship." Yasmin remembered how her dad went out all the time. Her mother complained that he spent a lot of time at Luisa's. She doubted that was the only place he went. "Nestor is probably like him."

"Don't make judgments. Regardless of what they went through, your parents stayed together many years."

"Until I caused their separation." Yasmin refused to believe otherwise, even if her mother denied it.

"Yasmin," Ani shook her head, frowning. "Sometimes we hide our pain in here." Ani pointed to her heart. "We suffer until we become numb, and then separation and divorce come easily." Ani gestured with her hand for Yasmin to scoot over and lay next to her.

"Why did you stay alone?" Yasmin asked. She had always wanted to know but until that moment never dared to ask.

"My husband had an affair with my best friend. Our families were close. We were like sisters. She lost her business and couldn't afford the house she bought. She filed for bankruptcy. I insisted she stay with us. When I realized what was happening, I packed and left. He broke it off, admitted it was a mistake, and begged for reconciliation. I loved him, but I couldn't forgive him. We got divorced." Ani paused and smiled. "When I forgave him, I was freed from the resentment, pain, and anger I had carried for years." She pointed to her heart. "Being depressed, isolating yourself, and suffering over the issues with your family are the result of not forgiving."

Yasmin wondered how it was possible to forgive Raul, Isabel, and her mother for mistreating her.

"I chose to be alone and refused to accept other opportunities for a relationship," Ani explained.

"Did you ever consider getting married again?"

Ani nodded. "Had I been with the Lord as I am now, I would have forgiven my husband, and we would still be together." She looked at Yasmin affectionately. "Have you seen Orlando again?"

"He was at the *rezos* with his mother and sister tonight." She made a conscious effort to be selective in what she said.

"You're frowning because?" Ani asked.

Yasmin disliked the transparency of her emotions. Orlando and Ani could easily read her gestures and reactions. "His sister doesn't like me. She gave me this look." She remembered Clara eyeing her up and down with antipathy.

"And his mother?"

"She's nice. Polite. Very sociable. Appears to be just as caring as Orlando."

"That's worth smiling about," Ani noted. "Your face changes when you talk about Orlando. Seems you like his company."

Yasmin pressed her lips together, annoyed at herself. She was unaware that her facial expression had changed. It was an unconscious reaction. Whether she admitted it or not, Orlando's presence had an odd effect on her.

During the *rezos*, she sensed his proximity and was overly conscious that he was sitting in the row behind her. She felt his stare, pretended not to notice, and refused to look back. During the rite of peace, she moved away from the crowd as she did every night. She watched him approach her and was stunned when his arm encircled her waist. His lips brushed her cheek lightly. Releasing her, he walked away leaving her frazzled with mixed emotions. Being in his arms gave her a sense of serenity and protection with a weird feeling in the pit of her stomach that made her feel anxious—awkward.

"No comment?" Ani asked, studying her gestures.

Yasmin shook her head and smiled. Ani wasn't making erroneous assumptions or judging her. It was a conversation. They listened to one another, exchanging opinions and ideas. Ani made Yasmin aware of things she had overlooked. She accepted and followed Ani's advice occassionally but not always as she should.

"The Lord brought Orlando into your life for a specific purpose," Ani said, a pleased expression on her face.

"Really?" Yasmin wrinkled her face with disapproval.

"Sometimes, because we're so focused on our problems, we miss the blessings we receive." Ani stood up. "Think about that, Yasmin."

Yasmin watched Ani exit the room. Ani was always attentive, her words encouraging. When they first met, it never occurred to her that Ani would become like a mother to her. She was grateful the Lord had united them.

Lying on her side, Yasmin closed her eyes. Was it possible that the Lord had brought Orlando into her life for a reason, that his presence was a blessing? It didn't appear that way. His presence was causing her strife and continous arguments with her mother.

Regardless of how she felt around Orlando or her facial expressions when she spoke about him, she had made her decision. Once the *rezos* concluded, the horrid encounters with Isabel and Raul would end, as would seeing Orlando. She could focus on what really mattered— reestablishing a close relationship with her mother.

* * *

Orlando sat next to Eva on the love seat. He picked up the glass of orange juice and drank some. He'd been looking forward to reinitiating the conversation they'd begun the night before. When he arrived, Eva informed him that Clara and Mario had gone to the supermarket. He was delighted.

"I'm not dating Yasmin," he affirmed, initiating the conversation.

"But you want to?" Eva asked, studying his features closely.

"Yaz is complex."

"Yaz?" Eva repeated. "What does she call you?"

"Orlando," he replied, ignoring the amused expression. "Sometimes when we talk, she's receptive. Other times she's evasive, argumentative, and stubborn."

Eva laughed softly, "Female traits."

"Yeah," he admitted, nodding.

"Seems you're drawn to her. When you're used to getting your way, a challenge can be motivating."

He had to laugh. Her observation was precise. He was intrigued by Yasmin's obsession with obscurity and eager to know why she thrived on being secretive. He wanted to know more about her. "Our conversations are brief. She doesn't say much about herself."

"Hmmm," Eva sang. "I don't think you're objective. You're emotionally involved."

"To a certain extent I am." He had been emotionally involved from the start, witnessing how the family condemned her. Their accusations, reactions, and description of what happened were excessive. "It's upsetting to see her suffering. Because of one mistake, she has to spend her life being mistreated?"

"Is that why you're so protective?"

"No, Mom. I question the validity of their accusations. They have no foundation or basis. I've been researching cases, interviewing clients, and going over statements and testimonies for years. She's the victim. That's my conclusion."

"You defend her and react strongly to any comment or criticism. You don't consider that protecting her?"

"I'm expressing my disapproval."

"Which almost led to a fight," Eva reminded him.

"Disagreement," he corrected. "My opinion hasn't influenced Raul. We've always disagreed. Yasmin has been the topic of many conversations. He delights in demeaning her and refers to her in offensive ways. He doesn't care if he humiliates her and makes her feel embarrassed or ashamed. There's nothing I can do."

"He asked you not to interfere, and you're resentful and angry?" Eva noted his angst.

"I agree with him. I'd prefer to settle any issue with my sister on my own." He refrained from adding that what disturbed him was that Raul was too aggressive and prone to overreacting. He was impulsive like Yasmin, Carmen, and Isabel. "Yaz is not how her family perceives her."

Eva grinned. "You're certain about that, even though she's complex?"

The knowing expression he had seen the night before resurfaced. He waited, certain she was going to convey what she discerned.

"Sometimes we're unaware of the obvious," Eva added. "We don't see it, and others do."

"True," he agreed, pleased that her view matched his own. "That's the issue with Yaz and her family." He changed the topic. "What do you think of her?"

"Why does my opinion matter?"

"It does, Mom." He gestured with his hand for her to tell him.

"She's beautiful, delicate, and reserved. She dresses conservatively and wears minimal makeup."

"You're very observant," Orlando complimented. "Now I know where I get it from. I've noticed the same. She does not merit the reputation she has."

"Orlando, you should understand why her family behaves that way. When you're deeply hurt, you need time to heal. By leaving, she either stopped it or prolonged it—maybe both."

"They need to resolve their issues or Carmen will be hospitalized again." He foresaw that possibility. Raul's and Isabel's attitudes had become worse since Yasmin's return. That could gravely affect Carmen's health.

"Unfortunately, Raul and Isabel, even Yasmin, might not realize that they have to avoid that. Yasmin returned recently because her father died, right?"

"No. She tried to go back home, but Roberto threw her out again. That evening, Carmen was hospitalized and admitted for several days. It was the first time she was diagnosed with high blood pressure and warned that she was at risk of having a stroke. Roberto was too self-righteous."

"Orlando, you shouldn't speak that way about someone who has passed away," Eva scolded.

"That doesn't change who he was or what he did."

Eva sighed aloud. "Be careful, Orlando. Good intentions can be misinterpreted."

"True," he agreed, convinced that her concerns were unfounded.

"You don't have to stay late again tonight. I'm going to finish packing my suitcase, shower, and lie down." She stood up. "I'll see you in the morning."

Orlando glanced at his watch. He would arrive after the *rezos* started, which wasn't a concern. He was looking forward to seeing Yasmin again.

* * *

Yasmin heard the door opening. Turning to the entrance, she saw Orlando enter. He stood next to Raul who was leaning against the wall. Orlando's chestnut-brown eyes fixed on her. It made no sense for him to arrive when the *rezos* were almost finished, but she preferred that to meeting him in front of the building afterward.

96

He acknowledged her with a smile. His confident stance assured her that his goals, once established, were achieved.

Carmen's words echoed in Yasmin's mind. What were his intentions? Was he like Manuel who sought to take advantage of her? She had realized that too late and then decided no one else would hurt her or take advantage of her again.

Shifting her gaze to the altar, Yasmin pretended to ignore Orlando. He claimed she should judge him based on merit. Her lips curled up. She supposed if he was cunning enough to convince females to trust him, he had some type of stature. Merit, which wasn't the word she would use, was given for achievement, good causes, and success after hard work and sacrifice, not for changing from one female to the next indiscriminately.

She scanned him from head to toe and then met his gaze. He was aware she was staring and grinned. She kept a serious expression, looked away, and turned slightly to avoid facing him. His prim appearance did not fool her. His black suit with gray shirt and plaid tie confirmed he wasn't a mechanic. She guessed he had an office job. He dressed lavishly and looked distinguished. She'd seen him casually dressed once on the evening he went to the emergency room with Raul. He'd worn black jeans with a short-sleeved, plaid shirt that exposed his muscular arms. He was fit. He probably lifted weights to keep himself in shape—another tactic to lure women.

Someone patted Yasmin's shoulder. Looking up, she realized Josefa was signaling her to stand. Embarrassed, she stood and listened to the chanted prayer. Looking in Orlando's direction from the corner of her eye, she saw him talking and laughing with Raul. Sitting along with everyone else, she tried to focus on what was being said, but she couldn't concentrate.

"Yasmin," Josefa whispered, tapping her on the arm.

She stood up abruptly. Josefa smiled warmly and continued singing. Her cheeks beet red, Yasmin kept her eyes fixed ahead.

Lula's vibrant voice echoed throughout the entire room as she sang and walked around the room with incense. Everyone sang along while embracing each other as a sign of peace and friendship.

Yasmin moved away from the row of chairs and pressed her body against the wall. An arm encircled her waist. Turning abruptly, she looked up. Orlando. As he had done the night before, he brushed his lips lightly on her cheek. The scent of his cologne lingered as he moved away. Still mesmerized, she watched him embrace Josefa.

Yasmin's cheeks flushed. She lowered her head. The mixture of emotions that overwhelmed her the night before returned.

"Yasmin, great to see you." Luisa kissed her gingerly on the cheek. "Rushing home today too?" She gazed at Orlando and then back at her.

Yasmin forced a smile and refrained from insulting Luisa to avoid another argument with her mother.

"Carmen must be pleased. She and Roberto argued all the time about whether you would return. How does it feel to be home again?"

Glad she kept her purse instead of giving it to Josefa, Yasmin walked to the door.

"Wait." Luisa placed her hand on her shoulder. "How's Manuel?"

Turning, Yasmin glared at Luisa with such intensity that Luisa stepped back and gasped aloud. Seething, Yasmin headed out.

"Talking about Manuel?" Raul blocked her path.

"Luisa was." She gestured in her direction, aware that everyone in the living room was staring at them and listening. She tried to walk around Raul.

"I asked you a question." He stepped closer to her, gazing downward.

"Ask Luisa." She gestured with her hand for him to move aside.

He allowed her to walk past him but followed her into the hall.

"More complaints?" she asked, stopping by the stairway. "Another list of *directions*," she stressed the word sarcastically, "that I need to adhere to?"

"Don't forget that I'm your older brother. You owe me respect."

"You earn respect; you don't demand it." She saw Orlando standing by the doorway several paces behind Raul and read the warning in his eyes to mellow out.

"Like you did ours?"

"I don't demand anything." She spoke in a calm, quiet tone although he was yelling. "All I want is for you and Isabel to leave me alone."

Raul laughed in response. "You wanted to see Ma, be with her. I'm going to make sure you do. I have your address and phone number. Anytime you decide to get lost, I'll be dropping by. If Manuel is lucky, he won't be there. If he's home, we have issues pending." He waved his fist in front of her face. "He'd better have insurance."

"I live alone," she said as she started down the stairs.

"Sure you do." Raul was sarcastic. "Dad wouldn't want you here."

Stopping, she turned back to face him. "I'll be here every day until the *rezos* end," she promised with a determination that surprised her.

Raul was stunned and didn't respond. Then his eyes became pitch-black. "Don't forget that Ma is the reason you're here."

* * *

Orlando lay on the bed, his hands crossed under his head, staring at the streaks of sunlight that filtered through the shades. He hadn't slept much. All night he'd thought about Yasmin. Raul loved to make scenes. He knew Luisa exaggerated and was just being spiteful, purposely stirring up conflict. Raul had used that as an excuse to embarrass Yasmin. Questioning her in front of the guests, following her out into the hall, and yelling at her ensured that everyone heard what he said.

Orlando shared Yasmin's frustration. Her family's reactions were extreme, and Carmen's attitude and comments were destroying Yasmin emotionally. She didn't need anyone else to do that. Whatever happened with Manuel and whatever the situation with Roberto, what she'd been through while away from home caused her to become self-destructive. He wanted to help her see the situation differently. But she refused to listen to sound advice, defiantly ignoring his advice not to contradict or confront Raul.

Orlando was confident that their attraction was reciprocal. Her smile and her body language contradicted her words. Although at times she acted self-conscious and embarrassed by his physical proximity, in his arms her body molded to his. She rested her head on his chest. He liked the scent of her perfume, her smile, and even her angry glares. As his mother pointed out, she was beautiful.

He sighed aloud. As he'd told his mother, it was complex.

Yasmin was leery of him, judged him based on his reputation, was distrustful, and questioned his integrity. He wondered if she was conscious of her reaction when she was around him. She studied him from a distance and took notice of his attire. She frowned often and eyed him with disapproval from the corner of her eyes. He could easily imagine what she was thinking. Did she realize she was treating him the same way her family was treating her? It bothered him, but that wouldn't deter him from taking advantage of every opportunity to spend time with her. Their conversations, though more like arguments, were gratifying.

There was a spark between them. Despite her misgivings about him, she enjoyed his company. When she let her guard down and was calm, she was a different person. Her responses were witty; her smile was jubilant.

Interestingly, no one he'd ever been involved with kept him awake nights or distressed him as much as Yasmin. Deciding not to delve more deeply into what that meant, he got up. It was Friday. After driving his mother to the airport, he'd head to work. He was still struggling to catch up and planned to go the next day to diminish the workload. He preferred working a few hours during the weekend until he caught up. During the week, he wanted to ensure that nothing would deter him from attending the *rezos,* seeing Yasmin, or meeting her as she headed home.

He hoped she would be in better spirits that night. She might surprise him and accept his invitation to chat for a while. He had chosen a few places where she'd feel comfortable and where they could talk leisurely. Despite the many times they had spoken, he knew nothing pertinent except what Carmen had mentioned.

Chapter 7

"Why didn't you tell me what happened at the funeral parlor, Yasmin?"

Placing her purse on the table, Yasmin turned around. "How did you find out?" she asked Carmen, skeptical that Isabel or Raul had divulged what had happened.

"We'll talk tomorrow. Raul mentioned that Josefa scheduled the *rezos* in the afternoon. We'll have a family discussion after that. Sit down." Carmen pointed to the chair next to the rocker. "Where did you go with Orlando?"

The abrupt change of topic startled her.

"Don't look surprised. I heard about it," Carmen said indignantly. "I'm tired of your lies, Yasmin. You and Orlando stopped to talk at the corner, and you took a cab. How convenient to forget mentioning that he went with you."

"Luisa," Yasmin yelled angrily.

"Lower your voice." Carmen rebuked. "She was in the neighborhood doing some errands and dropped by this morning. She seems to be doing well in her catering business. She started with birthdays and now is doing all types of celebrations, including weddings."

Yasmin rolled her eyes. The scowl on her face turned into a grimace. Luisa was talking about her business merely as an excuse. It was the preamble to end up gossiping. "When I see her . . ."

"You'll be polite, cordial, and respectful," Carmen demanded in a curt tone. "If you don't want people to talk, Yasmin Arias, don't give them reasons."

"Why did she tell you? She knows your condition."

"Are you concerned about my health or angry because she told me the truth?"

Yasmin pressed her lips together. Was she the only one who saw how malicious and impertinent Luisa was? It disheartened her that Luisa's lies were considered absolute truth and used against her. "Luisa's version is considered fact?"

"You're not denying you got into the cab," Carmen pointed out. "Where did you go?"

"Not where you think."

Carmen stood abruptly, "Don't be disrespectful, Yasmin Arias." She waved her hand in front of Yasmin's face.

"What will hitting me solve?" Yasmin challenged, unable to control her ire. "Dad's violence didn't resolve anything."

"You're right." Carmen lowered her hand. "It won't stop you from lying or doing what you want." She sat on the rocker. "Perhaps your father should have celebrated the occasion and congratulated you?"

"What did he really see?" Yasmin demanded, her eyes misty.

"Are you insinuating that Roberto lied?" Carmen shouted at the top of her lungs. "You tell me what he saw, Yasmin Arias. What were you doing when he barged in?" She paused, her glare daring her to contradict her. "I had no idea you were with Manuel, that you were bringing him here."

"You were home all the time," Yasmin reminded her, outraged by Carmen's inaccurate recollection of what occurred. Manuel had been there once.

"No, Yasmin. I went out frequently to do errands," Carmen pointed out. "Roberto accused me of condoning your behavior—blamed me for what happened."

Yasmin clasped her hands tightly over her lap and gritted her teeth.

"You get into a car with Orlando," she enunciated his name with disapproval, "and you expect people not to make assumptions?"

"I did nothing wrong. Luisa can think what she wants."

"Does that also apply to me?" Carmen demanded.

Yasmin wanted to grab her purse and leave. She inhaled through her nose several times, letting the air out slowly through her mouth.

"Breathe to calm yourself. Relax," Carmen mocked.

Yasmin knew it was wrong to lie, but she felt trapped and cornered. "We went to a diner and talked for a while."

Carmen leaned forward. "To talk," her smile widened mischievously. "About?"

It was the second time her mother had asked the same question. The double meaning in her words offended Yasmin. Without meaning to, she burst into laughter. There was no humor in her mother's accusations or how her reputation was marred by false notions. It reminded her of a dark comedy where the morbid prompted mirth that could not be explained. Exhausted both physically and emotionally, she leaned back on the chair and waited in silence for the bashing to continue.

The silence felt awkward—uncomfortable.

"Glad you're enjoying yourself, Yasmin. Continue living your life without caring how anyone else feels. Trust Orlando. Waste your time. You can do whatever you want. You live alone. You're independent."

Yasmin stood, intent on going to the bathroom. She needed solitude and prayer. She needed to reenergize, to compose herself.

"Are you leaving?" Carmen pointed to the door. "Go ahead. Come back in another year or two."

Yasmin envisioned herself holding up a white flag, admitting defeat, and leaving, if only to get a breather. Thinking about it and doing it were two different things. As much as she longed to run out, it wasn't an option. Unable to control her emotions, the tears she tried to hold back trickled down her cheeks.

"I'm . . . just going . . . to the bathroom." Without waiting for a reply, she hastened down the hall, weeping inaudibly.

"Tears won't solve anything," Carmen shouted. "Neither does lying, hiding, or being with Orlando."

* * *

"Yasmin did what?" Orlando asked, convinced that Raul was exaggerating.

"She told Ma what happened at the funeral parlor and purposely left out what she did."

Orlando shook his head. What Raul was saying made no sense. "Day after tomorrow, it's a week since she returned. Why would she wait to tell her?"

"Ma probably didn't mention it until now."

"Carmen wouldn't do that," he affirmed. Like Raul, Carmen confronted and questioned all disputes without delay. Yasmin was reserved. She simmered in her emotions, gave in to her fears, and refused to divulge anything pertinent about herself. Her silence sealed all the pain she experienced in her heart, making her defensive, sarcastic, and suspicious. "Someone else told her."

"Stop defending Yasmin." Raul skipped down the stoop and stood on the sidewalk. He looked ahead and whistled loudly as if letting out steam. "Here she comes. Good act, but not convincing."

Following his gaze, Orlando saw Yasmin approach. Her head down, she walked lethargically. She seemed drained physically and emotionally. Orlando forced himself to remain still. His impulse was to rush to her, embrace her, and reassure her that what she was experiencing was temporary, that she was strong and would endure.

He stepped down the stoop and stood next to Raul. It was apparent from Yasmin's body language that Carmen was continuing to pummel her without any regard to the duress she was causing. He wished there was some way he could stop Raul from badgering her.

"Good evening," Orlando greeted her politely.

"What's good about it?" she snapped without gazing at him and continued walking as if he hadn't spoken to her.

"You're rude and have no manners." Raul skipped up the steps and stood in front of the door. "Why did you tell Ma what happened at the funeral parlor?"

She stared at him, a sour expression on her face, and shrugged in silence.

Orlando watched them closely. They stood face-to-face, glaring at each other as if they were opponents. Straightening his shoulders, Orlando stood alert, ready to break the promise he had made not to interfere.

Yasmin gestured with her hand for Raul to move aside.

"Why didn't you mention what you did?" Raul asked.

Crossing her arms, Yasmin gazed back and looked at Orlando.

Her glare and the gush of anger directed at him stunned him. He wondered why she was furious with him. What had he done?

"Yasmin!" Raul hollered her name. "I'm talking to you."

The smirk that formed on her lips when she faced Raul exasperated Orlando.

"And?" Her voice rose considerably.

Speechless by her bravado, Orlando stepped beside her.

"You think I won't put you in your place?" Raul warned.

"You can." Yasmin challenged defiantly. "Do it. Then you won't see me again. The family name will be cleared, and I won't be around."

Orlando stood alert, waiting for Raul's reaction. It seemed her outburst had immobilized Raul. His intense glare would have made any opponent shudder. Yasmin stared back at him without flinching.

"Get out of my sight," Raul shouted, snapping out of his stupor.

Orlando relaxed when he saw Raul step aside and allow her into the building. He overheard Raul curse, watched him skip down the stoop, and followed him down the block.

"Can you believe her?" Raul griped. "She starts the problem and then has the nerve to stand up to me like she's my equal."

"Let's get a few beers," Orlando suggested.

"She's lucky she's a female. If she were a man," Raul grumbled. "Sometimes I wonder if she's really my sister."

"She is. She reminds me of Carmen," Orlando said. Raul turned toward Orlando, his brow creased with skepticism. "Also of you and Roberto—outspoken, fearless, and stubborn—family traits."

* * *

"We need to stop meeting like this," Yasmin complained.

When she saw Orlando leaving after the prayers ended, she was happy he would not be around to give her spies more ammunition against her.

"How was your day?" Orlando was suddenly walking beside her, appearing from nowhere.

"Where did you come from?" She looked around to try to figure out how she'd missed him.

Orlando ignored her question. "Never confront Raul like that again."

"I knew you were going to say that," she said grimly. "I won't make promises. He's too nasty. I'm tired of him and his accusations."

"Stop provoking him," Orlando ordered.

"If he expects me to act like a puppet the way Isabel does, I won't. I stayed away because of Dad's aggression. I won't tolerate it from Raul."

"Be careful what you say, Yaz. It's wiser to stay quiet."

She refused to allow Raul to bully, intimidate, and control her. "Why are you acting as if you're going to do something?"

"We're not going to discuss it further. Be prudent," Orlando stressed. "Think of your condition. You know stress causes your migraines. Find an outlet, or learn to control your emotions."

"The therapist is back," she said sarcastically. "You should speak to my family. Maybe they'll stop making my life more miserable than it already is."

"That's not an option. Another one might be some distraction."

"No," Yasmin interrupted, certain he was going to ask her out. "I need them to stop treating me like I'm worthless, blaming me for everything that's gone wrong since . . ." She stopped abruptly and looked away.

"What were you going to say?" Orlando asked, placing his fingers under her chin and turning her face gently toward him.

She pushed his hand away and kept her head down.

"Silence is not an answer, Yaz."

"Not the one you want." She lifted her arm as a cab approached. In silence, she entered the car and shut the door.

* * *

Orlando sat on the sofa holding his cell phone in his hands. There was no way to contact Yasmin. He still didn't have her home number, nor did he think she would provide it. Knowing where she lived was useless. He would not drop by without an invitation, and she wouldn't offer one.

Her abrupt departure worried him. He watched her get into the cab and leave. He stood there immobile as the car disappeared. He understood her plight and knew she had ample reasons to be upset. Refusing to let go or give herself time to recover from the constant onslaught kept her on an emotional roller coaster.

He envisioned her arriving in tears, rushing to the bedroom to take her medication, and then lying down sobbing. Despite the fierce storms, she gathered enough courage and strength daily to visit Carmen and attend the *rezos*. She was incredibly resilient yet withered under emotional strain.

He doubted she would confront Raul as fiercely during the discussion with Carmen the next day. Her fears that Carmen might end up in the emergency room was a good deterrent.

Raul's reaction may have given her a false sense of victory, creating confidence where none should be. Perhaps if they discussed the situation at length, she might understand the consequences and reconsider his warnings.

Orlando placed the cell phone on the table. It was a waste of time to concern himself with contacting Yasmin when he had no means to do it. Going into the bedroom, he started to undress. He would lift some weights. That would help him ease the tension he felt.

Raul's aggression and Yasmin's blind bravado tested his resolve beyond its limit. She had no idea how strongly he felt. It wasn't an act as she erroneously perceived. It was serious and would jeopardize his long-term friendship with Raul—a situation that could be avoided if she took his warnings seriously.

In boxer shorts and a T-shirt, he began to lift weights. He stopped an hour later, drenched in sweat. After a long shower, he donned his pajamas and lay on the sofa listening to music. He felt more at ease but still couldn't stop thinking about Yasmin.

Her words echoed in his mind. She was right; silence was not the answer he sought. Changing the subject, answering questions with questions, and escaping were her ways to avoid saying anything meaningful about herself. What made her so self-conscious and secretive? Perhaps she was hurt so profoundly that she'd sworn never to discuss it—an option that resolved nothing. Talking served two purposes. First, it helped her let go. Second, it helped her heal emotionally. Her silence prolonged the pain, maintained the excruciating load she carried on her shoulders, and made her bitter. It also kept her chained to the past.

* * *

Yasmin settled on the sofa, awaiting her demise. Raul was standing on her right near the door. Isabel was seated on the far end of the sofa to her left. Since the night before, she'd been plagued with worry, fearing the outcome of their discussion. Refusing to be alone, she'd slept at Ani's. They prayed for endurance, inner peace, and tranquility, which she did not attain. The night had been long, and sleep evaded her. The morning and then the *rezos* that afternoon seemed endless. The hours dragged on, the impending doom becoming heavier on her shoulders.

To her dismay, she missed Orlando. She wondered if he had taken the hint and finally decided to stay away. Admitting that she'd become accustomed to his presence was accepting failure. Acknowledging that her resolution was fragile made her determination stronger. She would pray for inner strength, self-control, and guidance. Giving in to emotions or false perceptions was not an option.

"Yasmin," Carmen said, "look at me when I'm speaking."

Yasmin straightened her shoulders, cleared her thoughts, and faced Carmen.

"Hasn't our family given the neighbors enough to talk about? If you behave that way at your father's funeral, what can I expect at mine?"

"That's a terrible thing to say, Mami."

"You're a great actress, Yasmin." Isabel sneered.

"*Hypocrite* is the right word," Raul said.

"Listen to you." Carmen was exasperated. "Family does not treat each other this way. I suppose when I'm no longer around, you'll remain enemies, each going your separate ways and acting like you're not related. It's disgusting. The seed your father planted has taken deep root."

"Why do you always blame Dad?" Raul was incensed. "You've never wanted to admit Yasmin was wrong."

It astounded Yasmin that Raul perceived that as true. Her mother condemned her just as much or more than her father.

"Wrong, Raul," Carmen answered. "I never condoned what Yasmin did. But this is her home, and we're her family. What happened shouldn't change that."

"She admitted she didn't want to live here," Isabel argued as she threw up her hands in frustration. "With all the freedom she has, why would she want to stay?"

"What freedom?" Yasmin asked. They spoke with authority and acted as if they knew everything about her, yet they had no idea what her life was like.

"You live alone and do as you please." Carmen's tone was sour. "How you grew up and what I taught you are all forgotten."

"Don't waste your breath, Ma. Yasmin has no idea what being decent is," Raul said.

"Orlando has probably been to her place already," Isabel said. "That's why he's always defending her."

"Watch what you say," Raul glared. "Orlando knows better than to get involved with her type."

"Meaning?" Yasmin demanded, grateful Orlando wasn't there to hear their horrid remarks.

"After using you, men move on to someone worthwhile," Raul replied.

Carmen looked directly at Yasmin and nodded.

The I-told-you so expression irritated Yasmin. She felt compelled to divulge that Orlando liked her company and treated her with respect and courtesy. Unlike them, he listened without criticizing or condemning her. But she realized that any comment she made would validate her mother's false perceptions. Yasmin prayed the discussion would focus on what had occurred at the wake.

"What makes you think Orlando isn't one of those men?" Isabel asked skeptically.

"Don't be like Luisa, spreading false rumors," Raul warned. "Like Ma, Orlando insisted I should forgive Yasmin. He kept telling me to allow her to mourn Dad. We argued about it many times, and he always defended Yasmin. He tried to convince me that if she showed up, I should allow her to be at the wake."

Yasmin was pleasantly stunned by the revelation and recalled that Orlando had mentioned they had different opinions. She felt a burst of energy spread throughout her body. She wanted to smile but remained serious.

"Orlando was right to feel that way, Raul, but he's not the topic here. The three of you are." Carmen refocused the conversation. "Why did I have to hear about it from someone outside the family?"

"You mean from Yasmin, right, Ma?" Raul said.

"I said outside the family," Carmen repeated.

"She shouldn't have been there," Isabel shouted.

"Lower your voice." Carmen turned slightly, glanced at Isabel, and then faced Raul. "You decided?"

Raul grunted aloud. "Yes."

Carmen stood up. "I . . ." she gestured to herself dramatically, patting her chest repeatedly, ". . . wanted Yasmin to see her father before he died, to be at the funeral parlor, at the church, at the cemetery. Why did you feel it was all right to overlook that? You ignored my wishes, Raul."

Yasmin noticed how distressed her mother looked. She rushed to her side and stood next to her. "Please calm down, Mami. You're going to end up in the hospital again. Did you take your medication today?"

"Do any of you care what happens to me?" Carmen dropped heavily onto the rocker.

"Yes, Mami." Yasmin kneeled before her.

"Stop pretending you're concerned for Mom or any of us," Isabel said angrily.

"Remember what I said," Raul said.

"What did you tell her?" Carmen demanded, turning from him to Isabel and back.

"Isabel knows," Raul replied, his tone indicating he didn't have to give explanations.

"That only applies to us?" Yasmin ignored the warning in his eyes. "You don't have to practice what you preach?"

"I'm warning you, Yasmin . . ."

"Or you'll what?" Carmen interrupted. "I forbid you to put your hands on Yasmin. Do you understand, Raul Ismael Arias?"

"You wanted her here, Ma. There she is." He pointed to her. "And you can thank Orlando and Josefa, not me, that she went into the funeral parlor. What happened inside was between them." He gestured to Isabel and then to Yasmin. "Had I been there, it wouldn't have happened, but I left. I wasn't going to stay in the same place with a hypocrite."

Yasmin watched him head to the door and pressed her lips together. Did Raul really think their mother would allow him to walk out? The battle was not over.

"I'm not finished," Carmen said.

Begrudgingly, Raul returned to where he had stood, the scowl on his face deepening.

"I don't know what else you want from me."

"You forget your place. Regardless of your age, you will respect me."

"I do, Ma. You want me to admit I was wrong? Fine. I'm sorry. My intent was not to hurt you. But I will not apologize to Yasmin. I disapprove of her lifestyle, her constant defiance, and her independent-woman attitude. I'm putting up with her presence here and at the *rezos* and ignoring her smart remarks—all to please you, Ma."

"All of you have done things I disapprove of, Raul. But I don't hate you for it, nor do I push you away."

"You're our mother," Isabel said. "It's different with Yasmin,"

"Am I not her mother too?" Carmen asked hoarsely.

Isabel was silent.

"If you want me to pretend that I'm glad she's back, I can't," Raul said.

"Neither can I," Isabel added.

A knot formed in Yasmin's throat, and her eyes filled with tears.

"I'm tired," Carmen spoke in a subdued voice. "I admit that it's my fault."

"Why?" Raul asked. "You have nothing to feel guilty about."

"She should have stayed wherever she was," Isabel said.

"Shut up," Raul snapped.

"Why can't I speak, Raul?" Isabel asked and then faced Yasmin. "You should have gone to your party even after you found out Dad was dead."

"Why would you say such a thing? Yasmin would not do that," Carmen said. "Both of you have to accept that this is and always will be Yasmin's home."

"Trusting Yasmin is a mistake," Raul declared.

Yasmin wanted to laugh aloud. Raul had no idea how wrong he was. Her mother trusting her was what she prayed for every night, waiting patiently for the blessing. She understood that her perception of time and when that would be resolved was the Lord's prerogative.

"Was it also my mistake to trust you and Isabel?" Carmen asked. "It's obvious with what took place at the funeral that none of you are concerned with my feelings or what I want. It's a shame that Orlando, who is not related to me, has more consideration than my own blood."

"He shouldn't have interfered."

"I'm glad he did, Raul," Carmen said curtly. "Thank God at least he had some common sense and knew what needed to be done. That was not his role. It was yours, Raul. In your father's absence or mine, you need to keep this family together. But that's too much to ask." She frowned. "This isn't a family and hasn't been for years, despite my wishes. Anger, resentment, and hostility have torn us apart." Getting up abruptly, Carmen walked down the hall.

"What now, Ma?" Raul called after her.

"What I want is not important to any of you." Carmen continued walking and then exclaimed without turning back to face him, "Do what you want. That's what you do anyway."

Yasmin watched Carmen amble down the hall. She knew she was crying.

"I hope you're happy," Raul said to Yasmin.

Yasmin looked at him and then at Isabel. Weren't they going to follow their mother into the room to console her?

"Why don't you leave right now? Forget us," Isabel said.

Yasmin ignored them and hurried down the hall and into the bedroom. Saw her mother sitting on the bed, her rosary and prayer book in her hands. Entering the room, she knelt before Carmen.

"Please forgive me, Mami. If I could change things . . ."

"Don't be ridiculous, Yasmin," Carmen said hoarsely. "Being sorry and apologizing never solves anything. You had many opportunities to end this situation and chose not to."

Yasmin realized her mother was right. She had postponed the repercussions by giving in to her fears.

"I didn't want to cause another scene," Yasmin said, tears streaming down her cheeks. "That's why I hid from you at the church and at the cemetery."

"You can't hide from life, Yasmin. You have to face it."

"I realize that now."

"It's never too late to change. Will you come back home?"

Yasmin lowered her gaze and looked at her hands. She recalled crying herself to sleep yearning for the security she had felt at home. Not being close to her mother during holidays, birthdays, and special occasions had been crushing. The desolation was oppressive, but as much as she cherished the thought of returning, the truth—although hard to accept—was that she no longer wanted to live there.

* * *

"Dinner was delicious, Clara—almost as good as Mom's." Orlando settled in the living room.

"Nobody cooks as delicious as Mom," Clara admitted, squeezing next to Mario on the love seat. Mario wrapped his arms around her shoulders and tapped a kiss on Clara's cheek.

"Finally you learned," Orlando said. "Before you got married, eating your meals was a punishment."

"Is it bash-on-your-sister night?" Clara asked, feigning anger.

"Just letting you know your cooking has improved. Right, Mario?" Orlando smiled.

"No comment." Mario shook his head, gesturing to Clara with his eyes.

"You're smart. No comment is the best option." Orlando grinned. Mario knew Clara well. Like Yasmin, she was always on the defense, ready to strike back.

"He'd better not say a word or he won't eat for a week," Clara warned.

"Clara's tough." Orlando's grin widened.

"Sometimes," Mario smiled.

"It's odd that you're visiting on the weekend. What happened?" Clara asked suspiciously.

"Nothing," Orlando shrugged. Raul had asked him to attend the family discussion, but he opted not to go. Their crude comments and demeaning remarks would upset him. Instead, he worked most of the day and visited Clara before heading home. "I had to reduce the pile on my desk. I needed to catch up."

"That's why you and Raul aren't hanging out?"

"I answered your question, Clara. I can't force you to believe me."

"You stopped going out, and there's no reason?"

"Clara, what are you so suspicious about?" Mario asked.

"She's still concerned about the disagreement I had with Raul when Yasmin showed up," Orlando replied, certain that was the issue.

"You almost fought," she corrected.

"We clarified that." He couldn't comprehend why Carmen, Yasmin, and Clara tied themselves to certain topics and brought them up repeatedly. "Since Roberto got sick, Raul and I haven't gone out like we used to. I'm not sure when or if we'll go back to that routine," he added. Going to a club, lounge, or bar no longer interested him. He was more concerned with convincing Yasmin to spend time with him, an endeavor that seemed unachievable given her reaction to Carmen's derisive comments and her own insecurities over his reputation.

Clara smiled and studied Orlando's features. "This is the first time in weeks that you visited on a Saturday."

He shook his head. "If I don't visit, you complain, and if I do, you question why."

"It's rare," she pointed out. "Unlike you."

"Or it's a beginning to make up for the times I should have been here and wasn't."

"Right answer, Orlando," Mario said with a thumbs-up.

"Hopefully, as Mom taught us, the promise will be followed by action." Clara smiled thinly. "Mom said the flight was smooth. Dad was thrilled to see her."

"I know." Orlando had called his mother the night before, and she had shared the same comment.

"Mom mentioned you spoke to her." Clara seemed pleased.

Orlando gazed at his watch and stood up. Although he had no plans for the night, he was ready to leave, looking forward to a full night's sleep.

In the morning, he wanted to drop by Raul's place. He hoped Raul would provide details of the family discussion, not that he expected any abrupt changes. He anticipated the situation would continue as it was or get worse.

"Leaving?" Clara said. "Going to meet her?"

"Respect his privacy, Clara," chided Mario.

"Yasmin is her name," he corrected. "And stop acting like we're together."

"Aren't you?"

"No," he replied calmly.

"You're not being realistic, Orlando. I doubt you'd do anything for your 'female friends,'" she made quotation marks in the air with her fingers, "without wanting something in return."

"Said by a true skeptic." It occurred to him that Carmen was drilling the same mentality into Yasmin, which explained Yasmin's unjust request that he stay away. "What do you think, Mario?"

"Once you get the reputation, it's hard to get rid of it."

"That's right," Clara said. "You plant the seed, it sprouts, it grows, and you get the fruit you planted—good or bad."

"Trust is an issue," Orlando noted.

"Didn't think that word was part of your vocabulary, not when you and Raul take advantage of every girl who falls for you."

"Remember, those girls also have a choice," Orlando clarified, winking at her.

"That doesn't change anything. You're still taking advantage."

He was reminded of Yasmin's reaction when he mentioned going to sleep in the wee hours. Despite what they both believed, he had stopped dating and was not seeing anyone. His reputation gave the wrong impression. Yasmin shunned it, Carmen was etching it on stone, and Clara affirmed it. As Mario pointed out, once a reputation was established, it became a serious problem.

"Does that apply to Yasmin too? Does she have a choice?" Clara shouted as he walked down the hall.

He exited the apartment, laughing. Nothing applied to Yasmin. She was a challenge—one he was struggling to overcome.

* * *

114

CHAPTER 7

"I don't like to see you depressed, Yasmin." Ani poured coffee into a mug and handed it to her. She took the sugar bowl from the counter, a spoon from the dish rack, and placed them on the table.

"I wish Mami understood why I can't come back home," Yasmin said, holding the mug in her hands. Leaving Carmen alone and destitute distressed her. She anticipated the living room would be empty as she exited the apartment. Without bothering to check on Carmen's condition, Isabel and Raul went about their business.

Ani placed the coffee pot on the stove after pouring herself a cup. "Look on the bright side. The Lord granted your prayer. Now your mother knows the truth. Everything has been cleared."

"It has," Yasmin agreed, saddened that her thoughts became a reality. The family discussion—or "battle" as she referred to it—was a disaster. She was grateful that her mother was aware of the reasons for her behavior. She also hoped that she understood why Orlando had not mentioned what occurred.

"Enjoy the small blessings. Be patient," encouraged Ani.

Yasmin smiled thinly. Her efforts to be patient were a challenge. She was coping with it as best as she could. Some blessings were easier to recognize than others, and although she was thankful, she had yet to experience the stability and tranquility she'd prayed for.

"Eventually, the Lord will open Carmen's eyes, and she will see you as God sees you."

"I hope so." Her mother refused to understand that returning home changed nothing.

"You doubt it?" Ani asked. "The Lord heard your prayers, Yasmin, and is working on them. It doesn't matter what you see or what's happening."

Yasmin nodded, poured a heaping spoon of sugar into the mug, and stirred vigorously. She sipped the brew slowly, enjoying the flavor.

"Have you seen Orlando again?"

Yasmin grinned. She was delighted by the news that he always defended her, and she felt self-conscious about misjudging him. She realized that although her mother was making assumptions, Orlando was not at fault. She had to admit that she was wrong about him.

"Every time I mention him, your face and eyes light up. That answers my question." Ani was delighted.

115

Yasmin laughed. Ani made it sound as if she were an infatuated teenager. There was no romantic link between her and Orlando. Her vow to stay alone remained intact. "He's just . . . a friend. That's all."

"That's a start," Ani said enthusiastically.

"To what?" Yasmin was quick to ask. If she ever suspected that he was interested in anything more, she would revert to her original plan.

The smirk on Ani's lips turned to a grin. "If we could rule our hearts. But what's up here," she pointed to her head, "doesn't dictate what's in here," and she pointed to her heart.

"He has a reputation," Yasmin stressed with disapproval. "He uses women like paper towels."

"If it's just friendship, why worry about that?"

It took a moment for Yasmin to think of a reply. It was true. Orlando's life was his concern. "Does friendship imply ignoring someone's faults?"

"That's part of our calling, Yasmin, to love one another despite our differences, social status, and way of life," Ani said. "We were given a model by our Lord so we could follow it. He accepted us and loves us as we are."

Yasmin disliked Orlando's inquisitive nature, how he probed in depth, scrutinizing every detail. He would make a good lawyer or detective. Still, even with his reputation and annoying questions, he was sincere—totally the opposite of how she perceived his character.

"Does Orlando go to the *rezos*?"

"Not all the time. He missed two sessions but met me after one of them in front of the building. He went with his mother and sister one evening and arrived when the *rezos* was almost finished on the other. Yesterday he was in front of the building with Raul when I arrived. He didn't go today."

"Wow!" Ani marveled.

"What?" Yasmin asked, puzzled.

"Seems you're very aware of his presence," Ani said, laughing.

Was she? That was a misconception. She wanted him to stay away. She was looking forward to *not* meeting with him nightly after the *rezos* ended.

"I'd like to go with you to one of the *rezos*, Yasmin."

"Three more days and they're over." She was ready to return to her regular routine of going to work, then going home or to Ani's, and visiting

116

her mother on weekends. She considered it a blessing to attend the *rezos* once a month.

She marveled that she had survived the week. It was the work of the Lord. Alone and in her own strength she couldn't have done it. "Josefa scheduled the *rezos* today and tomorrow at 3:00 in the afternoon. During the week, it's at 7:30 in the evening to make it easier for those who work to attend. The last day is Tuesday. When would you like to go?"

Chapter 8

"Want one?" Raul asked, following Orlando into the living room with a beer in hand.

Glancing around, Orlando decided to sit in the center of the sofa, the only clean area. Raul needed to hire some help. His shirts and pants hung over each of the four dining room chairs and on the sofa. Magazines, letters, and CDs littered the coffee table along with used mugs and empty beer bottles. Shoes, sneakers, and socks were scattered all over the floor.

"Best thing for a hangover."

"Long time since I had that," Orlando admitted. Getting drunk didn't appeal to him, nor would he have a beer in the early morning, not even to cure a hangover.

"You're not doing much lately," Raul said.

"Spending time with the family, catching up at work."

"Even if you visited family or worked, that didn't stop you before. What's going on?"

Orlando shrugged. "Taking time for myself."

"That what you call it?" Raul said. "When you're ready to join the living, let me know. Ma was complaining that you haven't called or dropped by since she was in the hospital."

"Hope you explained why I haven't been around."

"All Ma wants to talk about is her angel, Yasmin." Raul grumbled.

"I'll let her know," Orlando said, deducing from Raul's comment that the family discussion was unproductive. "I'll drop by when I leave and then go to the *rezos*."

"I'll meet you there. The lecture will be long. Glad it's you and not me," Raul smirked. "Can't wait for the *rezos* to end so I can focus on making space at the shop. I'm inundated with work. The offer's still open; you can own your shop or become a partner."

Orlando shook his head.

"I called you several times last night. You didn't respond. Figured you were busy and would contact me when you were ready."

"I meant to call," Orlando replied. He'd seen the messages after leaving Clara's place but waited to speak to Raul personally.

"Sure," Raul said. "Is it someone you've been with or a new one?" He studied Orlando's face.

"Neither," Orlando replied, meeting his gaze. He was eager to find out how the discussion fared and waited for Raul to mention it.

"Keep doing your thing." Raul shrugged. "Congratulations."

"For?"

"Ma thinks you're a hero. She was proud of your actions. She agreed that helping Yasmin was the right thing to do and thinks you're more considerate than Isabel and me. Ma approves of everything you say and do."

Orlando smiled in response. His sarcasm and belittling tone reminded him of Yasmin.

"Yasmin is with Ma right now, gloating over her victory," Raul griped. "Ma defends her and acts like she never did anything wrong. She told us we had to accept her."

"It's over," Orlando said, wondering how Raul expected Carmen to act.

"You're wrong. Yasmin will still be around after the *rezos*. Ma will continue demanding that we treat her like family."

Orlando laughed. "She is."

Their contradictions frazzled him. He could imagine how they made Yasmin feel. They didn't want her around yet complained about her absence. When she was there, they wanted her to leave. They loathed her ex and refused to believe she was alone. No matter what Yasmin did or said, she could never satisfy their whims. Most disconcerting, they didn't really know her. Had she been self-centered and immoral, she would disregard their comments and attitude and live frivolously. Instead, she suffered from migraines due to the emotional strain of their rejection.

"She didn't think about the family when she left with that coward or when she moved in with Ani and refused to come back home," Raul continued.

Orlando shook his head. Yasmin had to be insane to move back in. "That's the past," he pointed out. "We're talking about the present."

"That's where we differ. Yasmin hasn't changed. Our family's honor and name will always be soiled. But Ma doesn't believe me, and she's going to regret allowing her back in our lives."

Orlando disagreed. They would have disagreements as all families do. Regardless of that, Carmen would always want Yasmin close. "We've all changed, Raul. The only thing that's the same is that you, Isabel, and even Carmen refuse to let go. Move forward with your lives. Leave the past where it belongs."

"That's why you're Ma's hero." Raul lifted the beer, pretending to acknowledge him with a toast. Taking a gulp, he held it in his hand as he continued speaking. "I don't regret what I did, but I would redo it with just one change. I would have stayed and gone into the funeral parlor with Yasmin and Josefa."

Orlando knew that action would have made the situation worse. He frowned. The family discussion had clearly intensified Raul's animosity.

* * *

"You didn't eat anything, Yasmin," Carmen said. "What's wrong? You seem upset."

Yasmin glanced at the plate. Her appetite had vanished when she arrived. The mashed plantains with fried cheese, eggs, and salami remained untouched. When she saw Isabel and Maria sitting on the sofa, Orlando's words echoed in her mind. As he had said, she was confusing responsibility with being a martyr. Yasmin wished she had adhered to his advice and regretted not going to Ani's place after the Mass. His reasoning was valid. Visiting all the time was not mandatory; she only acted as if it were.

The willing victim, the martyr—that was her, Yasmin said to herself, trying to regain her composure.

"She probably had a problem with her man," Maria commented, wiping her mouth with a napkin and dropping it onto the plate. "As always, the food was delicious, Carmen."

"Yasmin is alone," Isabel mocked as she stacked her plate and Maria's on top of each other. Placing them on the counter, she returned to get the pitcher of orange juice and the glasses.

"You believe her?" Maria asked. "She's probably with Manuel and *several* others."

"Stop talking as if she isn't here." Carmen scolded. "Yasmin, you didn't answer me."

"I had breakfast already." She drank coffee at her place before she headed out.

Glancing at Maria, Yasmin maintained a blank expression. She disliked being around her and Luisa and avoided being anywhere they went. She would have gladly stopped going to the *rezos* to avoid them, but it wasn't a Christian way to act. She knew that, yet she couldn't control how she felt. She resisted the instinct to grab her purse and leave. She pressed back against the chair to control her impulse. She kept her head up and shoulders straight, ignoring their ridiculous banter.

"The list is *long*." Maria enunciated as she pushed the dining room chair in. "That's the rumor." She strode gleefully to the sofa and sat down.

"According to who?" Yasmin asked, Maria's smug expression making her livid. "You and Luisa?"

"We don't make things up." Maria picked up the remote.

"No?"

"Yasmin." Carmen called her name as if she were a disobedient child. "Maria is our guest."

Yasmin pressed her lips together. She could think of more descriptive words to articulate what Maria was.

Maria turned the TV on mute and switched from one channel to the next. "I can help Isabel clean up."

"Thanks for offering, Maria, but no need. Isabel can handle it," Carmen said.

"Why doesn't Yasmin do it?" Isabel yelled from the kitchen.

"I don't mind." Yasmin stood up, eager to keep herself occupied and her attention focused on something other than Maria's and Isabel's petty remarks.

"No, Yasmin." Carmen gestured for her to sit. "Isabel, make sure you put away Raul's and Orlando's food. I don't know what's going on with Orlando. Lately, he hasn't been around."

Yasmin felt her mother's heated glare and pretended to study her nails.

"Raul would say he's doing his thing." Isabel mimicked Raul's tone and then burst into laughter.

Yasmin noticed Maria's frown and her displeased expression. The reaction surprised her. Why would anything he did affect Maria . . . unless . . . She dispelled the thought. She was confident Orlando would never consider it, not when he could choose someone better.

"I wonder who he's with." Carmen looked at Yasmin out the corner of her eye and then gazed at Maria. "Except for you, I've never met or seen any of the women he fools around with. Unlike Raul, he's more prudent about his personal affairs."

Standing, Yasmin headed down the hall. Orlando and Maria? The mere thought made her stomach turn.

"Leaving already, Yasmin?" Isabel called as she passed by toward the bathroom.

Yasmin gritted her teeth.

"It's too early," Carmen noted. "The *rezos* are later this afternoon."

Yasmin paused. Turning, she spoke to Carmen. "I need to leave. Ani is going to the *rezos* today. I promised to pick her up."

"It's not midday yet," Carmen said.

"I know," she replied in an apologetic tone. "I'm helping her deliver some gowns. I promised to be there early. It's the only way to get to the *rezos* on time."

"Why aren't the clients picking them up?" Carmen asked with creased eyebrows while studying her face.

Yasmin spoke with the utmost concern. She wanted it to sound as if Ani were in dire need of her help. "Ani was supposed to have the dresses ready yesterday. She had to cancel the pickups. Since it was her mistake, I'm helping her deliver them."

"She'll help anyone who's not family," Isabel spouted.

"Watch your mouth, Isabel," Carmen said. "Why didn't you mention it before?"

Yasmin ignored the skepticism in her tone. "When I got here, we rushed to Mass. When we got home, you were busy preparing breakfast and serving the food. I didn't get a chance."

Carmen grunted aloud.

"And," Yasmin added quickly, "I'm going back to work tomorrow. I won't be able to visit during the week. I promise we'll spend more time together on weekends." Smiling, she walked down the hall.

"If you don't disappear for another five years," Isabel added.

"Enough, Isabel. Finish cleaning up. Why can't you call during the week, Yasmin?" Carmen called after her.

"She's probably too *busy.*" Maria stressed the last word.

"Standing on a corner is working?" Isabel shouted.

Thank you, Lord, Yasmin said to herself, thrilled that she would not have to stay a moment longer. She hated lying, but her mother would insist she stay. She was eager to leave and get away from Maria and Isabel.

"I'm grateful for everything Ani has done for Yasmin," she overheard Carmen say.

Isabel was shouting, evidentally so Yasmin could hear her insults. Entering the bathroom, Yasmin closed the door partially. She wanted to confirm if her predictions were correct. Her mother had always acted like Ani was an intruder and believed that if Ani had not helped her, she would have returned home.

"Although I always felt Ani shouldn't have intervened, I appreciate that she gave Yasmin a place to stay," Carmen said.

"What's to appreciate?" Isabel asked.

"That she let Yasmin be with her man while she lived there?" Maria said.

"Ani insists Yasmin is not the person we think she is," Carmen said with disbelief.

"For Ani, she's a saint," Isabel shouted. "Saint Yasmin." She repeated it several times, laughing hysterically.

"She has a great following—all men," Maria added with spite, laughing along with Isabel.

Yasmin grunted aloud, locked the bathroom door, and sat on the edge of the tub. Although she would have preferred to hurry out, it was best to pretend she needed to use the facilities and then leave. Staying a bit longer would not make her stay any worse.

There was a soft knock. Yasmin opened the door, expecting to see Carmen. It was Maria. "Excuse me," she said, gesturing for Maria to move aside.

"Soon, Orlando will get tired of you. Find someone else," Maria said.

Speechless, Yasmin stared at her, wide-eyed.

"He'll never take you seriously," Maria went on. "He'll use you, and when he's had enough, he'll shove you aside like every other man you've been with."

Yasmin forced herself to remain still and kept her arms rigid at her side, although she wanted to slap the smirk off Maria's face. "Stay out of my business," she demanded.

"I don't know why he would even look at you," Maria stressed spitefully. "Then again, he's a man. He'll take what's offered, even if it's worthless."

"Are you referring to yourself?" Yasmin said. Her face was flushed with outrage as she swept past her.

* * *

Instead of walking out of the elevator, Orlando stepped back, holding the door ajar for Yasmin to enter. His desire to see her was crushed by the acrid expression on her face. Her heated glare stunned him.

"What's wrong?" He let the door slam shut and pressed number one. She stood with her back to him. He deduced that there had been another argument during her visit with Carmen. "What happened?"

"I'm not wasting my time."

He placed his hand on her shoulder, turned her around, and lifted her face gently. The accusation in her eyes assured him that whatever had riled her up had nothing to do with her family. "Just say whatever it is. Give me the opportunity to defend myself."

"Rumor is that after you get tired of using a worthless . . ." she paused, "you'll move on."

"Who told you that?" He had an idea of who it was but wanted to be certain.

"Your girlfriend is jealous."

"Maria is not my girl."

"Obviously, she doesn't feel that way." Turning, Yasmin faced the wall. "Don't let me stop you from running to her."

"I was going to see Carmen," he said harshly.

"I should have slapped her. That would have wiped the smirk off her face."

"I don't see how that would have helped."

"I would have felt better."

"Maria won't approach you again after I speak to her." He pushed the door open, waited for her to exit, and walked beside her.

"She won't. Mami will. Luisa will do the honors of informing her about every detail of your chitchat."

"I assure you that's the last thing it will be." He was curt.

"Confronting her will only make the situation worse."

"You expect me to do what you do—nothing?"

Her glare was ominous. Without replying, Yasmin walked toward the entrance.

"That's the problem. You don't act, and then you get upset when the situation gets out of hand. It's ridiculous. Stop worrying about what others say. Demand the respect you deserve."

She swung around, her eyes glowing as brightly as her lip gloss. She looked beautiful with her hair loose. Her curly locks bounced lightly on her white V-neck as she stepped before him and lifted her gaze. She was incredibly attractive, even when angry.

"No matter what I say or do, your girl will always be rude."

"Never refer to her as 'my girl' again. She isn't."

"She was," Yasmin spat out.

The revulsion in her voice left him speechless. He hesitated, stunned by her reaction. "Over. Why can't I put her in her place? If you don't expect me to do anything, why are we arguing?"

"You're right," Yasmin said sarcastically. "Everything will be solved after you insult Maria. There will be no more rumors about us, and she'll respect me and stay away. And we'll be so happy after that."

"Or," he corrected, "you can let the situation blow out of proportion and then regret it as you did with your father."

Yasmin gasped. She turned abruptly and hastened toward the entrance of the building. He ran after her and placed his hand on her shoulder. She stopped but refused to look back.

"My intent isn't to offend you," he said in a calm tone, although he was livid. "Ignoring a problem doesn't make it go away. You need to be assertive, Yaz. Don't allow others to degrade you because you fear Carmen's reaction."

She turned slightly. "You're not the one who has to listen to Mami's accusations or hurtful comments. I'm the one being ridiculed and humiliated."

He walked around and blocked her path. "It's your choice. Let them get away with it, and stay upset. Or stand up for yourself, and face the consequences."

"Easy to say."

"That's how it appears to you. It's not the reality for either of us. At your request, I'm not getting involved. We won't discuss it again. The rest is up to you." Although her decision irritated him, he would follow her mandate.

He heard the door opening behind him and turned to see who entered.

"What a surprise to find you both here," Luisa exclaimed as she entered the lobby. "Yasmin, are you all right?"

* * *

"What happened?" Ani placed the sugar bowl next to the mug.

Yasmin stared at the dark brew, the color a reflection of how she felt. The confrontation with Maria, the argument with Orlando, and Luisa's impromptu entrance had ignited an inferno in her stomach. She felt ill. Her head was pounding; her stomach was burning. Covering her face with both hands, she wept.

Ani handed her a tissue. "You need to calm down. Be confident. He will resolve whatever it is."

When her tears subsided, Yasmin felt drained of energy. She went to the sink, washed her face, and then dried it with a towel. Crying served no purpose other than to prove how weak she was.

"You're not going to drink this?" Ani placed the mug in the sink. "Feel better?"

She did, somewhat. Yasmin nodded. "I'd prefer not to talk about what happened." Her voice was barely above a whisper.

"I'm here when you need me," Ani smiled warmly. Taking Yasmin's hand, she led her to the living room and picked up the Bible from the coffee table. They sat on the sofa. "Open your heart and your mind. Listen," Ani said. "Matthew 11:28 says, 'Come to me, all you who are weary and burdened, and I will give you rest.'"

* * *

Orlando considered going home but drove to Josefa's instead to attend the *rezos* that afternoon. Carmen had offered him breakfast, and although he was hungry, he declined the offer. He left shortly after arriving. He had found parking across the street from the building and strolled into a pizza shop at the corner. He purchased a slice and a soft drink and then selected one of the tables in the back. While he ate, he glanced around and frowned. He'd chosen an isolated table away from the crowd—Yasmin's preference. When they went to the diner after the cemetery, she'd selected a booth where the surrounding tables were empty.

Recalling their argument, his ire increased. Yasmin's glare felt like fire. She'd left without acknowledging Luisa who had smiled at him. He stood by the entrance of the elevator but decided to walk up the stairs. He jogged up the four flights briskly to work off the excess energy. He was greeting Carmen when Luisa arrived. He'd been prepared to correct any misleading comments. Luisa was savvy and did not dare mention she'd seen him with Yasmin. Eventually the encounter would be disclosed. At her convenience, Luisa would mention it, embellishing what she saw with lies and erroneous assumptions.

Maria hadn't dared speak to him. He ignored her and acted as if she weren't there. He directed his attention to Carmen, excused himself for not visiting often, promised to drop by more regularly as he had in the past, and hastened out. Yasmin was nowhere in sight as he walked to his car. He wondered if she'd gone to her apartment or to Ani's. A migraine would be the result of her emotional outburst over nothing.

The cursed relationship he had with Maria was meaningless. Yasmin's reaction disturbed him. He repressed any thoughts that would attribute her reaction to any feelings she might have for him and refused to dwell on false interpretations. That's what Yasmin did. She allowed Maria's hateful comments to dispirit her. He wished she would confront her family, Carmen included, along with Luisa and Maria, with the same gusto she confronted him. She lashed out at him as if he were the culprit of every malady that assailed her. It was interesting that the same treatment she wanted from her family she denied him. Oddly enough, her constant onslaughts had not diminished his craving to spend more time with her. She tried his patience beyond its limits and challenged his self-control and emotions. Yet none of that stopped him from thinking about her constantly or wanting to see her and be with her all the time. It made no sense. Nothing did.

* * *

Glancing from Orlando to the altar, Yasmin frowned. He was chatting amicably with Raul and the other male visitors who stood clustered near the door. Except for three elderly men who'd joined the women for the prayers, the rest avoided participating. They drank, made jokes, and laughed boisterously, oblivious to the ritual taking place.

She gazed at Orlando again, and he was aware of her stare. Their eyes met on occasion.

The verses she'd read with Ani before heading to the *rezos* appeased her until she arrived. The brazen expressions of victory gleaming from Maria's, Isabel's, and Luisa's faces revived her choler. They were pleased with themselves.

"Sit, Yasmin," Ani whispered in her ear.

Dropping heavily into the chair, Yasmin saw Orlando step out with Raul. Why did they even bother to attend? They wandered in and out as if it were a social gathering. Although outdated for some, the custom required respect from visitors and participants. It was apparent that most of the men attending, Raul and Orlando included, ignored that fact. Worse yet, they didn't care.

Ani tapped Yasmin's shoulder, and she shot up, pretending she was unaware of Ani's concerned look. She heard whispers and giggling. Turning back, she saw Maria, Isabel, and Luisa several rows behind her. With a broad grin, Luisa nodded, acknowledging her. Yasmin faced forward without responding.

The mother was as loathsome as the daughter. Yasmin had always shunned both of them and kept her distance, ignoring them as much as her parents allowed. Her father had confided details of family problems, shared his opinions openly, and encouraged their horrid meddling. Luisa and Maria felt privileged and empowered.

She sat down again. Orlando with Maria? Of all the women he could be with—Maria? The thought was nauseating.

She grunted aloud. Had Maria been as insignificant as the rest? What had he seen in Maria? Maybe he liked her physical attributes. She grimaced.

"Yasmin," Ani whispered her name. Everyone around her was standing. Her thoughts scattering, she stood up. Lula's melodious voice filled the room.

As she did every night when the rite of peace began, Yasmin leaned against the wall. It was her way to ensure she wouldn't be in the way as everyone hugged each other.

Ani embraced her and whispered in her ear. "All problems, no matter how serious, are resolved by the Lord."

Yasmin smiled thinly as Ani moved back and nodded. They would be leaving soon. She had endured.

Orlando approached them. When he stopped next to Ani, Yasmin hastened into the bedroom to get their handbags.

"Did something happen, Yasmin?" Josefa asked, entering the room.

"I'm sorry. I should have asked for your permission before coming into the bedroom," she apologized, embarrassed. "I didn't see you in the living room. I came to get my purse and Ani's."

"You're too proper." Josefa smiled. "You shouldn't pay attention to Raul. He likes being difficult."

Yasmin forced a thin smile and nodded. Surprisingly, he wasn't the cause.

Josefa patted her on the back, walked to the bed, and returned with two purses. "Go home, rest, and relax. I'll see you tomorrow."

Yasmin walked out and handed Ani her purse. She took Ani by the arm and led her out of the apartment, down the steps, and to the street as quickly as she could.

"Yasmin," Ani said out of breath, "hold on."

Reluctantly Yasmin halted. She needed to get away, to escape the mixture of emotions that overwhelmed her.

"What happened between you and Orlando?" Ani panted.

"Nothing," she replied, taking the car keys out of her purse. She was blessed that evening and had found parking in front of the building.

"It's obvious something did. That you refuse to talk about it is another matter."

* * *

Orlando showered after doing a strenuous workout. He stood under the running water, letting the questions wash away. Yasmin's anger, he decided, was the result of her passiveness. Her derailed emotions controlled her life and blinded her to reality. Even if she refused to admit it, she could make her life easier—empower herself and not allow others to humiliate and demean her.

He donned his pajamas. After taking a beer from the fridge, he turned on the stereo, lowered the volume, and sat on the sofa.

What verse had Ani whispered to him when he embraced her? He'd anticipated a greeting but instead she encouraged him to read a verse from the Bible. He'd watched as Yasmin came out of the bedroom, swept past him, grabbed Ani's arm, and dragged her out of the apartment.

He left shortly after. It felt odd to walk alone. It was weird that after a few days accompanying Yasmin to a cab or her car, he felt deserted. Placing the beer on the coffee table, he entered the bedroom. He had a Bible in one of the drawers. He looked thoroughly through each one until he found it. Then he walked back slowly into the living room. He sat down and opened the Bible. Philip 46? That name wasn't in the Old Testament. He read all the names in the New Testament. Philippians 4:6. That had to be the one. There were only four chapters. He read it. "Do not be anxious about anything, but in every situation, by prayer and petition, with thanksgiving, present your requests to God."

He smiled and reread the verse. Ani was giving him a message. Be thankful. Be calm. Ask for what you want in prayer.

"I thank you, Lord, for bringing Yaz into my life." He spoke his thoughts aloud. "You know my heart and my sentiments. I want her to be happy, to find peace and joy. I want her to break free of the shield of pain, misery, and fear she's built around herself. Please, Lord, clear her mind. Guide her so she won't allow her emotions to blind her."

That was part of what he wanted.

"You know how I feel, Lord," he mumbled aloud. "I want to spend time with Yaz. I want her to trust me and for us to have an enjoyable conversation."

He folded the page and placed the Bible on the table.

"Thanks, Ani." He spoke as if she were there.

There were two more days of *rezos*. Time sped by swiftly. It seemed like only yesterday that Yasmin had met him in front of the funeral parlor. The week had been intense—the chaos and relentless storms assailing both Yasmin and him. She had no idea that he was in the same situation, his own family questioning and judging him because he defended her.

None of that mattered. He would uphold his beliefs. He was convinced that Yasmin was the victim. Why he always felt that way was as inexplicable as his reactions whenever she was near. Her behavior, instead of repelling him, attracted him. "Lord, let her see my true intentions. Remove the blindfold of misconceptions she has about me and my reputation."

What happens now? The question echoed in his mind.

He planned to wait for her after the *rezos* the next day. He wanted to clarify again that he was not the source of her distress. Somehow, he had to convey that he wasn't the enemy and never had been.

He reached for the beer. The bottle tipped over. He grabbed the Bible before the liquid found it. After cleaning up the spill, he washed his hands and returned to where he had been sitting. Picking up the Bible, he noticed it was open to the same page he had folded. His eyes focused on Philippians 4:13: "I can do all this through him who gives me strength."

* * *

She sipped the brew slowly, enjoying the flavor. Her usual routine had begun again—waking up at 6:00 in the morning, showering, getting dressed, and leisurely drinking a cup of coffee before heading to work.

The afternoon before, after dropping Ani off, Yasmin had driven home. Her intention hadn't been to dishearten Ani who'd insisted she stay. She loved visiting, listening to hymns, praying, reading the Psalms and other verses, and talking about the Lord. All were an added blessing when she slept over. She found solace, strength, and peace when they read verses and discussed the meaning of Scripture. Although she disliked being alone, she sought the solitude of her own apartment to reflect on everything that had happened that day.

Yasmin knew her faith was not as strong as it needed to be. "A baby," she'd once overheard one of her sisters in Christ call someone who'd recently accepted the Lord. She understood what that meant—someone new in the faith. She had accepted the Lord a week before her father passed away, but she was still having problems renovating her mind, letting go of the past, forgiving, and being humble. Ani comforted her by saying that it took time to mature, that friends who'd been in the faith for many years faced all kinds of challenges.

Her progress, if she'd made any, was minimal. She was crawling, if that. But she was learning that she was never alone. The Lord was always there helping her as Psalm 46:1 proclaimed: "God is our refuge and strength, an ever-present help in trouble." When she felt trapped, weak, lost, or unable to withstand the pain and emotional turmoil, God was there, and He fortified her strength.

She acknowledged that she kept making mistakes. Her emotions overwhelmed her and controlled her. She felt ashamed and appalled by her behavior the day before. She'd acted as if others around her wouldn't notice. Raul, Maria, Isabel, Luisa, and even her mother thrived on degrading her. She made her feelings and reactions obvious to them and everyone else.

"You need to have self-control and be confident and brave." Ani's words echoed Orlando's sentiments. They were right. She could either continue to allow her family to control her emotions or stop worrying and overreacting.

That's what letting go meant. Finally, she understood and believed that she could accomplish it. The Lord was giving her discernment.

She drank the last of her coffee, rinsed the cup, and placed it on the dish rack. Leaning on the counter, she crossed her arms. Although she had hurried into the bedroom the night before, part of her longed to be in Orlando's arms. The other part of her was disgusted—sickened by the knowledge that he'd been with Maria.

Her cheeks reddened.

If Orlando accused her of being insane and never wanted to go near her again, she was at fault. She'd met his kindness, concern, support, and words of wisdom with contempt.

Following the Lord meant being thankful, tactful, and calm—silent instead of argumentative, not lashing out angrily, not condemning or criticizing as her family did to her.

"I hear You," she said aloud. The Lord was speaking to her, making her aware of her harsh and unacceptable actions. "You need to apologize for being childish, immature, and foolish," she rebuked herself.

It was a confirmation of what Ani had told her. Being respectful, tolerant, and loving to others was not as effortless as it seemed or sounded. It was difficult but achievable. With the Lord's help, she would have victory and overcome her flaws.

She prayed for fortitude to apologize to Orlando. Raul, Isabel, and the blabbermouths—well, she needed more intense prayer before she could demonstrate good sentiment toward them and forgive them. She could easily forgive her mother despite how harshly she'd treated her.

She realized her faith should not be affected by circumstances, emotional reactions, or what she saw. She had seen the Lord's deeds and blessings repeatedly through Ani's presence in her life and through her words, nurturing, and caring. She had to admit that Orlando's help was a blessing too. Yet instead of being thankful for his support and concern, she'd taken them for granted. She needed to address that and make the necessary changes.

* * *

"How are you, Yaz? How was your day?" Orlando asked, stopping next to her as she reached her car.

"Where did you come from?" she asked, turning and facing him.

"I was crossing the street as you exited the building. You walked down the block, unaware of your surroundings. You need to be alert, aware of who and what is around you."

"You know the exact time I leave the *rezos*," Yasmin marveled, dismissing his comment.

"Habit. Routine. *Rezos* ends. You're the first to leave."

"And you're watching, taking in every detail," she noted with disapproval. "Does anything escape your scrutiny?"

"Unimportant things, I suppose," he replied, admitting to himself that when it concerned her, he was aware of all details, regardless of how small. He scanned her casually from head to toe. She wore a black dress, a white blazer, and high-heeled sandals that matched the black purse she carried. Her hair was loose with black metal hairpins holding it away from her face. She wore no makeup, just a hint of lip gloss. Her casual office look was chic. It was a sign she had returned to work. "How about your day?"

"Long and tiring," she replied. "I wanted to speak to you."

"I have some things to clarify too." He wondered what caused the abrupt change in her attitude. She was calm, relaxed, and unconcerned about who was in the area that would see them talking. Whatever had happened, he was delighted. It was the first time he'd seen her calm and possibly happy.

"You go first. I'm listening." She lowered her gaze.

He placed the tips of his fingers gently under her chin and lifted her face. Her warm, hesitant smile was charming. "Now we can talk. I'm sure you've heard Matthew 7:12: 'So in everything, do to others what you would have them do to you, for this sums up the Law and the Prophets.'"

"From lecturing to quoting verses," she said playfully.

"You want Carmen, Raul, and Isabel to be considerate?" he continued, resisting the urge to smile. "You want them to forget the past, forgive, and trust you, right?"

"Yes," she nodded. She'd anticipated having a difficult time apologizing, but the Lord was making it easier. Orlando was setting the tone. After he spoke, she would admit she'd mistreated him and ask his forgiveness.

"You complain that they refuse to see you for who you really are, yet you're doing the same to me."

She nodded again.

Determined to make his point, he continued. "I've never approved of how your family treats you."

"I know."

Orlando hesitated. He had prepared an extensive discourse and a prolonged exchange as he strived to convince her.

"Please," she paused and then continued, "forgive me. I apologize. I'm sorry for taking out all my frustrations on you. You don't deserve it."

"Truce?" He extended his hand, although what he wanted to do was embrace her. Grinning, she shook his hand. "Great to see you in a good mood." Her smile was radiant—irresistible.

"Ever thought about becoming a pastor?" she teased, slipping her hand out of his.

"I have a right to express my feelings, no?"

"I wouldn't dare forbid it."

"You can be witty when you want to be. I like that."

"You can be obnoxious and nosy. I don't like that at all."

"There's a good and a bad side to everyone."

"True. Unfortunately, all my family sees is my bad side." She leaned against the car and paused before continuing. "It's like the good in me never existed."

"Keep the witty mood. It suits you best."

Her lips shone brightly from the touch of lip gloss. The natural look was extremely attractive. She leaned her head slightly to the side. "How do you know what suits me?"

"A guess."

"No," she shook her head. "You don't strike me as the type of guy who guesses anything. You're an observer. You analyze and study details."

"You disapprove?"

"There's good and bad in everybody," she mimicked him, and his smile widened.

"Let's go for a cup of coffee," he said, "and talk for a while."

She stared at him in silence, smiling.

"Don't think about it. Say yes." He urged her on, eager to spend more time with her. "It's a beautiful night. You decide where."

"Unlike you who can sleep a few hours and go to work, I need rest. Everything from last week has piled up on my desk. I need to be alert to tackle that pile again tomorrow." She smiled and got in her car.

Chapter 9

Picking up the cordless phone, Yasmin read the number and lowered the volume on the TV. Placing the remote on the center table, she sat up. Although there were times she longed for solitude, after spending so many nights at Ani's, her apartment felt barren, and the silence was unsettling.

She was careful not to mention or demonstrate any signs of how she felt and decided not to share with Ani that moving out and adjusting to being alone was still a challenge. The solitude, emptiness, and deafening silence were often unbearable. Although she insisted that she was fine, it was only to appease Ani's concerns. She loved staying over, but when she returned home, the nights were endless. She wandered throughout the apartment unable to sleep. She lay on the couch to watch TV until the wee hours of the morning, barely rested before getting up to get ready for work.

"How are you, Ani?" she said affectionately.

"I was expecting you this evening after the *rezos*. I prepared dinner and was waiting for you to arrive to eat."

"I'm sorry. I'm trying to get back to my routine."

"It must be old age. I forgot you were going back to work today," Ani said. "If you come tomorrow, I won't have to cook." She changed the subject. "Are you ready to talk about what happened yesterday, about why you were so upset?"

"I'll admit that I don't have self-control," she said, "that I should give myself some time to calm down." Recalling the sordid events, she felt ashamed.

Ani laughed. "I suppose that's a start."

"Yeah," she agreed and then explained in detail what had occurred. She realized as she described the unsettling scenario that Carmen never defended her and seemed oblivious to her feelings, unmoved by the humiliation others put her through. She had mixed emotions about that. It was painful, appalling, and also infuriating.

That realization along with Maria's offensive comments caused her to lose emotional control. She'd hastened out of the apartment, eager to leave the vicinity to somehow dispel the mixture of emotions that dampened her spirits. She felt defeated and worthless. The last person she'd expected to meet was Orlando. Unable to restrain her ire, she lashed out at him. His reaction and rebukes enhanced her anger. Then Luisa showed up—the perfect ending to a horrid morning.

"Defending myself, as Orlando suggested, or allowing him to put Maria in her place would lead to more arguments with Mami."

"Why get angry at Orlando for telling you the truth?" Ani asked.

Yasmin was glad they were talking over the phone. The question irritated her, and that would have been evident on her face. The truth had never spared her from being mistreated. All the lies her family believed were the results of their own suppositions. "That doesn't matter. I won't be respected, accepted, or looked at through a different lens because Orlando insults Maria."

"Right now they may not see or understand it, but eventually they will. Even if you disagreed with Orlando, he was only trying to help. Why insult him?"

"I shouldn't have," she said. Her conduct was inexcusable, but she had made amends—a small plus among so many mistakes. "I apologized when we saw each other earlier today."

"You met again today?" Ani sounded thrilled.

"He arrived as I was leaving the *rezos*." She had been disappointed when she hadn't seen him waiting in front of the building and was surprised when he showed up as she reached her car. "We spoke for a while."

"You did the right thing," Ani said. "Are you together?"

"No," she replied adamantly.

"If you're just friends, Maria can say and think what she wants," Ani said. "People always talk. They gossip without caring what's true and don't think about the damage they're causing. That's why we must be careful what we say."

Yasmin grinned. Ani and Orlando lectured her on the same topics. All Orlando had to do was encourage her to pray and insist that she stay firm in her faith, and he and Ani would mimic each other.

"Maria is jealous," Yasmin said, still disturbed that they had been involved.

"She still cares for him," Ani concluded. "Otherwise, she wouldn't have confronted you."

"He claims it's over—that Maria is and was *insignificant*." She stressed the last word.

"If he's just a friend . . ."

"I don't care who he's been with or why," she snapped. "Maria has some nerve speaking to me that way. She told me I'm . . ." She couldn't say the word. It took self-control that she had no idea she possessed to contain herself. "She's the one who's been with him already. He got tired of her and moved on. He said he doesn't want anything to do with her."

Ani laughed. "What offends you most, Yasmin? That they were together or what Maria said?"

Yasmin ignored the question. There was no humor in the situation. "Maria and Luisa need to focus on themselves, not on me. Every time Luisa has seen me with Orlando, she has told Mami."

"You're dating, but you're not interested in each other?" Ani asked, puzzled.

Yasmin sighed aloud, glad Ani couldn't see her grim expression. Denying it and arguing about it were futile. Ironically, when Orlando asked her out, she was tempted to say yes. The idea of spending more time with him was appealing. If they went out, it wouldn't alter the rumors or preconceived notions. What it would do is provide an opportunity to expand their friendship. Orlando was a good listener and genuinely cared about her feelings and opinions. He was interested in hearing what she had to say.

"Yasmin?"

"We're not dating," she said. "We've met several times after the *rezos*. We talked about Mami and how things are going with her. Unlike my family, Orlando is concerned about me and how I feel."

"I think your emotions are clouding your judgment."

"Not at all."

"I don't expect you to admit it. The Lord will open your eyes, and you'll see the truth. Then you'll have to ask for guidance to make the right decisions."

Unsure what Ani was referring to, Yasmin opted not to comment.

"I'm happy you're getting to know each other and becoming friends." Yasmin could tell that Ani was smiling. "I like Orlando. He's single, right?"

"With his reputation, I doubt it."

"You're being judgmental. That doesn't mean he can't get serious or won't fall in love."

"Love?" she repeated. Was Orlando capable of commitment?

"Yes, Yasmin, love," Ani said. "It can change a man."

"In movies," Yasmin quipped. "Tell me about Ismenia, Ismael, and Andres."

"We spoke last night. No word yet on when she's coming back."

"Did she mention me?" Yasmin asked eagerly.

"Yes. She asked how you were doing and wanted to know what was going on between you and Orlando, if you were still allowing him to drive your car."

She laughed along with Ani. "I hope she doesn't come back complaining that Ramona was making her life miserable. Ismenia shouldn't have set foot in her house again."

"Both of you need prayers so you can make wise decisions."

"I'm praying more often, too, asking the Lord to give me peace and help me control my emotions."

"Good," Ani said. "He knows what you need and will grant it in His time. Call me if you're not dropping by tomorrow."

Yasmin lay on the couch after hanging up and thought about Ani's comment. Her heart's desire was to be closer to her mother and be able to confide in her without being condemned. She wanted her mother to see her for who she was, not based on hearsay, the past, or erroneous perceptions.

It had nothing to do with Orlando, as Ani made it sound. She had more pertinent issues to address. "Help me change my ways, help me endure," she prayed aloud.

Be prudent, Orlando had told her. Although she continuously rebuffed his suggestions, his words were savvy. Prudence meant discipline, exercising good judgment, and being tactful. The Bible had many verses on that. She would look them up, read them, and study the Word. It occurred to her that prioritizing was a good start.

Visiting her mother was crucial. Restoring their relationship was her primary goal. Viewing it like an obligation and insisting that she had to visit every day were absurd. Her rationale and reasons were incorrect. She would carefully plan the time she spent with her mother and ensure they were alone.

She recalled Lamentations 3:22–23: "Because of the Lord's great love we are not consumed, for his compassions never fail. They are new every morning; great is your faithfulness." She could start over, begin anew, and get a fresh start daily.

The truce, as Orlando had called it, would be just that—an opportunity to start over. He knew too much about her. Their friendship would allow her to even the scale. It was time to level it.

* * *

Orlando set down the folder of the case he had been researching and glanced at his watch. He would leave with sufficient time to meet Yasmin as she exited the building. Since the night before, images of her smile, her soft laughter, and the smell of her perfume kept resurfacing. Her reaction had pleasantly surprised him as did the fact that she hadn't said *no* when he asked her out. Instead, she gave an excuse.

He was tearing down the wall she'd built around herself.

Her good mood had fascinated him. He enjoyed her banter and liked that she felt comfortable enough to tease him. He was thankful that Ani had encouraged him to pray but hadn't expected his prayers to be answered this soon.

* * *

What was Raul so angry about? He acted as if Yasmin's sole purpose for being at the *rezos* was to make him miserable. Yasmin supposed he was still upset about the family battle. It was his choice to fret. As her mother pointed out, his decisions were unjustified and reprehensible. Finally, her mother understood that she wasn't at fault, at least about that. It was a blessing, one she hadn't taken the time to be thankful for. She'd been so immersed in the darkness that she hadn't seen the small rays of light that shone upon her.

Shifting sideways so her back was to Raul, she studied the altar—a folding table covered with a white cloth. At its center was an 8" by 10" photograph of her father. It was a picture of him she had never seen. He was dressed in a black suit with a white shirt and checkered tie. He was smiling, and he had rarely smiled. His black hair sprinkled with gray was combed back. He looked like an older version of Raul.

In front of the frame was a white candle. Its light flickered, casting a glow on the picture. There was a glass of water on top of a small plate with rue inside. It was the traditional setup. She had seen it many times when attending prayers. A flower arrangement of white roses was usually included, but there was none. That evening as she walked past a flower shop on her way there, she stopped to purchase a vase with a dozen white roses. Josefa was delighted and placed it at the center of the altar. The flowers were in full bloom and looked beautiful.

Raul made his disapproval evident by reminding Josefa that he could provide everything and anything needed. He insisted that had she asked for a flower arrangement, it would have been on the altar when the *rezos* began. Josefa ignored his heated barks and thanked her for the gesture.

Yasmin had followed her instincts and was pleased with the results—another ray of light, she thought with a smile.

* * *

"Have you been to the South Street Seaport before?" Orlando asked, still astounded that Yasmin had accepted his invitation. She was in good spirits when they met in front of the building. He suggested they celebrate her survival of the nine days of *rezos*. She agreed without hesitation.

"First time," she replied, walking ahead of him toward the escalators. "Although I live in New York, I haven't done much sightseeing."

"I have the remedy for that," he said.

She looked back with creased eyebrows.

"I'll be your tour guide," he smiled.

"We'll see." She hopped onto the escalator.

He stood one step below her. Yasmin's body just inches from his, he inhaled slowly. The scent of her perfume was subtle yet enticing. It drew him to her like a magnet, awakening his desire to hold her in his arms.

He placed his hand near hers on the rail. She slid hers up to avoid contact. Her efforts not to be noticed were what drew his attention to her. A mere look at how she carried herself sufficed to know that she was totally inaccessible—a fact Raul always overlooked although he considered himself versed in the mannerisms of females.

Breaking the steel barrier she had constructed around herself was a challenge. The decision to discard the armor was ultimately hers. She had chosen to let her guard down to spend time with Orlando. Her company was confirmation that his prayer was answered.

"Pick any table," he said as they walked past the array of restaurants lined up one after the other on both sides of the corridor.

He wagered to himself that she would select an isolated area. He watched her stroll ahead, stop, and point. He nodded, approving the choice she made. It was a corner table by the wall in an area where the surrounding tables were empty.

He'd made a good choice taking her there. The place had occurred to him as he left the office. The smile was a sign that she liked his selection.

"Beer, piña colada, soda?" he offered.

She held up a peace sign with her right hand. Nodding, he headed to the bar.

"No liquor," she called out, watching him walk away. She followed through on her decision. They were spending time together and getting to know each other. What she planned originally and the results were opposites. Ani would say that the Lord took charge, settling the situation His way.

"Mind if I sit here?" he asked, gesturing toward the empty seat next to hers. She shrugged in response. "Hungry?" he asked.

She shook her head.

He noticed how she moved her chair to create a physical distance. He handed her the piña colada and placed his beer on the table. "Shall we toast?"

She lifted her cup. "To surviving."

"I knew you could do it." He tapped her cup and sipped his beer.

"Thanks for your support. Without you and Ani, things would have been worse."

He winked at her. "How's it going with Carmen?"

"I went back to work yesterday and won't be visiting until the weekend. When I mentioned it, she wasn't happy." Yasmin avoided his eyes. "I'm praying that nothing comes up when I go back."

"Think positive. I'm sure your relationship with Carmen will improve. Time and patience are the key."

She nodded. The situation was gradually getting better.

"Tell me about yourself," he urged.

"Actually, I'd prefer to talk about you."

He was flattered but eager to know about her relationship with Manuel. Carmen had mentioned that they weren't together. He wondered what happened between them and why she was alone. "I can be the focus some other time."

"You're very confident," she smirked. "Aside from what you know, there's not much to add."

"Sure there is," Orlando urged. "What have you been doing? Past? Present?"

She studied her cup that she held in both hands. "I worked as an accountant for three years in a textile company. I started as an assistant. When the accountant left, I got her position and a raise, and now I'm doing her work and mine."

He recalled Carmen's comment that she got her GED and took a course in accounting. "Life isn't just working, staying home, and focusing on problems. What else?"

"I visit Ani, Ismenia, and the kids," she replied matter-of-factly.

Picking up the beer, he drank and then set the bottle down. He wondered if she was purposely omitting information about herself or too engrossed in the past and the problems with her family to enjoy life.

"That's it?"

She shrugged in response.

"What do you do for fun?"

"Is that your favorite topic?" she teased. "It shows that unlike the rest of us, you and Raul don't take anything seriously."

"You think very highly of your brother and me," he grinned.

"Aren't you proud of the reputation you created?"

He laughed. "You know from personal experience that people exaggerate."

"I'll grant you that. The truth is, I don't see that people who enjoy themselves all the time like you and Raul are any better off than I am."

"Pessimists rarely do." He considered it an interesting point of view from someone who was believed to be gratuitous and indiscriminately wanton. Her own words verified that her reputation and behavior were opposites—as were his. When she got to know him better, her misconceptions about his reputation would end, at least he hoped they would. "But there is a big difference, Yaz. Happiness is part of life."

"I think you're in the wrong profession, Mr. Castillo," she said. "Ever consider counseling?" He shook his head. "Just a hobby, right? I'm assuming the first consultation was free. Am I getting a bill for this session?"

He shook his head, frowning. "All that to avoid talking about yourself."

"Wrong," she said. "I'm talking about myself. If you don't like what you hear, that's not my concern."

"What about relationships? Marriage, kids, family?"

Her brow creased. "What about them?"

"Settling down doesn't interest you?"

"What do you say about that?"

Orlando smiled. She would have been a difficult client to gather facts from. Even so, her answers gave insight to her perspectives. While other women thrived on talking about their relationships, Yasmin eluded the topic. Although Carmen doubted it, Yasmin hadn't lied about being alone. It was obvious she was unwilling to provide any tangible information about herself or why she and her ex had separated.

"If I find the right person, definitely. You?" He was aware that she was watching him closely, studying his face.

"If?" she repeated. "Right person? What does that mean?"

"Someone you want to spend your life with." He was curious where the conversation would lead or what she had to say about it. "I'd like to find that person. You?"

She lifted her cup, took several sips, and laughed softly in response.

Another subject concluded without much said. "How's Ismenia? The kids?"

"Fine." She met his eyes. "They're in Santo Domingo."

"On vacation?"

"Not the word I would use," she retorted. "I don't know when she'll be back."

"I thought you were inseparable and knew everything about each other." When he met Ismenia, he had been impressed by how close they were. They seemed more like sisters than friends. He and Raul had become the same way. "Weren't you meeting her Saturday night after you left the funeral parlor?"

"Yes, to celebrate her birthday."

He grinned, pleased that finally there was something tangible to discuss with her. Finding out she was going to see Ismenia and not out with her ex or on a date was good news. "What happened?"

Her silence and the way she averted her eyes and then shifted away from him were signs that she was reluctant to discuss it. He persisted. "Did she cancel after you told her you were at Roberto's wake?"

"We're not speaking to each other."

He was silent. From what he recalled, she'd spoken to Ani and told her she knew where the place was. From that, he deduced that Ismenia had been waiting and decided to go to the club. Who had been angry was unclear. If they weren't speaking, they'd likely had a disagreement. He rephrased the question. "Did you tell her that Roberto had passed away and you were at his wake?"

"I didn't want to spoil her birthday," she admitted glumly.

"It might have been best to tell her the truth."

"Too late," she admitted with regret. "Making the right choices is not my forte."

"Why do you demean yourself? Isn't it bad enough that your family and others do?"

"Others?" she asked, giving him a long, intense look.

"Please forget about that," he said, certain by the expression on her face that she was thinking of Maria. "I don't want you to get upset over nonsense."

"The only one who knows if it was nonsense or not is you."

He was about to speak, but she held her hand up.

"I'm not discussing it. It's not my business. My opinion is unimportant."

"Sounds good to me," he assured her, smiling and glad for the moment that the topic was cast aside. "You don't go out? You don't have any friends other than Ismenia? What about dating?"

Picking up her drink, she took several sips and held it with one hand while playing with the drops of water that trailed down with the tip of her forefinger. He watched her make squiggly lines up and down the glass.

"An answer would be nice."

"No," she replied, focusing on what she was doing.

"No to which question?" he insisted.

She lifted her eyes, shot him an annoyed glance, and lowered them again. "No to all."

She stood, ready to leave.

"Relax. Have another piña, and we'll leave after that."

She shook her head, walked to the trash bin, and dropped the drink in it. She headed to the escalators.

He hastened ahead to walk beside her and dropped the beer bottle into the trash.

"You'll go to work regardless of the time you get home. I can't do that."

Taking out his wallet, he handed her a business card. "If you need to contact me . . ."

She read it and lifted her eyebrows. "You work at a law firm?"

"I'm a paralegal. My address and personal cell are on the back."

"No wonder you ask so many questions," she said. "Do you give these out often?" She held it up by the tips of her fingers and waved it in front of him.

"To clients, but blank on the back."

"Yeah, sure," she humored.

"How do I contact you, Yaz? When can we go out again?"

She stopped as they reached the escalator. She recited her number as he entered it in his cell phone. "Next weekend, Saturday or Sunday. Call me."

* * *

Letting the door slam shut, Yasmin ran into the apartment and picked up the cordless.

"Hold on, Ismenia," she said after greeting her. She placed her purse on the sofa and rushed back to lock the door.

She was anticipating a call from Orlando. They had agreed to go out that weekend, and he had promised to contact her. She was eager to know where they were going and what time he would pick her up. It was Thursday night, and he hadn't called yet. Sitting on the sofa, she put the receiver up to her ear.

"I want to see you and the kids. When are you coming back?" She spoke in a jovial tone despite the disappointment she felt. Ismenia's contacting her meant that their quarrel was over—good news and something else to be thankful for. Orlando would call eventually. He still had that night and the next day to plan where they would go.

"I kept telling you that Orlando liked you." Ismenia ignored her question. "Are you convinced now, five years later?"

"I'd forgotten about that." She recalled that Orlando had visited often after Raul introduced him to the family. Ismenia harassed her constantly, insisting that they liked each other. Yasmin had disagreed.

"Now you're his girl. What did he do, go to the *Botanica* to get a love potion to bewitch you?"

She chuckled. "I'm not Orlando's girl. We're friends."

"Is that what you're calling it?" Ismenia laughed. "Mom told me he calls you Yaz. I love it. What do you call him?"

"Orlando," she replied, mindful that she was accustomed to the nickname now although she had disliked it at first.

"What does your darling brother say about your *friendship*?"

Yasmin noted the sarcastic emphasis on the last word. "Why would Raul have anything to say? What I do is my business."

"Knowing him, I'm sure he'll be delighted."

"Raul's opinion doesn't matter to me."

"Really?" Ismenia scoffed. "Since when? What happened to Miss I-can't-live-my life-without-my-family's-approval?"

"She's learning to let go and move on," Yasmin voiced proudly. It was difficult and challenging but not impossible.

"Bravo. Aside from Mom's preaching, it seems Orlando has had a good effect on you. Congratulate him for me."

"No." Mentioning he had been the focus of any discourse with Ani and Ismenia would pique his curiosity. It would prompt him to inquire what they had talked about. She would not divulge their absurd notions of a nonexistent courtship.

"Coward! I'll tell him myself," Ismenia chuckled. "I hope it lasts."

Yasmin laughed, amused by Ismenia's choice of words. They had gone out once, and Ismenia was already declaring misfortune. She was looking forward to spending time with Orlando, purposely ignoring all negative comments.

"Knowing you, Yasmin, who knows when you'll decide to end your *friendship*." Ismenia enunciated the last word. "When are you going out again with your so-called friend?"

"Saturday or Sunday," she replied, ignoring her sarcasm. "Orlando hasn't called me yet to tell me his plans."

"When was the last time you went out?"

"Tuesday night."

"Before that?"

She burst into laughter. Ismenia was worse than Orlando. "We just started going out this week on Tuesday."

"And already you're limiting the time you spend together?"

"Until I clear up the mess in my office, definitely." She'd agreed to go out with him on the weekend, determined to decrease her pending work. She planned to stay overtime that week and the next. Other projects had taken precedence, and a pile of files remained untouched on her desk.

"Mom is right. You need prayers."

"I'm good." Yasmin was at peace and content—feelings she had forgotten existed. The Lord had replaced her sadness with happiness. "When are you coming back?"

"Mom asked the same question. I'm not sure."

"Tell me about Ismael and Andres."

"They love being here. They play on the patio, swim, go to the beach, have fun, and enjoy being outdoors. Over there, they have to stay indoors in fall and winter."

Yasmin was tempted to say that she could research and find a variety of places that offered activities for kids indoors but changed her mind. "How are you doing?"

"I've had several arguments with Ramona. She doesn't want me around. The feeling is mutual."

"Why stay there?" Yasmin asked, irritated that Ismenia succumbed to such mistreatment just to be with Nestor. They needed to move into their own place, away from his mother.

"It's temporary. Nestor is adding another section to the house. It will have two floors. The first floor will have the living room, kitchen, dining room, guest room, and bathroom. There will also be a room for the maid and a laundry room near the kitchen. The second floor will be our room—a master bedroom with a bathroom, two bedrooms, and another bathroom. Once completed, I'll be staying there with him and the kids. It will be like having my own place. It has its own entrance, porch, and backyard. I won't have to see or speak to Ramona."

Yasmin disliked the idea. Ramona would still be close by, hounding Ismenia whenever she felt like it. "Couldn't you get your own place somewhere else?"

"Nestor likes to be close to his mom."

"Why wouldn't he do anything to accommodate you?" She spoke her thoughts aloud and regretted it.

"He does a lot of things to please me," Ismenia rectified in a stern tone. "I'm sure Orlando is doing the same, and you refuse to acknowledge how you feel about him. Unlike you, I have no issues admitting I want to be with Nestor. I'm willing to make sacrifices to be with him. Shouldn't you do the same?"

"There is no comparison. Our situations are different."

"I'm sure Orlando's version is different. You're the one fooling yourself, pretending it's something it's not. *Friendship* is the wrong word."

"Fine." She refused to argue. "Forgive me. I'm sorry I didn't tell you about Dad."

"I know you are," Ismenia concurred. "Whatever happens from now on, no matter what it is, you'd better confide in me."

* * *

"Dessert?" Orlando asked, as the waiter cleared the table.

Yasmin held up her piña colada and shook her head.

Instead of sitting across from her, he sat next to her. The scent of her perfume and the physical proximity were invigorating. He had no recollection of ever feeling that way with anyone he'd dated.

"I can order another," he offered.

"One is enough." She lifted her gaze and looked directly at him.

Orlando smiled. She looked radiant with a touch of eye shadow, powder, and lipstick. He couldn't help staring. He resisted the urge to comb his hand through her bouncy curls.

Picking up the beer, he sipped it slowly. Since Tuesday, he had been eager to see and speak to her. He had waited impatiently, concerned that she might get the wrong impression or feel hounded by his calls. To his surprise, she sounded pleased when he called the night before. She accepted his plans enthusiastically as if she'd been anticipating his call. He prayed the change would last a long time.

"Have things settled between you and Ismenia?"

"Yes," she nodded. "You forgot. Today we focus on you."

"I thought I was the investigator, the annoying inquisitor." It pleased him that she was interested in finding out more about him.

"You are," she affirmed, "but I'd like some clarification too. Aside from your reputation and Mami's complaints about all the trouble you and Raul got into, I know nothing pertinent about you."

He grinned. When they first met, she had been oblivious to his existence. Except for a timid greeting, they hardly spoke. She rarely stayed in the living room when he arrived with Raul. She went to her room, taking her schoolbooks with her and closing the door.

"What do you want to know, Yaz?"

"What was your childhood like? When and where did you and Raul meet?"

"I grew up in Washington Heights. My grandparents brought both my parents here from the Dominican Republic. My mother was a waitress. She met my father at the restaurant where she worked. He was a tailor and had his own shop for many years. When business slowed down, he sold it and purchased a house in Santo Domingo. He encouraged my mother to retire, and they live there now. He owns a *ventorrillo*, a grocery store. My uncle manages it. It's very profitable, so my parents and my uncle live comfortably. Dad doesn't like traveling back and forth. Mom doesn't mind."

"I like your mother. She's cordial. Your sister . . ." she hesitated purposely.

"Clara's set in her ways, a bit critical and argumentative but with a good heart."

"She doesn't like me," Yasmin noted.

"Clara doesn't know you. I'm sure she would feel differently if she did."

"Maybe." She was skeptical. "That answers the first question."

"When my parents moved to Santo Domingo, Clara moved into their apartment with Mario. I moved out on my own, got a full-time job at the law firm, and took courses after work and weekends to get my bachelor's degree."

"I thought you wanted to be a mechanic like Raul."

He shook his head. "It's a hobby, not a profession."

"If you could fix your car, why didn't you?"

"I can, but I prefer to take it to Raul's shop. I was too busy with Raul making the funeral and burial arrangements and overlooked taking it in. It was raining the day of the burial, but even if it hadn't been," he added to ensure she was certain he hadn't lied, "I was dressed to go to the cemetery and wasn't going to stain my clothes, hands, or nails with grease."

"Okay," Yasmin nodded. "And you met Raul . . ."

"Ninth grade. Initially we disliked each other. Raul was the class clown, making ridiculous jokes and provoking anyone who took him too seriously. He made some childish comments to another student, and it escalated to a fight. The argument began in class and continued after school. I was going home when I saw the crowd. I stopped to see what was going on. The guy and two of his friends were ganging up on Raul. I thought that was unfair, so I defended him."

"Not surprised. The two of you got into fights all the time."

His smiled widened. She knew more about him than she was willing to admit. "You have selective memory, Yaz. All you remember about us are the negative things—fighting, messing around with women, clubs, drinking."

Blushing, she nodded. "Mami complained about it to Dad. He ignored her. She got furious when Raul showed up with bruises on his face. She always asked Raul who he was hanging out with."

"Not with me," Orlando assured. "Raul had a lot of friends despite his temper. Most of them used him as a backup when they got into conflicts." He had brought that to Raul's attention. For a while, Raul ignored his advice and continued to stand up for the guys he partied with. "Raul began to be selective about who he went out with after getting into a conflict that could've resulted in serious injury, jail, or both. He thanked me for being honest. We became close and hung out together all the time. After several months, he invited me to meet his family."

"You were lucky," Yasmin said. "Mami made sure we understood she didn't want us bringing friends or boyfriends around. She told us not to bother if they weren't trustworthy or it wasn't serious. The same applied to Raul."

"I knew that," Orlando nodded. It was one of the reasons he questioned why Yasmin had taken Manuel to the apartment. She knew how strict her parents were and always adhered to their rigid rules. Taking such a big risk and acting so bold wasn't like her. "Anything else you'd like to know?"

"The interrogation is not over," she teased.

"When you want to continue, just ask. Did you visit Carmen today?"

"Yes," Yasmin nodded. "Luisa told her she saw us arguing in the lobby. Mami wanted to know why."

"Your explanation?" Orlando asked, unable to resist a smirk. Yasmin had been incensed and outraged by Maria's comment or the fact that they'd been an item—probably both. She was talking as if the incident had been trivial.

"I followed your example."

"That is?" he asked.

"I kept asking questions and redirected the conversation to other things."

He laughed heartily. "I won't take credit for that. You're very clever, more so when you don't allow your emotions to control your rationale."

"You always know the right things to say. That's your way to get any female you want. Is that how you got Maria?"

"Ouch." He pretended to be wounded, placing his hand over his heart and keeling over. "I need to go to the emergency room to get this wound treated."

"I'm serious." She gave him a disapproving look. "You courted her."

The fiery glow in her eyes delighted him. He didn't want to make assumptions but was flattered by the notion that she might be jealous. He wondered if she realized how her reactions could be interpreted. He guessed she was unaware of it and deduced that the minute she realized it she would become self-conscious, overreact, and stop seeing him.

"You've never done anything you regretted, that you wish you could go back and undo?"

"Are you being sarcastic?" She scrutinized his face.

"No." His tone was gentle. "It's how I feel. Maria was a mistake, one I wish I'd never made. I'm constantly reminded of it. It's frustrating."

"I know exactly what you mean," she said. "I feel the same way about the incident with Manuel."

Orlando waited, eager to hear what had happened. He doubted she would give much detail. She was an expert at evading the subject.

"I never imagined or thought one decision could change my life so drastically. It was as if who I was, the person everyone knew, never existed." She inhaled deeply and then exhaled slowly. Her eyes became blurry.

Orlando realized that whatever had happened that day, the wound remained open. That explained why she was so reserved.

"I didn't think lies could create . . ." She paused to wipe the tears that trailed down her cheeks. ". . . an image I could not erase."

He embraced her. She leaned her head on his shoulder and cried quietly. Her anguish troubled him. What decision changed her life? What lie was she referring to?

"Are you all right?" he asked when she moved back.

Yasmin dried her tears with the napkin he offered. "Thanks for understanding how I feel and being supportive."

"Of course." His intent was not gaining recognition or gratitude. He genuinely wanted her to be happy, to move on with her life and leave the past behind.

"When my family neglected me, you were there. And although your inquest was—is—annoying, you've given me good advice."

"Nobody is perfect, Yaz."

"Really?" she chuckled. "I wish my family would think that way too."

She was smiling again, in a good mood. He refused to spoil it by continuing to talk about the past. He stood, pleased that he had taken her to Olive Garden on 47th and Broadway. "Let's take a stroll around Times Square and decide where to go next."

Chapter 10

"I'm glad you decided to spend some quality time with me, Mami." Carmen had agreed to have lunch with Yasmin after Mass. They walked several blocks to a diner. "Do you like the grilled chicken?"

"Who knows how they cleaned and seasoned it," Carmen griped. Most of the food on her plate was untouched. "I can cook better than this, and you won't have to pay."

"That's the idea, Mami—no cooking," Yasmin chuckled.

"To eat junk and pay for it?" Carmen shook her head. "It's wasted money."

"I don't mind spending it. Why work and not enjoy the money you earn?"

Carmen picked up the glass of orange juice and took several sips. "That's what Manuel taught you? To squander money?"

"I don't misuse it," she defended herself, opting to refrain from the topic of Manuel. "I have savings, I pay all my bills, and I buy whatever I want."

"Ah yes, you're an independent woman. And you live alone." Placing the glass down, Carmen glared at her. "When you become a mother, you'll know how disappointing it is to see your children stray away, to watch them doing the opposite of what you taught them."

"I'm sorry I've caused you so much grief," Yasmin said.

"Just words," Carmen shrugged. "What were you and Orlando talking about in the lobby of the building?"

Yasmin cut a piece of chicken, chewed it slowly, and savored the flavor. The seasoning was delicious. She wished her mother would have

154

enjoyed the food and her company. Orlando and Ani would have been proud of her. She was faithfully adhering to their suggestions to be calm and at ease.

She had also followed through on her decision to get to know Orlando. The night before, after the date at Olive Garden, they went to the movies. It was the first time that she'd arrived home so late at night. Orlando was thoughtful, courteous, and respectful—gallant. He opened the door for her to get in and out of the car—a custom she'd seen only in movies. He placed his hand protectively on her back as they crossed the street. He held the door open for her to enter and exit. He was a gentleman, not what she expected from someone with his reputation. As promised, Orlando assumed the role of tour guide. She wondered where they would go next and was eager to see him again that evening.

Carmen cleared her throat, a sign she was waiting for an answer.

Yasmin sipped the glass of soda.

"Look at me when I'm speaking to you, Yasmin Arias," Carmen demanded. "Pay attention."

Yasmin placed the glass on the table and faced Carmen, smiling.

"Why do you deny what's so obvious? That glow in your eyes and that look on your face speak for you."

"Nothing wrong with being in a good mood," Yasmin replied, her smile turning to a grin. Ani had made similar comments, but it no longer bothered her. She was happy, at ease, going out, and enjoying herself.

"I'm sure there is a reason you're so happy," Carmen sneered. "Why were you arguing with Orlando?"

"Why do you believe everything Luisa says?"

"You were angry and didn't even greet her. Didn't we talk about that? It's rude and impolite. You almost knocked her down rushing out. What was the problem?"

"We were talking." She emphasized the last word purposely. Carmen's obsession with the topic made her realize that questions regarding Orlando, Manuel, and her past would be recurrent. Her prayers had been answered, however, and she was more adept at controlling her emotions. She remained calm, although Carmen's acrid attitude and censure continued. "Luisa and Maria need to focus on their own lives. Maybe then they'll stop worrying, gossiping, and lying about everyone else's."

"She didn't lie," Carmen defended. "You were in the lobby arguing," she said as if she'd been there. "Answer me. Why were you so angry?"

"That's Luisa's perception."

"You tell me what happened then." Carmen's eyes bore into hers.

"I wish you would give what I say the same importance you give Luisa's and Maria's comments."

"We both have a wish. Mine is for honesty," Carmen said. "Luisa may gossip about many things, but she's not blind, Yasmin. This isn't the first time she's seen the two of you together."

"And she makes assumptions and tells lies. She talks to you about them as if they were true."

"You're not interested in each other?" Carmen asked skeptically. "Yet you're always together?"

"Why doesn't Luisa worry about Maria? Hasn't she seen the way she acts around Orlando?"

"You're jealous," Carmen accused. "You do care for Orlando."

Leaning back, Yasmin crossed her arms. "I'm doing what Luisa and Maria do, observing and making my own conclusions."

"And you're right. Maria and Orlando had a thing a while back. It didn't last long, and I didn't think it would. Like you, Maria kept hounding him until he took what she offered. They're no longer together, and she's still at home." Carmen sniffed and wiped her mouth. "That's what happens to independent women."

"She's still interested." Yasmin didn't want to sound sarcastic, but she did.

"True," Carmen agreed. "She makes no effort to disguise it. Orlando doesn't want her near him. He got what he wanted. Like a mosquito, he stung and left."

Yasmin imagined the gross description and cringed.

"That's what men like Orlando do, Yasmin. They use women and leave."

She shared the sentiment and fully understood the repercussions. Orlando was a friend, one she could confide in. They conversed, they laughed, and they delighted in each other's company.

"Orlando is very nice to you, Mami." Yasmin reminded her. "He treats you like you're his mother. He's caring, considerate, and very thoughtful, more so than any of us. Why do you talk about him that way? I don't think he would ever do anything to disrespect you."

"You're defending him?"

Yasmin shrugged. She warned Orlando that being around her wasn't a good idea. Did he realize he was in the same predicament—judged by appearances and not reality? If he did, it didn't bother him. She supposed that was the reason he ignored her unjust decision to stay away. He made her realize that no matter what she did or didn't do, there would be innuendos.

* * *

Orlando watched with delight as Yasmin picked up her piña colada, sipped, and gazed up at him, smiling. They had gone to the wax museum on 42nd Street, and then he'd taken her to a Cuban restaurant in the vicinity.

"Part two of learning more about you," she said, holding the drink in her hand as the waiter cleared the table. "You and Raul went to the mechanic shop often, but you also went partying every weekend. Correction," she held her hand up, "every chance you got. I suppose that's how you earned your reputation."

He noted the disparaging way she said it. "You won't believe me, Yaz, but I've never taken it seriously."

"No?" She was shocked.

"It's not important. Gossip and rumors are based on suppositions. We both know that. Now that we know each other a little better, I hope you can focus on other attributes."

"I'll try, although it's Mami's favorite topic. Trusting is an issue."

"Just for the mother or for the daughter too?"

"Why ask the question if you know the answer?"

Her reply delighted him. She was witty and cheerful, signs that she enjoyed his company as much as he did hers. He decided to change the topic. His reputation didn't merit a lengthy discussion. Eventually she would overlook it as she had his fling with Maria.

"Everything wasn't fun and fights," he explained. "The Arias Mechanic Shop began as a hobby for both of us. We liked repairing cars. Throughout high school, we spent most of our free time doing repairs on the street. We purchased the tools we needed with the money we made and kept them in a van."

"Not what I thought you were doing," she admitted.

"What you imagine and what really happens are two different things." He waited for her to respond. She grunted aloud and remained silent. "We had a lot of customers by the time we graduated. As our clientele, profits, and demand grew, we needed to find a location. Raul continued working from the van while he got his mechanic's license. I accepted a full-time position as a paralegal in the law firm where I work now."

"I'm impressed. Both of you did something worthwhile."

"Glad you approve." He winked at her. "Not a total loss as you thought."

"Glad I was wrong," she said. "You and Raul own the shop?"

"Raul keeps insisting we become partners. I'm not interested."

"I'll have to admit I was convinced that you and Raul had nothing else on your minds but skirts, clubbing, drinking, and fighting."

"That's called an assumption," he pointed out, "which becomes a problem when it turns to gossip, kind of like what Luisa and Maria do with you."

"And your point is?" Leaning her head to the side, she looked at him with the corner of her eye.

"Why not get to know someone first and then decide if what you've heard about them is true?"

"Like you did with me?"

"Exactly."

She laughed along with him. He was glad she hadn't taken offense. They'd spent most of the weekend together, and the thought that they might not see each other until the next weekend bothered him. "We're back to work tomorrow, Yaz. When are we getting together again?"

She smiled. "You're the tour guide. You tell me."

* * *

Although her intentions were to eliminate the growing piles still cluttering her office, Yasmin had not worked overtime one day that week. The piles kept resurfacing daily despite her efforts to eliminate them as quickly as possible. Initially, the clutter disturbed her. She felt anxious and worried about not meeting all the deadlines of new reports and not catching up. Praying for peace of mind and tranquility helped her relax.

Able to think clearly, she became creative. She reorganized her office. She placed two crates under her desk, one for completed files and the other for pending work prioritized by due dates. The more pertinent files were on her desk near her computer. Thankful that the Lord had eliminated the cause of her anxiety and had facilitated her going out with Orlando after work, she hastened out of her office to meet him.

Since Orlando always wore suits, she chose her attire carefully. The array of blazers in her closet allowed her to mix and match outfits with dresses, skirts, and pants. Trying on an assortment of combinations before going to work, she paraded in front of the mirror to select the outfit she liked most. Before leaving the office to meet him, she retouched her makeup and sprayed herself with perfume. Orlando's grin and the way he nodded after scanning her casually from head to toe showed his approval. She pretended not to notice and smiled jovially.

"How was your day?" he asked, as she got into the car.

Leaning forward, she tapped a kiss on his cheek. Shocked by her own spontaneity, she sat back, blushing. She hoped he realized it was an affectionate greeting and nothing more. "Busy day," she replied, glad that although he seemed pleasantly surprised by the gesture he made no comment. "I worked through lunch and didn't finish what I was working on. You?"

"The hours dragged on," he shared. In the short time they had been dating, the change in her attitude was impressive. The kiss was a welcome perk that he wished she would adhere to whenever they met.

"Really?" she laughed softly. "Doesn't the day go faster when you're doing research on whatever cases you have?"

"Sometimes." He was reluctant to share that the workload was not the issue. Time was. Waiting to see her made the hours endless.

"It's Friday," she said to comfort him. "The week is over, and now you can enjoy your weekend. Where is the tour guide taking me?"

Her emphasis on the words *tour guide* made him chuckle. "Have you been to the Cloisters in Washington Heights?" he asked as he drove on 56th Street toward the West Side Highway. Her office was in midtown Manhattan not too far from his, making it easy for him to pick her up. He had suggested dropping her off at work in the morning, but she refused, preferring to take public transportation. They agreed that he would use his car, which made it easy for him to drive to his place after he took her home.

"No." She shook her head.

"We'll go to the restaurant and then walk around the park. There is a museum that closes at 6:00 p.m. It's best to go on weekends in the afternoon."

"I can leave Mom's place early or skip Saturday and go Sunday," she suggested.

Her putting off being with Carmen so they could spend time together surprised and delighted him. It was also a blessing. The Lord had granted him so much more than he'd prayed for.

He turned on the radio, and they listened to salsa as he drove uptown. There was a lot of traffic, but they moved forward at a good pace. He noticed how she surveyed the area with creased eyebrows when they arrived. The restaurant entrance was in the park. All she could see were barred windows, two huge, wooden doors, and the walkway that led to the parking lot.

"Not much to see on this side," he said.

"And on the other side of the mural?" she gestured forward.

"Let's find out," he said, getting out of the car. He waited for her to join him, and then they stood by the concrete wall. Below was the park, the Inwood area, and beyond was the Bronx.

"Quite a view," she said. "I had no idea this place existed. I've never been this far uptown."

"That means the tour guide is doing a good job," he praised himself. It had been two weeks since they started dating, and in that time, she had become accustomed to his company. Did she yearn to see him as much as he did her? Were the hours long, the work tedious, her thoughts inundated with memories of the time they had spent together? They were questions he wouldn't dare ask. He met her eyes, and the glow lit his heart with hope, igniting emotions he'd never felt before.

"What?" Yasmin asked, aware that he was studying her. The warmth in his eyes seeped through her, causing her stomach to flutter.

"For someone who had a busy day, you look calm and happy," he commented gently, combing back her hair. She was wearing it loose, the way he preferred it. He almost blurted out that she looked radiant and that he wanted to see her, be around her, and talk to her all the time.

"I am." She was candid. The pastor was right. Letting go, as he had preached, had brought incredible results. She felt at peace—blessed with the stability and tranquility she'd sought.

"No more migraines?" he asked, thrilled to see the transformation she had undergone since they'd met in front of the funeral parlor. She was a different person—self-confident, content, at ease.

"They stopped as suddenly as they started. They began when I visited Mami and Dad dragged me out of the apartment, threatening to leave Mami if I visited again. After that, I've had them on and off."

"They're caused by stress." Orlando noticed that she mentioned what Roberto did without remorse or emotional strain. She was finally moving forward, leaving the past where it belonged. It was what he had prayed for, and that prayer was being answered.

"The doctor returns." She tilted her head slightly and smiled.

"And leaves right away." He placed his arm around her shoulders, and they walked toward the restaurant. "Hungry? I'm starving."

"Me too." The yogurt she'd had instead of lunch at 2:00 that afternoon had left her famished. "I might have to chip in for the bill. I'm that hungry."

"No, you won't," he assured. "Get whatever you want from the menu. Money is of no concern."

"All right." She strolled past the entrance to the other side of the building. "Can we sit in the back? There's a garden."

Joining her, he noticed the tables on the patio were strategically positioned to provide ample space to move around. It was empty, and he knew she would like the privacy. Placing his hand on her waist, he led her through the entrance, past the tables inside the restaurant, and into the garden. Except for another couple seated near the bar, they were the only ones there. He gestured for her to select a table and followed her to the far end. He liked her choice. They could talk freely, and she would feel at ease. Placing a chair next to hers, he sat down.

"Are you finished with your interrogation, Yaz?" he asked after they ordered drinks and food.

"I think in comparison to everything you know about me, you haven't shared much," she said. "But I'm not interested in hearing details about your flings."

"Good." He preferred that she focus on more positive things about him. "No part three?"

She shook her head. "Why? Are you starting your inquisition again?"

He waited in silence until the waiter placed their drinks on the table and walked away. "I'm curious as to why you dropped out. You were an honor student your senior year. You would have received several scholarships."

"I want Mami to stop focusing on the past. I'm trying to do the same. Why talk about it?"

He rested his arm on the back of her chair and turned slightly so they were face-to-face. Her lips were inches from his. He imagined himself lowering his head and kissing her.

She cleared her throat and leaned back against the chair, distancing herself from him. Again, her stomach was queasy, a strange mix of anxiety and glee. She smiled timidly and then lowered her gaze.

"Last time, Yaz," he said, noticing the red hue on her cheeks. She was bashful and demure, the opposite of her reputation and what her family chose to believe. It saddened him that he could not change their erroneous perceptions. Praying and believing were the solutions. He was certain that through prayer their hearts would be touched, and they would see her as she really was, the way he saw her. "I promise it's the last time we'll talk about the past." He refocused his attention.

"I'd rather not," she said, her lips curling down.

"We won't discuss it again." He placed the tips of his finger under her chin, and she looked up, smiling coyly.

"I'll remind you of that," she warned.

"Please do." He winked playfully. "Carmen still doesn't understand why you dropped out."

"How do you know?" He spoke as if they were confidantes. He'd mentioned that he discussed pertinent issues with her mother. Ironically, despite their close friendship and candid talks, Carmen continued saying disparaging comments about him.

"Carmen and I talked about you often. I kept encouraging her to have faith, telling her you would return eventually."

"Really? What made you so sure of that?"

"Prayers answered," he replied. "Carmen told me that she prayed all the time that you would return."

"Ani says we just have to wait for God's perfect time. It's true. I can give testimony to that."

"Me too." He'd been convinced she would never go out with him. Somehow the Lord had made it happen. She accepted dating him every day that week and seemed pleased with his company. She was more apt to talk about herself, although the topic of Manuel never arose.

"You," she stressed the word, "go to church?"

"Sometimes," he said. "A colleague at work is a Christian. He always invites me when they have special events and conferences for men. I attended a few."

"I also attended some conferences for women with Ani," she said. "Amazing topics. Ani goes every year. When she invited me to church, I was reluctant to go, but I noticed the change since she became a Christian. I wondered what happened. Ani is a different person now. Before, she was always arguing with Ismenia. Their fights were intense. They became enemies and wouldn't see or speak to each other for weeks. Ani would get depressed and cry all the time. Now she's calm, at peace. It's not that she doesn't get upset. Now she handles situations without yelling, cursing, or getting offended. She always talks about the Lord, praises Him, gives testimony, and is grateful for all the blessings she's received."

"Ani's a wonderful person." Orlando recalled the verse she'd suggested. It changed his perspective on things. It made him realize he needed to be closer to the Lord. He continued to pray about many things in his life, mostly for Yasmin. He wanted her to break the chains of the past that kept her stagnant. She seemed in control of her emotions, confident, calm, and happy, confirmation that his prayers were being answered.

"Ani is a blessing in my life. If she hadn't taken me in and nurtured me, I would have been out on the streets. She treats me like a daughter. I wish Mami would treat me the same."

"In time," Orlando said.

"His time," she quoted Ani. "Although Mami's accusations and insults drain me emotionally, we're getting along a little better. I just wish I hadn't stayed away so long."

"Making mistakes is part of life. Thankfully, God helps us stand and picks us up when we fall."

"True," she agreed. The Lord was the father she always yearned for— loving and caring, her companion. He diligently took care of all her needs. "Everything He does for us is beneficial."

Orlando nodded. "About dropping out . . ."

Yasmin took several sips of her drink. Unsure of how to begin, she was silent. It was the first time she would speak about it. Ani had never pressured her. Certain that Ismenia would divulge to Nestor whatever she confided, she never explained to Ismenia what happened either.

"I wasn't planning to drop out," she began. "At first I was depressed and refused to go out. Then Ismenia told me Maria was spreading lies. She was telling everyone what happened—her spiced-up version of it."

"Maria started the rumors?" He had heard the comments and knew that whoever began the gossip had to be close to the family. He'd suspected Isabel, but now he realized he'd overlooked Roberto's close friendship with Luisa. He recalled Carmen complaining that Roberto didn't need to confide everything that happened in their home to her, not that Roberto listened. Like Raul, he did as he pleased. "Carmen doesn't know they started those rumors. If she did, I doubt she would continue confiding in them."

"She knows they gossip and accepts it as fact. She accuses me of providing proof with my behavior," she shrugged. "I don't care anymore. I ignore it, and even that upsets Mami. No matter what I do, she's not satisfied."

"Give it time, Yaz." Although Yasmin would not mention it, he knew the evidence was that Luisa saw them together and then divulged her assumptions of a fictitious relationship. "Raul knows Luisa likes to gossip. He's told Luisa and Maria to stop meddling."

"He's worse than they are the way he refers to me." She shook her head and felt her cheeks stinging with embarrassment. "If I were a man . . ."

He shook his forefinger in front of her, gesturing not to consider it. "We already discussed that. Be prudent."

"Do you think it will stop him if I stay quiet?"

"Provoking him isn't a good idea. We both know that." He feared Raul would become violent. "Don't challenge him, Yaz. Please."

"Fine," she agreed, tired of the subject. "I couldn't go back to school after that. I imagined everyone in the school whispering to each other as I passed by, pointing, laughing, and saying horrible things about me."

"You have a vivid imagination," he said. "Like any other emotion, fear must be controlled or it paralyzes you."

"I allowed it—past tense," she corrected. "Ani had no idea I'd dropped out. I got up every morning and pretended to get dressed until she left. Then I went back to bed. When I got up, I kept myself busy doing chores and made sure dinner was ready when Ani and Ismenia got home. Ani insisted that cleaning and cooking were unnecessary. I felt it was essential, a minimal way to show my gratitude and appreciation for not being homeless. When Ani realized I had dropped out, there were no lectures, insults, or demands that I leave. She gave me an ultimatum: work or school. I got a job at a supermarket and worked there while I got my GED. I enrolled in a business institute in the evenings and worked days at the supermarket until I got a certificate in accounting and was hired."

"Maybe you should tell Carmen what you went through. That might help her understand why you dropped out and how you became financially independent."

Yasmin shook her head. "The problem with my family since the incident with Manuel is that they ask questions but don't want to hear the answers. So here's my dilemma. Should I lie so they think I'm telling the truth, or do I tell the truth so they think I'm lying?"

He laughed heartily.

* * *

"What are you so happy about? Are you with Manuel again?" Carmen leaned forward and took hold of Yasmin's chin, examining her face.

"No," she grinned.

"Continue lying to yourself." Carmen leaned back on the rocker. "That glow on your face, eyes lit up, that smile." Carmen noted them with disapproval. "When a woman is in love, it shows."

"*Amor, amor, amor,*" Yasmin sang humorously in Spanish, repeating the word *love* three times. What her mother called the look of love was peace of mind. She was cheerful and had been for an indefinite time. As Ani mentioned, the Lord placed Orlando in her life for a purpose—to revive her and bring joy to her drab life.

"I don't understand why you're upset, Mami," Yasmin said, daunted by her crude attitude. Instead of sharing and celebrating along with her, Carmen was pessimistic and kept focusing only on negative things.

"Happiness over what, Yasmin? Tell me the reason, and then I'll decide if I should join you."

"It's beautiful outside," Yasmin crooned, unaffected by her mother's acrid view. The day was bright and sunny, chilly but not too cold. After leaving, Yasmin would visit Ani for a while and then go home to get ready. Orlando was picking her up at 6:00. He suggested she dress up. She was excited and looked forward to seeing him. She was eager to find out what they were celebrating and where he was taking her that required formal attire.

"That's what you're happy about? The day?" Carmen reproached her in a cool tone. "Admit you're with Manuel or with Orlando."

Yasmin laughed and shook her head. "I'm single."

"Really?" Carmen asked with disbelief. "Something is going on, if not with Manuel then with Orlando. Admit it."

A sly smile formed on Yasmin's lips. "We're just friends."

"Friends?" Carmen asked with disbelief. "You are so naïve, Yasmin Arias. Men are not your friends. That's just an excuse to take advantage of you. They take you to fancy places and restaurants, hold your hand, and open the door for you. They are very polite and act like gentlemen. After they get what they want, they forget about you. Get serious with someone else."

The smile faded from Yasmin's face. Images of the many times she and Orlando had gone out flashed through her mind. He behaved just as her mother described. An arctic chill spread down her spine and throughout her body. She shivered.

"You can't hide the truth, Yasmin," her mother said. "Eventually, it will be revealed."

The phone rang. Yasmin handed the receiver to Carmen and rushed to the bathroom. Locking the door, she leaned against it. She closed her eyes and fought the intense desire to cry.

"The truth?" she murmured aloud. Was it possible she had fallen for Orlando? When? How? It was friendship. They talked about all types of topics. They laughed, enjoyed each other's company, and went out frequently.

Scenes surfaced of being in his arms, holding his hand, and their faces and lips inches apart. The mixture of emotions she felt was vivid as if he were there. She yearned for his kiss and imagined herself responding. Was that friendship? She recalled Ani's words that she would have to face reality and make some tough decisions.

Had everyone noticed except her? She felt as if she'd been struck hard across the face and was awakened to a horrid and crude realization.

"It's not true," she whispered inaudibly, painfully aware that the pretence was over, ended.

She felt wretched and covered her mouth with her hands as tears clouded her eyes. She wanted to scream that her mother was wrong and deny that her feelings were real. Instead, she paced from one side of the bathroom to the other, feeling trapped. Taking several deep breaths, she tried to control her emotions, although her first instinct was to grab her purse and leave. That was not an option. Her mother would see through any charade she made up.

She washed her face several times, patted it dry with the towel, and then returned to the living room, masking the discontent she felt with a calm outward expression.

"Orlando is dropping by with Raul," Carmen announced, smiling. "Hopefully, they'll start coming every Saturday like they used to and then go back to their regular routine of going to clubs and discotheques. Orlando hasn't come around in months. It seems he's been busy with whoever he's taking advantage of."

Stopping abruptly, Yasmin stared at Carmen in silence. How could she face him and act as if nothing happened when she had fallen voluntarily into his trap?

"I have to go." She took her purse from the dining room table and grabbed her jacket from the back of the chair. When he arrived, she would not be there. "Ani's expecting me."

"Call and tell her you'll go later," Carmen ordered, daring her to challenge her. "You'll set the table, serve them, and clean up after they eat. Then you can leave."

* * *

"Ma is thrilled that you're visiting." Raul patted Orlando's shoulder as they entered the building, walked toward the elevator, and stepped inside. "She's used to seeing you every weekend. She was fussing that you have not been around for months. When I told her we were dropping by today, she was so happy. She was already planning what she'd cook today and next weekend."

"I know how Carmen is." Orlando was unconcerned. He pressed the number four and moved in so Raul could stand next to him.

"If you haven't called or been around, I'm sure it's because you're enjoying the honeymoon phase as I call it."

"No," Orlando shook his head, smiling thinly. Although they spoke occasionally, he had not seen Raul since visiting him after the family reunion. Time had passed swiftly. Five months had lapsed since Roberto's wake, the funeral, and the nine days of *rezos*.

"I know it's not work," Raul said as he studied Orlando's features. "It's not the first time you've disappeared when you're with someone. I have no problem with it. Enjoy yourself. Don't get serious."

"Not yet."

"Meaning you're considering it?" Raul noted the undertone in his words.

Orlando didn't respond. He had said the first thing that occurred to him, and it was a mistake. Not getting serious *yet*? What did that even mean? Yasmin believed whatever they had was a friendship, even though the way she acted hinted at something more substantial.

He was having difficulty being objective and maintaining his original standpoint of just getting to know her. His life was not as orderly and organized as it had been before dating her. The confidence he felt making choices and decisions was faltering. He worried about what would happen when she realized the term *friendship* no longer applied. "There's nothing to consider," he complained in a grim tone.

"And you're upset about that?" Raul asked, incredulously.

He laughed dryly. His apprehensions were irrelevant. Discussing a situation he had no control over was pointless. His angst was unwarranted.

"Why haven't I heard about this one? Who is she?"

"No one to meet," Orlando assured him, weary of the conversation.

"We've known each other for a long time. The fact that we're talking about it means whoever she is, it's getting serious." He spoke with disapproval. "Once that happens, you're doomed," he forecast with derision. "I won't let that happen. When it starts getting too intense, it's over."

"That was the pact," Orlando jested, as they exited the elevator.

"Was?" Raul repeated, slapping him hard on the back and bursting into boisterous laughter. "For you, yeah. I still live by that motto. I'm the best man, right?"

Orlando forced a smile. "If it happens."

"I can't believe you're letting some girl put a noose around your neck. Think about it seriously. Move on to the next one while you still can."

Orlando smiled as he walked beside Raul down the hall. Although well intended, the advice did not apply to him or his situation.

Raul banged repeatedly on the door.

It occurred to Orlando as they waited that if Yasmin were still there, it would be the first time they would meet at Carmen's since they began dating. He doubted she had ever considered that possibility. His gut feeling assured him that she wasn't ready for that encounter.

"Open up, Ma," Raul shouted, hitting the door with his fist.

* * *

Yasmin set the table while Orlando and Raul sat on the couch chatting. She placed the rice, stewed beans, fried pork chops, and salad on the table.

Every course was on a different plate so they could serve themselves. That was the nightly routine. The habit, enforced by their father, was followed strictly by their mother who sat on the rocker supervising every move Yasmin made.

Yasmin's hands trembled. She held firmly to everything she transferred from the kitchen to the dining room table, focusing on what she was doing while avoiding eye contact with everyone there.

"You can eat now," she announced, gesturing to the table. As Orlando and Raul sat down, she walked down the hall to the bathroom.

"Yasmin cooked today," she overheard Carmen say.

She held the door partially open so she could hear their conversation without being physically there. It wasn't as though she could stay away very long. Her mother would notice that, too, as would Orlando. He seemed aloof, but she was certain he was aware of her distress, acting nonchalant as if she weren't there.

"Why do you always defend her, Ma?"

"I'm defending her because I said she cooked?" Carmen asked. "She did. I went to visit . . ."

"You went out, and she stayed and cooked?" Raul interrupted, "And?"

"Forget I mentioned it," Carmen said.

"It's delicious," Orlando commented. "She takes after you, Carmen."

"That's your opinion," Raul muttered.

"Yasmin cooked all the time when she lived here," Carmen responded, "and you never complained, Raul. Isabel is the one who doesn't like to cook."

"Isabel dresses like an old lady," Raul objected. "She'll never find anyone to look at her twice, not that any guy who goes near her won't need my approval first."

"Stop talking nonsense," Carmen said. "Isabel is not your daughter; she's your sister."

"That won't stop me from putting any guy who wants to take advantage of her in their place."

"Yasmin has always been more conscious of her looks. Even as a child she was very fussy and kept her clothes neat and clean," Carmen said. "I want to thank you, Orlando. You were right when you told me I would understand after I spoke to Raul, Isabel, and Yasmin."

"No need. Glad things worked out."

"For Yasmin," Raul corrected. "If you and Ma want to talk about that, I'm leaving."

"Like your father, you want to force everyone else to do as you order."

"Nothing wrong with any similarity I have with my father. I'm proud of it."

Proud of what? Yasmin thought. Raul's arrogance and his misconception that being like their father merited any pride were absurd.

"Sometimes I don't have patience, Raul. Thank God you have your own place," Carmen sighed aloud.

"You wouldn't say that about Yasmin. You want her to move in."

"She made her decision. I accepted it." Carmen sounded disheartened. "I can't force any of you to do what you don't want to do, not even you, Raul. At least she's kept her word and is visiting on weekends."

"For now," Raul stressed, his voice trailing off. "I already told her what would happen if she does her disappearing act."

"And that is?"

"Leave that to me."

"Stop imposing your will on others, Raul. Focus on yourself."

"That's what I'm doing," Raul chuckled.

"I hope your family is different, Orlando," Carmen said loudly. "Here, nobody wants to accept the truth or face the consequences of their mistakes. They prefer to hide behind lies and pretend everything is fine."

Yasmin knew Carmen was speaking directly to her and sucked her teeth aloud. It was time to return to the trenches.

"I'm sure that happens in all families," Orlando said.

With measured steps, Yasmin walked past the dining area to the sofa.

"Not eating, Yasmin?" Carmen asked.

"Not hungry, Mami."

Orlando gazed at Yasmin. She avoided meeting his eyes. He noticed the disparaging way Carmen glared at her and then looked at him. He continued to eat slowly although his appetite had waned. Whatever they had discussed before his arrival had caused Yasmin to revert to being suspicious. He deduced from her facial expression and stance that the condemnation, accusations, and dread of being misused had resurfaced.

His fears had materialized. A feeling of doom draped over him. He veiled the pain and assumed it would be a long night that would end with no victor, just loss, emptiness, and shattered hopes.

"The food wasn't bad, but we know that isn't why men are interested in you," Raul prodded Yasmin.

"I'm sure there are other things to talk about, Raul," Orlando said.

"The defense has spoken." Raul banged his hand three times on the table as if he were a judge. "Case closed," he mocked with authority.

"What woman would tolerate you?" Carmen asked, incensed.

"Single. Love it," Raul smiled.

Yasmin gazed at Orlando from the corner of her eye. He wiped his mouth with the napkin and dropped it on the empty plate. Raul was leaning against his chair. Both had finished eating—her cue to start cleaning.

Another reprieve, she murmured to herself.

Orlando and Raul returned to the sofa. Carmen reseated herself on the rocker. Relaxing somewhat, Yasmin began washing the dishes, grateful she could focus on something to do while listening to their conversation.

"Orlando knows exactly what to say and when," Raul humored. "You have to be born with that gift."

Yasmin agreed. Orlando had a way with words. He also had character, determination, confidence, and a reputation she had ignored. All along he intended to add her name to his grimy list. She gritted her teeth and blinked repeatedly to clear her vision. Her mother had predicted it—warned her countless times.

Growing up, Yasmin had experienced and witnessed the power of Carmen's words. Her mother could forecast doom with uncanny insight. Whatever fate she declared was everyone's inescapable path, the dark pit into which they would eventually fall. She proclaimed their mishaps, and when they happened, she smeared the shame, guilt, and pain like tar on their faces.

Yasmin recalled the pastor preaching about the tongue and how vile it could be. He quoted Proverbs 18:21: "The tongue has the power of life and death, and those who love it will eat its fruit." He encouraged the congregation to be alert, to guard their words with the same cautiousness they did their hearts.

Clearing her thoughts, Yasmin focused on the conversation.

"Orlando can get any woman he wants," Raul said. "He can convince a rock to move."

"You're exaggerating," Orlando laughed.

Yasmin found no humor in Raul's comment or Orlando's placid response. The tar was smeared all over her face, and as her mother predicted, she had fallen into a bottomless pit.

"And you don't do the same, Raul?" Carmen asked.

"We have different styles. I go for the kill. Orlando takes his time. He's patient, sets his goal, takes it one step at a time, and waits patiently until he succeeds."

"Enough about me," Orlando said, attempting to direct the conversation away from his reputation. He knew Yasmin was listening intently to every word, and he anticipated the consequences would be grim.

"I doubt either of you will get married," Carmen commented wryly.

Yasmin wiped the counter, turned off the faucet, and leaned against the sink. It was absurd for her mother to mention marriage. It was apparent that neither Raul nor Orlando wanted a commitment.

"Never," Raul proclaimed with certainty. "But Orlando might consider it."

"Really?" Carmen's interest was piqued. "Have you met *someone*?"

Yasmin noted the emphasis on the word someone. She straightened her shoulders, held her breath, and waited for his answer.

"Not yet." His reply was casual, his tone lighthearted.

"Excluding the one we were talking about?" Raul was skeptical.

Her hands over her mouth, Yasmin walked to the window. There was another woman? She stifled the sobs that were choking her. Why was she surprised? She knew his reputation yet she had taken the bait and convinced herself he was sincere, trustworthy, and reliable. She believed he genuinely cared about her and her plight.

"A commitment has never occurred to you, Orlando?" Carmen insisted. "Surely there must have been at least one girl who made you consider it."

Straightening her shoulders, Yasmin listened attentively.

"No," he replied simply.

Yasmin wiped angrily at the tears that trickled down her cheeks. Why did she feel disheartened, betrayed, and outraged? What had she expected him to say? He had no sentiments. Like Raul, he just cared about fulfilling his own needs.

"It sounded to me like you were considering it," Raul insisted.

"Who is she?" Carmen asked.

"There's no one to get serious with," Orlando replied calmly, although Carmen's insistence irked him.

Closing her eyes tightly, Yasmin leaned against the wall for support. She had been warned countless times yet made her choice. Orlando wasn't at fault; she was.

"I know you're seeing someone," Raul affirmed. "I don't care who she is. Enjoy it. Move to the next when you're ready."

"Why the mystery?" Carmen asked. "Is it someone we know?"

"Why all the questions, Ma?" Raul demanded. "Something I need to know, Orlando?"

"Just asking." Carmen spoke loudly so Yasmin could hear her plainly. "I feel sorry for whoever she is."

Chapter 11

Orlando parked in front of the building and turned off the engine. Adjusting the heat, he leaned back. The temperature had dropped, and it was windy and frigid. He had no idea how long he would wait, and he needed warmth. He reflected on the events of that evening and analyzed his course of action. Yasmin was still there when he left. She'd gone to hide in the bathroom again, no doubt to gather the energy to face Carmen's scalding accusations.

He considered calling her to cancel their date or not showing up, but neither option appealed to him. He decided to wait for her to get home. He doubted she would go to Ani's. She'd head from one hiding place to another.

Her frailty and inability to stand up for herself disturbed him as much as Carmen's lack of empathy. Carmen thrived on demeaning and hurting Yasmin. Every question had come with the assumption that trusting him was a mistake. All the effort he'd put into gaining Yasmin's trust melted with each gush of disdain that came out of Carmen's mouth.

Like a marionette, Yasmin allowed her emotions to be manipulated. Flustered and agitated, her only recourse was to isolate herself in the bathroom or kitchen. Carmen, whose eyes were as sharp as an eagle, discerned Yasmin's apprehension and attributed it to the false notion that she and Orlando were intimately involved and that he was taking advantage of her.

Yasmin's prolonged absences, her unnerved demeanor, and her transparent glare were absurd. What was she feeling guilty about? Going out proved nothing. Orlando had always treated her with respect and courtesy. He had gone out of his way to please her. It appeared as if he had.

Carmen's comments and Yasmin's unrealistic scenarios had prompted the drastic change.

Then there was his reputation—his past. Whatever mistrust Yasmin harbored was solidified by Raul's caustic and obnoxious comments. His endless babbling over meaningless conquests and marriage anchored Yasmin's erroneous perceptions. Orlando had never taken Raul's chatter seriously. He considered it comical and harmless. But he realized how wrong he was. Now he saw himself through Carmen's and Yasmin's eyes. He understood that his past created footprints of a shallow life. No female stayed long enough to make an impression. He and Raul had ensured that an array of women entered and exited their lives continuously. Surprisingly, Yasmin had made an impact without trying. She was oblivious to the effect she had on him.

Orlando glanced around, wondering when Yasmin would get home. They had tickets to a Broadway show. When they went to the movies, he noticed her interest in seeing a musical. Casually he'd asked which one she preferred to see. He purchased the tickets in advance to celebrate the five months they'd been dating. He planned everything meticulously. He made reservations at a nearby restaurant for after the show and requested a corner table. He wanted Yasmin to enjoy the outing as much as his presence. He hoped she would feel as delighted as he was that they'd been dating for an extended time.

"Orlando?" Yasmin knocked on the car window.

A thin smile crossed his lips as he exited the car and met her on the curb. His perception of her persona and demeanor was keen. Deciding to make their conversation brief, he was straightforward. "We need to talk, Yaz. It's warm in the car."

She shook her head. She wrapped her unzipped leather jacket around herself and hugged her purse against her chest. "Talk about what?"

"Correct me if I'm wrong, but we're not going out tonight?"

She avoided his eyes purposely. His grasp of her emotions, reactions, and decisions daunted and disturbed her. Still frazzled from the hours of stress, she decided to ignore her outrage over his ability to read her so accurately and focused on their discussion. While driving home, she had been preoccupied with how to notify him of her decision. He'd taken the lead and spared her from contacting him.

"An answer would be nice," he commented, aware that she was struggling to choose the appropriate words, trying to gear up enough courage to speak.

"This," she began and paused, "is a mistake. We can't continue seeing each other."

Facing her, he responded with a serenity that was the opposite of the turmoil raging within. "I'm not sure what you mean by *this*. But I'd like to clarify that there's no *we*. This is your decision. The word you should use is *I*."

She gazed down the street, her expression a mask of pain and disappointment. Over what? It couldn't be just his reputation. Hadn't they resolved that already? She'd cast that aside and dated him. They had gone out repeatedly and enjoyed each other's company. They had talked about all topics, including her past. Although there were things about what happened with Manuel she hadn't shared, she'd confided in him and expressed her feelings.

Her behavior that night and the abrupt change baffled him. Hadn't Carmen always criticized and objected to his reputation, ingraining mistrust, reinforcing his ill intent, and questioning his character? Something was amiss. There was a piece of the puzzle missing, and it distorted his view.

"Why are you interested in me?" she asked, looking up at him.

It was rare for him to stop and reflect before responding. He was agile with words and always quick to respond. In his attempt to come up with a reply, a question surfaced. What had he done to merit her distrust? Did she realize her suspicions were like a dagger piercing through him and causing unbearable pain and deception?

"Wrong question, Yaz," he replied, snapping out of his stupor. "Be direct. Say what you're really thinking and why you behaved the way you did."

She turned away, her eyes blurry.

"Yaz." He wanted to embrace her and console her. She looked destitute and disheartened. "You deserve to be happy." Even if she refused to admit it, that's how he felt. She'd led a miserable existence for years. She had just begun to enjoy life, to be happy, discarding all the baggage that kept her stagnate. Suddenly, for no cause apparent to him, she wanted to stop seeing him and revert back to isolation and depression.

"With you and your reputation?" she stressed with disgust, lowering her brows. Did he really think she wouldn't see through his horrible charade, that she would remain blind and unaware of his ludicrous plan?

"You've been dating me and my reputation," he mimicked her pronunciation, "for months. Why has that become an issue again?" He felt as if he had reverted to the past. Again, without justifiable reason or the opportunity to defend himself, she had convicted and sentenced him.

Her intuition warned her to remain silent and not say anything else. Instead, she blurted out her thoughts. "What have you been expecting in return?"

Orlando laughed, although he felt wretched. "Should I lie so you think I'm telling the truth, or do I tell the truth so you think I'm lying?" He quoted her in the most sarcastic tone he could muster.

* * *

Yasmin was out of her pajamas and into blue jeans and an oversized cotton T-shirt as fast as she could muster. Walking to the dresser, she combed her hair back, tied it, and went into the kitchen.

It was unusual for Ani to visit impromptu. Yasmin anticipated the sermon would be lengthy. Deciding not to dwell on what they would discuss, she kept herself busy while she waited.

She brewed four cups of coffee, took out two mugs, and then decided to use her fine china. She got two cups, two saucers, and the matching sugar bowl from the top shelf of the cabinet. She washed it, dried it, and then set it neatly on a tray on the dining room table. She had just placed the matching spoons on each saucer when the doorbell rang.

Yasmin took a deep breath before opening the locks. She stepped back and held the door ajar as Ani entered.

"Hiding again?" Ani tapped a kiss on her cheek and moved back to study her face. "You look awful." She walked into the living room, placed her purse on the coffee table, and sat down facing Yasmin. "What's going on, Yaz?"

Yaz? It annoyed her to be called that name by someone other than Orlando, a realization that made her squirm.

"Coffee is done," Yasmin said as the aroma filled the living room.

"Let's talk," Ani patted the empty space next to her, "and pray."

Yasmin curled into a corner of the sofa next to Ani and hugged her own legs.

"You left me waiting with the table set and the food ready last Saturday. I've called you dozens of times here and at work. You don't answer. I prayed for you and asked the Lord to guide and help you through whatever it is."

Unable to speak, Yasmin shut her eyes and fought the onslaught of tears that overwhelmed her. Asking Orlando to stay away felt like part of her had been ripped out. She dragged herself to work and then back home to solitude, loneliness, and misery. Her migraines returned. She was taking the prescribed medication with no relief. The pain was constant and unyielding.

"Yaz?"

"Please . . . don't . . . call me that," she managed to say, her voice so hoarse it was unrecognizable.

"Only Orlando can?" Ani laughed softly.

Yasmin allowed the tears clouding her gaze to trickle down her cheeks and sobbed silently.

"Isolating yourself in these padded walls solves nothing. The Lord is the only one who can help you through this." Ani hugged her.

"How?" She rested her head on Ani's shoulder.

"Focus on the outcome, not the process. What you're going through now is preparation for the Lord's goal and purpose in your life. Let go, Yasmin. He can't help you if you try to resolve your problems on your own. Surrender. Hand over your problems and let Him resolve them."

Taking a tissue from Ani, Yasmin moved back, blew her nose, and dried her face. "I've been humiliated, shamed by my own mother, and used by a man I thought was sincere."

"Problems are part of our lives. God is with us, supporting us and guiding us. But we must accept His help, present our issues, and wait patiently and calmly for Him to act in His time. I'm sure you've already made your decision without praying on it or waiting for His response." Ani paused and then asked, "What happened?"

"I told . . . Orlando . . . to stay away." Her last words were barely above a whisper.

"Because?"

Yasmin cleared her throat several times and spoke clearly. "Mami warned me about him. Like a fool, I thought it was friendship."

"That's what you wanted to believe, Yasmin. It has always been more than that. The way he says Yaz—it's not a friendship tone. How he looks at you and how he acts—he feels the same way about you."

"It was a mistake. I should have followed my instincts."

"You did. You were attracted to Orlando. You liked his company and the security you felt. The problem is that you refuse to admit it or acknowledge how you feel about him."

"What feelings?" She couldn't be in love with him. Loving a man who had no respect for women was absurd.

"Admit the truth. You love him," Ani rebuked.

"That's impossible."

"Is it? The Lord united you. All these months you've been so happy, at peace, enjoying yourself. You acted like a different person. The Lord transformed and healed your heart through Orlando's love. Accept it. It's a blessing."

Yasmin stared at Ani through a mist. Her feelings and thoughts were jarred. At work, she had difficulty concentrating. His name and gestures constantly popped into her mind, shrouding her thoughts. She couldn't stop thinking about him. "He's a womanizer. He's not interested in becoming serious."

Ani laughed. "Seems that bothers you as much as his past with Maria. Jealousy and fear that you love a man who won't make a commitment are painful. That doesn't change the fact that you fell in love with him. Admit that you love each other."

"No, no," Yasmin repeated, shaking her head.

"Why not?" Ani challenged. "For some, it takes just a look, a moment."

"In romance novels and fairy tales. In real life, men like him take advantage and leave." She paused and added, "He was seeing another woman while he was going out with me."

Ani's laughter was so boisterous it echoed throughout the living room. "Your proof is?"

"Raul said . . ."

"Did you see him with someone else?" Yasmin shook her head. "You merely assumed from Raul's comment that it's true?" Ani's tone implied that Yasmin should be wiser. "You've been going out with him after work and on weekends. When did he meet and get serious with this other woman?"

Yasmin wiped her tears. Even if he wasn't seeing someone else, her name was just one on his long list. "I won't allow Orlando to hurt me the way Manuel did. I thought his feelings were sincere. Like Orlando, he just wanted to take advantage."

"Why are you comparing them?" Ani reproached. "Is there something you're not telling me? Has Orlando been disrespectful?"

She could make no accusations. He had always been attentive and was not pushy or coercive like Manuel. She'd been in his arms willingly, and he'd never been indiscreet.

"He was a perfect gentleman," Yasmin admitted as the tears trickled down her cheeks again. It was all she had been doing for days—crying erratically and taking her medications to ease the throbbing pain.

"Yasmin, you've found someone you can share your life with. What are you afraid of? Don't make the same mistake I did, denying yourself the opportunity to be happy because your previous relationship ended the wrong way. You'll regret staying alone. Loneliness is not a good companion."

Yasmin knew that already. Loneliness waited for her in the apartment and hovered over her when she entered. At times, its presence was asphyxiating—overpowering. When she felt most vulnerable, Ani's place was her harbor, the one place she could escape the oppressive grip of loneliness.

Ani placed her hand under her chin and lifted her face. Yasmin smiled, remembering that Orlando lifted her face the same way when he wanted her full attention. Making eye contact was essential for him. Each time their eyes meet, she felt the warmth in his eyes seep through her like rays of sunshine. Its heat melted the icy wall she'd built around her heart. She had to admit it—she loved him.

"Have you called or visited Carmen? Did you go to church with her this morning?"

"No," she replied, unsure of when she could visit again. "Mami delights in my misery. She's cruel and heartless." She still felt emotionally ravaged. She planned to visit her mother eventually but needed time to regain emotional strength. "I need peace of mind. I need to be alone."

"You're not. Our Father is always with us."

"I don't feel His presence, even when I pray."

"You either believe or you don't. You can't make your own decisions without His guidance, solve things on your own, and claim to have faith. It doesn't work that way."

Yasmin was silent. She realized that reverting to past behaviors led to a dead end. "Help me. I want to follow Your path. Instead, I fall deeper into the mud," she prayed quietly.

Covering her face, she wept.

"No more crying." Ani embraced her. "Let's pray." Helping Yasmin up, Ani led her to the bathroom and waited while Yasmin washed and dried her face. Together they walked to the bedroom. Yasmin took the Bible from the night table, and they walked back to the sofa where they sat huddled together.

"I foresee making your wedding dress in the near future," Ani proclaimed with delight, opening the Bible.

"Wedding?" Yasmin was astounded. "Orlando said he wasn't interested in getting married, that he hadn't met anyone he could take seriously."

"It would be foolish of him to say otherwise when there is no relationship yet."

Speechless, Yasmin stared at her. She'd planted the seeds and tended to the garden, but when the plants began to grow, she stepped all over them.

"Don't look so discouraged, Yasmin. The Lord always finishes what He starts. You and Orlando will go through hardships, but He'll make sure you get together." Ani grinned. "Your love for one another is a blessing. Be grateful, accept it, and give thanks."

How could she give thanks and accept their love as a blessing when she'd pushed him away? She had no idea if or when they would see each other again.

"Call Orlando. Apologize. Tell him how you feel. Everything will work out. That's what the Lord does—He heals."

* * *

"What's wrong, Orlando? I haven't heard you so unhappy in a long time."

He muted the stereo with the remote. He'd listened to both voicemails from his mother but had been reluctant to call back, wanting to avoid worrying her unnecessarily. This time, he answered her call.

"Lots of work. How are you and Dad?"

"He's been sick. Bad cold. But we're fine." She paused and added, "I'm worried about you. Clara said you've been doing a lot of overtime, that you're miserable. Are there problems with Raul over Yasmin or with Yasmin?"

"Neither, Mom," he said, annoyed at Clara's lack of common sense. They discussed being discrete, not mentioning anything that would upset their parents. Like Yasmin, Clara refused to listen to sound advice and adhere to it. "No need to worry. I have lots of new cases and have to get the work done."

"On weekends too?" Eva marveled.

"On occasion. Not regularly, as Clara implies."

"It's enough that she noticed and mentioned it. She's worried about you for a reason. Work also keeps the mind occupied, more so when we're upset about something or someone."

"I won't deny that's true," Orlando agreed. Yasmin's absence in his life made everything bland and lackluster. After their argument, he avoided all possibilities of seeing her again. Almost a month had gone by with no contact. He was struggling not to give in and call her or drop by as she left work.

"What's happening with Raul?"

"Our friendship is the same." They had gone out a few times. The sense of adventure and eagerness he'd always felt when going to a club or discotheque had vanished. Ironically, Raul's notion that he was in the "honeymoon phase" gave him the opportunity to stay away without explanation. When they saw each other or spoke on the phone, Raul continued to tease him. He kept asking when Orlando would introduce him to his future wife. He insisted on meeting the woman who'd put a noose around his neck and tightened it. Then he would change the subject and refocus their conversation on other topics. Raul stopped inviting him to hang out and asked him to contact him when and if he wanted to join "the living."

Like a boat anchored at a pier, Orlando was stationary with no idea what would happen next. Nothing interested him. He had no plans and no direction. Work kept him occupied—his mind busy, as his mother reasoned.

"How's Carmen?" Eva asked.

"She's fine. Feisty."

"Interesting word." Eva noted his dissatisfaction. "You always joked about the comments, advice, and lectures Carmen gave you and Raul. You never took it seriously. What changed?"

"Carmen doesn't realize the impact her criticism has on Yasmin." He regretted his words the instant they left his mouth. His mother picked up easily on his emotions and ailments. One word, a comment, and his expression enabled her to discern that something was amiss.

"Criticism about you or about Yasmin's past?"

"Doesn't matter."

"It does. You just don't want to discuss it with me," she said in an affectionate tone. "Has it occurred to you that you're interested in a lot more than a casual friendship, that perhaps Carmen's comments express her concerns over your reputation, her fears that you're taking advantage of Yasmin?"

"No longer relevant," he admitted with defeat. Yasmin had been aware of that and had apologized. She had asked him to forgive her. They had settled that issue. Why it had resurfaced intrigued him. Carmen's harsh criticism and acidic comments never ceased, and Yasmin had been at ease. She appeared unconcerned and seemed to be enjoying the time they spent together. He analyzed every date, his gestures, and hers. He found no reason or cause for her reaction. He had concluded that their attraction was reciprocal, their feelings mutual.

"Orlando?"

His mother's voice refocused him. "Sorry, Mom."

"Clara is right. You're distressed and unhappy. That's a big change from the last time we spoke. Why is what Carmen thinks important?"

He debated if he should continue and decided to be candid. As always, his mother had already deduced what was wrong. "Until recently, Yasmin disregarded Carmen's harsh criticism about me. Suddenly, without cause, she asked me to stay away."

Eva was silent and then said, "I warned you that good intentions are often misunderstood."

"You did," he admitted, recalling Yasmin's accusations. Her questions were branded in his thoughts: *Why are you interested in me? With you and your reputation? What have you been expecting in return?* He felt offended and hurt. Was that the impression he'd given her? Why couldn't she be honest and express how she felt and why? Instead, she passed sentence. "Everything you said was true, Mom," he replied with finality, not wanting to discuss it further.

"I'll continue praying for you," Eva said affectionately. "Remember, when the storm ends, the sun shines again. Pray for guidance."

"That's what I'm doing," Orlando replied. Without intervention, he would have never dated Yasmin. He was thankful and grateful. He would pray for fortitude. Following Yasmin's request was arduous. He longed to contact her, to convince her that she was wrong about him. But he reconsidered. Despite how wretched he felt, he would follow her request.

"Time is a cure. It helps you heal slowly. Everything will work out, Orlando."

"In the meantime, I'm focusing on work and keeping myself busy."

"That's the best option right now," Eva said. "Call if anything changes between you and Yasmin."

"All right." Hanging up, he glanced at the Bible on the coffee table. He sat on the sofa and reread the verse Ani suggested. If the Lord had united him with Yasmin once, he could do it again.

Waiting was the only solution.

Even if they weren't meant to be together, he would continue to pray for her and ask the Lord to help her realize she needed to take care of herself. Not eating when she was upset and allowing her emotions to spiral uncontrollably were what sparked her migraines. She needed discernment and wisdom to make the right decisions when she was distressed. Only the Lord could provide that.

* * *

"Finally remembered I'm alive?" Carmen griped.

A pained smile formed on Yasmin's lips. She'd anticipated that reaction before contacting her. "Sorry, Mami. I was . . ."

"Don't bother giving me explanations."

She held the receiver at a distance and could still hear Carmen clearly. "Okay, Mami."

"You broke your promise. You lied to me."

"I'll see you Sunday morning," Yasmin changed the subject. "We'll go to church together."

"Don't bother. I can continue going alone. Don't pretend you want to spend time with me or do anything that pleases me. I'm just reminding you that day after tomorrow is the sixth monthly *rezos*. I'm sure you didn't remember or weren't planning to go."

"I've attended all of them. I highlighted all the days on my calendar. I'll be there."

"Good for you," Carmen sang sarcastically. "We're going to the cemetery with Josefa Saturday morning. We'll get together in front of Josefa's building and leave from there."

"I'll join you." She noted that Carmen was making it sound as if it wasn't mandatory.

"Let's hope you don't have something better to do."

Yasmin remained silent. A month could not compare to five years. She needed the time to recoup, to energize before reentering the battle zone.

"No comment?" Carmen asked and then added, "Seems Orlando is terribly busy. Since his visit with Raul when you were here, he's only dropped by twice and was in and out as if avoiding meeting someone."

"What does that have to do with me?" Yasmin feigned indifference.

"How you feel about him is obvious. You disappeared after his visit, and when he was here, you hid in the bathroom and refused to eat. You stayed in the kitchen listening to our conversation. Were you crying when he admitted he didn't take any woman seriously? Your eyes were red and puffy when you came out of hiding."

It was no surprise that her mother noticed every gesture and reaction. Carmen surveyed everything and used it like ammunition. She made it unbearable to be around Orlando in her presence. Yasmin wished that, like him, she could mask her emotions—act as if *he* were invisible. But as Carmen foretold, she cared for him, a realization she had to confront. Admitting she loved him took courage. She'd spent the last few weeks praying, studying the Word, and listening to hymns. She felt more at ease and calm—composed.

After Ani's impromptu visit, Yasmin had spent every weekend at her place. She was still debating her course of action. She wondered how she would feel or react if Orlando attended the *rezos* and they were face-to-face again. He hadn't attended it the previous month, and she felt strange walking down the block alone.

She missed him—his physical proximity, talking to him, going out with him. She longed to see him and be with him. She continued praying for enlightenment and wisdom, asking for strategies on how to approach and resolve the situation with him. Ani stressed that if she loved Orlando, she should reconsider her decision, take the initiative, and call him. She had asked the Lord for a sign, a confirmation that they were meant to be together.

"Why so quiet?" Carmen asked.

"Nothing to say." She was candid.

"Still not convinced it was a mistake to get involved with Orlando?"

* * *

When Orlando spoke with Eva the day before, the possibility of seeing Yasmin was nonexistent. Now he was standing in front of Yasmin's door next to Raul. They'd met after work, and Orlando assumed they'd go to a lounge or bar. Instead, Raul asked him to accompany him on an errand. He agreed but realized Raul's intention as they drove downtown.

Orlando's feelings were mixed. He was looking forward to seeing Yasmin, stunned by how the Lord had worked in his favor. Still, he felt uneasy about dropping by unexpectedly.

"We'll find out why she disappeared," Raul said, pounding on the door.

Orlando couldn't comprehend why Yasmin's first recourse was to isolate herself. He hoped her disappearing act, as Raul called it, wasn't to avoid him.

"Yasmin," Raul shouted.

"What do you want?" she said in the same pitch, flinging the door ajar.

"Are you in the habit of opening the door without knowing who it is?" Raul demanded, walking past her.

"I'm sure everyone in the building heard you," she replied, "and for your information, this building is safe."

Orlando disagreed. Until something happens, all buildings are "safe." Entering the apartment, he stood by the arch that separated the hall from the entrance to the living room and ignored the inquisitive look Yasmin shot his way as she walked by.

The elation he felt seeing and being close to her startled him. Her influence on his emotions was powerful. Had it always been that way? When it happened was unclear to him. The question that surfaced worried him. What would he do if her decision was concrete?

"Why are you here, Raul?" Yasmin placed her hands on her hips.

Without answering, Raul peeked into the kitchen and then walked through the living room to the bathroom across from the bedroom. "Who's in there?" he asked, knocking on the door.

"Me when you leave," Yasmin said. "I was about to take a shower."

"Really?" Raul glanced back at her and pushed the door open.

Orlando heard her mutter a prayer as she watched Raul step into the bathroom, walk out, and then enter the bedroom. She stood there barefoot with her back to him, wearing a white cotton robe tied at the waist. Her hair cascaded over her shoulders in disarray.

She sensed Orlando's stare, gazed at him, and then turned away. She looked beautiful despite her sultry demeanor. She seemed healthy. Her face was slightly thinner, a confirmation she was barely eating. He didn't detect any sign of a migraine. She wouldn't be standing and waiting for Raul to finish his inspection if she were in pain. He was glad she was all right but disconcerted that she appeared unaffected by her decision to stop seeing him. Had he imagined that their feelings were mutual?

"Get out of my room, Raul," she yelled, walking down the hall.

Orlando scanned the living room. He'd been there once before but hadn't paid much attention to the décor. Yasmin's attention to detail and order was extreme. The living room looked like a photograph from a magazine. The brown leather sofa with matching love seat had a set of brown-and-cream-striped pillows at the corners and the center. The curtains matched the pillows. The shade was not lighter or darker; it was similar. The candle holders, vases, and knickknacks placed strategically throughout the room had a hint of brown or cream.

The living room was impressive, and everything matched impeccably. She had spent some time putting it together, something to preoccupy her from what was most important—being healthy, enjoying life, and moving forward. He surveyed the place again. It lacked something—pictures. There were none, not even of herself.

"Did you look under the bed? In the closet?" She was curt.

Lifting his gaze, Orlando saw her trailing after Raul into the living room. Hadn't he warned her sufficient times to watch her tone when addressing Raul?

"Too bad you didn't suggest that to Manuel. You could have kept your secret, and we wouldn't have known what a great actress you are." Raul sat on the sofa with his legs crossed and his arms stretched over the back of the sofa, gesturing with his hand for Orlando to sit down. "Make yourself comfortable."

"Welcome," she said sarcastically. Crossing her arms, she remained standing in the center of the room.

Orlando walked to the love seat and sat, hoping Raul wasn't planning to stay long. It was obvious from Yasmin's stance that she expected them to leave right away.

"Is Manuel coming later?" Raul demanded.

"Not your business."

He grunted quietly. She was stubborn and disregarded his warnings.

"You talk to him the way you do to me?" Raul asked.

"That's why you're here? To ask ridiculous questions?"

"You deserve each other. You're both low lives," Raul grinned.

"Thanks for the compliment," she shrugged. "You know the way out." She pointed to the door.

Her blatant disregard of his warnings frustrated Orlando. He sat on the edge of the sofa, eager for Raul to have his say so they could leave.

"I thought I made it clear to you that Ma's health is a priority," Raul barked.

"For Isabel and me, yeah."

"I'm going to ignore that remark." Raul eyed her from head to toe. "Did you forget what I told you?"

"You've said so many things that I have no idea what you're referring to."

Orlando suppressed a smile. She was daring. If she used that energy and determination to be more assertive, she would be an incredible woman.

"I'll refresh your memory," Raul informed her. "I'm going to make sure you continue to visit Ma. I'll be at the door reminding you or taking you personally to visit her."

"I spoke to Mami before you came barging in like you own the place. I'm going Friday to the *rezos* and Saturday morning to the cemetery."

Orlando watched Raul take out his cell phone and touch the screen several times. It occurred to him that he was calling Carmen to verify what Yasmin had just told him.

"Hi, Ma. You're on speaker," Raul greeted Carmen warmly. "Has Yasmin called you?" He held up the phone.

"She remembered I'm alive, called about an hour ago. Why?"

Orlando studied Yasmin closely. She stood glaring at Raul intensely, her face flushed with anger.

"I dropped by Yasmin's place to see if she was all right. She looks great. Can't imagine what kept her from visiting you for four weeks."

"Without a word," Carmen grunted. "Yasmin is independent. She doesn't need her mother or her family, just whoever she's with."

"Told you not to trust her," Raul said. "We'll speak later, Ma." He held the cell phone in his hand, grinning. "At least you didn't lie about that."

"Get out."

Raul stood up and hovered over her. "I've seen that look on my opponents' faces before I knocked them out."

Orlando controlled the impulse to grab Raul by the arm and escort him outside. "Time to go," he said and stood, gesturing toward the door.

"When I'm ready." Raul sat down again. "You don't use your phone?" He pointed to the cordless on the table.

"When I want," she stressed. "Do you call and visit Mami all the time?"

"We're not talking about me."

"Right." She placed her hand on her chest. "You're the one who makes sure everyone else does exactly what they're supposed to, but you don't."

Orlando watched Raul spring up, grip her chin with his hand, and force her to face him. He waited, watching him intently.

"I'm not impressed, Yasmin." Releasing her, he stood next to Orlando. "If you don't visit this weekend, I'll come back to escort you."

"Should I clock in to show you proof?"

Orlando straightened his shoulders as Raul turned around abruptly and glared at her. She froze but kept her chin up, her gaze fixed on Raul's icy glare. In silence with a deep grimace on his face, Raul walked out, slamming the door.

There was no denying that Roberto's blood ran through both of their veins. Orlando hoped he was wrong, but he had an unnerving feeling that if Yasmin kept challenging Raul, they would both regret it.

* * *

Yasmin held tightly to the cell phone, resisted the temptation to hang up. Her heart was thundering loudly, her mouth dry.

"Who is this?"

Hesitant to speak, she remained silent. Orlando wouldn't recognize her number. It was the first time she had called him on the phone she purchased during lunch.

"Hello?" He repeated it several times, and then a click and silence.

"Coward!" Yasmin rebuked herself. She paced impatiently from one side of the living room to the other. Her heart raced as though she had run a mile. "Give me strength, Lord." She sat on the sofa, cell phone in hand.

That evening, she anticipated seeing Orlando at the *rezos*. She rushed out, hoping he was downstairs. She was disappointed. While in the cab, she decided to contact him. She had not bothered to get comfortable and was still in the outfit she'd worn to work.

She took a deep breath to calm herself. What was she afraid of? The past could no longer dictate the type of life she would lead. As Ani said,

God placed Orlando in her life to give her a new perspective but more importantly to become a part of her life.

She had believed that falling in love and trusting again were unachievable. The Lord had changed that by bringing them together.

She glanced at the spot where Orlando had stood and wished he were there. She envisioned herself rushing into his arms and closing her eyes as their lips met.

Taking a deep breath, she gazed at her cell phone. When Raul stormed out, Orlando was still standing in the center of the living room. She turned to him, and their eyes had locked. The disheartened expression made her feel wretched. She perceived his pain and was struck by the realization that she had caused it. Mindful only of herself, she had been oblivious to his feelings.

"Don't open the door without verifying who it is, Yaz. Never take chances with your safety," he had warned before exiting. Despite her withdrawal from his life, he continued to be attentive, kind, and considerate—her protector, friend, advisor, and confidante.

The man she loved.

He had managed to extract her from the decorated prison she'd created for herself. She repaid him by using his reputation and his past against him. She had judged and condemned him just as she was judged and condemned. Apologizing and getting into a relationship with him, if he still wanted to be with her, would not undo all the anguish she'd caused him.

She sighed aloud.

Fear could not stop her from trying. She pressed redial. Orlando didn't answer. Cell in hand, she lay on the sofa and stared up at the ceiling.

She was tainted by the past. The wounds left from the ordeal with Manuel were still unhealed. She'd sealed the atrocious experience in the back of her mind—suppressed it. It was her secret, one she promised herself to never divulge. Accepting she was in love with Orlando meant exposing the truth.

The mere thought of voicing what had occurred made her tremble.

She recited Hebrews 11:1 aloud: "Now faith is confidence in what we hope for and assurance about what we do not see." The Lord would provide the strategy necessary to tell Orlando the truth.

When they were together, she would open her heart. Her relationship with Orlando would not be initiated with lies and secrets. The truth would be exposed. She would be free. They would begin anew, writing their story on a clean slate with the Lord as their guide.

Feeling confident, she pressed redial.

"Who is this?" His voice startled her.

"It's . . . me."

"Yaz?"

"I got a cell phone," she explained.

"What happened?" he asked with concern. "Are you all right? Carmen?"

"No, I . . ."

"Just say it."

"I need to speak to you," she blurted out.

He was silent.

She waited, holding her breath.

"About?"

"Can we discuss that when we meet?" she asked, preferring to speak to him in person.

There was a long pause before he spoke. "When? Where?"

"My place."

"No. What time are you leaving from Carmen's tomorrow?"

"Aren't you going to the cemetery?" Yasmin asked, hoping he'd attend so she could see him.

"I haven't decided. Are you ready to be around me in front of Carmen?"

She was tempted to reply with "not yet" but realized that once they became a couple, everyone would know. The pretense was over. Her mother would have to accept her decision, even if she disapproved. A sour thought surfaced. Was it possible that her relationship with Orlando would hinder her attempts to get closer to her mother? She decided not to dwell on negative thoughts. If the Lord united them, He would ensure that her mother approved. Yasmin had no idea how that would happen but trusted God to do what He did best—transform and mold situations. "Hopefully, we'll be back around 3:00 or 4:00 from the cemetery. I'd like to spend some time with Mami. I don't want to leave right away."

"I'm curious as to the rationale behind not calling or going to see her."

"Isolating myself is a bad habit," Yasmin admitted, "and not easy to stop."

"That's a start. You should do something more productive like exercise or yoga, anything that will help you steer away from secluding yourself."

She smiled. Her well-being was always his focus. She needed to do likewise. "I'll consider those options."

"Finally agreeing with me?" he taunted. "Did you stop visiting Carmen because of me?"

"I was selfish and thought only about myself and my needs, a family trait I'm not proud to share with Raul and Isabel."

"There's hope for you yet," he humored dryly.

She laughed and envisioned herself in his arms. The image of their lips uniting stirred a fluttering in her stomach.

"Glad you're in a good mood, Yaz," Orlando said. "What's the plan?"

His tone had softened. She relaxed and thanked the Lord inaudibly. "I'll leave around 6:00, the latest 7:00. Where do we meet?"

"Go straight home. Call me when you're on your way, I'll meet you in front of the building."

"I was thinking about the last time we were going out. I hope cancelling wasn't a big expense."

Orlando grunted aloud. "That's not an issue, Yaz. Never has been. We'll talk tomorrow."

Before she could comment, he hung up.

Lying on her side, Yasmin dismissed the gloom that overcame her. The next day would determine their future.

Chapter 12

Orlando decided not to work that morning. He would meet Yasmin in front of Josefa's and then accompany them to the cemetery. Her call had surprised him. Hearing her voice and her expressed desire to see and talk to him prompted the notion that she was reconsidering her decision. Still, he refused to speculate, opting to hear what she had to say before making erroneous assumptions. Based on her remarks, he would determine how to respond when they spoke. He would decide what his course of action, if any, would be.

He was astounded by how miraculous the Lord was. He had granted two blessings that week—seeing Yasmin and getting a call from her.

The drive to Josefa's was shorter than he'd anticipated. Traffic was light. He double-parked next to Raul's car and noticed that Carmen, Yasmin, Angel, and Raul were cluttered together as he exited the car.

As he approached them, he wondered what Angel was doing there. He overheard part of the conversation as he stopped next to Raul who was standing in front of Angel with a menacing stance.

"Relax, Raul," Angel urged, his voice quivering. He held up his hands in front of his chest as if that would stop Raul from striking him. "When we spoke last time, I mentioned that I saw Yasmin in front of the club and spoke to her."

"Yeah, you did." Raul's chin was lifted, his hands curled into fists. "You conveniently forgot to mention that her man interrupted you?"

The question startled Orlando. He had discussed with Yasmin what occurred after she left the wake. Had she purposely omitted that her ex was there? How had Raul found out? Orlando gazed at

Yasmin. She was flustered and agitated. His hopes shattered, he wondered if she was going to talk to him about her ex. Had they made up?

"We were talking, and her man interrupted us. He got loud and nasty." Angel's comment disrupted Orlando's thoughts.

"Manuel?" Carmen asked Yasmin.

"No." Yasmin shook her head.

Her angst triggered a multitude of questions, and Orlando promised himself they would address them when they met.

"I don't know him or his name," Angel blurted out quickly. "With his attitude, I doubt he was just a friend."

"That's your opinion," Yasmin corrected curtly.

Orlando studied Angel from the corner of his eye. Who the guy was or how he was related to Yasmin should not concern Angel. Why it did was obvious. Angel liked Yasmin. What prompted her to stop and talk to such a bigot made him furious. She should've ignored Angel and not spoken to him at all.

"We almost got into a fight," Angel added, noticing that Raul was becoming agitated.

"Your man is lucky, Yasmin." Raul spoke to her although he was leaning toward Angel. "Had I been there, I would have taught Manuel some manners."

"And ended up in jail," Carmen assured. "Were you in the club with Manuel, Yasmin? Did you leave to get away from him? Is that why he followed you?"

Carmen voiced the same questions that Orlando had. All eyes directed at her, Yasmin shrank back, cheeks flushed. He waited for her response, along with Carmen, Raul, and Angel.

"No." Yasmin shook her head.

Her reply was vague, inconclusive. She provided no clue of what had really occurred. When they spoke, Orlando would demand clarity and specific details.

"Your sister needs to be careful who she gets involved with. Jealous men are a big problem," stated Angel.

"If you were just talking, why would that concern you?" Raul glanced at Yasmin and then moved forward, his fist raised.

"Control yourself." Carmen stepped in front of Raul who stopped abruptly and took several steps back. "I knew you were lying when you said you weren't with Manuel," Carmen spoke to Yasmin and then faced Angel. "When did this happen?"

"That's what I'd like to know," Raul snapped.

"It was the night we celebrated Papo's birthday," Angel said. "I thought you had gone with her to the club."

"I've never gone to any club with my sisters," Raul noted proudly.

"I invited you the day I took my car to your garage," Angel explained. "When we met at the bar, you mentioned you couldn't go because you were at your father's wake."

Orlando gazed at Yasmin. He recalled her borrowing his cell and telling Ani that someone was angry. Had she been referring to Manuel? On their first date, they had spoken about why Ismenia was upset. The topic of her ex, the argument, and Angel's presence were never mentioned.

Orlando studied Yasmin's face. Her anxious expression disturbed him. While they dated, the possibility that her ex was still around had not occurred to him. Confident that his conversation with Carmen verified that fact, along with her behavior and comments, he believed she was single. The trust he'd harbored was shattered like a glass falling on concrete. His mind raced through every encounter they'd had. Nothing she'd said or done corroborated his findings as false, but doubt still plagued him. He needed verification to be certain she had been alone and that she hadn't made up with her ex.

His thoughts banished as Raul turned abruptly and took hold of Yasmin's shoulders. "You went dancing after going to the wake?"

It was Orlando's cue to move closer. He stood next to Raul, alert.

Angel tapped Raul on the back. "We'll get together some other time."

"Coward!" Orlando hissed, watching Angel almost run away.

"She would never do such a thing," Carmen said.

Raul gripped Yasmin's arm. "All that nonsense in front of the funeral parlor, the scene inside, and you went to a club afterward?"

"I didn't go . . ." she began, teary-eyed.

"No?" Raul interrupted her. "I should have known. You and your man, Ismenia and hers—I never bought your act. I'm just sorry Ma did. Get out of my sight." He shoved her back.

Orlando caught her and helped her regain her balance. He avoided her gaze, certain that she'd discern his misgivings. He stood next to her on guard.

"I didn't go inside the club," she repeated, "I wasn't with Manuel."

"You're a hypocrite—a liar," Raul shouted, his eyes blazing.

"Who are you to judge me?" Yasmin responded in the same tone. "You don't know me, who I am, or what I consider right or wrong. You're just like Dad. You condemn others based on lies and ridiculous assumptions."

"Don't call him *Dad*." Raul lifted his hand.

Orlando was about to step in front of Yasmin when Carmen grabbed Raul's arm.

"Don't you dare," she ordered, her face flushed. "Enough scenes. We'll discuss this at home."

* * *

Taking a deep breath, Yasmin stepped out of the elevator. Carmen swept past her, keys in hand. Yasmin dragged herself slowly toward her doom.

"I know You're with me, Lord. Thanks," she whispered a prayer.

Entering the apartment, Yasmin watched Carmen hasten down the hall without speaking. She heard a door open and close in the distance. Unsure where to sit for this trial, she glanced around the living room.

The hearing wouldn't begin until the district attorney showed up. Raul was parking the car. His assistant, Isabel, was with him.

Although Yasmin would have preferred company—Orlando's—on the long drive, she drove to the cemetery alone. From Orlando's facial expression and stance, she knew he was judging and condemning her. She knew nothing would be accomplished that night when they spoke—if he did, in fact, meet with her.

The silence in the apartment echoed that of the cemetery. No one dared to speak. It was apparent that something was horribly wrong. The atmosphere was unsettling, dense with friction. Yasmin braved the questioning stares, Raul's recriminating attitude, and Orlando's distant stance and probing stare. Orlando had taken the wrong side. He was no longer her ally.

Was he jealous? She noticed the disdainful way he looked at Angel when he greeted him. He discerned that Angel liked her. Yasmin frowned. Angel was irrelevant, a thorn that, like Manuel, had caused her undue grief.

If how the day began was a sign of how it would end, she doubted anything good would occur. Was it bad luck or awry karma? Was it a lesson the Lord wanted to teach her? She had no idea.

When she arrived, Angel had seen her parking and rushed over. He greeted her as if they were old acquaintances and started talking nonsense. Raul arrived with Carmen before she got rid of him. Raul overheard Angel's remark that "her man" was nasty, arrogant, and dangerous. He confronted Angel and demanded to know what they were talking about. Orlando arrived as he questioned him. He assumed, as everyone else did, that Angel's erroneous perceptions were true.

It seemed that was her fate, always being judged and condemned on mere appearances.

She glanced at her watch. Would the trial be over in three hours? It hardly seemed enough time to be convicted. Her initial instinct was to tell her mother that she was going home. She didn't dare, deciding it was best to address the issue right away.

"I don't know you anymore," Carmen said in a husky tone. "What have you become? Who are you?"

"Please, Mami, just give me the opportunity to explain what happened."

Carmen was silent, a steel mask covering her face. Looking directly into her eyes, Yasmin expounded on what occurred after she left the funeral parlor. "I went to tell them I wasn't staying. Nestor argued with me in front of Angel, not Manuel."

"With that explanation, everything is solved?" Carmen turned away from her and sat on the rocking chair.

"No," she knelt before her, "going to the club was the wrong decision— one more to add to the long list I already have."

"Why are you so unwilling to change?"

"Am I the only one who needs to change, Mami? Why is it that you have no faith in me? For you, Isabel, and Raul I'm a horrible monster without feelings, principles, or morals. How can I prove that's not who I really am?"

"Actions speak, Yasmin."

"It isn't just my actions; it's how they're perceived. If I apologize, I'm a good actress just saying what you want to hear. If I don't, I'm cold-hearted, snobbish, and proud. Either way, I lose."

"You only worry about yourself and your feelings."

"That's not true. It's unfair for everyone to think that everything I do is to purposely hurt and embarrass the family."

"You're the victim?" Carmen asked.

"Am I the only one to blame for everything?"

"You don't know the answer to that question?"

"My answer isn't acceptable to you, Raul, or Isabel. You're right that actions speak. What about Raul's actions? Isabel's? Why are they excluded? Their behavior is worse than mine, although you believe otherwise."

"What I believe?" Carmen mocked, placing her hand on her chest. "When did that become important to you?"

Yasmin sighed aloud. "What do you want me to do?"

"What I want has never been important to you, Yasmin Arias."

"You're wrong. Getting your approval and doing whatever pleased you has always been my goal, but you find fault in everything I do."

Carmen stared at her in silence.

"I've learned the hard way that not facing the consequences of my actions has made my life extremely difficult. I know I've made a lot of mistakes and wrong decisions. I hurt you with my absence, but does that justify how I'm treated? I have feelings too."

Yasmin saw the tears trickle down Carmen's face and realized her own cheeks were wet. "There are mistakes I won't make again. I promise." She took Carmen's hands and kissed them. "Are you taking your medication? Getting upset can affect your blood pressure."

"You've changed, Yasmin. All those years on your own made you a different person."

"Am I that bad? Are you ashamed of me, of what I've become?"

Carmen shook her head. "You're my daughter. I love you."

Yasmin stood with open arms, and Carmen embraced her.

"I love you, Mami. I'm sorry I hurt you so much. I love you," she whispered hoarsely, resting her head on her shoulder. "Please forgive me."

Carmen held her tightly and cried silently. Yasmin thanked the Lord. For the first time in years, their pain had united them, melting that thick coat of ice that had kept them apart.

The door was unlocked. Isabel entered followed by Raul.

Carmen tapped Yasmin's cheek gently before she sat on the rocker. Yasmin smiled thinly as she took one of the dining room chairs and sat next to her.

"Why are you crying, Mom?" Isabel knelt before Carmen. "Are you all right?" Isabel turned toward Yasmin. "What did you do to her?"

"Nothing," Yasmin replied, astonished that Isabel would accuse her of harming Carmen.

"Get out. I don't want you to set foot in our home again," Raul shouted as he stood in the center of the living room pointing at the door.

"I'm not going anywhere." Yasmin remained seated.

"I don't want any more arguing," Carmen said quietly. "It's over."

"No," Raul declared. "Dad was right to throw her out. She should have never come back."

"I won't leave unless Mami asks me to," Yasmin said.

"Get out!" his voice echoed throughout the apartment.

"Do I have to remind you that this is my home?" Carmen stood up.

"You don't need her." Isabel placed her arm over Carmen's shoulder. "You have us, Mom."

"I was in front of the club talking to Ismenia. We planned to go there to celebrate her birthday," Yasmin explained, hoping it would calm Raul down. "It wasn't Manuel. It was Nestor I was arguing with."

Raul faced Carmen. "If you allow her to stay, I'll never set foot in this apartment again."

"Are you threatening me?" Carmen was appalled.

"I'm tired of pretending, Ma. Either she leaves or I will."

"I'm not leaving." Yasmin stood up. "You do what you want, Raul."

He grabbed her upper arm and led her to the door.

"Let me go," she cried out, squirming to set herself free of his painful grip.

"Stop it, Raul." Carmen rushed forward, blocking his way. "Release her."

"She will never set foot in this apartment again," he replied, his grip tightening.

Yasmin wriggled to free herself from his infernal grip, her eyes filled with tears from the pain.

"That's not your decision, Raul."

He released her. She stumbled back, regained her balance, and stood next to Carmen.

"You're choosing her over us?" Raul pointed to Yasmin and then to himself and Isabel.

"I won't turn my back on Yasmin or any of you, Raul."

"You would let her stay as if nothing happened?" Raul said with disgust. "I don't understand."

"You don't have to understand my decisions. Just accept them."

"And she gets away with everything she did?" He turned toward Yasmin and looked at her with enmity.

"Why is it so easy to believe the worst about me, Raul?"

"Don't ever speak to me," he turned swiftly, hitting her across the face with the back of his hand.

She knocked over the rocking chair and felt a sharp pain in her back as she crashed on the floor. The side of her face was throbbing. Placing her hand over her cheek, she stared up at him, horrified.

"You may fool Ma with your act, but not me." He pulled her upright, took hold of her shoulders, and shook her. "You're a liar, a fake."

Carmen grabbed his arm and uttered some unintelligible sounds. Stumbling back, she placed her hands on her forehead, swayed to the side, and collapsed.

"Ma!" Raul hollered, catching Carmen's limp body. He placed her on the sofa and patted her face gently. "Ma?"

Isabel knelt beside him. "Call an ambulance."

"Who knows how long it'll take them to get here?" Yasmin commented, hastening to the sofa. She stood by Carmen's feet, maintaining a safe distance from Raul. "Take her to the emergency room for immediate treatment."

Raul lifted Carmen's limp body and headed out of the apartment. "Pray nothing happens to Ma."

Yasmin heard him yell at her as he hurried through the hall and down the stairs.

* * *

Orlando finished drying his hair, placed the towel around his neck, and sauntered into the living room to answer his cell phone. His muscles were sore from the extraneous exercise routine he just finished. Focusing on the repetitions helped him keep his mind occupied. After his workout, he stood under the shower and let the water wash away the grim thoughts that plagued him.

He'd kept his distance from Yasmin at the cemetery. He would not add to her misery by lingering around her. The temptation to question her had been uncontrollable. The uncertainty about what had really happened in front of the club distressed him.

He made several hypotheses with the bit of information he'd overheard. Yasmin and her ex broke up that night, and on the rebound, hesitant to get back with Manuel, she was reluctant to become emotionally involved. The meeting she arranged was to express her apology and then return to her life of bliss with her ex.

If that wasn't the case, perhaps Yasmin was telling the truth. The man she argued with was not Manuel. Who the man was and what the quarrel was about were questions he would pose when they spoke.

His final supposition was that she had been with Manuel all along and deceived him. He dreaded that possibility most. If she'd lied purposely, if Raul was right, he was a miserable judge of character. He would be a failure in his profession, his insight and his ability to make inferences and use evidence and facts questionable.

His cell rang and he picked it up and read the number. "Yaz? What happened?" he asked, alarmed. All he could hear were her sobs. "Why are you crying? What's wrong?" Horrid scenarios flashed through his mind. "Where are you?"

"Corner . . . of . . . Mami's building."

"Wait for me there."

He ran into the bedroom, donned his jeans and sneakers, put on a T-shirt, pulled a sweater from the closet, and slipped into his leather jacket as he grabbed his car keys, wallet, and cell phone. The door slammed shut as he dashed out.

He wondered if it had been wise to decline Raul's offer. Knowing that an argument was inevitable, he had opted out. He preferred not to witness the name-calling, accusations, and offensive comments.

Perhaps he had been too hasty. Raul lost control easily when he was furious. If Raul had hurt her . . . Dismissing the thought, he ignored the sense of culpability that draped over him. Overwhelmed with the uncertainty of losing her, he had gone home to whimper. He overlooked her safety since he was too engrossed in his own emotions.

Now he sped through the streets, swerving from one lane to the other, leaving any car behind that was slowing him down. Living in the same neighborhood gave him the privilege of arriving swiftly if traffic wasn't bad. That gave him some solace. He needed to see her, to ascertain that she hadn't been seriously hurt.

He refused to consider what his life would be like without her. He had to be straightforward with himself and accept that he loved her.

After double-parking, he rushed out of the car and ran toward Yasmin in front of the building. She didn't appear to be hurt.

"What happened?"

"Orlando!" She embraced him. He held her tightly. Her body against his dispelled the horrid scenarios he'd imagined.

"Thank God you're all right," he muttered, kissing her forehead. "Yaz," he lifted her face gently and saw the reddish bruise on the left side of her face and the black-and-blue mark on her swollen lips. "Raul?"

Her shoulders shook as she sobbed.

"Calm down." He held her shoulders firmly. "Close your eyes, inhale deeply, and exhale." She did as he instructed, "Good. Let the air out slowly. Do it again, several times more. Open your eyes." When she did, she smiled at him with tears trailing down her cheeks. "Feeling better?" he asked.

She nodded. "Raul took Mami to the hospital. Mami grabbed him by the arm to try to stop him from throwing me out of the apartment. When she spoke, her words were slurred. She stumbled back and then fainted." Yasmin inhaled slowly to control the desire to sob. Then she exhaled and wiped her tears.

"Come on." Slipping his arm around her waist, he led her to the car. He waited until she made herself comfortable on the passenger side. "When is it going to stop?" he asked, voicing his thoughts aloud as he started the engine.

"What are you talking about?"

He stopped at the light and faced her. "The three of you know Carmen's health is delicate. Why would you argue in front of her?"

"Now that's my fault too?"

"Is that what I said?" His tone was unintentionally rough. It outraged him that she ignored his warnings and his fears had materialized. Raul had hit her. Worse was that he'd had the opportunity to prevent it yet chose not to. Carmen was in the emergency room again, and he was as much at fault as Raul, Isabel, and Yasmin. From what Yasmin described, Carmen might have had a stroke. He cursed inaudibly. Instead of going home, he should have been there. It might have prevented the situation from becoming volatile.

"That's what you're assuming. Just like you assumed from what Angel said that I'm with Manuel."

He looked at her and then at the road ahead. She was mindful of his reactions, another indicator she might have feelings for him. Suppositions and inferences weren't enough. He needed to be certain. "If you weren't so secretive, Angel's words would be meaningless." He was too angry to be subtle. His tone was rough and heated.

Yasmin laughed harshly. "Thank God Angel didn't say he saw me in front of a hotel."

"You never denied speaking to him," he reminded her curtly.

"I'm guilty, right? The truth, what really happened, is irrelevant to you and my family. So much for us being together."

"Was that what you were going to tell me, Yaz?" Had she considered being with him? The revelation yielded no satisfaction. If she expected him to get into a relationship with no clarification of her past, she was mistaken. He needed verification that she was single and wanted to know the facts about her supposed breakup with her ex.

She ignored his question. "You're a hypocrite, pretending you cared about my feelings, that you wanted to help me and believed in me. I was foolish to believe you."

"Don't change the subject. Were you with your ex at the club? Did you go there to meet him?"

"One remark from Angel and you're convinced that I'm . . . what? Worthless as Raul believes?" She paused and wiped the tears streaming down her cheeks. "You think I want to be with a man who's suspicious of me and questions my actions because of what some snob says?"

From her comments, it was easy to deduce that she'd decided to be with him. Until he knew all the facts, though, and was clear that their union would not be hindered by Manuel's reappearance, there would be no relationship.

"Answer the question, Yaz," he insisted. "Did you argue with your ex in front of Angel?" She was purposely avoiding the subject, focusing on his reactions.

"That's what Angel said, and you believed it." She was sarcastic. "His words are your evidence."

Orlando parked across the street from the emergency entrance. He was silent, giving himself time to calm down. Facing her, he spoke in a tempered tone. "No, Yaz, *your* words are. What happened?"

"I don't care what you think or what you want to believe, Orlando." She gazed toward the hospital and then back at him. "I just want to know if Mami is all right."

"She won't be around long if the three of you don't get it together."

"For your information, Mami and I were having a quiet conversation when Isabel and Raul walked in." Orlando gestured with his hand for her to lower her voice. She hesitated and then continued in a restrained tone. "Raul demanded that Mami throw me out and made threats that he would never visit Mami again if she didn't. He told me to leave. When I told him I wouldn't, he slapped me. And you blame *me*?" She opened the door and then hesitated. "That's coming from you, the man who supposedly cares for me. There's no need for enemies. With you and my family, I have enough."

He took hold of her wrist. "I warned you not to antagonize Raul."

"What was I thinking when I called you?"

He pulled her toward him and tried to embrace her. She shoved him back angrily. "Thanks for nothing. I'll go to the hospital by myself."

"No! Listen to me." He spoke calmly though he could barely contain his agitation. "What are you going to do when you go inside? Get into another argument in the emergency room? If Raul is that upset, you shouldn't go near him."

"Let him kill me if that's what he wants." She sobbed through the words. "Maybe then I can . . . have peace."

"Don't ever talk like that."

"Please," she hissed, tears streaming down her cheeks, "as if you care what happens to me."

Resisting the desire to embrace her, he took a deep breath. He was allowing his emotions to control his rationale, making the situation worse. She was too upset to listen. The bruises on her face made him feel as if a ton of bricks rested on his shoulders. He felt guilty—livid—by his lack of common sense. He'd allowed her to go alone when he knew Raul's temper. He was outraged and furious with himself. He realized that reprimanding himself and feeling guilt served no purpose, nor did arguing when she'd been through such a horrid experience.

"Let's prioritize, Yaz." He had to give her time to calm down. He had to ignore his own emotions and support her. "Carmen's health is what's important. We'll address the issues between us later."

"Us? There is no us," she spat out. "Find yourself someone you can trust."

He placed his hand gently under her chin and guided her face toward his. "I apologize," he whispered and then tapped a kiss on her forehead. "I shouldn't have taken what Angel said so seriously, but I need to know who you argued with and why."

She remained silent, her eyes blazing with ire.

"I overreacted," Orlando admitted. "I allowed my emotions to cloud my judgment. That wouldn't happen if . . ." He was about to confide that he loved her but hesitated, ". . . if I didn't care for you. I do, Yaz, a lot more than you can imagine."

Without responding, she gazed toward the hospital and crossed her arms.

"Promise me you'll wait here while I go inside to find out Carmen's condition," Orlando pleaded.

She looked at him out of the corner of her eye, frowned, and then nodded.

"Any message you'd like me to give Carmen?" he asked, opening his door.

"Tell her I . . ." she took a deep breath, ". . . love her."

"I'm sure she knows that, but I'll tell her anyway."

As he crossed the street, he glanced back and saw her slumped against the door. It was inhumane for Raul to abuse her physically and unforgivable that again he was excluding her from her mother's bedside in the emergency room.

Orlando saw Raul standing against the wall in the waiting area.

"What are you doing here?" Raul asked when Orlando stopped next to him.

"Yasmin called me." It appeared as if Raul realized the seriousness of what had occurred. He looked wretched, a sign that perhaps the experience would prompt him to reconsider his behavior and make his mother's health a priority. "How's Carmen?"

"The doctor suspects she might have had a stroke." His voice was drenched with guilt.

"Carmen is strong. She'll be fine."

"I should have gone to my place. I thought about it, but I didn't want Ma to get angry if I didn't show up. I promised myself I wasn't going to say anything. When I walked in, Ma's eyes were swollen from crying. I . . ." He paused and then continued. "The last thing I want is for anything to happen to Ma."

"It isn't easy, but you have to control your temper, Raul. Carmen is back in the hospital, and you could have really hurt Yasmin."

"She should have stayed away."

Orlando placed his hand on Raul's shoulder. "Do you really mean that?"

Raul sighed. "What I want or think doesn't matter. Yasmin wins."

"Maybe you need to stop looking at it as winning or losing." Neither had won, Orlando concluded, recalling the image of Yasmin leaning on the car door, sobbing. "See it as an opportunity to finally put the past aside and move forward. What Carmen wants is unity in the family. She wants to know you care for one another, especially in her absence one day. It's a legitimate sentiment."

Raul sighed, "Nothing is more important than Ma's life."

"I know that." He considered adding that Yasmin felt the same way but decided against it.

"Ma has an IV, a heart monitor, and some medication to lower her blood pressure. They took some blood and plan to do an EKG and more tests to ensure the stroke didn't affect her vital organs." He shook his head, "Seeing her like that . . . I told Isabel to stay with her. I'll go back later."

"Carmen will be home soon." Orlando patted his shoulder. "And Yasmin?"

"I can't deal with her right now."

Orlando wanted to remind Raul that eventually Carmen would ask to see Yasmin, but he decided it was best for Raul to hear that from Carmen.

Raul looked at him, a pained expression in his eyes. "How could I live with myself if anything happens to Ma?"

Orlando empathized with Raul. He felt the same way about Yasmin.

* * *

She looked at her watch and then at the entrance of the emergency room. As planned, she was with Orlando at the time agreed, but it wasn't a date. Convinced that would not deter him from questioning her, she frowned. He would demand details, clarifications. Emotionally drained and physically exhausted, she wished their conversation could be postponed.

She saw Orlando running across the street. "Is Mami all right?" she asked as he got into the car and started the engine. He nodded. "Thank God. Did you find out what's wrong?"

"Relax. The doctor is doing some tests to make sure everything is fine. Then they'll decide if she'll be admitted."

"You would tell me if her condition was serious, right?" She studied his face closely. Orlando looked directly into her eyes and nodded. He

206

seemed sincere, but she was still skeptical. "Did you see her? How did she look?"

"I didn't see her."

She glanced anxiously toward the entrance. "I wish I could be with her."

"We discussed that."

"Raul gets his way, as always."

"Funny, he said the same about you. If that's all that concerns the three of you, this won't be the last time Carmen is hospitalized." Stopping at the light, he gazed at her.

"I'm not the reason she's in the hospital," Yasmin stated.

"Stop pointing fingers, and focus on what's important—Carmen's health."

"You can't imagine how it feels to know that Mami is in the emergency room . . ." She paused to take a deep breath and clear her throat. ". . . and not be with her."

"I do." Reaching for her hand, he squeezed it. "Give Raul time to calm down. When Carmen asks for you, he'll get you like he did the last time. Right now, he needs to analyze what happened and make some tough decisions."

"He brought that upon himself." Yasmin regretted the words instantly. She recalled the pastor preaching about praying for those who hurt you, sharing joy and sadness with one another, and living in harmony. He said to enjoy the company of all without conceit, pride, or criticism. Raul was her brother, and she wanted their relationship to be different. Instead of gloating over his troubles, she needed to pray for him.

"Raul is just as upset as you are about Carmen's condition. Hopefully, this will help him realize he needs to be more civil and accept Carmen's decisions." He'd noticed that Raul was visibly distressed and even anguished. He hadn't seen him like that before. "Let's get something to eat. I'm starved."

"I'd rather go home." She longed for peace and quiet and had no desire to be in a public place where there was music, people talking, and boisterous laughter.

"You'd rather?" he repeated, looking directly at her.

"You're being difficult," she replied as she placed her hands on her throbbing temples. They were pounding, a sign that the migraine was getting worse. She rummaged through her purse looking for her medication and then remembered that she had left the bottle on her bureau. "You know, I've been through a horrid day, Orlando. Is it too much to ask you to take me home?"

"I'd like the same consideration. My day was just as bad. I need peace of mind too."

"Truce." Their roles were switched. It was her turn to be tactful. He needed to vent his frustrations, to dissipate the misgivings that haunted him. She needed to provide answers, be supportive, and understand how he felt. "Can you please drive me home? I don't have my migraine medication. I need to take it before this headache gets stronger. After that, we can go to any restaurant you like."

"I'm going to reserve my comments about your medication," he commented sourly as he made a U-turn. "What were you going to talk to me about? I'm listening."

Yasmin studied him as she considered where to begin. He had fixed his gaze ahead and was holding on to the steering wheel tightly. His shoulders were erect, his jaw tilted up slightly. It was a side of him she had never seen. The somber expression reminded her of Raul. She realized his severe reaction was triggered by her silence and inability to trust. She'd had ample opportunity to tell him the truth, to be sincere, but she had lacked the courage and determination.

She repeated the same version she had told her mother. "I was walking to my car when Angel appeared, talking nonsense."

"And you listened," Orlando added.

Although Orlando's comment irritated her, she decided that Angel didn't merit further comment. "Nestor left Ismenia in the club and caught up with me. Angel made some ridiculous comment to him. While they argued, I left."

"The best thing would have been to go straight home."

"True."

He looked at her with lifted eyebrows. "What about your ex?" Orlando disliked Manuel so much that he refused to say his name.

She suppressed a smile. "He wasn't there. Angel was referring to Nestor. I . . ." She hesitated. Being honest might stir up more conflict, but she had decided to tell him the truth. "I haven't seen my ex since . . . that day."

Parking, he turned off the engine and faced her. "Two questions: Why did you go home that day? And what do you mean you haven't seen him since 'that day'?"

208

CHAPTER 12

Glancing around, Yasmin realized he had parked in front of the entrance to her building. She wanted to run out of the car and escape. Instead, she faced him.

"The one thing I will demand in our relationship is *honesty*." Orlando stressed the last word as his eyes locked on hers.

"I haven't seen or spoken to him since that day," she reiterated firmly. Orlando's eyes were like a magnifying glass, meticulously studying her face. It was the same prying look she'd received from Carmen many times. She kept her gaze steady; there was nothing to feel guilty about.

"We were supposed to spend time together. The semester was ending, and I was taking finals. I told Mami I was completing a research project for one of my classes. I planned to get a stack of books from the library to take home as proof that I had been there all day. My library card was in my wallet, but I had left it on the bureau, so I went to the apartment to pick it up."

"Why didn't you leave after getting it?"

Her face beet red, she lowered her gaze. "After Dad threw me out, I left the apartment, crying. Manuel took me to his car and drove me to his mother's place. When we got there, he told me to wait in his room."

She recalled standing behind the door, crying inaudibly, while Manuel had a shouting match with his mother. The atrocities they said to each other still made her blush. Manuel had no respect for his mother. He used crude, foul, offensive language. "That's when I overheard his mother ask him how he expected her to allow me to live there when he was married and had a son. She said his wife would find out, and that would cause serious problems. While they argued, I left."

He stared at her, an expression of disbelief on his face. "He didn't notice and didn't follow you?"

"His room was near the entrance to the apartment. They were screaming so loud they didn't hear the locks open. I ran down the stairs and out the building." She remembered looking back as she dashed to the corner and hailed a cab. In her disheveled condition, the driver must have thought she was in danger and took pity on her. He drove her to Ani's and waited patiently while she dragged herself upstairs to get the money to pay the fare.

"You ran?" he asked, repeating the word she used. "Because?"

Her mouth was dry, and it was uncomfortable to speak. "I didn't want to be with Manuel anymore. I thought he was single. I never suspected he was deceiving me."

209

Orlando studied her features. She was looking directly at him, her gaze steady. He wondered if she was purposely omitting information. Her ex's deceit would upset her, cause a heated argument, and even lead to a breakup. Running away without confronting him was triggered by something other than finding out he'd lied. "Why would you sneak out and run away without telling him it was over? That doesn't make sense."

She looked toward the entrance of her building and forced herself to sit still. She yearned for the quiet refuge of her apartment where the silence demanded nothing except patience.

"After what he did to my father, how could I stay with him?" She lowered her gaze and stared at her hands as she spoke.

"That may have influenced your decision, but that wasn't the reason you ran away." He stressed the last two words purposely. "What happened, Yaz?"

Lowering her eyes again to avoid his, she grimaced. Convincing herself she could say what occurred was different from doing it. Divulging what she had hidden for years in the depth of her heart wasn't as easy as she thought. *Help me. Give me strength*, she prayed, trying to gear up courage to voice what she'd vowed never to reveal.

"As long as it's over and you're certain you don't want to go back with him, I accept that. But I refuse to believe you left without his knowledge, that all this time he never attempted to contact you." He paused and then asked, "You never saw him? Not once?"

"No," she retorted, shaking her head. The cynicism in his tone angered her. He was acting like her mother, questioning her with the same degrading attitude. "That's what happened. It's your choice to believe it."

"You're hiding something," he accused, indignantly. "I don't want half-truths, and I won't get into a relationship based on deception and secrets."

Chapter 13

Orlando sat motionless, staring at the entrance. Yasmin exited the car and hurried into the building. The clarifications he'd sought were not addressed. Her reluctance to divulge whatever she was concealing irked him. Why call and ask to meet him when she was unwilling to tell him the truth?

He started the engine, drove to the corner, and stopped at the light.

Like a roller coaster, his emotions were spiraling up and down. The turbulence continued. Walking out meant what? That she opted to stay alone rather than tell him the truth? Why was it his choice to believe it? He was questioning why she'd snuck out, not the validity of her words.

The car behind him honked. He gestured with his hand for the driver to move around him, backed into the parking space he had just exited, and turned off the engine.

He figured she would curl up in bed or on the sofa and weep. He hoped she took her medication, although it wouldn't help if she didn't calm down.

"Control yourself. Be rational." He voiced his thoughts aloud. He also needed to calm down. He couldn't allow his emotions to minimize his reasoning, which wasn't easy when it concerned the woman he loved.

He refused to leave but wasn't ready to face her either. He needed time to think, to sort out the smog of confusion her incomplete version generated.

"Help me calm down," he prayed aloud. "Clear my mind. Give me the strategies and wisdom to handle this situation so it will unite and not separate us." Leaning his head back, he closed his eyes.

Motionless, he cleared his mind of all thoughts and remained still for an indefinite time. More at ease, he opened his eyes. He reexamined her comments. She had gone to the apartment to pick up something she forgot. Instead of leaving, which would have been the wisest decision, she stayed. If she had done so willingly, why not admit it? Why skip to what happened when Roberto threw her out?

He supposed she might feel uncomfortable talking about what transpired before Roberto barged in. He did not want or expect her to talk about that. He understood that she was flustered and emotionally distraught by what occurred and had allowed her ex to take her where he lived. She explained that in her ex's room she overheard his argument with his mother and confronted the harsh reality that her ex had deceived her.

It astounded him that her ex expected her to move in without qualms. The fool believed that after pretending to be single, she should overlook his deceit. What he could not fathom was what prompted her to leave without his knowledge. Did her ex even know she'd overheard his conversation?

There had been no closure, no breakup. Yasmin ended it in a manner that was questionable and unusual. He presumed that her ex had to accept her absence and disappearance as an end to whatever they had without knowledge of why she left.

Orlando created a mental outline of how the events occurred. They met, and instead of going to the library, they headed back to get her library card. She omitted what occurred before Roberto arrived. His version, crude as it was, painted a picture of Yasmin taking her boyfriend home without caring if her parents showed up. That was how Roberto, Carmen, and everyone else discerned it.

Perception. The word popped into his head. When they spoke, she had alluded many times to how she was perceived. He recalled her saying "unlike mine, which is based on appearances and false judgments." When she made that comment, he wondered what she was referring to. He believed she was naïve and had not considered the consequences of her decision. From what she divulged, her intent was to pick up something and leave right away.

"No!" he gasped aloud, imagining a horrific scenario. If the scene he'd envisioned was correct, that would explain why she kept alluding to false perceptions and why she objected to Roberto's comments, claiming his words condemned her. He finally knew why she said that Carmen didn't understand what she experienced or how she felt. He understood her comment that what happened wasn't her fault and that everyone blamed and treated her like dirt. She had voiced her discontent about how one mistake changed her life drastically. Initially, he concluded that going back home was the wrong decision, which was misconstrued by her family and perceived as preplanned. It never occurred to her that her ex might take advantage of the opportunity that they were alone. That was the mistake.

He sighed aloud, disheartened by the gross situation she had endured. His eyes became misty. He blinked several times to clear his gaze. He felt overwhelmed with outrage, antipathy, and aversion.

If he ever saw her ex . . .

He took several deep breaths and forced himself to refocus.

Revenge wasn't important. Yaz was. He regretted his behavior and his selfish attempt to force her to explain to his satisfaction what had occurred.

How could she voice such a demeaning and humiliating experience? As if that wasn't devastating enough, Roberto's sudden appearance, his distorted view of what was happening, caused her reputation to be smeared. She lost her home, her respect, and the love and affection of her family just because her ex took advantage of her trust and innocence.

Anguish draped over him. She had suffered so much degradation, Raul's abuse, and Carmen's constant chastisement. He'd always suspected she was the victim, not the culprit. The confirmation that he was right yielded no satisfaction. He'd prided himself on defending her and acting as her advocate, yet he'd just questioned, judged, and condemned her. He was supposed to be her protector, the one who empathized with her, always preoccupied and conscious of her pain. He had failed her. All his convictions had evaporated over a jealous fit. Yasmin's outrage and accusations were justified.

She needed his support. Consoling her and assuring her that he loved her—those were his priorities. Her past would not alter his feelings. He loved her and wanted to formalize their relationship.

He exited the car and walked toward the building. Entering the foyer, he pressed the call button and waited.

"Who is it?" he heard her raspy voice ask.

"Orlando."

"Go home."

"Not leaving, Yaz. I'll be here all night until you buzz me in."

"You wouldn't do that."

"I'll keep ringing the buzzer to remind you I'm here," he promised.

Silence.

Orlando prepared himself to stay in the foyer all night, if necessary, but the buzzer went off, and he went inside. He ran up the two flights of stairs, knocked softly on her door, and entered the apartment. He walked into the living room and expected her to follow him. Instead, she stood near the entrance, head down and shoulders slumped. She was wearing pajamas—a tank top with capris. Her hair was tied back in a bun.

"Yaz," he walked back and stood behind her. "Please forgive me," he whispered. "The last thing I want to do is hurt you, offend you, and make you cry."

She remained motionless and made no attempt to respond.

"As much as I'd like to promise that in our relationship we won't have disagreements and arguments, that's not the reality. What I can promise is that I won't take your feelings for granted as I just did. I'll wait until you calm down for the appropriate time to discuss whatever it is." He was aware she was listening and noticed how she tilted her head slightly to the side. "Let's not waste more time and energy hurting one another." Slipping his hands around her waist, he pressed her against him.

Turning around, she looked up at him, tears trickling down her cheeks. "You're right. I have a secret. I just don't know . . . how to begin."

He wiped the tears gently from her cheeks. "I understand. What's important now is that we're together."

She stared up at him. "I agree with you. I don't want our relationship to begin with secrets."

"Let's sit down." He led her to the couch and placed his arm over her shoulder as she nestled next to him and met his gaze. "I shouldn't have reacted the way I did," he told her. "I let my emotions control me. The possibility that it was your ex and that I was wrong about how we felt for one another distressed me." He reconsidered adding how irate he'd been at himself for rushing home. "I wish I could erase all the pain and shame you've felt all these years over what happened that day."

Yasmin lowered her head, embarrassed. "I told him to wait for me in the car," she began in a husky voice.

"It's okay. You don't have to talk about that now—or ever."

"No," she said firmly, her cheeks damp. "I want you to know the truth. I want us to start anew with no ties to the past." She placed her hand on his mouth to silence him. "Please listen." She cleared her throat and spoke clearly, although tears were streaming down her cheeks. "I told him to wait for me in the car, but he got out anyway. So I said to wait by the entrance to the building. He refused. He followed me into the elevator and stood next to me while I unlocked the apartment door. I was afraid someone would see us together and tell my parents. I rushed inside, glad no one saw us. I told him to stay in the living room, that I would be right back. I got my wallet and was about to leave my bedroom when he walked in." She paused and closed her eyes tightly.

"No need to say any more, Yaz." He embraced her, and she rested her head on his chest and wept. He blinked to clear his gaze. "Enough crying." He stood to get her a napkin and a glass of juice. "Did you take your meds?"

She nodded.

"Good. I want you to lie down for a while. You'll feel better after you sleep."

She drank some juice and placed the glass on the coffee table. She combed his hair back with her hands. Patting the sofa, she pulled him by the arm so he would sit next to her again. She cuddled in his embrace and rested her head on his shoulder. "I've never spoken about it," she said quietly, "not even to Ani. When I showed up at her place, she accepted me with open arms without criticism or reproach. She held me while I cried and then got a towel and pajamas for me. She prepared the bed while I took a shower. Ismenia wasn't home. She arrived later and found me in her room sleeping. By that time, I had promised myself no one would ever know my secret. Ani never pressured me to speak about it. I volunteered no information."

"Yaz," he moved back so their eyes met, "I won't ever force you to do anything you don't want to do."

"I know," she affirmed, smiling. "I'm sorry, Orlando. Forgive me. I planned to tell you. I just . . . couldn't."

"I should have been more patient," he admitted, remorse pressing his shoulders down like a boulder. "We can put all that behind us now." He cupped her face in his hands and met her gaze. Her eyes, sparkling with warmth, reassured him that their feelings were mutual. "I love you, Yaz."

"I feel the same way about you," she said, grinning.

He kissed her softly on her forehead and embraced her again. She was finally calm and at ease. The storm had been fierce, but they were together. He thanked the Lord silently, grateful that he had made the right decision by praying and asking God for guidance.

Resting his head back, he relaxed. The silence was a blessing as was holding her and knowing they had a future together. A new beginning, she had said. He agreed. There would be challenges, but with the Lord at the center of their relationship and lives, there would also be victories.

He dozed off and awoke when she stirred in her sleep. He studied her. She was resting peacefully. He lifted her, carried her to the bedroom, and placed her gently on her bed. He stood near the bed, watching her. She'd endured so much drudgery, pain, and disillusionment because of false impressions and malicious gossip. There had been so many years of unnecessary misery. He would ensure with the Lord's blessing that their relationship was based on mutual respect and do everything within his means to nurture, love, and make her happy.

"Orlando," she called groggily as he was walking toward the door. "Are you leaving?"

"I should," he said, sitting on the edge of the bed. "You need to rest. I'll come back in the afternoon."

Sitting up, she shook her head. "I don't want to be alone. Please stay."

"I can come back later," he insisted. "It's been a long, draining day for both of us. Relax. Sleep."

"Please. I can rest while you're here."

Deciding not to contradict her, he took off his sweater, hung it on the doorknob of the closet and slid onto the bed beside her. She lay on his chest, her head nestled under his chin. He draped his arms over her back. The silence in the room enhanced the serenity and happiness he felt. The Lord had provided so much more than he'd asked for.

"Thank you," he whispered. He yearned for an even closer relationship with the Lord, to know more about Him and serve Him as He deserved.

Yasmin stirred in her sleep, and he recalled Carmen's comment that when he found the right girl, he would be eager to get married and start a family. When she said it, he was confident that would never happen. His grin widened. Carmen was right. Marriage and a family were forthcoming.

* * *

An incessant ringing awakened Yasmin. Groggily she lifted her head and listened. It was the doorbell. Sitting up, she glanced at the alarm clock on the night table—3:34 a.m. She supposed it was Raul. He was probably there either to pick her up or provide information about her mother's condition.

She gazed at Orlando as she slipped slowly out of bed. He was asleep.

"Thank you," she whispered, gazing up to heaven. There was peace between them. Finally, they were together, their relationship established.

The doorbell rang again. Yasmin tiptoed out as quietly as possible. Closing the bedroom door, she ran through the hall and past the living room to confirm it was Raul.

"Who is it?" she asked, trying to keep her voice as low as possible.

Recognizing Raul's voice, she opened the locks as quickly as her hands allowed and stared at him, wide-eyed.

"Ma was admitted," Raul explained, entering the apartment. "She was transferred from the emergency room to a regular room about two hours ago. I waited until she was settled in before coming here."

Unsure if he was sincere, Yasmin studied his face, looking for a sign of bereavement. He looked tired and somber but not overwhelmed with grief. Scanning him from head to toe as she joined him in the living room, she noted that he was still wearing the same jeans, sneakers, oversized sweater, and leather jacket he'd worn the day before. He and Isabel had probably spent the night at the hospital.

"The doctor confirmed that Ma had a mini stroke. She'll be hospitalized until they make sure her blood pressure is back to normal. They'll be observing her and doing more tests."

"A stroke?" Yasmin gasped aloud, gazing toward the bedroom door. Orlando knew her mother had a stroke and kept it from her? She tried to recall how long she had waited after Raul drove their mother to the hospital. She was too shaken up emotionally to discern the length of time, and she couldn't blame Orlando. He was protecting her from another violent dispute.

"Mini stroke," Raul clarified. "The doctors explained the difference between the two. A stroke causes damage that may be permanent. Mini-stroke symptoms are like a stroke but are short-term, and recovery is much quicker."

"Mami could have . . ." Yasmin began and then became silent. She couldn't fathom the idea much less the actuality of losing her mother.

"The doctors assured us that she'll be home soon." Raul placed his hand on Yasmin's shoulder and squeezed it gently. "If it makes you feel better, you can speak to the doctor. He'll discuss her condition and treatment."

Motionless, Yasmin looked at Raul. It was the first time in years he had shown any affection or concern for her feelings.

"Seeing Ma will reassure you," he added, forcing a smile.

"You forbade me to go to the hospital. Did you forget?" she reminded him in a quiet tone.

He turned her face slightly to study the bruise. "Doesn't look . . . too . . . bad."

"I'll live," was all she could think of saying. There was a black-and-blue mark on the side of her face where he had struck her, and her lip was still swollen.

"I didn't mean to hurt you. I . . ." Lowering his gaze, he shook his head.

Stunned by his admission of guilt, she smiled thinly. Acknowledging he was wrong was difficult for Raul. She was grateful for his attempt and stunned that the Lord touched his heart so he could voice his regret.

"Apology accepted," she said, nodding.

He winked at her. "The doctor stressed that Ma needs rest and tranquility. She needs to take her medicine regularly."

"That was the same recommendation last time." It seemed like an eternity since he'd made the same comment to her at Ani's.

"It's different now."

"How?" she interrupted. "Are you and Isabel willing to take care of Mami? Will you ensure Mami gets the peace of mind she needs?"

He nodded. "Ma's health is what's important."

"You and Isabel need to make that a priority."

"You're right." He combed his hair back with his hand. "I just came to tell you Ma's condition. You can visit her anytime. I'm going home to shower and rest for a few hours. I can pick you up on my way to the hospital."

"No need." She shook her head, opting to go with Orlando. She imagined the acrid expressions and rumors that would start when they showed up together, but she was at peace. If her mother accepted him, that was sufficient. "I'll meet you there."

"Always have to do things your way," he grumbled, frowning.

"A family trait we both share."

"Can't deny that. Visiting hours are 1:00 to 8:00. Ma's on the fourth floor, section B," he explained as they walked toward the door. "I'll be there when you arrive. Get some rest. You look tired."

"Practice what you preach," she said, opening the locks. "The doctors will contact you if Mami gets worse?" she asked anxiously.

"They have my cell number," he assured her.

She heard footsteps and a door closing in the distance. They turned simultaneously toward the living room.

"Manuel is here?" Raul's eyes darkened. "Ma was in the emergency room, and you were here with him?"

* * *

Orlando blocked a right punch and then pranced back with his fists lifted. Raul lunged toward him. Orlando ducked and landed a right on Raul's jaw. He watched Raul stumble back, regain his balance, and spring up.

"Don't hold back because I won't." Raul gestured with his hand for Orlando to move forward.

"Stop!" Yasmin ran between them.

"If you don't control her, I will," Raul promised.

"By hitting her?" Orlando demanded sarcastically. "Only cowards hit women." Grabbing Yasmin's arm, Orlando blocked her path by standing in front of her. "Stay out of the way, or you'll get hurt," he yelled, frustrated by her senseless attempts to stop them.

Horrified, Yasmin watched them prance around the living room as if they were in a boxing ring, swinging at each other, ducking, blocking, and landing punches. She gasped aloud as Raul crashed into the love seat, blood trickling from a cut on his lip.

"Enough!" she screamed at the top of her lungs. Standing between them again, she extended her arms to keep them apart.

"It wasn't just gossip. Ma, Maria, Luisa, and Isabel were right," Raul accused as he stood up, glaring at Yasmin and then at Orlando. "I never suspected it, although I should have known. That's why you defended her all the time."

"Wrong," Orlando clarified. Taking hold of Yasmin's wrist, he pulled her toward him and stepped in front of her.

"Yeah," Raul scoffed, lifting his fists. "You took advantage of our friendship and got involved with my sister, knowing I wouldn't approve."

"No."

Yasmin attempted to get in between them again. Orlando gestured with his arm for her to move back.

"You're here," Raul stressed. "You're a hypocrite, a traitor." Prancing forward, Raul landed a right on the side of Orlando's face.

"No!" Yasmin shouted, horrified. Her gaze fixed on the trickle of blood trailing from Orlando's eyebrow to his chin and then onto his white T-shirt.

"Relax, Yaz. I'm all right," Orlando said, realizing it was a futile attempt to calm her down. She looked so distraught that he feared she would have a nervous breakdown.

"Yaz?" Raul repeated with disgust. "You have pet names for each other?" He bolted toward Orlando, punching him repeatedly.

"Stop! Stop!" Yasmin cried out as they fought. Her heart was beating so fast she was breathless. She felt lightheaded—faint.

"Let's finish this outside," Orlando said, heading toward the door.

Yasmin watched, terrified, as Raul hastened after him. "No, no, no!" she yelled repeatedly. The room swirled around her, and she felt as if she were floating before darkness engulfed her.

Orlando stopped abruptly when he heard her frantic screams. Turning swiftly, he saw her collapse. He darted back and lifted up her limp body.

"Satisfied, Raul?" he asked, laying her gently on the couch.

"Should we take her to the hospital?" Raul squatted down beside him.

"If she doesn't come to." Propping a pillow under her head, Orlando gestured toward the bathroom. "Get the alcohol from the medicine chest."

"You would know where everything is," Raul complained.

"Isn't her health what you should be concerned about?" Orlando asked, sickened by Raul's lack of sensitivity.

"I'm not a hypocrite like you."

"You don't care what happens to Yasmin, but you're fighting me because you think I took advantage of her?"

"You betrayed my trust. You knew I never wanted any friend of mine messing with my sisters."

"Are you going to get the alcohol?" He shot him a stern glance.

Cursing, Raul ran to the bathroom and soon returned with the bottle.

"Yaz," Orlando knelt before her, patting her face gently. "Can you hear me?" A horrible thought occurred to him as he took the cap off and placed the alcohol bottle under her nose, moving it from side to side. Carmen would have a heart attack for sure if she heard Yasmin was admitted to the hospital.

Yasmin coughed several times, opened her eyes, and pushed his hand away.

"Yaz?" Her blank expression was like a dagger thrust into his heart. She had been through enough emotional turmoil that night. He wanted to spare her the anguish of witnessing them fighting. "Are you okay?" He leaned forward and studied her face. She was pale; her lips were ashen.

"Does she need to go to the emergency room?" Raul asked. Yasmin shook her head. "If you need to go, you will, even if you don't want to," he added, his tone implying she wouldn't have a choice.

"Get some water, Raul." Orlando pointed toward the kitchen. He heard Raul cursing aloud as he rushed away. "I can take you to the hospital for treatment, Yaz."

"No." She lifted her head, placed both hands on her temples, and lay down again.

"Where is the medication for your migraines?" Orlando was about to stand, but she pulled his arm and shook her head. Kneeling before her again, he took the glass of water from Raul and placed it to her lips. "Drink some," he urged.

She took several sips and then gestured for him to put it away.

Orlando placed the glass on the coffee table and studied her expression. She was more alert, but she still looked pale.

Turning on her side, Yasmin covered her face with both hands and cried softly.

"That's the answer to everything," Raul griped.

"Why are you so insensitive?" Orlando asked, standing and facing him.

"Don't you dare correct me when you've been with my sister all this time pretending to be my friend. You're a snake."

"Are you going to start fighting again?" Yasmin asked hoarsely, sitting up.

"We haven't even begun," Raul vowed, waving his fist.

"You know where to find me," Orlando replied, looking directly at him. He wasn't intimidated by Raul's menacing stare.

Yasmin gazed from one to the other, aghast. They'd gone from best friends to enemies because of her.

"I do," Raul stressed, smiling maliciously.

She looked at them again. Raul had a red mark on his right cheek and a cut on his upper lip. Orlando had a minor cut over his left eyebrow and on his jaw, and the side of his face was red and swollen. She pointed to the door. "Get out, Raul."

"I should have known you'd be enjoying yourself instead of worrying about Ma. You two deserve each other. You're both scum."

"Don't come back," she ordered.

"No reason to," Raul assured indignantly. "Better be alert." He spoke directly to Orlando. "Not finished with you yet."

"You decide when and where," Orlando shrugged.

"Get out!" Yasmin screamed.

"You need to take it easy, Yaz," Orlando said, squatting before her. "Lie down and rest. If you don't have a migraine already, you'll get one later."

She ignored him and turned to see if Raul had followed her mandate. "Thank God," she murmured as the door slammed shut.

Orlando took a deep breath and sat on the edge of the couch next to her. There was a deafening silence in the apartment, a stillness that marked the end of a friendship. That wasn't the way he'd wanted Raul to find out about their relationship, but he also didn't want Yasmin's reputation more soiled than it already was. His hands were tied.

"Are you sure you're all right?" He focused on her, putting aside the turmoil brewing within.

"Are you?" she asked, concerned by the grave expression on his face.

"I wish I could have spared you from such a horrible experience," he said with regret. Embracing her, he rested his head on hers. At least she wasn't hurt physically while they scuffled. Raul was a fierce opponent, vicious when he wanted to be. Unknown to Yasmin, Raul had held back and controlled himself, a sign that he had taken her presence and constant interference into consideration. That would not be the case when they confronted each other again. They were the same height—5'6"—similar weight, and both agile fighters. They had been in a multitude of fights as a team. They knew each other's weaknesses and strengths, which would make their confrontation fierce.

Yasmin stared at Orlando, speechless, noting the grim expression on his face. Raul's threat disturbed her as much as Orlando's comment and challenge. They would fight again; she was certain of that. Since neither of them backed down in her presence, she envisioned a horrid scenario if they met again. She swallowed the knot in her throat and forced a smile.

"I'm going home," Orlando said, standing up. He needed time to sort out his feelings, reflect on what happened, and decide what his next steps would be.

"What if Raul is downstairs?" she asked, reaching for his hand and squeezing it.

"I'm not going to hide." He pulled her up and embraced her. "I won't instigate it, but I'll defend myself."

"I'm supposed to pretend this is not happening?" she asked anxiously.

"Trust my judgment, and remain calm. This is between me and Raul. I will handle it."

"It's not Raul's business if we're together," she stressed. "We don't owe him any explanation. His approval isn't necessary. You've done nothing wrong, and you don't need to apologize."

"I'd rather not talk about that now." He needed to pray and ask the Lord for clarity and direction. She probably needed to do the same.

"Okay." She kissed his lips. Embracing him, she nestled her head on his neck. "Please stay."

He caressed her back gently. What did he want to rush home for? Nothing he did would change what happened. He had to accept the crude reality that the confidence and esteem he'd earned with his friend through years of loyalty had vanished and with it the opportunity to clarify the situation.

"All right," he said, "but I'm leaving in a few hours. I need to go home for a while. We'll plan our agenda when I get back."

She nodded in response.

Orlando walked alongside her back to the bedroom. He lay on his back, staring at the ceiling. She rested her head on his shoulder and pressed herself against him. She seemed at ease, but he knew she was anxious—distraught.

Retracing the order of events, he recalled waking up when she exited the bedroom. Convinced it was Raul, he lay on the bed waiting, reflecting on how he would inform him and Carmen of his relationship with Yasmin. Although he wanted Carmen's blessings and Raul's approval, he worried about how to convey that his feelings were genuine. He anticipated a backlash due to the history of mischief he shared with Raul. But nothing would deter him from his goal of proposing, getting married, and having a family. That would not change.

He squeezed Yasmin gently. Staying was the right decision. She wasn't asleep, and although her body was motionless over his, she was not as relaxed as she had been earlier. He wanted to say something to alleviate the turmoil assailing her, but he lacked the energy to talk. The appropriate words eluded him.

Losing Raul's friendship disheartened him, but his relationship with Yasmin took precedence. Her comment that she was at fault and her sense of culpability concerned him. He hoped the situation with Raul would not deter her from accepting his marriage proposal. Deciding not to dwell on false notions or fret about situations that might not occur, he focused on relaxing.

I need your help to resolve this conflict with Raul, Lord, he prayed silently. *I don't want Yasmin to continue suffering. Lord, guide me so I can become the husband, provider, and companion she needs and deserves. Give her strength to endure this situation. I put myself, her, and the situation with Raul in your hands.* Closing his eyes, he attempted to rest.

Yasmin was motionless. She knew Orlando was awake and felt him pressing her closer to him. She sensed his apprehension and was aware of the angst he felt. Just hours after the issues that kept them apart were resolved, Raul's appearance was like a tornado, creating havoc and chaos and disrupting the serenity and happiness they shared.

"Why, Lord?" she murmured, repressing the desire to cry.

Orlando had enough to worry about, and she refused to distress him further by weeping. The silence was a reminder of the disarray prompted by Raul's presence, but it was best for the moment.

"Please help us," she prayed.

* * *

"What happened?" Ismenia asked, alarmed, studying the bruise on Yasmin's face. "Who hit you?"

"Long story," Yasmin replied. The image of Raul and Orlando exchanging blows was still vivid.

Yasmin surveyed the room in silence. Orlando had cleaned up while she slept. He had swept all the debris from the broken knick-knacks scattered over the floor. She'd clung to him teary-eyed before he left, wishing he would stay. Convinced he was determined to leave, that he needed time alone to reflect on what occurred, she watched him exit, her heart overwhelmed with fear and sadness. She had not fulfilled her promise to lie back down and rest. Instead, she lay on the couch, sobbing, and then slept from exhaustion and pain. Her temples pounding, she could barely lift up her head. She awoke hours later when Ismenia knocked.

"Yasmin?" Ismenia called anxiously.

Unable to speak, Yasmin shook her head. It wasn't fair. After they became a couple, their bliss had immediately turned to chaos. If Raul reacted that way, she could only imagine what her mother would say. Why, God? The question kept resurging. She didn't understand why the Lord would unite them and then allow Raul to maliciously threaten Orlando with the intent to harm him.

She burst into tears, surprised she could still cry. Her body ached as if she had been the one fighting. Sudden movements caused a stabbing pain in her temples. She had taken the medication before Orlando left to pacify him, but its effects were minimal.

"Tell me what happened, Yasmin," Ismenia said, distressed.

In response, Yasmin covered her face with her hands, curled up in a corner of the sofa, and continued sobbing. She craved falling into a deep sleep. She wanted to dispel the images of her brother fighting the man she loved. She never imagined witnessing another fight between a family member and someone she was involved with. She couldn't really call Manuel's attack on her father a fight. Although her father tried his best to defend himself, younger and more agile Manuel took full advantage of his strength. What Yasmin had just witnessed the night before was the opposite. She knew Raul and Orlando had gotten into many street fights, but she never imagined they would fight as if they were total strangers. Orlando said he had no choice, that he had to defend himself. It was true. Raul had run back into the apartment when he heard footsteps and punched Orlando as he stepped out of the bathroom. Agile on his feet, Orlando had blocked the repeated blows.

"Yasmin," Ismenia knelt before her. "Drink this."

Yasmin cleared her throat and sat up, wiping the tears that trickled down her cheeks. She drank some of the water and handed Ismenia the glass.

"Come on," Ismenia urged, pulling her up.

"No." She tried to sit down again.

Ismenia forced her to stand. "You're going to take a shower and get dressed. We're going out. You need to get out of this place for a while."

"No."

"I'm not taking no for an answer, Yasmin," Ismenia said firmly. "Do it."

Yasmin had no energy to argue. She went into the bathroom, turned on the shower, and stood under the hot water, praying it would wash away the horrid images of what had occurred just hours before.

Chapter 14

Orlando exited the bathroom wearing pajama pants and a towel wrapped around his neck. He glanced at the clock on the night table. Noon. He hoped Yasmin had gone back to bed and slept a few more hours before getting up.

He was happy that she'd taken her medication while he was there. After everything that had happened, he could tell she wasn't feeling well and was exhausted both physically and emotionally. He felt the same. While she slept, he was awake, thinking and replaying the whole ordeal he and Yasmin had been through. Like a row of dominoes falling in succession, one mishap led to the other.

"Lord, everything happened all at once," he spoke his thoughts aloud.

The serenity he had shared with Yasmin was brief. He felt as if the rug had been pulled out from under him and he'd fallen into an abyss of uncertainty. He had no idea how Yasmin would react after his bout with Raul. She seemed edgy and distressed when he left. He doubted she had grasped the full realization of what happened.

He adored her, but she tried his patience to its limits. She was stubborn and impulsive. He couldn't protect her and guard himself simultaneously. It annoyed him that she was so reckless.

His cell phone rang, and he strolled over to the nightstand. Sitting on the edge of the bed, he read the number and frowned.

"How are you, Orlando?"

He tried to sound cheerful as he greeted Eva, although hers wasn't the voice he longed to hear. He wanted to hear Yasmin's voice, which was the only way he would be able to gauge her stance on the situation. He had called her, but her cell phone went directly to voicemail. He left several messages. She didn't reply. The only option was to drop by. He wasn't sure how wise that would be without contacting her first, so he would wait until she called him.

"What's wrong?" Eva asked. "Problems with Yasmin again?"

"Never mind." He preferred not to discuss it. "How are you and Dad?"

"Have you spoken to Clara? Did she give you my message?"

"No."

"If you had spoken to your sister, she would have informed you that your father was admitted yesterday. I stayed with him last night. I'll head back to the hospital after we speak. He's had a cold on and off, and then it got worse. The doctor said he has pneumonia."

"Sorry, Mom. Should I come and be with you?" It wasn't the most convenient time, but he would go if he had to.

"No need. The doctor promised he'll be home in a few days. He's taking antibiotics. But like me, he's upset with you. Clara spoke to me late last night and said she left you several messages. You didn't call or drop by her place to find out what happened. What if it had been an emergency?"

Orlando was silent. The image of dominoes cascading one after the other surfaced. *What's happening, Lord?* he asked silently, disconcerted that the trail of ongoing problems continued.

"Did I catch you at a bad time, Orlando? I get the impression you're not in the mood to talk."

He sat up straight and spoke in a firm tone. "I must admit I'm not in the best of moods. I've been through some rough times."

"I dread what that means," Eva commented anxiously. "Is Yasmin the reason?"

"She's the victim." He opted not to provide details, thinking it served no purpose to expose Eva to his plight. She had enough to contend with.

"So you're back to being her protector?" Eva sighed. "What's going on between you?"

"I'm going to propose to Yaz and marry her if she accepts."

"What?" Eva hollered with disbelief. "I knew you were in love with her and that you were protecting her because you cared."

Orlando couldn't resist smiling, although he felt wretched. His mother shared Raul's point of view. He realized his deeds would be shaded a different color when the news spread that they were in a relationship.

It bothered him, but not because he cared about the gossip, which he considered irrelevant. Yasmin was too susceptible. It was another issue that might affect their relationship.

"If she accepts?" Eva asked, puzzled. "Why would you propose if she doesn't feel the same way about you?"

"She does." The happiness he should have felt by admitting that wasn't there.

"You're getting married!" Eva said, astounded.

He laughed in response. The thought astonished him as much as it did her. Despite everything that had transpired, his decision was solid. He loved Yasmin and wanted her to be his wife.

"Wow! If she loves you . . . there's something you're not telling me, Orlando. What really happened?"

He had said too much already. Eva was worried without knowing about his fight with Raul. "You taught me that our expectation and what happens are often opposite."

"That's the way it is sometimes," Eva agreed with concern. "But all relationships have problems, some more serious than others. You need to communicate. It's the only way you'll have the stability to overcome whatever obstacles are keeping you apart."

"You're right." It amazed him that his mother's perception, though she had limited information, was so keen. He and Yasmin had been through so much emotionally that it was normal to overreact. Was he reading too much into Yasmin's behavior? Was he overanalyzing the situation?

"What do Carmen and Raul think about your relationship?"

The frown on his face deepened. Like Raul, Carmen might not approve—a reaction that might be widespread. "Carmen was hospitalized yesterday. She doesn't know. No one does except Raul."

"Oh my God!" Eva gasped with disbelief. "Why was she admitted?"

"It might be a stroke." He recalled Raul's comment when they spoke in the emergency room.

"I'm confused." Eva sounded puzzled. "You're with Yasmin? She agreed to be with you? That's why you want to propose to her, right?"

"Raul doesn't approve. He showed up at Yasmin's place while I was there." He shared some details to provide clarity.

"And you're concerned Yasmin won't accept your proposal because he disapproves?" Eva asked skeptically. "Why would his opinion matter to her? For you it would. You were like brothers."

"Past tense," he admitted glumly. Their close friendship was over. He doubted Raul would have accepted his relationship with Yasmin even if he told him personally. His reaction might have been the same.

"You have to choose between your friendship and being with Yasmin?" Eva deduced, her tone expressing disapproval.

"I made my choice," he said, realizing the situation with Raul was irreconcilable. "I want Yasmin to be my wife."

Eva sighed aloud. "I think you've been in love with her for a long time without realizing it."

Orlando tried to recall when he had fallen in love with Yasmin. Was it when they first met? He remembered her timid smile as she lifted her gaze to greet him the first time. Despite her aloof attitude, there was something about her that intrigued him. He looked forward to seeing her. He liked her quiet, reserved personality and her enthusiasm for education. She selected fashion trends as carefully as her friends. She was close to one, Ismenia.

"Are you still there, Orlando?"

"Yes, sorry."

"Don't exclude me. As soon as she accepts your proposal, you'd better call and let me know. I want to be there for all the celebrations and ceremonies."

"Easy, Mom. One step at a time. I need to propose first. Right now, things are a bit hectic. I'm not sure when they'll become stable."

"Soon I'll be having a grandchild," Eva said with delight.

He laughed boisterously. The idea of family and children appealed to him. Having a child with Yasmin would be a blessing, one he would cherish infinitely. But that was in the far future. There were more urgent matters to resolve in the present. Their relationship had to solidify. He loved her and was willing to make any sacrifice to be with her. She claimed she cared for him, but words and actions were different. How committed she was to the feelings she professed was yet to be proven.

He wanted to establish a firm relationship with her and live a life centered on Christ. The Lord had blessed him immensely by bringing her into his life and uniting them. Although eager to propose, he had to be patient and continue praying so Yasmin would be strong and resilient enough to endure the challenges they were facing.

"Grandchildren—not for a long time," he said.

"Maybe not," Eva said. "When I left, you were convinced you hadn't met anyone worthwhile. Now you're talking about marriage. That's just the beginning. What follows naturally is a family. Our expectation and what happens are different."

He chuckled. "Yes." He had no idea what the Lord's plan or purpose was. He just knew that whatever happened, the Lord was in control.

* * *

"When did you get back?" Yasmin asked as she sat on the bench next to Ismenia. They had walked leisurely to Riverside Park, Yasmin's grim mood slowly dissipating. It felt good to be outside. The wind was mild and soothing on a bright, sunny day.

"Last night, I called Mom from the airport when I got home," Ismenia began. "We spoke for a long time. She told me you've decided to be Orlando's girl." Ismenia was clearly delighted. "I tried calling you, but your phone was busy. So I decided to drop by this morning. I didn't expect this," she gestured to the bruise on Yasmin's face.

Yasmin bit her lip. Her cell phone wasn't charged, nor was her cordless. After rushing upstairs and leaving Orlando in the car, she forgot to take her cell phone out of her purse and charge it. The cordless had fallen off the base while Raul and Orlando were fighting. She placed it back the next morning, but it was still charging. She was certain Orlando had called dozens of times trying to contact her. For the moment, she disregarded calling him. They would see each other later that afternoon or evening. Before Ismenia left, she would call him and explain why she hadn't contacted him.

"Tell me about the kids," Yasmin said, eager to focus on any topic that kept her awry thoughts at bay.

Ismenia embraced her and smiled. "They're fine. Are you ready to talk about it?"

Yasmin inhaled deeply and then exhaled. "Raul and Orlando fought."

Ismenia's eyes widened.

"That nonsense about his friends not messing with Isabel or me—it's ridiculous. He just wants to control everyone's life."

"You should ask Raul if he has a rule for not getting involved with his sister's best friend and then remind him that he didn't follow it."

Yasmin laughed. Ismenia and Raul had been together for a while. "Raul gives orders for others to follow. He gets to do what he wants," Yasmin said.

"Which is why you should not make the same mistake twice. Things didn't work out with Manuel. That's the past. Forget Raul and everyone who is against your relationship. You love Orlando, and he loves you. That's what matters."

"One thing has nothing to do with the other."

"No?" Ismenia faced her. "Weren't you in love with Manuel and left him because he beat up your father? Everyone in your family disapproved, right?"

"I'm not talking about that." She shook her head. "I've wasted too many years brooding and suffering over the incident with Manuel. No more," she said decisively. "My life is taking another direction."

Ismenia clapped enthusiastically. "Mom was right. Being with Orlando has had a positive effect on you."

"You have no idea," she whispered, her eyes becoming misty. As much as she loved him, she wondered if they should stay together. Their relationship had barely materialized, and already he was the target of Raul's aggression, a direct effect of being involved with her. Perhaps she was not worthy of loving or being loved.

"Don't start crying again," Ismenia warned. "Be happy. Orlando will not give you up because of what happened."

"I don't want them to fight again." She dreaded the thought and knew Raul would carry out his threats.

"I'd like to tell you that they won't," Ismenia commented, frowning, "but just like your father, Raul doesn't know the meaning of forgiveness. Something terrible would have to happen for Raul to realize that you can't mistreat the people you love."

"What am I going to do?" she spoke her thoughts aloud, overwhelmed with anxiety. She had found the man she wanted to share her life with, yet they could not be together.

"Relax. Wait and see what happens. Maybe they won't fight again. Orlando has more common sense than Raul. He'll avoid it."

"That's what I thought," she said grimly, recalling Orlando's comment. "But he told me he won't hide from Raul."

"Why should he? Raul is a bully and acts like everybody must do things by his standards. Orlando should stand up to him," Ismenia pointed out.

"Weren't you listening to me? I don't want them to fight again."

"How are you going to stop them? Raul won't care if Orlando doesn't want to fight him. He's too selfish. If he had any common sense or valued your feelings or his friendship with Orlando, we wouldn't be having this conversation. Raul has always been insensitive, rude, and obnoxious."

Yasmin grinned. Ismenia sounded like she still hadn't gotten over Raul. Their torrid relationship had lasted two years, ending because of his infidelity and her jealous fits. Ismenia constantly showed up to whatever club Raul frequented, fought with whoever Raul was with, and insulted him in front of his friends. They spent several weeks apart, made up, and then repeated the same scenario. Raul ended the relationship. Ismenia had been dating Nestor on and off whenever she and Raul temporarily stopped seeing each other. Shortly after Raul's decision, she moved in with Nestor and announced she was pregnant, something Yasmin considered suspicious, although she never mentioned it.

"Stop staring at me like that," Ismenia said. "Whatever you're thinking, it's not true."

"Are you sure about that?"

"You know Raul is arrogant, hateful, unbearable, and many more things I won't bother to mention."

"Are those the great qualities that made you fall in love with him?"

"That wasn't love," Ismenia said. "I don't know what it was."

"You were crazy about each other," Yasmin reminded her. "And in Raul's honor, you named your first child Ismael." She said it purposely to see Ismenia's reaction. Ismael was Raul's middle name. Yasmin always wondered why Ismenia hadn't named him Nestor, the normal thing to do with a firstborn son.

"I chose that name because I liked it."

"Yes," Yasmin sang sarcastically. "Why not name him after his father? Nestor Junior?" She suspected Ismael was Raul's son. She had seen pictures of Raul as a baby. The resemblance to Ismael was astonishing. She often wondered if Nestor knew or if he objected when Ismenia chose the name. Surely Nestor had no idea the name was associated with Raul or he would have been suspicious.

"I can name my child whatever I want," Ismenia stressed. "If you want to talk about the past, let's focus on you. Remember when I kept telling you that Orlando liked you?" She nudged her on the arm. "You denied it. "Don't talk nonsense to me," she mimicked in a child's voice. "I don't want to hear it. Me and Orlando? No!" She pretended she was singing and then stopped and laughed loudly. "It's interesting how things change."

Yasmin agreed. "It's interesting how some things don't. I think you still care about Raul."

"When has Raul taken any woman seriously? The word *relationship* is a curse to him. Loving and caring for anyone other than himself is not up here," Ismenia pointed to her head, "or here," and she pointed to her heart.

Yasmin smiled. Ismenia was fooling herself. Her attitude and tone were of a woman who was indignant, offended, and still suffering from Raul's infidelity. "I don't see much difference between Raul and Nestor. Both are promiscuous."

"You're not the one who needs to see it," Ismenia retorted. "I do."

"If you say so." Yasmin was skeptical, but it occurred to her that perhaps Nestor was a better candidate. Ismenia was right; Raul wasn't interested in a relationship.

While dating Orlando, she had called it a friendship, but he'd expressed his love in ways she'd never imagined. He respected her, attended to her likes and needs, and was always eager to please her. During the months they dated, he'd never gone to her apartment and never asked or insisted that she invite him—a courtesy she appreciated and acknowledged as his way of showing that his intentions were noble. It was sad that her mother had never received that type of attention or affection from her father. Roberto was oblivious to her mother's emotional needs and the simple actions and selfless deeds that would have nurtured their relationship.

Those things were important to Orlando. Their relationship would be different. He would ensure that they spent quality time together, traveled, and celebrated special days and holidays. He would be loving, courteous, and devoted to making the place where they lived a loving home.

She sighed and shook her head.

"Worrying isn't going to solve anything," Ismenia said.

"There has to be something I can do," Yasmin said, her somber mood returning.

"Mom would say trust the Lord and have faith." Ismenia mimicked Ani's calm, quiet tone.

"She would," Yasmin smiled, thinly. "Why aren't the kids with you?"

"I left them with Ramona."

"Why would you leave your kids with a woman who can't stand you?" Yasmin marveled.

"Because it's me she doesn't like. She pampers and spoils her grand-children," Ismenia said. "Nestor convinced me to let them stay a while longer. I decided it would be nice to spend quality time with him since we're alone in the apartment."

"I hope that's what's happening." Yasmin was skeptical.

Ismenia rolled her eyes. "We just got back late yesterday. But unlike you, I'm optimistic. You should follow my example in your situation."

"There's hope for him yet," Yasmin quoted Orlando's phrase. "Tell me about your trip."

Ismenia averted her eyes. "The kids are fine. I spoke to them before dropping by. They're going to the beach today."

"When are you bringing them back?"

"In a week or two, a month at the most. We'll probably stay a while and then come back."

"Shouldn't you be saving money just in case?"

"In case of what?" Ismenia challenged.

"Have you considered a career? Going back to school? Working? Maybe you need to think seriously about what you would do if one day Nestor can't support you."

"Don't be so civil. Just say it. What you mean is if he is arrested, hurt by one of his customers, or killed. I can't live my life worrying about what-ifs. You're the one who does that. I enjoy life."

"You have kids, Ismenia," she reminded her in a sour tone.

"They have everything they need," Ismenia shrugged happily. "I hope now that you're with Orlando you'll enjoy the present, forget the past, and stop worrying about the future."

Yasmin stared at Ismenia, a blank expression on her face. The present and future looked bleak. Her happiness was no longer the priority.

"We'd better go." Yasmin glanced at her watch and stood up. "Visiting hours at the hospital have started already." Focused on their conversation, she had overlooked the time.

"I'd like to go with you to see Carmen."

Yasmin nodded. "Mami would like that. Perhaps Ani would like to go with us too. Call her so she can get ready. We'll pick her up on the way to the hospital."

Orlando glanced around the waiting area as he entered the hospital and saw Raul sitting across from Maria, Luisa, and Isabel. It was odd that they were still in the waiting room since visiting hours had already begun.

"You'd better leave right now." Raul stood abruptly when he saw Orlando approaching.

"Why?" Luisa asked. Standing, she gazed from Raul's face to Orlando's. Her eyes lingered on the bruises on their faces.

"Mind your own business, Luisa," Raul said as he stopped, gesturing for her to return to her seat. "Do you need to be dragged out?" Raul challenged Orlando.

"No," Orlando replied calmly. "What are you going to tell Carmen when she asks for me? In her condition, do you want her worrying unnecessarily?"

"How considerate."

"Your decision," Orlando said, ready to walk out.

"Did the two of you get into a fight?" Luisa asked, still standing behind Raul. Isabel and Maria walked over and stood next to her. Both of them studied the bruises on Raul's and Orlando's faces, gasping aloud with shock.

"Sit down," Raul said to them, pointing to the waiting area. "This doesn't concern any of you."

"Did you get into a fight over Yasmin?" Maria asked.

"Mind your own business." Raul's voice rose considerably. He gestured for Orlando to follow him as he walked toward the entrance.

"Incredible!" Luisa spoke loud enough for everyone in the lobby to hear. "They fought over Yasmin. She destroyed their friendship."

"Yasmin returned to make us miserable," Isabel spat out.

Orlando smiled. They wanted him to hear their comments. He didn't care what they thought; their reactions were meaningless.

"Orlando will find out the hard way that taking her seriously is a mistake," Maria commented.

"What he does is not your business," Luisa told Maria. "Orlando never cared about you. He used you. Now it's his turn. Yasmin will use him and then leave him like he left you. He'll find out for himself how painful that is."

Their exchange amused Orlando. They would fester in jealousy and outrage when they heard he planned to marry Yasmin.

"Are you going to tell Ma you're with Yasmin, or are you going to wait until she finds you together like I did?"

"I'll tell her when Yaz is with me."

"Where is she?" Raul asked, his lips curling up. "Probably with her ex, and you're here. But that doesn't matter—because you *love* her."

"She'll come later," he replied, ignoring Raul's comment. He thought Yasmin would be in the waiting room or with Carmen when he arrived, but now he was certain she was at Ani's and would contact him eventually.

"She's alone, and you're here now?" A scowl replaced Raul's sinister smile. "You go on up, but I'm not going up to the room until you come down."

"You don't think Carmen will find that odd?"

"Did you think I would find it odd that you pretended to be my friend all the time you were with my sister?" Raul raised his chin. "I'll be outside. The three of you can go up with Mr. Sincerity," he called out to Luisa, Maria, and Isabel.

"No," Isabel said, gazing at Orlando with disapproval. "I'll wait until he leaves."

"I'll go up with Isabel," Maria replied in the same tone.

Turning slightly, Orlando looked at Maria. Her insistence on acting as if he'd jilted her was comical. There was no justification for her to feel that way. He'd made his stance clear—being with her had been a waste of his valuable time.

"Do what you want." Raul faced him. "We have business pending." He bumped purposely into Orlando's shoulder as he exited.

Orlando nodded and watched Raul walk out. Leisurely he strolled to the security desk.

"Yasmin has some nerve," he heard Isabel comment.

"She must be happy," Maria said with disdain. "Now she has someone else to add to her long list."

"Orlando!" Luisa called.

From his peripheral vision, he saw her rush toward him. He waited reluctantly.

"Visiting hours start at 2:00, not at 1:00 as the recorded message says when you call. We arrived too early."

He glanced at his watch. Ten minutes wasn't a long time, but he wasn't going to spend it listening to gibberish. He walked to the far end of the waiting room and sat in an isolated area.

Not being able to contact Yasmin was frustrating. He scanned his cell phone. She hadn't called. That was not a good sign.

"Because you're with Yasmin, you can't sit with us?" Luisa asked, sitting down on the empty chair next to him.

Turning slightly, he looked at her in silence. Whatever she had to say did not interest him.

"Men like you always end up with the wrong type of woman."

"Men like me?" he repeated, smirking.

"You think it's funny now. Eventually you'll find out that Yasmin isn't worth any sacrifices you've made—including losing your friendship and fighting with Raul."

"Who told you we fought?" he demanded in a curt tone.

"Why else would Raul ask you to leave? It's obvious you had a problem because of that . . ."

"Be careful what you say about Yaz." Standing, he started walking away.

Luisa dashed ahead and blocked his path. "Yaz? Since she came back, she's been lying to Carmen that she wasn't with you. That's why Raul is furious. All these years you were with *Yaz*," she said the name with disdain, "and pretended not to know where she was."

"Keep your assumptions to yourself," he warned.

"You'll regret taking her seriously."

"Finished?"

"It's sad when you can choose the best and end up with the worst."

"I agree. I didn't want the worst, so I chose Yasmin."

"When you realize you're wrong, it'll be too late."

"Or I'll realize that I'm right, and I'll be delighted." He winked at her. "Stay away from her. Keep your comments, opinions, and lies to yourself."

"I have nothing to say to her," Luisa hissed indignantly. She turned abruptly and then hesitated. Turning back, she faced him. "You know he's looking for her?"

"Who is?" He was certain she was referring to Yasmin's ex.

"As if you don't know," Luisa said. "Her man, Manuel. I saw him recently at a wedding I catered."

"Gossiping and spreading lies isn't enough? Now you have to bring messages too?"

"Lies?" Luisa repeated, offended. "Everything I've said about Yasmin is true."

"That's a matter of opinion," Orlando corrected her.

"Wow!" Luisa laughed scornfully. "You're blind."

"Why should that concern you?"

"It doesn't," Luisa stressed. "Why do you think Manuel wants to see her? I'd ask myself that question."

"If I were you," he strolled back to where Luisa stood and hovered over her, "I'd be cautious what I say and to whom."

"Are you threatening me?" Luisa stared at him, wide-eyed.

"I'm letting you know that your mouth can cause serious trouble."

"What makes you so sure Yasmin isn't using you to make Manuel jealous so they can get back together?"

"Do you know where he lives?" he demanded. "Can you give me his address? Cell number? That's useful information."

"Now you're acting like Raul—foolish. Even if I did have it, I would never give it to you."

"Don't mention his comments or any information about him again."

"Afraid that *Yaz*," she sang the name spitefully, "will go back with him?"

"For someone who talks so much about regret, it seems to me that you'll be the one who will regret meddling and gossiping."

"Before that happens, you'll be sorry you got involved and took Yasmin Arias seriously."

* * *

"Why did you bring them?" Raul demanded, gesturing toward Ismenia and Ani.

"I need your permission?" Yasmin asked, embarrassed that he would make such a nasty comment in their presence.

"So much for changing for the better as you get older," Ismenia retorted.

"We can wait for you in the lobby," Ani said, turning toward the elevator.

Yasmin placed her hand on Ani's shoulder. "Only two people can see Mami at a time." She repeated what she'd been told by the guard at the security desk. "You and Ismenia can see Mami while I wait here." She wanted to speak to Raul about the situation with Orlando.

"The doctor said Ma needs rest," Raul emphasized.

"Meaning what?" Yasmin snapped. "That no one can see her? Is she alone?"

"Isabel and Maria are with her now."

She turned to Ismenia. "Let Isabel know you're here to see Mami. They can wait wherever they want until you're ready to leave."

"If we can't go in, we'll come back another day," Ani said, reluctant to go up to Carmen's room.

"No. We came to see Carmen, and we will," Ismenia said, taking Ani's arm and leading her towards the elevator.

"Watch what you say in front of Ma," Raul warned.

Ismenia stopped and turned toward him. "You think everyone is like you, Raul, without common sense or self-control? You're the one who needs to think before you speak or act."

"You," he pointed to her, "are you lecturing me?"

"I curse the day I ever considered you more than what you are—a fool."

Raul laughed. "You and many, many more. You have the same option I gave them. Stay angry, or calm down. Neither will make me lose sleep." Turning his back to Ismenia, Raul gestured for Yasmin to follow him. He walked down the hall toward the window.

"He needs prayer," Ani commented.

"That's exactly what I need," Raul shouted, chuckling. "Hopefully, God will hear it and change me."

Touch his heart, Yasmin prayed, dragging herself toward him. "Did you purposely forget to mention that visits for Mami were restricted?" she asked before he spoke. He mentioned her condition but overlooked or purposely refused to mention the doctor's restrictions on visiting.

"Now you know," he replied, unconcerned.

Yasmin decided not to pursue the subject. Her mother was getting the treatment she needed, and that was all that mattered. Changing the subject, she spoke to him in the same acidic tone. "What is it you want to talk about?"

"I don't want Ma to know what happened with that traitor."

"You know as well as I do that Orlando is a trustworthy and valuable friend," she corrected, "one you don't deserve."

"Don't tell me what he is or isn't," he corrected. "You won't be around next time I see him," he muttered smugly. "Then you'll visit him in the emergency room."

She felt her knees weaken and pressed her body against the wall to stop herself from collapsing. The dull ache on her temples began to throb. She pushed the tips of her fingers on her temples and closed her eyes for a moment.

"You should see a doctor about those migraines."

Straightening her shoulders, she lifted her chin and looked directly at him. "Orlando has never been disrespectable of your friendship or of me."

"Not my concern. I would have taken full advantage and made sure the beating was earned."

"That's what you wanted to tell me?" She was eager to get away from him.

"Ma is in a delicate condition," Raul began.

"That's your accomplishment, not mine."

"I don't know how long she's going to be hospitalized. I don't want her to be alone," Raul continued as if Yasmin hadn't spoken. "I already told Isabel when she should be here, and now I'm telling you. This week, you'll be here from 12:00 to 2:00 every day. If Ma is not sent home by the weekend, I'll make another schedule. Be here on time. Don't leave her alone to make any calls or to see anyone. Come alone. Understood?"

Crossing her arms, Yasmin stared at him with lifted eyebrows. He made plans without considering her needs. He didn't care what her work hours were or if she could take the time off. Leaving the office early or arriving late was impossible with the time he scheduled. He stood before her, a smug expression on his face, as if he expected her to adhere to his demands without question.

"When are you and Isabel going to be with Mami?"

"You just worry about the time you should be here."

She pressed her lips together. Telling Raul what he could do with his mandates was as futile as arguing.

Straightening her shoulders, Yasmin steadied herself. She knew responding in a nasty or curt way was easier than following the Lord's example of being humble. She decided to refocus her thinking and perceive his request as a gain, not a loss.

She wanted to visit her mother without worrying about disputes. His plan provided the serenity and privacy she preferred. She decided to take the week off. The next morning, she would notify the supervisor that her mother was hospitalized and add that she needed to take some vacation time. Oddly, just days before, she had attended a meeting to discuss excess vacation and sick days. She agreed to get paid for some and take the others at her leisure.

"Thank you," she murmured, gazing up. The Lord had prepared the path before the calamity struck. She could be with her mother without consequences or issues at her job. It was an unexpected blessing, she thought, astounded by God's immense grace and mercy.

Their conversation over, Yasmin walked away. She stopped by the entrance to glance back. Raul was looking out the window, his shoulders erect, his chin lifted high. The relentless warrior was always controlling everyone and everything.

"Help him, Lord," she prayed. "Change his icy heart so he has empathy for others."

Chapter 15

"Where's Clara?" Orlando asked.

"She's at a baby shower for a colleague." Mario handed him a glass of soda and sat. "I'm waiting for her call to pick her up. She'll be happy to hear you dropped by. She's complaining that you've been ignoring her calls."

"To you and to Mom." He took several sips and then held the glass in his hand as he continued speaking. "Clara doesn't understand that things get hectic."

"Violent too." Mario's eyes lingered on Orlando's injuries. "She'll be upset when she sees those bruises."

"It's nothing," Orlando shrugged. "But she'll overreact."

"I agree with you," Mario nodded. "Clara complains she wants to spend time with me, and I'm always at work. Today I'm home, and she's with coworkers at a baby shower. She was annoyed when I suggested we go out. She complained that if she hadn't had an invitation, I wouldn't have made plans."

"Relationships are complicated." He still hadn't heard from Yasmin. Her silence bothered him and reinforced his intuition that their relationship would be affected by the scenario the night before.

Mario nodded, grinning. "I don't argue. I stay out of Clara's way until she calms down."

"Is that the trick to staying together?" Orlando smirked and sipped his soda.

"It's my way to handle the situation. When Clara is upset, she won't listen. Arguing is a waste of time and energy. I let her have her say. Then when she calms down, we talk and work it out."

"Working out problems is a challenge," Orlando said, aware that Mario was describing the same scenario he experienced with Yasmin.

"It's about being perceptive, knowing when to bring up issues, address problems, and come to an agreement. It's not about winning or losing." Mario smiled. "I hear you're getting married."

Orlando burst into laughter. His mother was excited and thrilled that he was finally making a commitment. "I told Mom I'm considering getting serious. She's already planning grandkids."

"One leads to the other. With Yasmin?"

He nodded. "She can be as stressful as Clara."

"That's part of being in a relationship. Like everything else in life, there are good and bad times," Mario said. "Clara wasn't thrilled with the news about you and Yasmin."

"I'm not surprised. She'll object, joining a few others that share her misguided opinion."

Mario smiled. "Clara keeps complaining that you had many to choose from and picked the worst."

"I'm sure Mom feels that way, too, although she won't admit it." Orlando wished there was a way they could know and see Yasmin the way he did. "Eventually they'll realize they are wrong about her."

"True. Your parents weren't too fond of me when I married Clara. It took time for them to accept me. I think that happens with many couples. At least you're close to her family."

Orlando shook his head.

"Carmen disapproves?" Mario lifted his brows and stared at him in surprise. "Raul?"

"Not sure about Carmen," Orlando clarified. "Raul is definitely opposed."

"Did you tell him you're serious about Yasmin? That you're proposing?"

"Never had a chance to discuss it, and now he won't listen."

Mario gestured at the cut over Orlando's eye. "Raul is a fighter. Talking is not how he handles any situation. Clara kept saying Yasmin would cause the end of your friendship."

"She didn't. I wanted to tell Raul about us, but before we could speak, he visited Yasmin and found me there. He assumed the worst."

"That's when you fought?"

"Yasmin was frantic. If Clara or Mom knew, they would be too. I don't want to rile them up." Although he knew Mario wouldn't mention anything they discussed, he stressed the last three words. "I haven't spoken to Yasmin about it yet. From the grim expression on her face when I left this morning, she's envisioning horrific scenarios."

"She witnessed it?" Mario asked with disbelief.

"Raul doesn't think when he's angry. He just reacts. And thus why Carmen is in the hospital again." He worried about Carmen's reaction when she found out what happened. Her curiosity would spark questions that Raul would ignore. Even for his mother's well-being, Raul refused to pretend everything was fine between them. From his crude attitude, she would discern something was amiss.

"Carmen, Clara, and Eva have reasons to be concerned, and so does Yasmin," Mario commented. "This situation is serious." Mario leaned forward with a solemn expression on his face. "Raul is not the kind of guy you want to have as an enemy."

"He'll get over it," Orlando said. The Lord was in charge. He had prayed and placed the situation in His hands, and now he would wait calmly for a resolution. "I still consider Raul my family despite what happened. Sometimes your own relatives can be your worst enemies."

"You're in a tough position. I hope things work out."

Orlando nodded. His cell phone rang. He didn't recognize the number but answered it anyway to see if it was Yasmin.

"Orlando?"

He gestured for Mario to wait as he stood up and walked into the kitchen. "Where are you, Yaz?"

"I'm at the hospital walking Ani and Ismenia to the elevator. After they leave, I'm going to spend some time with Mami. I borrowed Ismenia's cell phone to call you."

"Where's yours?" he asked, annoyed.

"With everything that happened, I didn't get a chance to charge it."

"How do you feel? Are you all right?"

"The migraine is back, although I'm taking medicine as prescribed."

"You should be home resting. Did you eat?"

She was silent.

"You need to take care of yourself, for both of us. When are you going home?"

"Visiting hours are until 8:00. I'm not sure when Raul will ask me to leave. He's in charge."

"Don't antagonize him." Orlando paused, refusing to worry her more than she already was by adding that he wouldn't tolerate it. "Did you drive?"

"Yes. I'm staying at Ani's tonight."

"Best place for you to be right now." He approved of her decision. Being alone in her apartment would only depress her. "Call me when you leave the hospital. I'll meet you there."

* * *

"I don't understand." Yasmin propped the pillows behind her and lay back. She wiped the tears from her cheeks with a tissue Ani gave her. "This had to happen now when I finally decided to change my life. It doesn't seem fair."

Ani sat on the bed and smiled slightly. "The only one who knows why and when things happen is the Lord. I'm sure there is a purpose for all of this. Something good will come from this situation."

Placing her hands on her temples, Yasmin sat motionless. The pain became numb if she remained still.

"Wait, and be patient," Ani advised. "Asking why serves no purpose. It happened. Accept it."

"You should have seen them fighting as if they were enemies—strangers." With the horrid scenario still vivid, Yasmin shivered involuntarily. Her worst fear was that Raul's threats would materialize. She closed her eyes and prayed without speaking. *Please don't let them meet again. Keep them far apart.*

"I'm sorry you had to go through that dreadful experience again. With Carmen hospitalized, it's rough. Remember, our Lord never gives us more to handle than we can manage. You need to remain calm, continue praying, and ask for guidance."

"I'm trying my best." Yasmin longed to be as tranquil and at ease as Ani, but instead she felt agitated and troubled. The issue between Orlando and Raul wasn't her only concern. When she entered Carmen's room after Ani and Ismenia left, her mother burst into tears, sobbed uncontrollably, and tried to speak, but her words were incomprehensible. Anxiously, Yasmin ran to the nurse's station to inform them. The doctor was still doing rounds and rushed to Carmen's room behind the nurses.

He prescribed a sedative that was added to the IV. A few minutes later, Carmen was asleep.

Before the doctor left, she took the opportunity to inquire about her mother's condition and the restricted visits. His reply worried her. Stress and anxiety were a strong factor in causing the minor stroke. He added that Carmen needed a change of lifestyle. Because her agitation caused her blood pressure to be unstable, it was best to limit visitors to ensure rest and relaxation. He stressed that they were lucky. The test results showed that her internal organs were not affected. Yasmin knew it wasn't luck; the Lord had intervened. He was merciful and knew the load on her shoulders was enough.

Ani cleared her throat. Lifting her gaze, Yasmin refocused.

"Mami slept most of the time I was with her." Yasmin blinked several times to clear her vision. "I prayed until she woke up. We spoke for a little while. Mami was groggy, her speech a bit slurred. She said Orlando had dropped by for a few minutes. She asked if I was crying because Orlando and Raul had fought over me." Yasmin laughed dryly, despite her grim mood. "I thought Mami was asleep. I had no idea she was watching me. Raul arrived with his usual attitude. I rushed out, and we didn't finish our conversation."

Raul made no attempt to be civil and didn't try to lessen the emotional stress on their mother. He continued to blame her for their mother's ailment. He followed Yasmin down the hall as she left, demanding to know what she'd said to upset Carmen. Without replying, she entered the elevator and turned her back to him as the doors closed.

"Stop brooding, Yasmin. Overthinking things does not resolve anything. How did Carmen find out they fought? In her condition, who would dare tell her?"

"Luisa," Yasmin replied angrily.

"Pray that the Lord touches her heart and Raul's."

Yasmin shook her head. Praying for Luisa and Maria seemed like rewarding them for their malice. As for Raul, she was praying for him but doubted he would ever change.

"You should see the look on your face," Ani chided. "Walking with the Lord requires a change of heart and mind, Yasmin. That includes praying and asking for blessings for everyone, even our enemies. The Lord is the only one who can change people. As much as we want to believe we can do it, we can't." Ani stood up. "What time is Orlando coming by?"

"I'm not sure. He said he'll meet me here." She was glad she would have some time for herself before he arrived. She needed to organize her thoughts and plan how she would tell him her decision.

* * *

Orlando watched Ani enter the bedroom and close the door. Then he directed his attention to Yasmin. She was dressed in a T-shirt with jeans and slippers, her hair loose. She looked pale, and her eyes were swollen. The solemn expression confirmed his anxieties. He was about to encounter the effects provoked by the incident of the night before.

"Yaz." He took her hand and led her to the sofa. He waited until she sat down and then sat next to her and put his arm around her shoulders. He studied her face. "Why aren't you in bed?"

"I'd prefer to talk."

"You think it would matter to Ani if we're here or in the bedroom?"

She shook her head.

"We can talk some other time if you don't feel up to it."

Without responding, she wrapped her arms around his neck and rested her head on his shoulder. He held her tightly and felt her shoulders heaving. "How are you going to get better if you don't control your emotions?" he whispered in her ear.

She pressed herself against him. He held her firmly, resting his head on hers until she calmed down. Moving back, she looked up at him and smiled.

"I spoke to Raul," she began, clearing her throat. "I tried to convince him . . ."

"Why did you waste your time?" he interrupted. "Let me handle that situation. You worry about us."

She shook her head, "I don't want you to fight again."

"That's the least of my concerns right now."

She lowered her gaze. "Did you meet with Raul when you went to the hospital?"

"He was there. He waited outside until I left. Nothing happened."

"That should make me feel better?"

"Why not?" He was irked by her question. "Discussing it with Raul served no purpose. I meant what I said. What happened isn't going to change my routine. My life continues as is."

248

"I was . . . worried."

"It's absurd for you to make yourself sick about nothing."

"Your life is nothing?"

"Don't exaggerate. Raul is not going to kill me."

"He will hurt you. That's his intent."

"And before he does, you'll have a nervous breakdown and end up in the hospital. It's ridiculous."

She stood and walked to the window. "Call it what you want, Orlando." She lifted her chin and crossed her arms. "You really expect me not to worry about your safety? Raul is vicious. Just imagining what he'll do . . ." She shook her head.

"You can't allow your fears to overwhelm your emotions and reasoning to that extent."

"I'm not crazy." She was indignant.

"You're not rational." He stood before her. "There's no reason for you to worry about ifs or maybes. Don't create scenarios that may never happen. It's a waste of time and energy." He gestured toward the sofa. "Sit down, please." Sitting next to her, he turned her head so they were facing each other. "Our relationship—you—that's what's important to me, Yaz."

"All I've caused you is grief."

"Also meaning and joy. My life was empty and routine before you returned." Orlando wanted to add that she had stirred a new need in him for a serious relationship. Marriage and starting a family was now a priority.

"You can't deny the complications, rejection, and loss."

"That's your perception, Yaz, not mine."

"I've always wondered if Dad would have ever forgiven me, if we would have made up."

"Why bring that up now?"

"Do you think Raul will ever forgive you?"

"Probably not. I accept that fact."

"You're deceiving yourself. Just like I would if I said I didn't care that my father didn't forgive me. I do, and I regret it." She placed her hand on her chest. "I've learned to accept it, but it hurts. I can't say I shared the good times or the years of closeness with my father like you shared with Raul." She paused to take a deep breath and clear her voice. "You're lying to me and to yourself if you say it doesn't matter. It does."

"You matter to me too."

"Is that enough?" She lowered her gaze, "Do you love me so much that you'll never regret losing Raul's friendship or getting hurt because of me?"

"Let it go, Yasmin," he ordered, annoyed by the direction the conversation was taking.

"You know me more than my family does. You know that since I was thrown out, I've lived with guilt, regret, and fear. That was the reason I stayed away."

"Let's focus on the present. Be direct. Tell me what you really want to say." He wanted her to get to the point.

"I dread the consequences of your confrontation. I feel guilty because whether you want to admit it or not, I'm at fault. You are and always have been a trustworthy friend. Raul refuses to believe that. He's just like Dad. The truth, as hard as it is to accept, is that my father would have never forgiven me."

"You're making assumptions without basis. Who knows what would have really happened, what Roberto would have done if he'd gotten to see you before he passed away?"

She shook her head. "You knew my father and what he was capable of, how rigid and coldhearted he was. Raul is just like him. Dad would have done the same or worse. I don't want that to happen to you."

Orlando was silent. She had just explained the reasons for her decision, which he perceived wasn't going to be favorable. "And your solution to that is?"

"I was thinking that . . ." She paused and bit her lip.

He waited, studying her. She lowered her gaze and then her head. She stared at her hands that were clasped tightly on her lap. He had seen the same gestures repeatedly. She was struggling to be straightforward, afraid to speak up.

"Just say it, Yaz."

"We can't," she was crying softly, "stay together." She blurted out the last words quickly and then covered her face and sobbed.

"Look directly at me when you say that, Yasmin Arias."

Refusing to face him, she kept her gaze low and continued hoarsely. "I know," she cleared her throat, "that you didn't want to fight with Raul. If . . . if we're not together, he'll have to leave you alone."

"Raul doesn't have to do anything," he corrected, irate by her decision. "He won't care if we're together or not. Our friendship will still be over."

"There won't be a need to fight," she stressed, her gaze still lowered.

"He knows where I am. It's not a choice, Yaz. If we meet, I have to defend myself."

"If he hurts you or you hurt him, then what? Again, I must live with guilt and regret for the rest of my life. I won't. I can't." She raised her tear-filled eyes. "I've lived that way for too long. I refuse to go back to that type of life."

"Who's asking you to live like that?" He waited for a reply and continued when she stared at him wide-eyed in silence. "Not me. You choose to see the glass half-empty instead of half-full. You never want to see the bright side. You're too pessimistic, emotional, and unrealistic to face the facts and see the situation from a different perspective."

"Think so?" She straightened her shoulders, speaking in a clear, firm, tone. "I'm trying to get you out of a situation you don't want to be in so you'll be safe and your life will be back to the way it was. I'm making the sacrifice so neither of you gets hurt."

"Don't expect me to be thankful or show any gratitude for your grand sacrifice." Orlando tried not to sound as distraught as he felt. "You misunderstood me. I don't need a protector, a referee, or a problem solver. I need a woman who will love me, be brave enough to stay with me, and share the best and the worst. I want someone who is supportive and loving, who trusts my judgment and accepts my decisions."

"You know the way out." She pointed to the door without facing him.

He watched her stand and drag herself to the bedroom with her shoulders slumped. Without looking back, she entered and closed the door.

Taking his leather jacket, Orlando headed out.

"Orlando." It was Ani. "Can I talk to you for a moment?"

He nodded and followed Ani to the kitchen. She sat opposite him. He wasn't in the mood for conversation. He wanted a stiff drink to numb the desolation he felt.

"I was praying while you spoke. It's obvious from the pained expression on your face that Yasmin made a drastic decision."

"For both of us. It ended before it started."

"That's how it seems," Ani said calmly. "You felt the same way a few weeks ago, and the situation changed. Now, in the middle of the storm, you can't give up. This is the time to be strong. You," she pointed to him, "managed to bring her this far. Are you going to give up now when she needs you the most?"

"She just broke up with me," he reiterated. He was certain Ani misunderstood the situation.

"Mere words," Ani smiled. "Yasmin loves you. It took time for her to accept that and let go of the past, to be brave enough to date you. I know she confided in you about Manuel."

"You knew?" he asked, stunned by her revelation.

Ani shrugged. "Her behavior, the way she spoke, her determination to avoid him, her fear of getting into another relationship—sometimes words aren't necessary."

"True. Everything you're telling me is accurate, but I'm not sure I can accept or be in a relationship that's this unstable. This time it's the issue with Raul. Who knows what the next reason will be?"

"It's a tough situation. Yasmin's fears are valid and real. Don't expect her to see things through your lens. She can't. Look at it from another perspective. In every relationship, one of the two is weaker in different areas. You're the stronger one right now. As you did before, open her eyes and help her understand her misconceptions. With the Lord's help, what we see as impossible can become a triumph, a victory. There is a purpose for all of this. Our Lord doesn't make mistakes. I can assure you that this situation will make your relationship and love stronger."

Her words appeased him. Still, he felt ambivalent. What was he supposed to do? "Truthfully, I'm not sure what the next step is. Her decision is premature. She never gave us a chance."

"Time," Ani replied simply. "I agree with you, Orlando. Yasmin should have waited, thought about it, and made a reasonable decision. Unfortunately, not everyone handles pressure the same way. You know she crumbles under it. She isolates and secludes herself. Despite her difficult character and frustrating behavior, you love her. Yes?"

He nodded.

"Is she worth the sacrifice?"

Grinning, he nodded again.

"Then give it time. Let the Lord handle it. As He did in the past, He will provide and give you so much more than you can possibly imagine."

* * *

Yasmin was headed to the bathroom when she saw Orlando exit. Stopping abruptly, she covered her mouth with both hands to silence her sobs. She wanted to run after him but forced herself to remain motionless.

She'd made her decision and knew full well the consequences. Straightening her shoulders, she walked into the kitchen. "What were you and Orlando talking about?"

"Time, the importance of not making hasty decisions," Ani replied as she poured herself a glass of water, placed the pitcher in the refrigerator, and then sat down.

"It's the best option," Yasmin said. Pulling back one of the chairs, she dropped limply onto it.

"Is it?" Ani challenged. "The first serious problem in your relationship and you give up. *You*," she stressed the word, "decide. Forget there's two that need to communicate, to come to an agreement, and act. One, which is you, forgets the needs of the other and makes a final decision. Is that how you think the Lord wants you to solve this?"

She stared at Ani in silence. Calmly and in a quiet, loving tone, Ani destroyed her rock-solid resolve. Although Yasmin had prayed for guidance, she'd made the same mistake again and used her own judgment. She reacted swiftly instead of waiting.

"When are you going to stop focusing on yourself and start thinking about Orlando? How he feels? His pain and his loss?"

"I am thinking about him. That's exactly why we can't stay together."

"What makes you so sure your decision will fix the issue with Raul?"

Yasmin lowered her gaze. Orlando told her it wouldn't matter if they broke up. Perhaps he was right. "I'll pray it does," she blurted out.

"You could have done that without breaking up with Orlando. You forgot that the Lord brought you this far and united you. Fear and faith don't go together. It's one or the other." Ani paused and stared at her in silence. "It is during the challenges and rough times that you have to remain firm. Remember that as the Lord did before, He will act again, take charge of the situation, and give you victory."

Yasmin wiped her damp cheeks. "Why would God continue helping me when every time He does, I mess it up?"

"He doesn't keep a manual of our mistakes and point them out to us when we come to Him. He wants us to trust him, to believe, to be firm in our faith. There are no limits or maximums. He is there when we need him—always."

"Orlando deserves better. All I've done is cause him misery."

"I recall someone being delighted and very much in love when she was dating. That someone was brave enough to call Orlando to start a relationship. Why give up now?"

"I've caused him endless grief. Pain."

"We were never promised a life without challenges. There will always be problems along with happiness. If you think Orlando deserves better, pray for wisdom to become the woman he deserves. You have the tools. The Lord empowers us for every challenge. He never puts on our shoulders more than we can handle. He molds our character through our experiences so we can become more like Him. Our lives become an example for others. Remember that."

"I prayed for guidance," Yasmin murmured.

"And instead of waiting for His reply, being patient, you decided to help the Lord by doing what you thought was best. He doesn't need your help. All He needs is for you to hand Him your problems and allow Him to act."

* * *

Orlando placed the bottle of liquor on the table after pouring a shot. He held it in his hand and stared at it. Drinking was not the solution, nor would it erase the emptiness or sense of loss he felt. Placing the shot glass on the coffee table, he lay on the couch and stared at the ceiling.

Ani's eloquent words had grounded him and temporarily halted the emotional whirlwind Yasmin's decision prompted. Just two nights later, and he still felt wretched, his rationale battling with his emotions. Understanding Yasmin's weaknesses and why she behaved as she did in no way stopped the misery he felt. Ironically, he had anticipated her regression—expected it. What he'd overlooked was how devastated he would feel.

Yasmin took on the martyr role with excellence. She willingly punished herself and gave up anything and everything that would provide happiness. To Orlando's misfortune, that also included him.

"Lord," he said, unable to think of anything else to add to his prayer. The past two days and nights seemed endless. He couldn't fathom how he would endure weeks or months without her. Work had become a drudgery. Lifting weights helped him forget his anxiety temporarily. But that evening, he didn't even have the energy for that.

He picked up his cell phone and looked for Yasmin's number.

Was she asleep? Thinking about him? Crying over giving up her happiness for a worthless cause? He doubted she had come to that realization; otherwise, they would be together.

He was tempted to press dial. Would she answer? She would recognize his number and know it was him. Perhaps it was best not to call, to stay distant as she requested.

He paced from one side of the living room to the other, the cell phone in his hand. Life had been simple when there was no emotional attachment. Moving on had been easy. His routine and social interactions had continued uninterrupted. But Yasmin changed that. Since they'd met in front of the funeral parlor, everything had been different.

He loved her and wanted her to be his wife, to be part of his life. He continued praying, asking the Lord to open Yasmin's eyes and give her discernment to understand that self-sacrifice was not necessary. She deserved to be happy.

Sitting on the sofa, he leaned back and closed his eyes. He envisioned Yasmin in his arms, her head nestled under his neck, her body pressed against his. It felt so real. It was as if she were there.

Opening his eyes, he pressed dial on his phone.

"Orlando?"

He hesitated before speaking. Hearing her voice was a sour reminder that they were separated.

"Do you know what time it is?" she asked.

"Yes," he replied, glancing at the cable box. "It's 4:32 in the morning." She sounded wide awake and alert, and she spoke clearly. Like him, she was unable to rest. "I needed to hear your voice," he said. "Are you taking care of yourself? Taking your medication? Eating?"

"Doing my best," she replied.

"How can you take care of Carmen if you get sick too?" he asked, bothered by her self-destructive behaviors.

"I'm all right."

"Saying it doesn't mean you are," he stressed. "Please take care of yourself. How's Carmen?"

"It's been tough. She's been getting sedatives to keep her calm and control her blood pressure, which is still fluctuating. Thank the Lord that the EKG and CT scan were normal. The doctor said until her blood pressure becomes stable, she won't be discharged."

"Sedatives to keep her calm?" he repeated, noting her concern. "What happened?"

"She's depressed and cries all the time. She looks . . . very sad."

"You need to be strong, Yaz, for Carmen and for yourself. Everything will be fine."

"The counselor is back," she humored.

"And too far away to take you into my arms and console you."

She was silent.

"At least the tests results are positive. That's good news," he said to reassure her everything would be fine. "Soon Carmen will be going home, probably by the end of the week. She is strong like her daughter. She might surprise you one of these days and perk up."

"Mr. Fortune Teller?"

"If I recall correctly, in a conversation we had at the diner after going to the burial, you were the fortune teller," he reminded her. "Or was it an assumption?"

"Yeah. Seems like an eternity since that happened."

"Time moves quickly." Over the past two days, time had dragged on at an unbearable drudge. "I miss you, Yaz," he said softly. "I want to see you, be with you."

"Mami found out the two of you fought over me," she said anxiously.

"We know who told her. Luisa or Maria, or both. Only they could be so foolish and thoughtless."

"If you hadn't fought with Raul because of me, you would have visited her with them. They wouldn't have had anything to say."

"Wrong, Yaz. They look for anything to gossip about, to make it bigger and more outrageous than what it actually is."

"I'm sure when Mami gets better, she'll have plenty to say about it."

"Maybe not." He didn't share her grim outlook. "Positive thinking gives you a better perspective on everything."

"The therapist is back?"

"I love you, Yaz. Whatever role I need to play in your life to make you happy, to support you during a crisis, to help in any way I can, I'll do it."

There was silence, and then he heard her whisper hoarsely, "I know."

"I'm not giving you up. This situation with Raul will end, and instead of calling, I'll be taking you in my arms."

She was silent again and then spoke. "Get some rest. You have to work tomorrow."

"You don't?" he asked, noting she hadn't said we.

"I took the week off. It was the only way I could be with Mami during the time the boss scheduled."

"Please, Yaz," he began.

"I know," she interrupted, annoyed. "You think I want to give either one of you more reasons to fight? Raul did me a favor. He scheduled me first, and I found out that family can visit earlier, so I'm spending more time with Mami. I'm happy I don't have to see him, Isabel, or those two blabbermouths."

"Great," he said, delighted. "I'd like to see Carmen. What time do you get there?"

"Raul can drop by at any time," she warned, sourly.

Orlando remained silent. He didn't care about that. He wasn't afraid to meet him, nor would he make any attempt to avoid him. Had Raul been serious about his threat, he would have already fought him, not that she would understand, listen, or agree with him. He decided not to press the issue any further. "Please take care of yourself, Yaz, for yourself, for Carmen, and for me."

"Good night, Orlando." She hung up.

He lay down on the sofa. Hearing her voice appeased him somewhat. She was still apprehensive and edgy, which meant waiting.

Time was the key, as Ani had said.

He realized it would be foolish not to follow Ani's keen advice. She'd been instrumental in uniting him with Yasmin. Her insight and support were a blessing. The Lord had strategically placed her in his life and Yasmin's to light their path, union, and relationship. She was like a guardian angel, one he was grateful to have.

Ani reminded him that he had weathered the storm and persevered with the Lord's help. He could not take credit for that on his own. His prayers had been answered. He was blessed twice—when Yasmin started dating him and when she called to admit she loved him. As Ani pointed out, Yasmin was brave. Telling him the truth and speaking about such a horrific experience took courage.

Orlando had tried to persuade Yasmin to be strong for herself and for Carmen, but the same applied to him. After all, Ani stressed that he was the stronger one in the relationship. Caving in and allowing his emotions to overpower him was straying not only from the Lord's purpose but also from his principles, character, and beliefs. Actions spoke, as his mother had taught him. His vow not to give up Yasmin had to be backed up with actions. He had the best ally working beside him to achieve victory—the Lord.

How many times would the Lord bless him or anyone for that matter? He didn't know, but he knew that he had to trust. Believing and praying were the only ways to restore his relationship with Yasmin. The Lord had united them once, and if He intended for them to be together, they would be. All he had to do was wait patiently and calmly without allowing the pain, anguish, and solitude to diminish his faith.

More at ease and filled with hope and anticipation, he refocused his thinking. To propose, he needed to buy an engagement ring.

"Is that what you want me to do, Lord?" he asked aloud, grinning.

At work that day and the day before, he couldn't shake the thought of purchasing the ring, but he resisted the idea. He questioned the purpose of buying a ring when their relationship hadn't materialized. Buying it and being prepared to propose when the time arose was trusting the Lord completely.

He would take a shower and snatch a few hours of rest. He would return to his routine the next day and work diligently and enthusiastically as he always had. He would continue visiting Clara after work, enjoy dinner, and chat with her and Mario. He planned to call his parents more often and share with them his aspirations, joy, and strength in the Lord.

While waiting for the Lord to resolve the situation with Yasmin, he would search for a ring, take his time, view available styles, and compare prices. Once he purchased it, he would carry it with him.

Flowers. The word occurred to him as he entered the bathroom. Returning to the living room, he sat at his desk and searched for flower shops online. He ordered two flower arrangements, one with red roses and the other with yellow. They would arrive that morning and the day after, each before Yasmin headed to the hospital. He would make sure she knew he was constantly thinking about her. Until they were together again, he would send gifts, trinkets, and flowers—daily reminders of his love and dedication.

Chapter 16

Yasmin looked outside at the beautiful, sunny, brisk day. It was another day to be thankful—a new beginning.

Her eyes filled with tears. "I know You bring light where there is darkness and hope where there is desperation, but I feel like I've lost everything. After so many years living in fear, immersed in my pain and in the past, I finally moved forward and started again. Then everything crumbled before me."

Her relationship had begun and then disintegrated within hours. As happened with her father, Raul's impromptu arrival caused a radical change in her life. If there had been a purpose the first time, she'd yet to see it. For the second, she was just as lost. She knew the Lord hadn't brought Orlando into her life and filled her heart with love just to rip them apart. How could any good come from the situation with Raul? She wanted to have hope, to see the bright side as Ani did.

Yasmin gazed at Carmen who was asleep. It was gratifying to see her resting. Had she been home, she would be cooking, cleaning, fussing about, and not following the doctor's orders. Although she hadn't been given any sedatives that morning, she was sleeping soundly.

Yasmin sat on a chair near the window. She thought about Orlando's call and missed him. She thought about him all the time, about being in his arms and cuddling next to him.

Hearing his voice had delighted and distressed her. She had been praying that the Lord would unravel the conflict between him and Raul. Then, as Orlando promised, instead of talking over the phone, they could be together.

His vow that he wouldn't give her up had made her self-conscious. She was unable to rest after speaking to him, and then she revisited her conversation with Ani. She'd been hasty and focused on her fears rather than Orlando's feelings. Being considerate and empathetic had never occurred to her. She'd forged ahead, oblivious to his pain. She did not deserve him.

His comment had hurt, but it was true. He needed someone in his life who would support him, accept his decisions, and stand by him. All she'd done since they'd met was cause him grief with her distrust, accusations, and criticism.

Yet he loved and accepted her as she was. He continued to be patient, indulgent, caring, and incredibly romantic. She had received a bouquet of red roses that morning. Ani had carried it into the bedroom, all smiles. Yasmin sat up, took the card out of the tiny envelope, and read his message. "I'm here for you, Yaz. Always will be. I love you."

Now she leaned her head back, trying unsuccessfully not to cry. Was her decision worth the pain she and Orlando were enduring?

Please guide me. I know fear and faith don't go together, but I'm scared, she admitted silently, overwhelmed with sadness. *I don't want them to fight again. Please ensure they don't see each other.*

"What are you so upset about, Yasmin?"

Startled by her mother's voice, Yasmin wiped her face quickly with her hands and blinked repeatedly to clear her gaze. She placed the chair closer to the headboard and sat down. She cleared her throat and spoke firmly. "Nice to see you awake. How do you feel, Mami?"

"Better. Rested." Carmen took the remote and adjusted the bed so she was sitting up. "It's difficult to sleep at night. There's too much noise— nurses talking, coming in and out at all hours."

"I've been here a while, but I didn't want to wake you," Yasmin explained, happy that she'd allowed her to sleep several hours. "All test results are good so far," she told her. "The doctor said you'll be going home soon."

"Thank God! I'm tired of being here. I don't like hospitals, and staying in bed all day is a waste of time," Carmen complained. Then she added in a serious tone, "I'd like an answer to my question."

"I was just praying . . ." she paused and then added, "so things work out."

"I've been doing the same," Carmen agreed in a disheartened tone. "Our family is a mess. I've been here four days, and I notice you always come alone. Raul and Isabel come together or with Luisa and Maria."

"Your blood pressure is still unstable. Worry and stress won't help that." Yasmin wondered if Raul had considered how their mother would feel about his obnoxious schedule. "You need tranquility and rest. The doctor keeps stressing that."

"You expect me to ignore everything that's happened?" Carmen pointed out. "The three of you must think I'm blind. You come at different times. You ignore each other. Who would think you're related or family?"

"Raul went to my apartment to pick me up and even offered to give me a ride," Yasmin said, hoping to appease Carmen's anxieties.

"That's what he's supposed to do." Carmen reached for the box of tissues on the bed. Taking several, she dried her tears.

"Please, Mami." Standing, Yasmin embraced her. "You need to . . ."

"I'm your mother. You don't correct me," Carmen scolded her and moved back so they faced each other. "Now everything is a big secret? No one wants to tell me the truth? Why did Raul and Orlando fight?"

Yasmin sat down again and stared at her hands in silence. She refused to discuss what happened. She wouldn't cause her mother undue grief or stress.

"Yasmin," Carmen said her name softly. "Please, no more lies."

"I love him." Yasmin was blunt. She was surprised she could say it without bursting into tears.

Carmen stared at her, wide-eyed, and then spoke. "Finally, you admit the truth."

"We haven't been together since I returned, as you believed," she clarified.

Carmen shook her head, "Our thoughts and our minds can deceive us. What we believe to be true isn't necessarily reality. It's a harsh lesson to learn at my age."

Yasmin was stunned by the revelation and realized that her mother was right. She had deceived herself and believed she could resolve the conflict between Raul and Orlando. Only the Lord could do that. It was what Ani meant by helping the Lord. Her faith continued to be frail. She was still allowing her fears to control her.

"Why hasn't Orlando come to see me, to tell me about your relationship?"

Yasmin kept a blank expression to disguise the remorse she felt. Had she trusted the Lord and been patient, Orlando would have spoken to her mother and clarified everything. Her decision made it appear as if he were irresponsible and disrespectful.

"Am I talking to myself?" Carmen asked. "Talk to me about your relationship. Tell me why they fought. What was the cause?"

Yasmin wanted to get up and pretend she needed to step out, but she knew that evading the conversation by walking out was useless. Her mother would keep harping on the subject until she got the answers she sought.

"Why do I always have to find out everything that happens with my family through someone else?" Taking more tissues, Carmen dried her tears.

"Why are you crying, Ma?" Raul stood at the foot of the bed, glaring at Yasmin.

"Stop looking at her like that," Carmen rebuked him. "We've had enough violence and problems in our . . . I don't even know what to call it. It's not a family."

"Ma, you need to take it easy." Raul walked over and kissed her forehead. "I spoke to the doctor. He says you might go home soon."

"Home," Carmen laughed. "That's what you call that inferno?"

Raul gazed at Yasmin from the corner of his eyes, a deep scowl on his face. Yasmin stood up and took her coat, scarf, and purse from the back of the chair. Raul was early, and although she could have stayed longer, his appearance was her cue to leave.

"Yasmin can't stay?" Carmen pointed out, disgusted. "Why does she have to leave when you and Isabel get here? Whose idea was that?"

"It's best that way, Mami," Yasmin said, kissing her on her cheek. "We get to spend time with you and take care of other responsibilities."

Carmen looked at her, frowning, and then faced Raul. "Your idea?"

Without waiting for him to reply, Yasmin landed another kiss on Carmen's other cheek. "See you tomorrow, Mami. I'll call you later."

Yasmin noted Carmen's disheartened expression and controlled her own desire to cry as she hastened out.

"Wait!" Raul followed her into the hall and grabbed her arm.

Yasmin gestured toward the entrance of the room with her hand. They were close enough that their mother could overhear their conversation. Holding her wrist, Raul led her to the elevator and stood in front of her. "Don't give Ma explanations for any decision I make."

"Fine." She was curt. "I wasn't going to tell Mami the schedule was your great idea, but not coming together, which is what Mami wants, makes it obvious that nothing has changed."

"Now you're the expert on what Ma needs?" Raul scoffed.

"No, you are," she replied calmly, looking directly at him.

"I told you to come from 12:00 to 2:00. Why are you coming earlier?"

She locked eyes with his. "I found out family can come at 10:00 in the morning. You overlooked that, so it's not my problem. I get to spend more time with Mami."

"What lies are you feeding her? She's depressed and crying all the time."

"And according to you, I'm the cause?" she laughed. "You and Isabel don't do anything at all to upset her?" She paused purposely and then added, "That wonderful schedule just proves to Mami that we don't get along. Hint, hint. Maybe that's why she's depressed. Or is it because she almost had a heart attack after you hit me in front of her? You decide." She started to walk away.

Raul was still holding her wrist. He pulled her back. She took a deep breath and stepped toward him. She waited in silence for him to growl at her.

"You're lucky you're a female," he stated in an acrid tone.

"Yes," she nodded. "If I wasn't, I'd be next to Dad in the cemetery, and you'd be rid of me. Mami would be overjoyed by your accomplishment of finally putting me where I belong."

He cursed just loud enough for her to hear him. "Have you brought that fraud to see Ma?" Raul demanded.

"We're not together."

"Wow!" he chortled. "He left you already. I knew Orlando would never take your type seriously."

She forced herself to remain serious and pressed her lips together so she wouldn't grin.

"That fake," Raul continued. "All this time you thought he defended you because he liked you."

"You're the phony," she corrected, regretting mentioning that they were separated. "For years you pretended he was like family, and in an instant, you threatened to hurt him. You never deserved his friendship."

"Maybe," he shrugged. "Truth is he used you and then discarded you like trash. That's what you are and always will be."

Without responding, Yasmin pulled her wrist from his grip and entered the elevator. She didn't care what Raul or anyone else thought.

Orlando knew who she was and what she had been through. He loved and respected her, and he deserved a firm commitment.

"Schedule stays as is," Raul exclaimed, holding the elevator doors open.

"Great. I'll continue coming at 10:00 in the morning," she said. "I'll just make sure to leave before 2:00, which is your time, not 12:00." She pointed to her watch. "I'm leaving early today. Next time I'll stay. Remember, we all have to face the consequences of our actions."

"No argument on that. Orlando will feel the results of his decisions soon enough." Raul smiled, winked at her, and then stepped back allowing the doors to close.

His ominous threat made her laugh. He thrived on intimidating others. It was sad. He'd become what he despised most—an ogre, just like her father. She would continue praying for him and for herself.

Her comment about facing the outcomes of erroneous decisions applied to her just as much as it did to Raul. She had to admit that her misery and Orlando's were the direct cause of allowing her fears to control her rationale and diminish her faith. She had made a horrid mistake. She'd foolishly believed that breaking up with Orlando would resolve a situation only the Lord could control.

* * *

"The food was delicious, Clara." Orlando dropped the napkin onto the plate and watched her stand to clean up. Mario, who sat opposite him, handed her his plate.

"I'm going to ask you for a food stipend. You've joined us for dinner every day this week," she teased, collecting all the dishes from the table and placing them in the sink.

"Really?" Orlando laughed. "How about that, Mario? First she complains I don't visit, and now she wants to charge me for dinner because I dropped by several nights."

"Ignore her," Mario chuckled.

"Good idea," Orlando grinned.

"Are you on my side or his?" Clara tapped Mario on the shoulder. "When are you bringing your fiancée?" she asked Orlando, placing her hands on her hips.

Orlando leaned back on the chair and sipped homemade lemonade.

"Did you hear me?" Clara waved her hand in front of him.

"Our engagement is . . . on pause," Orlando said. Mario lifted his eyebrows and smiled.

"On what?" Clara asked. "What does that mean?"

"Yaz needs time," Orlando replied, ignoring the questioning look Clara shot his way. "One of these days we'll surprise you."

"Please let me know in advance," Clara commented with an expression of disapproval on her face.

"I will," he promised. "I'd like you to be on your best behavior. Yaz is sensitive. She'll be timid and shy until she gets used to coming over."

"I can't believe it. Yasmin trapped you. I told you she would," Clara grumbled. "A spider's web."

"Wrong," he shook his head. "You can't imagine how difficult it's been, but it's worth it. I'm ready to start a new life with her."

"After the pause?" Clara was sarcastic.

He nodded.

"And that wouldn't have anything to do with the marks on your face?"

"Don't tell Mom," he said firmly. "It's the last thing she needs to know. Carmen shouldn't have found out either."

"So you had to choose between Yasmin and your friendship with Raul?" Clara was indignant. "And you were considered family?"

"I am," he replied simply.

"You proposed already?" Mario asked.

"Not yet." Orlando was still searching on the internet for a ring, but he wasn't impressed with what he'd seen. "I'm working on it."

"What if she says no?" Clara asked.

"Yasmin will be my wife," he said confidently. "The Lord brought us together, and He'll make sure we get together again."

"Where's Orlando, Mario?" Clara pretended she couldn't see him. "This guy who's pretending to be my brother can't be him."

"That's what love does," Mario laughed. "Congratulations."

"You wouldn't mind being the best man, would you?"

Mario stood up and shook his hand. "I'd be honored."

"The best man should be Raul," Clara said.

Orlando nodded. "He won't be, but that won't stop me from making sure Yaz becomes my wife. She's the priority."

"Wow!" Clara said. "She's changed you."

"You're right. She did. I'm ready to settle down." As Ani had wisely pointed out, Orlando realized he couldn't force Yasmin to discern the situation as he did. It had been a drastic decision, painful for both. He was confident. He would wait patiently for the Lord to finish the work He started.

"Since her return, there have only been problems, and now your friendship with Raul is over," stated Clara.

"Dear sister, you share Yasmin's wrong point of view."

Clara's eyes widened. "What are you talking about? What do we share?"

"She blames herself and believes she caused the issue with Raul. That's why she broke up with me—and thus the pause."

"To be with another man?"

"Listen, Clara," he spoke firmly. "She's trying to stop us from fighting again. She released me without bail. No return date. Case is pending."

"And you're acting as if nothing happened?" Clara marveled. "Since Sunday you've been miserable and depressed. What happened after you left last night? Did you get drunk?"

"No," he laughed. He'd made a solid decision to dismiss all negative thoughts and ill feelings that were a waste of time and energy. "Yaz is going to be my wife. I just need to be patient."

"You haven't proposed?" Clara asked. "She broke up with you, and you're sure she's going to marry you? Oh my God!" Clara placed her hands on her head. "You need a shrink."

"It's believing in the Lord and what He is capable of doing."

"Am I dreaming?" She put up her hands in awe. "Now you're religious?"

"It's a relationship with the Lord, one I'll nourish by becoming a member of the church Ani and Yaz attend."

Clara stared directly at him. "Who would have said or believed that with your reputation you would voluntarily put on a leash and become a man of faith?"

"Without the Lord's grace, I wouldn't be with Yaz. He united us."

"I'm impressed," Clara smiled. "I worried it was one-sided."

"I'm sure Yaz will reconsider, and then we'll move forward with our lives."

"Relationships are tough, Orlando," Mario said. "If you love each other, you'll learn from your errors. If she's the best thing that's happened to you, convince her that not being with you is the biggest mistake of her life."

"Good insight, Mario. I'm already doing that."

* * *

"I told Ismenia not to open the gift," Ani said, irritated, and handed Yasmin the box. "She didn't listen."

Lifting the cover, Yasmin smiled. Inside were 10 giant strawberries dipped in dark and white chocolate with a variety of toppings. "It's okay, Ani." She didn't mind. She was thrilled that Orlando had sent a gift instead of flowers. The day before, he'd sent an exquisite arrangement of yellow roses. "Have some." She held the open box up to Ani.

"Maybe later. You enjoy it, Yasmin. I'm sure Orlando paid a fortune for that gift and the roses."

"They're delicious." Ismenia took another strawberry before Yasmin placed the box on the table. "I love this," Ismenia said after taking a bite and swallowing. "Here." She handed Yasmin the card. "It's closed."

"Thank the Lord for that," Ani griped.

Sitting on the sofa next to Ismenia, Yasmin opened the envelope and read, "Not giving you up. Love you, Orlando." She blinked several times to clear her eyes. She put the card back inside the envelope and placed it next to the box. She stared at the yellow roses that adorned the center of the table.

The Lord took mercy on her. Despite her error, Orlando remained firm, committed to her and their relationship. It filled her with hope and reassured her.

"Tell me you just came back from making up with Orlando," Ismenia said, tapping her on the shoulder.

"I was at the hospital with Mami until 12:00 and then dropped by the apartment to dust and pick up some clothes," she replied, wishing she had done what Ismenia described. "The doctor said Mami will go home this weekend," she added before Ani and Ismenia asked. "Most likely on Sunday. He would have told us if it was tomorrow."

"Good news. I hope she behaves when she's home." Ismenia chuckled. "Tell me the date and time you're planning to make up with Orlando. You need to stop this foolishness. Otherwise, you'll have a flower and candy shop here."

"Stop it, Ismenia," Ani said. "This is between them and the Lord."

"Right," Ismenia smiled. "Why aren't you reminding Yasmin that if the Lord united them, she shouldn't have broken up with Orlando? Convince her it's unfair to make him suffer unnecessarily."

"Do you listen when I tell you what to do?" Ani asked.

Ismenia grunted aloud. "You're the ones who are always talking about the Lord, claiming all your prayers are answered. Your faith that everything will work out doesn't apply to this situation?"

"One word," Ani held up her index finger. "*Patience.*"

Yasmin laughed without meaning to. Like Ismenia, she not only lacked patience but was also guilty of being impulsive and overly emotional. They were weaknesses she prayed the Lord would help her overcome.

"You think it's funny?" Ismenia asked, tapping Yasmin on the shoulder again. "If I were you, I would have gone to his place when he sent the first flower arrangement, admitted I was wrong, apologized, and stayed the night."

Although she had seriously considered it, Yasmin made no comment.

"No reaction?" Ismenia gasped, frustrated. "You're waiting for him to find someone else? Take care of your man, or someone else will."

"Stop being so dramatic," Ani chided. "Orlando isn't interested in anyone else. His gifts are proof of that. He'll wait."

"You agree with that, Yasmin? He's not going to wait forever."

Nor was she, Yasmin thought, grinning.

"What's the big smile for?" Ismenia reached for her buzzing cell phone and read the number. "Got to go." She stood up and answered it. "I'll be right down, Nestor." She hung up and dropped her phone into her purse. "Please promise me you'll think about what I said." Bending down, she kissed Yasmin on the cheek.

"I'm already doing that."

"Thank God!" She kissed Ani on the forehead. "I'll call you later, Yasmin. Give me good news."

"Like Raul, Ismenia speaks her thoughts. She can be reckless, imprudent, and too impulsive," Ani said.

"Like me," Yasmin admitted, aware she'd behaved the same way with the situation between Orlando and Raul.

"Seems the Lord is giving you discernment." Ani studied her face. Yasmin nodded in reply. "Good. Follow Him, and He'll take the lead."

"I will. Why haven't you insisted that I get back with Orlando?"

"This is a process for both of you. I'm sure the Lord has a purpose."

"I have no idea what it could be. I still don't understand why all this happened," Yasmin shrugged.

"No need to know why. God will complete what he started. You'll understand it later, or maybe you won't. That doesn't really matter.

What's important is that He knows what's best for us. Wait patiently and peacefully. He will give you so much more than you expect or ask for."

"You're right."

"Complete trust—that's all He wants from us." Ani sat next to Yasmin on the sofa and embraced her. "And patience. He will do the rest. I have some errands to do." Ani gave her a hug and then stood up. "Eat. Dinner is ready. Rest. You need it. Staying up most of the night worrying doesn't help. Saying you're going to do something and just thinking about it are not the same as doing it. Remember that."

Yasmin watched Ani walk into the bedroom and out again with her coat, hat, scarf, and purse in hand. She heard the door shut and her footsteps grow distant.

The apartment felt empty, the silence awkward. It was rare to be alone in Ani's place. The reason she stayed was to have company and avoid being alone.

Taking off her boots, she lay on the sofa, her gaze fixed on the box and the card. Closing her eyes, she lifted her arms in praise.

"Please forgive me for not trusting You, for relying on my intelligence to solve my problems. I surrender to You. The situation with Orlando and Raul is Yours to handle as You wish."

She cuddled in a corner of the sofa. Exhausted from barely sleeping, she dozed off and dreamed that the Lord was standing before her. The light was so bright that it inundated the room. She saw herself lifting her arms to hold on to His hands, overwhelmed with joy and peace.

Believe. It was the one word she heard clearly.

Opening her eyes, Yasmin sat up. Was it a dream? A vision? Had she imagined it? She had felt His presence so strongly. It was as if He'd been physically there. *Believe*, the Lord told her.

"Thank you," she said aloud, overwhelmed with joy. Even if it was just a dream, she was with God. She marveled, ecstatic.

The peace and tranquility that overcame her was indescribable. Taking the card from the coffee table, she curled up on the sofa again and held the card close to her heart. "I love you, Orlando. I want to spend the rest of my life with you," she said. "I believe the Lord will unite us again and that everything will work out for the best." She closed her eyes and fell into a deep, restful sleep.

* * *

Orlando placed the heart-shaped box on the desk along with the keys. He considered calling Yasmin but decided against it. He would give her time to make up her mind. His plan was to continue sending gifts, anything that would remind her of his love.

Placing his cell phone next to his keys, he strolled into the bedroom and took off his tie. He would lift some weights, shower, and lie down for a while. He had already eaten breakfast at Clara's and gone to several jewelry stores. He found an engagement ring he deemed appropriate. He guessed the size. If it didn't fit, he could either get it enlarged or made smaller, or Yasmin could select another style.

* * *

"You look calm and rested this afternoon," Carmen commented as Yasmin took off her coat and placed it on the back of the chair with her purse.

"You're up and walking around," Yasmin marveled, embracing her warmly.

"The doctor is finally sending me home tomorrow." Carmen was delighted.

"Sorry I came so late," Yasmin apologized, placing the chair closer to the headboard and sitting down. She had arrived after noon. "I haven't slept well for several nights. When I got home yesterday, I lay down to rest and woke up at 10:00 this morning."

Ani had arrived and found her sleeping on the couch. She did not wake her. The aroma of freshly made coffee roused her. She felt refreshed when she got up. After showering, she sat and explained her dream, sipping coffee. Ani concurred that it was a confirmation from the Lord that trusting meant no fears, doubts, or questions. Yasmin had to believe and be patient.

"I'm not surprised to hear that you can't rest. Plenty of worries are keeping you awake," Carmen said. "I can imagine how horrible it was to see them fighting."

Yasmin noted that Carmen used the word *see*. The only one who knew she witnessed it was Raul. She wondered if he had told Isabel. It was the only way Luisa would have known and mentioned it to her mother. God help her, she prayed. Luisa needed to be touched by the Lord so she could realize that gossiping was harmful, that rumors spread darkness and cause problems, and in her mother's case could be disastrous.

270

"Are you going to tell me what happened? Why they fought?"

"Please, Mami. I'd prefer not to talk about that." She refused to discuss anything that would dampen her mother's good spirits.

Carmen shook her head. "It's foolish to try to shield me from the truth, to hide things that eventually I'll know."

"You're right, and we'll talk about it some other time."

"I'm sure Ani and Ismenia already know. You tell them many things you won't share with me."

"I don't want to upset you, Mami." Yasmin reached for Carmen's hand and squeezed it gently.

"Say whatever it is. I'm listening," Carmen urged in a quiet voice.

"I just feel that in our family, the truth, listening, and trying to work things out aren't important." She was candid.

"I've always wanted you to confide in me and trust me," Carmen said. "But I realized after what happened that my attitude hasn't helped. We have to make big changes in our family. I have to admit that your father and I are to blame. He cherished the grudges he had, and he was unforgiving, relentless, and sometimes surprisingly cruel. I accepted it, lived with it, and forced the three of you to do the same."

"That doesn't matter anymore," Yasmin said, finally convinced that leaving the past where it belonged and moving forward, along with trusting the Lord, were the best course of action.

"It does, Yasmin. While here, I've had time to think about a lot of things. Roberto's character was remarkably like my father's. Mamá lived with Papá 50 years before she passed on. She always told me that when your husband is upset, be calm. Talk afterward, come to an agreement, and resolve your problems. Don't hold grudges. I never saw the agreement or any of the solutions. I just saw that Papá always got his way while Mamá submitted to his demands."

Stunned by Carmen's revelation, Yasmin waited eagerly for her to continue. They were having a real conversation. Her mother was confiding in her. It both surprised and delighted her.

"I didn't want to marry a man that in any way resembled Papá, but I did," Carmen lamented. "I was willing to accept my choice, to live with it despite the sacrifices and the deceptions until the incident with Manuel."

"Maybe we should talk about that another time, Mami." Yasmin could tell that Carmen was getting emotional. She feared it would affect her blood pressure.

"Your father never asked how I felt. I tried to speak to him, but he refused to listen. I was miserable. We became distant, led separate lives, and focused on our own problems. Neither of us was willing to forgive, communicate, or try to find a solution. Our separation was inevitable."

"If I hadn't brought Manuel . . ."

"No," Carmen interrupted, shaking her head. "You were wrong to do so, but your father's attitude was like Raul's—extreme. I understand now why you feared Roberto. When I saw Raul hit you, I envisioned your father doing the same. I remembered the last time you visited. You seemed so happy. I was certain you'd decided to move back home."

That had been Yasmin's intention, but she wasn't going to make her mother feel worse by admitting it.

"Like Raul, your father threatened to leave if you returned. It broke my heart when your father dragged you out." Covering her face with her hands, Carmen cried softly.

Getting up, Yasmin embraced her. "Please calm down."

Carmen lifted her hand to silence her and continued speaking. "Even then I fooled myself and kept thinking he wouldn't hurt you. I believed your fears were just an excuse to stay away."

"Please, Mami," Yasmin repeated, moving back and studying her face.

"Sit. I'm fine." Taking a stack of tissues from the box on the bed, Carmen dried her face, waited for her to sit, and then cleared her throat and continued. "I knew you wouldn't return."

"If you want to be discharged, you need to relax."

"I'm all right." Taking Yasmin's hands, she held them tightly in her own. "We've all exaggerated and behaved horribly. I wanted you to come home so badly that I refused to believe Roberto would hurt you. I kept telling myself it was a phase he would get over. It wasn't. He never budged. Raul is doing the same now."

Although Yasmin was concerned for her mother's health, tears of joy filled her eyes. Finally, her mother understood her plight. It was a blessing—a confirmation that her prayers were answered.

"It's over, Mami." Her mother had suffered her absence, battled with her conscience, and been torn between accepting her father's decision and standing up for her beliefs. Yasmin realized her mother had suffered just as much as she had or more.

"I hope it's clear that our divorce had nothing to do with you," Carmen said, looking directly into Yasmin's eyes. "Problems don't end a relationship, Yasmin. How the couple handles it does."

Yasmin nodded. That was a lesson she'd just learned and intended to rectify. "Do you regret divorcing Dad?"

Carmen stared at her in silence.

"You don't need to answer if you don't want to," she added quickly, embarrassed for asking.

"Why not?" Carmen smiled. "Sometimes I wonder if things would have been different or if I should have tried to communicate more. I blamed him for my weaknesses and convinced myself that he forced me to accept an inhumane decision. I disagreed but did nothing but try to force you to return home. I was just as cruel and insensitive as he was." Her voice was filled with remorse. "This is the first time I've talked about it. Reality isn't easy to accept or live with."

"I know," Yasmin nodded. "Thanks for confiding in me, Mami." Standing, Yasmin leaned over and hugged Carmen.

Carmen kissed Yasmin's forehead. "Tell me what happened between you and Orlando. You denied you were together but admit you love him. If you weren't dating, how could you have fallen for him?"

Yasmin laughed as she sat down again. She wondered where to begin or how to explain all the hurdles and conflicts they'd endured. She decided not to expound too much. "When we met after the *rezos*, it was to talk about you and how we got along. Orlando was always encouraging me, telling me I was strong and that things would work out between us."

"Sounds like Orlando," Carmen agreed, smiling, "the opposite of Raul. He's thoughtful, sensitive, and supportive. I should have never said such horrible things about him. He didn't deserve it."

"He cares about you, Mami. He worries about your health and encourages me to take care of you. He insisted I visit you the day of the burial and drove me to your place to make sure I went."

Yasmin wondered if Orlando was home. She had no idea what he did on weekends or if dropping by without calling was a good idea. She dispelled her apprehensions, willfully erasing all negative thoughts. She smiled, determined to remain in good spirits.

"Orlando respects and admires you, Mami. He's genuinely concerned about your well-being. That's one of the things I really like about him." Yasmin was grateful she'd fallen in love with a man who had high esteem for her mother. "I don't know when I began to care for him, but I did. Raul feels Orlando betrayed him and their friendship. That's why they fought."

"I'm surprised Orlando didn't talk to him about it."

"Everything happened at the same time. We've barely had time to clarify things between us, much less tell anyone."

"I knew there was a reason you were depressed," Carmen affirmed. "You've suffered so much."

"Everything will be fine," Yasmin said, recalling her dream.

"I believed my prayers hadn't been answered, but they have," Carmen admitted. "I need to be grateful and thankful."

"Me too," Yasmin nodded.

"Tell me about Manuel."

"I never lied to you about him. We broke up the same day Dad threw me out."

"You never saw him after that?" Carmen asked with disbelief.

"No."

"And Angel?"

"Angel?" she repeated, disgusted. "I never liked him."

Carmen grunted aloud. "Neither do Raul and Orlando. Raul held back because I was there. Otherwise, they would have fought. And the way Orlando looked at him, he was jealous. He knew that Angel liked you." Carmen shook her head, frowning. "Those two have a long history of doing wild and crazy things."

"I ended that," Yasmin confessed. "It's not fair for Orlando to have to choose between me and his friendship with Raul."

"No, it isn't, but fair doesn't exist in life," Carmen noted dryly.

"It exists with God. He's just and merciful."

"True. I've always wanted to ask when you became Manuel's girl."

"It was when we went on summer vacation with Dad to Santo Domingo, and you stayed here in New York. Manuel knew my cousin Alfredo; they were attending college together." Yasmin had met Manuel the day she arrived. She was thrilled, flattered that he liked her. "We went out a few times with Alfredo and his girl until Raul found out. He told Manuel I couldn't go out unless he joined us, which he never did. Manuel stopped visiting." She was certain that Raul demanded Manuel to stay away. He had probably threatened him.

"When you returned from the trip, Raul mentioned you liked some guy and that he'd spoken to him," Carmen shared. "I never imagined that he and the man your father found you with were the same person."

"When we came back from vacation, I forgot about him. Then I went to a party with Ismenia, one of the few you gave me permission to attend. Manuel was there. He went crazy when he saw me and started saying I was his girl."

"You wanted to be?"

"Yes," she admitted. "We saw each other daily after that. He picked me up after school."

"You were never late."

"He gave me a ride so we could spend time together."

"You always find a way to do what you want," Carmen marveled. "Roberto accused me of knowing that he was your boyfriend and keeping it a secret. I didn't even know who he was referring to."

"Dad always complained that you were too lenient."

Carmen shrugged. "I tried to be flexible. Why did you take him to the apartment?"

Yasmin was silent, considering the best way to answer. "I was naïve and foolish."

"You broke up with him because?"

"When Dad threw me out, Manuel took me to his mother's place. I heard them arguing. His mother asked him about his wife and kid. He had pretended to be single. I felt deceived. I refused to stay and left."

"It must have been horrible for you." Carmen gestured for her to come over. "I'm sorry, Yasmin." She embraced her.

Yasmin squeezed her mother lovingly. "No need to apologize, Mami."

"Forgive me for being so hard on you." Carmen caressed her face gently and looked directly at her. "Why is Manuel looking for you? What does he want?"

"What?" Stepping back, Yasmin stared at Carmen in shock. It was the first time she had heard that. "Who told you he's looking for me?"

"Are you aware that Luisa knows his family? They live in the same neighborhood as your father and Luisa in Santo Domingo. I think your father knew his parents and Manuel when he was a child. Luisa told me she saw him and his sister at a party she catered. He asked Luisa about you."

Yasmin grimaced. "How did he find out Luisa knew me? She must have been talking to them about us, telling them stuff he didn't need to know. That's why I . . ." She hesitated and reconsidered what she was going to say. "I don't want her to know anything about me. She needs to worry about herself and her daughter. Luisa needs to stop meddling."

"What difference does it make what Luisa tells Manuel? If it's over, what she tells him shouldn't make a difference."

"I disagree, Mami. Why does Luisa feel she has the right to announce everything that happens in our family? Don't we have a right to our privacy? We don't know everything about her, and I don't want to know. It's her business what she does and why. I think we deserve the same courtesy."

"You're right. Your father and I argued about that many times. He wouldn't budge, and I just accepted it as I've accepted so many things that should have ended long ago," Carmen said decisively. "I was convinced you were with Manuel and were denying it. But that's the way life is when you make assumptions. What you think and what is really happening are opposite."

Chapter 17

Orlando heard someone knocking. Donning a pair of jeans, he grabbed a T-shirt from the drawer and dashed out of the bedroom. He'd taken a long shower after lifting weights. He planned to prepare something to eat and try to find something entertaining on TV or listen to music.

"Who?" he asked, anticipating that it might be a salesperson. No reply. He started to turn away. Whoever was knocking was persistent.

After asking a few times without a response, he opened the door, prepared to get rid of whoever it was.

He saw the last person he expected.

"Can I come in?" Yasmin asked, smiling coyly.

"Please." He stepped back, allowing her to enter, and controlled the impulse to embrace her as she swept past him. Following her inside, he wondered how she got his address. He stood several paces behind her as she stopped by the doorway of the kitchen.

"I've never been to a bachelor pad." She smiled and entered the kitchen, studying her surroundings, and then walked past him to the living room. "The place is neat and clean." She took off her gloves and coat and placed them on the leather chair.

Her approval pleased him, and he stood near the desk watching her as she gave herself a tour of the apartment. As she entered his bedroom to look around, he hid the heart-shaped box in one of the drawers of his desk and admired her from afar. She wore jeans with a pink sweater and a matching print scarf. Her hair was loose as he preferred, the curls bouncing lightly as she moved about. Her lips shone brightly.

Forcing himself to stay still, he envisioned himself taking her into his arms and kissing her.

"You decorated it yourself?" she asked.

He nodded. When he first moved in, he took a few months to decide how to decorate. He chose a modern, crisp look. The walls were completely bare. A black leather sofa and two chairs were placed selectively away from the walls with the coffee table at the center. The solid metal wall unit was black and held a flat-screen television, a CD player, and some CDs. An avid music lover, Orlando kept his collection arranged by genre on several shelves. The space around the furniture was ample. His desk was by the window. His laptop, charger, car and apartment keys, along with his cell phone and current mail were habitually there.

"I like it, but it needs something," she said.

"What?" he asked, studying her facial expression. She was relaxed, jovial, and unusually bold. He never imagined an impromptu visit, much less a daring tour of his apartment. Both were gratifying. Stepping closer, he slipped his arm around her waist.

"My touch." She wrapped her arms around his neck and tilted her head back to look up at him.

"You can redecorate all you want," he said.

"I came to . . ."

"I know why you're here." Lowering his head, his lips covered hers. She returned his kiss eagerly and stepped back breathlessly when he moved back. He noticed the red hue on her cheeks. She was always bashful and demure. He grinned. "How did you get my address?"

"I kept the business card you gave me at the South Street Seaport."

"Yeah?" He was thrilled by her answer. "Although you didn't want to have anything to do with me and my reputation, you still saved it?"

She pinched him playfully. "Your reputation is going to change now."

"That's the past. Being with you is my present and future." He kissed her forehead and gestured for her to sit on the sofa. She did so, and he put his arm over her shoulders. She snuggled next to him, eyes sparkling with glee as she looked up at him. "Are you taking your medications? Eating?" he asked. She nodded. "Still at Ani's or back home?"

"I went to the apartment to clean up, but I've been staying with Ani." She kissed him gingerly on the lips. "Thanks for the flowers. Ismenia loved the chocolate strawberries."

"You didn't have any?"

"I planned to," she said apologetically.

"It's all right." He was happy that Ismenia enjoyed them. "As long as you got the message I sent with it."

Yasmin nodded. "I just came from the hospital."

"When is Carmen going to be discharged?" he asked, troubled that the next day would be a week since she was admitted.

"Tomorrow. She's excited and ready to leave," Yasmin exclaimed. "Today we clarified a lot of things and confided in each other. We even talked about you."

"I'm happy to hear that, Yaz. That's something you've wanted for a long time. What did you tell Carmen about me?"

"That I'm in love with you."

He kissed her. "Did you mention that I feel the same way about you?" He rested his forehead on hers.

"You'll have to do that yourself."

"No problem." He planned to do that anyway. "Are we official? Together regardless of whatever problems we encounter?" He wanted to be certain she understood the commitment she was making to their relationship and to him.

"I'm here to stay."

"Ready to make it public?" he asked.

She smiled nervously and nodded.

"I want to ask Carmen and Ani for their blessings," Orlando blurted out. "Mom wanted to be the first to know when things worked out. We'll call her before I take you home."

"Eva knows about me?" Yasmin asked, wondering if she heard him correctly. She was prepared to stay and willing to get her clothes and move in with him. His comment that he was taking her back to Ani's surprised her.

"You're not a secret in my family, Yaz." He noticed the red hue on her face. "No need to feel embarrassed. It'll take time for you to get used to them, to feel comfortable when we visit. We'll take one step at a time."

She nodded and rested her head on his shoulder.

"Are you still going to the hospital tomorrow morning?" he asked, caressing her back. He felt her nodding. "Great. We'll go together. I'll pick you up at Ani's."

Moving back, she looked at him with creased eyebrows. "I said I'm here to stay." She repeated the words to make sure he heard her.

"As much as I'd love that," Orlando shook his head, "it's not happening—not yet. I refuse to validate all the lies and assumptions that have ruined your reputation. I want you to be respected, to be treated the way you deserve."

"How will you do that?" she asked skeptically.

"By doing things in the correct manner," he assured. Her disappointment saddened him, but he intended to wait for the precise moment to propose.

"Correct manner?" she repeated, a puzzled expression on her face.

"Stay with Ani for now." She would understand what he meant when he posed the question. They would plan the ceremony and then move in together when they were married.

Yasmin was silent, her eyes locked on his.

"Part of our relationship means trusting me, Yaz."

"I do," she nodded, a serious expression on her face. "I just don't see the point in waiting."

"If I had left that night, Raul wouldn't have seen me. He did, and now he's convinced that all the lies spread about you are true, more now than before. I'm not happy about that."

"You were right. Raul doesn't care if we're together or not. He just wants vengeance. Why let whatever he thinks or does affect our plans?"

"I'm doing this for you. Regardless of what anyone thinks, you and I know the truth. I refuse to smear your reputation or name more than it has been."

"Okay." Yasmin smiled, an expression of awe and admiration on her face. "If you feel that strongly about it, although I don't agree, I'll accept it." She took a deep breath, preparing herself for the topic she was going to address. "There is still something I need to tell you about the day Dad threw me out. I don't want anything from the past smearing our relationship."

"No need to talk about that, Yaz. We love each other, and we're moving on. Let's leave the past where it belongs."

She placed her hand over his lips. "I want you to know everything that happened."

"No." He knew enough. She had provided sufficient details. "I don't want you to relive that horrid experience again. Erase it from here," he pointed to her temples, "and here," and he pointed to her heart.

"I only told you part of what happened," she said.

"That was enough to conclude that coward took advantage of being alone with you. That's not love. Had he really cared about you, he would have waited and respected your decision."

"All these years I stayed alone," she went on despite Orlando's objections. "I wasn't interested in a relationship, much less being physically close to anyone."

"That's understandable." He realized Manuel's hideous behavior caused her to build a barrier around herself and her heart.

"You were right. I ran away because I didn't want him near me. Just the thought of being physically close to him disgusted and sickened me."

"Enough, Yaz." He cupped her face in his hands and kissed her gently on the lips. "Leave it in the past where it belongs."

She shook her head. "I need to talk about it, to finally take this load off my shoulders and to confide in you completely."

"All right." He leaned back, took hold of her hand, and gestured for her to continue.

"When he walked into the room, he took me in his arms. He kept kissing me. I tried to convince him that we needed to leave. I pushed him away and begged him to stop." She paused and took a deep breath.

"You don't have to continue."

"I do." She nodded and smiled thinly. "I heard the door being opened and closed and footsteps. I thought I was imagining it. I was shocked when Dad grabbed Manuel by the shoulders and shoved him out of the room. Dad was screaming all types of profanity as he confronted me." She closed her eyes. "When Dad attempted to strike me, Manuel intervened. I watched, horrified, as they exchanged blows."

Orlando thought about what she'd just revealed. It sounded as if they hadn't been in the room for a long time. "Roberto arrived shortly after you did?" he asked to confirm his suspicions.

"He assumed we had been there for hours. He became violent. I . . ." she paused, recalling how her father lashed out at her and Manuel, ". . . I had never seen him so angry. I'd never been so afraid, so ashamed." She gazed at her hands.

"Yaz." Orlando lifted her face up, expecting to see her crying but was stunned that she wasn't. "You have nothing to feel ashamed about."

"Manuel led me to his car. Still in shock and sobbing, I had no idea where he was taking me. I didn't really care. When we got to his apartment, he told me he needed to speak to his mother. That's when I realized we were at her place and that he lived there. I felt trapped and desperate. I had no idea where to go or what to do." She laughed dryly. "I gazed out the window . . . considered . . ." She shook her head.

"Thank God," Orlando exclaimed, horrified at the vision that arose. "The Lord stopped you."

She nodded in agreement. "Even then He was with me." It had never occurred to her that when she was going through such turmoil, the Lord was guiding and taking care of her. "It was then that I decided to leave. I opened the door and stepped out of the bedroom. Manuel was in the living room with his mother, and they couldn't see me. I froze and stood by the front door a long time. I kept glancing back as I opened the locks. They didn't hear it and kept arguing. I ran out." She relaxed. Finally, she could speak about it without feeling degraded or condemning herself. "I felt used, dirty, and disgusted. I was also devastated. I realized my reputation would never be the same, that my family would believe the worst."

"Yaz," he said tenderly, embracing her. She rested her head on his shoulder. He held her firmly to reassure her that it was over, that he was with her, that he would protect and care for her always. His eyes misty, he prayed silently, *Lord, heal her. Help her forget all the pain and suffering she's carried in her heart all this time.*

He was glad she wasn't crying. She had become stronger emotionally, able to face that crude reality calmly and peacefully. It was the Lord's work.

He realized the sentence she imposed on herself was more severe than the one her family had inflicted. She'd condemned herself to a life of solitude, fear, and remorse. Her inability to trust, to be in a relationship, and to open her heart to be loved and to love was caused by her ex's betrayal. Without knowing it, Roberto had stopped Manuel from finishing what he had started. The Lord had protected Yasmin.

"Yaz." He waited until she faced him to continue. "What happened wasn't your fault. You said no, and he should have stopped and respected your decision. Too bad we didn't find him. He deserved the beating he was going to get." Then Orlando realized his mistake.

Yasmin was staring at him, appalled.

"I'm not saying I'm going to do anything, Yaz. It upsets me that your ex treated you that way, that you've suffered so much unnecessarily because he refused to listen to you." The last thing she needed to hear after confiding in him was that he would seek vengeance. His goal was for her to focus on their future, not the past. The outrage and anger over her ex's actions were irrelevant. What mattered was reassuring her and making her aware that he understood what she'd been through. "I'm sorry, Yaz. I don't want you to stress or worry. The Lord is in charge."

Her gaze fixed on him. He maintained a calm semblance and smiled.

"The past doesn't matter anymore," she said. "I let it go. I forgave myself, and I forgive Manuel. I'm free, and it feels as if an enormous weight has been lifted from my shoulders."

"You're strong and brave. I appreciate your sincerity. Thanks for telling me the truth." He kissed her, regretting his outburst. She had witnessed her ex fighting with Roberto and Raul fighting with him. The last thing Orlando wanted was to cause her more anxiety over the possibility of another fight between him and her ex.

She looked up at him lovingly. "I couldn't have come here or told you what happened without God's grace."

"I've been praying for that, Yaz. Did it ever occur to you to tell Carmen what happened?"

"If you tried to explain the truth to Raul, he wouldn't believe you," Yasmin said. "The same thing would have happened with Dad and Mami too. Today, she finally accepted that I have suffered a lot and that I was the victim."

Orlando nodded. "You're right. I doubt it would have changed anything."

"Questions?" she asked.

"None." Everything was clear. All the pieces of the puzzle were in place, and the picture was atrocious. He realized that her revelation of everything that happened was a sign from the Lord, a confirmation that their relationship had been established by Him.

* * *

"I told you that He never fails us." Ani was ecstatic.

"I wish I'd listened to you before," Yasmin said, teary-eyed.

"Afflictions teach us to be humble, to seek His help, and to grow and mature in our faith. All of it has a purpose."

Yasmin hugged Ani, unable to contain the tears that trailed down her cheeks. "Words can't express how thankful I am for all you've done, Ani."

"Gratitude is to Him." She pointed up. "He made all this possible, not me. I just provided the guidance. I was obedient and gave you all the messages He put in my heart."

Yasmin embraced Ani again. *Thank you, Lord, for bringing Ani into my life. Bless her, and provide whatever her heart desires most,* she prayed silently.

"Where's Orlando?" Ani asked.

Moving back, Yasmin took the paper towel Ani had torn from the roll and dried her tears. "He's looking for parking. He wants to come up and see you before he goes back home in a cab."

"He's driving your car again?" Ani chuckled. "Although you're happy, I sense that something isn't quite right. What is it?"

Yasmin wasn't aware that her eyes revealed her disappointment. She had gone to Orlando's place, convinced they would start their relationship immediately. She had even planned to pack some of her clothes and stay at his place. Now she was glad she'd reconsidered. His decision surprised and amazed her. His intentions were noble and showed how much he loved her, but she doubted it would have the effect he desired on Raul, her mother, or anyone else.

"It's nothing really," Yasmin began, smiling happily. There was nothing to feel sad about. They were together. She accepted his decision, agreed to trust him, and would keep her promise. "Orlando wants me to stay here until we make it official, whatever that means."

Ani laughed. "As if you don't know him. He's a planner. He likes to organize and ensure all details, no matter how small, are taken care of. Get used to it, accept it, and enjoy it. Few men are like that."

Yasmin laughed. "You're right."

"Although you're a couple, it's important to remember to give yourselves some breathing room. Do things you enjoy on your own and things you enjoy together. Balance your relationship. It's not separate all the time or together all the time."

"I'll remember that," Yasmin promised.

"I'll remind you if you forget," Ani smiled. "How did Carmen react when you told her?"

"We're planning to surprise her tomorrow morning," Yasmin smiled ecstatically.

"She'll be as delighted as I am." They heard a soft knock. "I think Orlando is here." Ani walked out of the kitchen to answer the door.

Yasmin saw Orlando enter and embrace Ani.

"Congratulations." Ani gave him a peck on his cheek.

"Thanks," he said, walking into the kitchen. "You were crying, Yaz?" he asked as he gave her a kiss on her lips.

"I got a little sentimental when I was telling Ani about my visit to your apartment."

He placed a chair next to her and sat down. "I'm grateful for all your help, advice, and sincerity, Ani."

"I won't take merit for that. Thank the Lord," Ani said, returning to where she sat. "I'm happy and thrilled to see the two of you together. I'm sure Carmen will feel the same way."

"We'd like her blessing and yours," Orlando replied. "Mom already knows. She's planning for grandkids."

"You've always had my blessing and my prayers. You will continue to have them." Ani clasped both of their hands and squeezed. "I love the idea of being a grandmother, too, but you should wait until you're ready. Give yourselves some time to enjoy being a couple. When you begin a family, the focus, responsibilities, and routines change."

"I'm in no rush," Orlando agreed and then added, "Before we have kids, we need to be prepared."

"I'd definitely prefer to wait," Yasmin said.

"I won't stay too long." Orlando stood up. "I just came by to thank you and give you the good news personally."

"Can't you stay a while longer?" Yasmin asked, looking up at him.

"I'd like to stop and get something to eat before I head home," he replied. "After visiting Carmen tomorrow, we'll spend the day together."

"If you don't mind having leftovers," Ani offered, "there's plenty of rice, beans, and stewed oxtail. I can make a salad. You can stay as long as you want."

"Yes?" Yasmin asked eagerly. They had barely spent time together, and she wasn't ready to be apart again.

Orlando nodded, grinning.

Ani stood up. "You can wait in the living room while I prepare everything."

Yasmin followed Orlando to the living room. She stopped to admire two wedding gowns that Ani had hung over the curtain pole. One was white; the other was cream. She recalled Ani's comment that she would make her wedding dress, although not anytime soon. Whatever Orlando meant by "doing the right thing" sounded like he wanted to wait a while.

Orlando stood behind her, slid his arms around her waist, and rested them on her stomach. Leaning her head on his shoulder, she closed her eyes. How long they waited was unimportant. She needed to enjoy the present and savor their union.

"Ani's work is incredible," he commented. "She should have her own shop."

"She did when I first moved in with her," she replied, opening her eyes. "Rent was horrible, and the workload was overwhelming. She prefers to work by recommendation. She chooses her clients and doesn't allow the workload to interfere with her church activities. She's highly active at the church."

"If Ani's happy, that's what counts," he said, walking around to face Yasmin. "Why were you crying?"

"I wasn't upset. I was just so happy and amazed at how everything has fallen into place."

"I don't want you to worry about the situation with Raul."

"God will resolve that, too, as He has everything else."

"Yes," Orlando concurred, "which is why you need to be at peace." She kissed him. "I am."

"Love birds," Ani called, "food is ready."

They walked into the kitchen together and sat where Ani had set their plates. "Aren't you eating?" Yasmin asked Ani.

"I ate already." Ani placed a soda on the table and then sat down.

"I'd like to attend service at your church, Ani," Orlando said, handing Yasmin the bowl of rice.

"Yasmin accompanied me every Sunday before she started attending Mass with Carmen," Ani said.

"That was temporary," Yasmin chimed in. "From now on, I'll be going to church with you and Orlando. We'll visit Mami afterward," Yasmin explained, as she served herself two spoonfuls of rice and poured beans over it.

"It's a pleasure that you'll join me. There are a lot of young couples at our parish."

"We'll be there," Orlando promised. "Yaz, I'd like you to get used to eating more," he joked as he passed her the bowl with the meat.

"A few more pounds couldn't hurt," Ani said. "I'd like to use a little more fabric to make your wedding dress."

"Not for a long while," Yasmin assured them both as she poured a glass of soda for Orlando, handed it to him, and then poured herself some.

"Really?" Ani asked, grinning. Orlando smiled, winked at her, and then turned to Yasmin.

"What?" Yasmin asked, looking from one to the other. "Anything I should know?"

"It doesn't matter when. I'm making your dress," Ani sang the words.

* * *

"Just the person I wanted to see." Carmen greeted Orlando with a hug.

"Great to see you. How do you feel?" Orlando was pleasantly surprised to see Carmen fully dressed. Her discharge was definite.

"Fine," she replied, turning to hug Yasmin.

"You're packing already, Mami?" Yasmin kissed her on the cheek. "We can drive you home."

"No need. I already spoke to Raul. He'll come around 2:00. Discharge papers take forever, and the nurse needs to speak to me about the medications and follow-up appointment." She gazed at Orlando and then at Yasmin. "You're here because you're together?"

"Yes," Orlando replied. Turning slightly, he studied Yasmin's face. Her smile and the glimmer in her eyes delighted him. He faced Carmen again. "It's great that you're going home."

"Thank God. It seems like I've been here an eternity."

"You'll have to take it easy, Mami," Yasmin commented.

"Certain things have to be taken care of right away," Carmen said, a serious expression on her face. "We're having a family meeting this evening at 7:00. Raul will tell Maria, Luisa, and Isabel. I was waiting to tell you, Yasmin, and I was going to call you, Orlando. Prayers are answered, for here you are. Both of you need to be there."

Orlando exchanged glances with Yasmin. Her surprised expression matched his. A meeting the same day she was discharged meant she had something urgent to discuss. "Then 7:00 it is," Orlando agreed.

"Will you excuse us?" Carmen said to Yasmin. "I want to speak to Orlando."

Yasmin looked at Carmen and then at Orlando, not masking her surprise.

"Private conversation," he winked at her, smiling.

"About me?" Yasmin asked, gesturing to herself. "And I have to leave?"

"Go drink some coffee . . . and bring me one," Carmen urged.

Orlando slipped his arm around Yasmin's waist as she turned to leave, kissed her cheek, and whispered, "You told me Carmen wanted to speak to me about our relationship. This is the time."

Yasmin nodded and took her purse. Whatever they discussed could be done in her presence, but deciding not to press the issue, she walked out of the room. Stopping by the doorway, she said, "Call me when you want me to come back."

Orlando smiled as he watched her exit.

"Sit. Let's talk." Carmen sat on the bed.

Placing a chair in front of Carmen, Orlando sat down. He had been looking forward to this conversation and was pleased it was happening earlier than he had anticipated. "I'd like to apologize if I've been disrespectful or caused you any grief," he began.

"I'm the one who should be apologizing, Orlando. Until the past few days, I had no idea how much harm . . ." she paused and took a deep breath, ". . . our family has done to Yasmin."

He had seen the same self-criticism and regret reflected in Yasmin's behavior and words countless times. He noticed the blurry eyes and grieved expression. "Are you okay?" he asked and was about to stand. Carmen shook her head and held up her hand, signaling him to remain seated. Taking a tissue, she dried her eyes.

"It's tough when we recognize we've hurt the ones we love unnecessarily, that we can be cruel, heartless, and destructive."

"True," he agreed and considered to add that Yasmin battled with that continuously and was just beginning to accept her mistakes, forgive herself, and move forward with her life.

"Yasmin has suffered a lot," Carmen continued. "I'd like to exclude myself, but I'm just as guilty as the rest."

"You're her mother. You have every right . . ."

"No," Carmen cut him off. "Nurturing, consideration, kindness, and caring—she received those things from Ani who's not her mother." Her words were saturated with remorse. "I thought I was doing the right thing,

288

but I fooled myself. We all have in this family. Unfortunately, Yasmin was the target—the blame for everything, guilty or not."

Orlando stared at her in silence, stunned by the accuracy of her words. It was apparent that Carmen had been analyzing the situation and had accepted her culpability and made some vital resolutions. It occurred to him that such would be the topic of the family discussion she scheduled that evening.

"Forgive me, Orlando. Instead of uniting you, I caused problems and misunderstandings."

"I would have spoken to you and Raul before, but until yesterday there was nothing solid between Yaz and me."

"Yaz?" Carmen repeated, grinning. "It's obvious you're very much in love and happy."

"You told me that when I found the right person, I would get serious, establish a relationship, get married, and start a family."

"I did?" Carmen asked, her brow furrowed. "When?"

"The night we spoke in the emergency room, the same day I took Yaz to the cemetery and dropped her off at your place."

"Ah, yes," she nodded. "Isabel arrived while we were talking and started arguing with Yasmin." She sighed aloud. "Our family is a mess."

Orlando waited for Carmen to continue speaking. He was pleased that she finally realized how much they'd hurt Yasmin. Her discernment of the situation could only be brought about by the Lord.

"What are your plans?" Carmen asked.

Meeting her gaze, Orlando spoke with authority. "I'd like your blessing and your permission to marry Yasmin." He'd been tempted to bring the engagement ring, but since he was dressed in jeans and a sweater, he had no place to hide it. He didn't want Yasmin to see it until he proposed.

Carmen's eyes were misty, although she was grinning. "I have to be honest, I thought she'd become another Maria."

Orlando shook his head. "Raul has the same concerns," he said, regretting his past choices. "I couldn't speak to you or to Raul until everything was clarified between us. It took time for Yaz to accept that she cared for me, to trust me, and to believe I was serious about our relationship."

"I'm sure all the horrid suspicions I drilled into her didn't help."

"Don't blame yourself, Carmen. Yaz had her own doubts. Nothing you told her was worse than what she believed. Her experience with her ex was also an issue."

"She told me they were never together."

"He destroyed her trust in men. She didn't want to get hurt again if she got into another relationship," he explained. Although he wasn't planning to retaliate, Manuel's offenses still angered him. He was praying about it, asking the Lord to help him forgive him. "She feared being deceived and was convinced I was trying to do the same."

"Did I hear in your tone a desire for revenge?" Carmen eyed him sharply. "I expect that from Raul, not you. Whatever happened, that's over. Leave it alone. Focus on your future with Yasmin. You have my blessings. It's an honor that you'll be my son-in-law." Standing, she embraced him affectionately.

"Thanks. I already purchased the ring. I don't want Yaz to see it until I propose."

"I wouldn't have had any objections if you'd asked her before telling me."

"Your approval was necessary," Orlando corrected in a gentle tone. "Yasmin is your daughter. Out of respect and because I have high regard for you, Carmen, the right thing to do was to ask you first."

"You're so formal," Carmen smiled, pleased. "Yasmin's very fortunate. After all she's been through, she deserves to be happy." She kissed him on his cheek, sat down, and pointed to the chair so he would do the same.

"It's not luck or fortune. It's the Lord's work. I've been blessed twice—first with your treating me as your son and now that you're accepting me as your son-in-law."

"I think it's the other way around, but either way, I'm happy that you and Yasmin are together. Does Eva know?"

"She's thrilled. She spoke to Yaz yesterday. She's already planning to buy a crib and all sorts of things for the grandkids."

Carmen burst into laughter. "She's way ahead of me, not that I don't look forward to that. First, some things need to be put in order."

* * *

Yasmin anticipated that Orlando would share what he discussed with Carmen when they left the hospital, but she was disappointed. When she returned from window shopping at the gift shop, they were talking amicably and laughing.

His silence piqued her curiosity, but she was hesitant to question him about it. They stopped at a restaurant to have lunch and then headed back to Ani's. Still, he made no attempt to mention what they discussed.

"Everything all right, Yaz?" Orlando asked as they waited for Ani to open the door.

She nodded. His keen sense of her feelings and emotions always daunted her. She needed to get used to that.

"Sure?" he studied her face carefully.

"Yes," she replied. She was certain he'd mention it eventually.

Entering the apartment, she kissed Ismenia on the cheek and walked to the living room. Trust, she told herself as she greeted Ani with a hug and placed her coat and purse on the sofa. She was being childish and immature. It was obvious that whatever Orlando and Carmen had discussed, it had been positive. Otherwise, they wouldn't have been smiling. She decided not to dwell anymore on whatever they had spoken about.

"It's been years since we've seen each other, Orlando," Ismenia said, following him into the living room. She sat opposite him on the love seat. "But I've heard a lot about you."

"You have?" he asked, taking off his leather jacket and placing it on his lap as he sat next to Yasmin.

"You've been a topic of interest since Roberto passed away," Ismenia said.

"That so, Yaz?" He placed his arm over her shoulders.

"Yes," Yasmin said, "except Ismenia forgot to mention that she was the one who was always mentioning you."

"She admits it!" Ismenia clapped enthusiastically. "That friendship nonsense—I never believed it. I knew it was more than that. I was right," Ismenia sang proudly. "And by the way, I'm the maid of honor."

"Not anytime soon," Yasmin corrected, shaking her head.

"Not yet?" Ismenia leaned forward eagerly. "Fine. When are you moving in? Are you staying in your apartment or Orlando's?"

Yasmin smiled and looked at Orlando, tilting her head slightly, gesturing for him to reply.

"Ismenia," Ani yelled from the kitchen.

"Not right now," Orlando replied as Ismenia stood up.

"Meaning?" Ismenia asked. She looked at Orlando and then at Yasmin, a puzzled expression on her face.

"Eventually," he replied casually.

"In the meantime?" Ismenia demanded.

"I'm calling you, Ismenia." Ani walked into the living room, took Ismenia by the hand, and led her into the kitchen. "Excuse us."

Yasmin laughed and watched them enter the kitchen. "Ismenia is very outspoken," Yasmin said.

Orlando chuckled. "She hasn't changed much since we first met."

"What were you going to answer?" she asked, hoping that would provide the rationale she sought.

"In the meantime, we enjoy being together and continue going out."

She frowned in response. He grinned. The reason would be clear to her that evening during the family discussion. Without knowing it, Carmen had provided the time and place for him to propose.

"All right, Mom," Ismenia clamored as she walked out of the kitchen and reseated herself across from them. "So you'll be dating for a while before settling in together," she commented with disapproval. "That's not what I expected, but if you're both happy with that decision, great."

"When are you getting the kids?" Yasmin changed the subject.

"Next week," Ismenia said. "I just wanted to remind you again that whenever you decide to get hitched, I'm the maid of honor."

Orlando nodded in agreement. "Point noted."

"You'll have to wait a while for that," Yasmin said. Orlando had not addressed the topic of marriage, engagement, or commitment, which confirmed that they would continue dating. She was disappointed. She had expected their relationship to solidify right away.

"I'm just making sure no one takes my place," Ismenia said.

"Want something to drink, Orlando?" Yasmin asked him.

He shook his head. Yasmin walked into the kitchen and stood next to Ani who was doing the dishes. "Why do you and Ismenia keep talking about making a wedding dress and being the maid of honor? Do you know something I don't?"

Ani ripped a paper towel off the roll, dried her hands, and faced her. "Yasmin, remember what I said. There's a right time and place for everything. Believe. God will complete what He started."

"I just thought . . ." She let the sentence hang. Eventually, she and Orlando would solidify their relationship. What she knew with certainty was that when he asked, whenever that was, there would be no hesitation and no need for extra time to decide. Her response would be swift.

Chapter 18

"Are you ready to face the family by my side?" Orlando asked, studying Yasmin's features as they entered the elevator. She appeared at ease, but he wanted her to voice any concerns or fears she might have. Embracing her, he waited for her response, prepared to remind her that the Lord worked in every situation they'd encountered and would continue to do so.

Tilting her head back, Yasmin smiled. His concern was unwarranted. As they left Ani's place, she anticipated feeling nervous and edgy. Instead, she felt serene. "We have the Lord's blessing along with Ani's and Mami's. That's what we needed," she sighed. "It would be wonderful if Raul and Isabel approved, but that's in the Lord's hands. Only He can touch their hearts."

Planting a kiss on her lips, Orlando led her down the hall. Her confidence and smile appeased him. He took it as a sign that as the Lord had done countless times, they would be surprised by the results of the evening.

Isabel opened the door. Orlando noticed how her eyes widened in awe as they entered. Yasmin muttered a greeting to her, Maria, and Luisa as she walked toward Carmen. The grimaces on their faces deepened as their gazes shifted from her face to Orlando's hand at her waist. Isabel mumbled an array of obscenities as Orlando stepped forward to embrace Carmen. If Yasmin overheard, it was not obvious in her mannerism or facial expression. Orlando was pleased that Isabel's, Maria's, and Luisa's animosity no longer distressed Yasmin.

"Remain where you are, Raul," Carmen ordered as she sat on the rocking chair. "Thank you for coming on time, Orlando. We were waiting for you to begin."

Orlando nodded, gazing at Raul. Sitting with his arms crossed, Raul eyed Orlando from head to toe, his eyes stopping at Orlando's hand on Yasmin's waist.

"Sit." Carmen pointed to the area designated for Orlando and Yasmin.

As they sat down, Orlando reached for Yasmin's hand and held it on his lap. Glancing around, he was impressed by Carmen's planning. She had strategically placed a chair on the right side of the rocking chair for Raul. To her left, she placed two chairs, one for Yasmin and one for him. They faced the sofa, where Maria, Isabel, and Luisa were huddled together, glaring at Yasmin and him with displeasure. Orlando smiled. If they were that upset just from seeing them together, he imagined they would be livid when he proposed.

Yasmin looked around casually. She could barely contain the glee she felt. It was evident that her mother had established a protocol of behavior for her arrival with Orlando. Otherwise, Isabel would have blasted her disapproval when they arrived. The Lord had given her victory.

"We're not going to argue," Carmen began, instituting the rules. "No shouting, no violence." She looked at Raul. "No gossiping. Whatever is discussed here doesn't go out that door." She faced Maria and Luisa.

Yasmin gazed at Orlando with lifted eyebrows and then faced Carmen. Her mother was defending her and making sure Luisa and Maria stopped spreading malicious lies. It was Yasmin's heart's desire. She felt overjoyed, overwhelmed with gratitude.

"I know all of you are concerned about my health," Carmen continued. "That is the least of my concerns when Orlando and Raul, who are like brothers, are now enemies. I still can't believe they fought one another. I'm glad I found out. It gives me the opportunity to stop it. There won't be another fight." She looked directly at Orlando and then at Raul. "Do I make myself clear?"

Orlando nodded and said "Yes" aloud.

"Raul?"

"I have nothing to say."

"Lack of communication is what's destroying our family and your friendship with Orlando," Carmen said.

"Wrong, Ma. Orlando's been defending Yasmin all these years because he was with her. He probably gave her the address of the funeral parlor and pretended someone else did."

"I told Yasmin that Roberto had passed away," Luisa admitted. "She acted like it was the first time she'd heard about it."

"I . . ." Yasmin started but Orlando waved his hand, silencing her. She complied calmly.

"That's right, Raul," Carmen said. "Like the rest of us, you've made assumptions based on your own ideas and not on what really happened."

"I didn't *assume* they were together. I found him in her apartment in the wee hours of the morning the night you were admitted to the hospital."

"Lower your voice. We can hear you clearly. Does that give you the right to judge them or to assume? No. I made the same mistake. I was convinced they were involved."

"Why so apologetic?" Raul demanded as if it were incomprehensible for her to take that stance. "Now you're going to defend them and act like what they did was acceptable, just like you did with the situation with Manuel."

"We're not going to discuss the past. Let's focus on the present, on what's happening now. Luisa kept mentioning that she saw Yasmin and Orlando together."

"I wasn't lying," Luisa interjected, defending herself.

"True," Carmen agreed, "but you have to be honest. You assumed, as I did, that something was going on. Your intent was to cause conflict. And you did. I would get upset, argue, accuse, and condemn Yasmin and Orlando."

Her face flushed, Luisa lowered her gaze.

"Is that the purpose of this meeting, Ma?" Raul interrupted, "to ask us to act like nothing happened? To accept their relationship?"

"Listen, Raul." She held up her hand to silence him. "You went to the apartment and found Orlando there. What does that prove?"

"That he sleeps over whenever he feels like it," Maria concluded.

Yasmin shook her head, frowning.

Orlando leaned closer and whispered in her ear. "Everything will be fine, Yaz. Remain calm. Let them clarify things among themselves." She nodded in response and smiled. Orlando was impressed with the way Carmen was handling the discussion. She was maintaining control and being clear and concise.

"Please, let us discuss this without interference," Carmen said to Maria directly.

"Why are we even here?" Maria asked.

"Are you being disrespectful to Ma?" Raul leaned forward.

Maria shrank back apprehensively. "Just asking."

"Is there a reason why we're here?" Luisa asked. "Whatever happened between Orlando and Raul and the issue with Yasmin has nothing to do with us."

"No, it doesn't," Carmen pointed out. "But I'm tired of the gossip, rumors, and misinterpretation you spread about all of us. I want you to hear our discussion and be part of it so there will be no more assumptions and so our family issues will remain private. That's why I will repeat what I said so it's clear to you. What we discuss here and now doesn't go outside that door." Luisa cleared her throat but made no comment. "We're all guilty of assuming. I include myself and everyone in this room except Orlando and Yasmin."

"I found Orlando in her apartment, just like Dad found Manuel with Yasmin," Raul pointed down the hall.

"Can we focus on the real issue? Your concern should be what Orlando's intentions are."

"Not interested in what he has to say. I already know."

"Yeah?" Carmen gestured to her ear. "Listen. Orlando?"

"I'm in love with Yasmin," Orlando declared.

"Like you've loved every female you've been with," Raul crooned.

"I've never felt this way before," he said, meeting Raul's heated glare.

"I'd put on a good act too. Fact is, Yasmin is worthless, and you're pretending you care. We both know that."

"Don't ever speak about . . ." Orlando began and then stopped when Carmen lifted her hand, signaling for him to be quiet.

"Never refer to your sister that way again, Raul," Carmen said. "The abusive language and name-calling stops now. That includes the three of you." She pointed to Maria, Luisa, and Isabel. "Understand?"

"That's what Yasmin is, even if I don't say it," Raul reproached.

"Is she?" Orlando leaned forward.

"You're defending her because she's with you."

"Wrong," Orlando corrected. "When you found me at her place, it was because we got into an argument. I refused to leave until she clarified some things."

296

"Which is why you were in your T-shirt, came out of her bedroom, and went into the bathroom?" Raul stood up.

"I knew it," Maria hissed.

Carmen stared directly at her in silence. Maria cleared her throat and leaned back.

"All this time I've been asking who you were involved with," Raul explained. "I've been telling you to enjoy the honeymoon phase, and you never admitted it was Yasmin."

Yasmin glanced at Orlando nervously. Placing his arms over her shoulders, he whispered. "Nothing is going to happen, Yaz."

"Sit down," Carmen demanded calmly and waited until Raul complied. "If you can't discuss this in a civilized manner, how can I expect you to have self-control? How can I be certain you won't fight with Orlando again over issues that don't concern you?"

"What?" Raul hollered, facing Carmen. "Anything any friend of mine does with my sisters concerns me."

"Yasmin is not a child. She is a woman. We have to accept that fact along with the decisions she makes."

"Yeah? I suppose we should have accepted the fact that she brought her boyfriend to the apartment. That was her decision too."

"Enough, Raul," Carmen ordered, exasperated. She placed her hand on her chest.

Orlando feared the emotional strain was too much. "Perhaps we should continue this conversation some other time."

"Please, Mami," Yasmin said, "I don't want you to end up in the hospital again."

"As if you care," Isabel commented.

"We're going to finish this conversation." Carmen lifted her hands and waved them repeatedly. She took a deep breath and was silent for a few minutes. "Remain seated, Raul. Control yourself. You don't have to agree. Just *listen*." She stressed the last word. "Isabel, Yasmin does care. She shows it through her actions, unlike you and Raul."

"Now she can do no wrong?" Raul put up his hand in frustration.

Carmen glared at him until he leaned back. "What I need most of all, Raul, is tranquility. I can't go on like this. It hurts me that you and Orlando aren't speaking to each other. He's like a son to me and a brother to you. I know if anyone tried to hurt him, you would defend him. Orlando would do the same for you." She paused as if thinking and then continued. "We've been mistreating Yasmin for a long time. It stops today. It's time to let go of the past, forgive, and move forward. We have to learn from our mistakes."

"The only reason I brought Orlando to meet the family was because I trusted him, and he . . ."

"He what?" Carmen interrupted. "Fell in love with your sister? I suppose life would be easy if we could control our hearts, if we could follow the ridiculous social rules imposed by society, friends, and family. But that's not reality."

"You don't understand, Ma. Orlando knows what I'm talking about and why I feel the way I do. He's doing to my sister," he punched his chest loudly, "what he's done to other women he's been with. And I have to accept it?"

"I won't deny that in the *past*," Orlando stressed the word, "I didn't take any female seriously. I respect, love, and want a serious relationship with Yasmin."

"I believe you," Carmen nodded. "I'd like Raul to explain why he's so convinced you're lying."

"I know him, Ma."

"Really?" she said. "I lived with your father many years. I had no idea he could be so coldhearted. He threw Yasmin out, spoke about her with hatred and offensive foul language, and refused to see her or speak to her. The only time she visited, he shoved her out the door as if they weren't related."

"There's no comparison, Ma."

"There is, Raul. You choose not to see it. Reality is hard to face. Admit it. We think we know people, but we don't."

"You're right," he agreed with disdain. "I thought I knew Orlando. I confided in him and allowed him to become part of our family."

"And he still is," Carmen affirmed. "All of us make mistakes and need to be forgiven. Do you think I thought you were capable of hitting Yasmin? You're her brother. Your role is to protect and care for her, not abuse her physically, insult her, and humiliate her."

Raul sighed aloud. "I didn't mean to hit her. It just happened."

"Like the fight with Orlando just happened?" Carmen asked. "You need to consider seriously the consequences of your actions. What if you had hurt Yasmin, if I had become seriously ill, or if your confrontation with Orlando had led to one of you getting hurt or arrested? What is it you want, Raul? What's your goal? To destroy our family and then regret it? Your father never considered that. Shouldn't you?"

Raul's shoulders slumped. He lowered his head. "I'm sorry, Ma."

"Being sorry solves nothing. It's mere words. Actions speak. You can't force others to do what you want, Raul. You can't impose your beliefs or make assumptions about how anyone will behave in any given situation. That applies to all of us. I trusted you. I believed you would take my feelings and my illness into consideration. I thought you would treat Yasmin as what she is—your sister."

Orlando noticed that Carmen's words struck everyone in the room. There was a long silence, a sense of regret mixed with sadness. Yasmin dried the tears that trailed down her cheeks. Orlando pressed her against him. She gazed up at him and forced a smile.

"I know you regret it, Raul," Carmen continued, "that you didn't mean to do it. What makes you think Yasmin didn't feel the same way about what happened with Manuel?" Carmen's tone was quiet and firm. "Think about that, Raul, and ask yourself if it's really so bad that Orlando and Yasmin love each other?"

Raul gazed at Orlando from the corner of his eye and then looked at Carmen.

"The question you should be asking is how serious this is." Carmen turned toward Orlando. "What are your intentions?"

It was the opportunity he had been waiting for. Orlando took out the gift box from the pocket of his shirt and knelt before Yasmin. Her eyes widened as he handed her the box. "Yasmin Arias, will you marry me?"

He ignored the surprised gasps of Luisa, Maria, and Isabel who stood up and gazed at him as if he were insane.

"When I told you that you'd get married when you found the right girl," Carmen said, delighted, "I had no idea Yasmin would be the one."

"Please!" Maria rolled her eyes.

"My God," Luisa uttered.

"Blind fool," Isabel sneered.

Focusing his attention on Yasmin, Orlando watched her open the box. She took out the ring and handed it to him to place on her finger.

"Yes. Yes. Yes!" He slipped the ring on her finger, and she wrapped her arms around his neck. He squeezed her tightly, released her, and turned to Carmen. "As we discussed this morning, Carmen, until recently there was nothing concrete between us," he explained, sitting next to Yasmin again. He placed his arm over her shoulder as she cuddled next to him. "Yasmin called me when Raul and Isabel took you to the hospital. She was agitated. I drove to the emergency room with her and spoke to Raul."

"You told me she called you," Raul admitted. "I didn't pay attention to what you said."

"Afterward, Yasmin and I went to her place to clarify the situation between us."

"If you weren't together, what were you resolving?" Raul demanded.

"I don't want to hear anything else," Maria said indignantly.

"I don't recall Ma saying this discussion is ended," Raul said, casting Maria a scowl.

"How can you take her seriously?" Isabel asked. "You don't care what she is?"

"Orlando won't listen, Isabel. Men like him prefer worthless women," Luisa commented.

"Those are the types of comments you will stop making," Carmen ordered in a stern tone. "You will stop making derogatory comments about my daughter."

Luisa placed her hands on her chest. "I have never . . ."

"You just did, and you always have," Raul corrected her. "Thanks to you, the neighborhood knows all our business, past and present."

"Add talking to Manuel about me," Yasmin blurted out, recalling her conversation with Carmen.

Orlando was stunned by her comment. Luisa had mentioned that Manuel was asking about Yasmin when he went to see Carmen. Orlando wondered how Yasmin had heard about that. "How do you know, Yaz?"

"I mentioned it," Carmen explained. "I wanted to know why he was looking for her."

"You knew?" Yasmin asked Orlando, a puzzled expression on her face. "Who told you?"

"Luisa," Orlando replied, gazing at her.

Raul stood up. "What are you talking about? What's going on?"

"Ask her," Orlando replied, gesturing toward Luisa. "You told Carmen, right, so she would tell Yasmin? Sneaky."

"That true?" Raul turned to Luisa. "What about Manuel?"

"I saw him at a party I catered. He asked me about Yasmin," she replied nervously. "That's all."

Raul turned to Yasmin. "What does he want?"

"Don't know, don't care," she shrugged.

"You believe that?" Raul asked Orlando.

"Yasmin has no reason to lie," Orlando replied.

Raul swung around and gazed at Luisa. "What did you talk about? Why did he ask about Yasmin?"

"He wanted to know how she was and if I had seen her."

"What information did you give him?" Raul demanded.

Orlando scrutinized Luisa's face. She spoke quickly and anxiously. Her face red, she looked guilty and embarrassed. Her reaction made him suspicious. He doubted she would admit or voice what she had discussed.

"What did you tell him?" Raul rephrased the question.

"Nothing," Luisa replied, her voice quivering. "I said Yasmin was fine, that I had seen her at her father's *rezos*. That's all."

Raul grunted aloud. "You'd better be careful what you say."

"First Orlando threatens me and now you?" Luisa was indignant.

Raul looked directly at Orlando. Their eyes met, and Orlando read the message in Raul's eyes. It confirmed his own suspicions. If Yasmin's ex was asking about her and looking for her, there was a reason. Not knowing his intent disturbed him. He shared Raul's misgivings.

"Some things don't change," Carmen said. "I don't like that look between you two." She gestured from Orlando to Raul. "We've had enough violence in this family. Manuel can ask about Yasmin all he wants. Maybe he's curious about how she is and knows that Luisa is in contact with us. Maybe he asked out of curiosity. Why are you acting like there's a problem?"

"I just want to make sure. I can ask him personally," Raul smiled mischievously. "You know his address, Luisa?"

"You're both exaggerating," Yasmin said, sharing Carmen's qualms. She noticed the exchanged looks between Orlando and Raul. It concerned her. She'd witnessed enough fights among her loved ones and couldn't fathom seeing another physical confrontation between Raul or Orlando with Manuel. Her mother was right; there had been enough violence. "Mami is right. Forget it."

"I trust no one," Raul gazed directly at Orlando. "No one."

"I have no idea where Manuel lives, and thank God I don't know Yasmin's address or how to contact her," Luisa announced as she stood up. "Time to go, Maria."

"Can you get Manuel's information for me?" Raul asked.

"I'm going to give you the same answer I gave Orlando when he asked. No."

Carmen turned simultaneously with Yasmin and stared directly at Orlando. All eyes were focused on him. Orlando faced Luisa as he spoke. "What I told you was that instead of bringing me messages, you should provide information that was worthwhile."

"What would you do with his address?" Yasmin demanded anxiously.

"Nothing," Carmen replied. "Raul will also do nothing. Forget about Manuel and the past. What he said or didn't say is irrelevant. Let's focus on what needs to be resolved here and now."

"I can cater your wedding, Yasmin," Luisa said as she walked over to Carmen. She tapped a kiss on her cheek. "Take care of yourself, and rest. I'll call you later this week."

"Catering their wedding?" Maria exclaimed. "You're joking?"

"No, thanks," Yasmin replied, appalled by the suggestion.

"If you change your mind, let me know," Luisa said. Maria following her out of the apartment.

Isabel locked the door behind them. "I'm going to my room."

"Sit down," Carmen told her. Isabel stopped, stood next to Raul, and rolled her eyes. "Let's finish our discussion."

"What now, Ma?" Raul asked, frustrated.

"I want to be certain you and Orlando are going to act like grown men."

"Men fight."

"Foolish men, Raul," she corrected. "Is this problem ended?"

"For me, nothing's changed," Orlando said. "We had a disagreement, but I still value our friendship and will continue to think of you as a brother, Raul. I apologize for . . ."

"You've nothing to regret, and there is no need to apologize," Carmen interrupted. "Raul?"

"It's over, Ma," Raul said. "I'm not going to pretend that what you did didn't bother me," he said to Orlando. "You betrayed me. I won't forget that. You're with Yasmin. Fine. But don't expect me to congratulate you. I'm stepping aside, Ma," and he turned toward Carmen. "I'm following your advice. I'm letting people do as they want without imposing my will or opinions on them. But don't expect me to participate in any activities that involve him and Yasmin. I'll visit when they're not here."

"How sad," Carmen's eyes filled with tears as she continued. "You're punishing yourself, Raul. You'll be miserable if you don't let go of all that anger and hostility and forgive."

Raul shrugged, walked over to Carmen, bent down, and kissed her on her forehead. "I'll be at my place. Call if you need anything, Ma."

"Fine," Carmen replied dryly.

"I won't be involved in anything they do, either. Can I go to my room?" Isabel asked, her eyes lingering on the engagement ring. The scowl on her face deepened.

"Go," Carmen gestured with her hand and watched Isabel hasten down the hall. "After everything that's happened, Raul and Isabel still refuse to change."

"Change isn't easy. It requires time," Orlando noted.

Carmen stood up, gave Orlando a kiss on the cheek, and said, "Always the right words."

Orlando laughed. Yasmin had made the same comment countless times. From the grin and the knowing expression in her eyes, he knew she was thinking it now.

"Thanks, Mami." Yasmin embraced Carmen.

"For what?" she asked, hugging her. "I did what I was supposed to do years ago." Taking Yasmin's hand, Carmen studied the ring. "It's beautiful, Orlando. Congratulations on your engagement. Orlando, would you mind if I plan a dinner to celebrate, even though your parents aren't here?"

"I'd rather you wait. Otherwise Yaz might become a widow before the wedding," he chuckled. "I'm calling Mom tonight to give her the good news. I'll ask when she can travel and then let you know."

"Any idea when you'll get married or what type of ceremony you'll have?"

"Yaz?" Orlando gestured toward her.

"When we decide, we'll tell you," she replied.

"In the meantime, I'll plan the menu and speak to Ani and Ismenia about the decorations," Carmen said, thrilled. "We'll set the date for the dinner after you speak with Eva."

* * *

"What's on your mind, Yaz?" Orlando asked. He had driven around the block several times looking for a parking spot. Finally, someone was leaving as he drove up. He parked a block from Ani's building, but instead of getting out, he faced Yasmin. Since they'd left Carmen's, he had noticed a serious expression. She had been quiet during the ride, preoccupied. His guess was that the comments about Manuel concerned her. "I want you to feel comfortable talking to me about anything that bothers you, no matter what it is."

She nodded and shifted slightly to face him. "I got the impression from the way you and Raul looked at each other that you might retaliate. Now that the issue between you and Raul is over, there's a problem with my ex?"

"We both feel the same way, Yaz," he replied casually. "We don't trust Luisa or her comments. Neither do you."

She nodded.

"Who knows what she told him or why she mentioned that he asked about you. Your safety is our concern."

"Raul cares about what happens to me?" she marveled.

Orlando laughed. "He loves you, Yaz. He might not show it the way you like, but why else would he get so offended because I'm with you?"

Yasmin shook her head. "He expects everyone to do as he says. He wants to control everything."

"I agree that he has some wrong ideas, that he's complicating his life by being so rigid, but the truth is, he's ensuring nobody takes advantage."

"Who ensures that he does what's best for Mami or anyone else in the family?" she asked. "Like Ani says, he needs lots of prayers, and I'm doing that, praying God will transform his heart. Getting back to what we were discussing, revenge is not for you or Raul."

"Do you feel Manuel is a threat? Does hearing that he is looking for you and wants to know about you and where you are frighten you? Worry you? Make you feel uncomfortable?" She hadn't expressed how she really felt, and he needed to ascertain if he should consider her ex a real threat or a trivial fact, as Carmen suggested.

"It makes me uncomfortable," she admitted, her gaze meeting his, "not because I'm afraid but because I'd rather he stay away. I don't want to see or speak to him ever."

"What would you do if he showed up, if you met him unexpectedly?"

She lowered her gaze and stared at the purse on her lap. For weeks after she'd run out of the apartment without his knowledge, she'd dreaded meeting him. Part of the reason she'd dropped out of school was that he picked her up and drove her home. She wanted to avoid seeing him.

"Yaz?" Orlando looked at her until their eyes met.

"At first I was afraid," she admitted, candidly. "Months later, when Ani demanded I go back to school or get a job, I had no choice. I worried I might see him, but I did what I had to do. As time passed, I forgot about it."

"That answers only part of my question," he pointed out.

"If we met, I would keep my distance. If he approached me, I would tell him we have nothing to talk about and demand he stay away and leave me alone."

"If you met by coincidence, if he called you, would you tell me?"

She hesitated before answering. "What would you do if I did?"

"The answer is yes or no."

"I know that, but I don't want . . ."

"I know what you don't want, Yaz. That's understandable, given everything you've been through. You need to trust me, to trust my judgment. That means confiding in me, right?"

She nodded. "Yes."

"To which question?"

Laughing, she crossed her arms and feigned being annoyed. "To both, Mr. Castillo."

"Okay, you did just agree to be Mrs. Castillo," he laughed. She leaned forward and kissed him on the lips. Embracing her, he kissed her again. "No need to worry, Yaz. Let's focus on our wedding."

"And allow the Lord to handle the situation with my ex, right?"

"Definitely," Orlando replied firmly. He would pray for guidance. It bothered him that Manuel was seeking information or trying to contact her, but there was no reason to assume he had ill intentions. His main concern and focus was on getting married and starting a new life with Yasmin. "You're right, Yaz. Please accept my apology."

She nodded, held up her hand, and admired the ring. "Can't wait to show it to Ani and Ismenia."

The sparkle in her eyes returned. She sounded excited and eager to share her joy. Orlando felt the same way. It was a mistake to allow her ex or her past to taint their happiness.

* * *

"I'm so happy for you. Who would have thought you'd end up getting married before me?" Ismenia laughed.

"I'm still in shock," Yasmin admitted.

Orlando's proposal had been unexpected. Yasmin finally understood Ismenia and Ani's comments. Her engagement, which was made official before everyone in the family, filled her with awe, respect, admiration, and appreciation for Orlando. The Lord had united her with a man who loved and cherished her. She had no idea such bliss, joy, or peace existed. She couldn't resist repeating "Thank you, Lord" again and again. The words felt insufficient and did not really convey all the gratitude she felt.

"I never imagined my own mother would solve the situation between Orlando and Raul or that she would bless our union," Yasmin marveled. "It seemed as if she was totally against it."

"That's how the Lord works," Ani said. "It's all about believing, Ismenia."

"I might," she shrugged, "one day."

"And you'll find out as I did that He won't fail you. All I wanted was reconciliation with Orlando. I thought we would move in together, that it would take years for him to consider marriage. I was shocked when he knelt in front of me and proposed with everyone watching us."

"God blesses us with so much more than we expect or think we deserve. I told you that Orlando was a man of character," Ani said. She handed Yasmin a glass of juice and then sat on a dining room chair opposite her and Ismenia. "Few men are so detailed and romantic."

"He thinks of every detail, no matter how small," Yasmin said.

"One thing is for sure. Orlando adores you," Ismenia said. "Where is the future groom?"

"He said he had an errand to do after work and will pick me up after. We're dropping by his sister's and then going to a restaurant to celebrate."

"Why are you staying here until you get married?" Ismenia asked with a disapproving tone. "Now that you're engaged, what's wrong with moving in together?"

"Orlando is against it. He said we're doing things *the correct way*," Yasmin mimicked his serious tone. "I agreed."

"That doesn't make sense. What's this nonsense about the 'correct way'?"

"Orlando loves and respects Yasmin and is willing to wait until she's his wife to live with her," Ani explained with admiration. "It's commendable."

"Its old-fashioned," Ismenia corrected sourly, "and unnecessary."

"Not for me or Orlando," Yasmin stated.

"Both of you have been around Mom too long. Forget what everyone else says. Live your lives! Enjoy it."

"That's how you choose to live, Ismenia," Ani pointed out. "Orlando is a man who recognizes the value of marriage. He is also aware that when you're doing God's will, marriage comes first."

"All right," Ismenia lifted her arms in defeat. "Three against one. No sense fighting a battle I'm sure to lose. Congratulations." She hugged Yasmin affectionately. "You deserve to be happy. I always knew Orlando was the one."

Yasmin nodded. "We haven't spoken about where we'll live, but since he has a co-op, that's where we'll probably stay." A thought occurred to her. "Want to move into my place, Ismenia?"

"No." Ismenia shook her head. "Ramona is moving permanently to Santo Domingo. Nestor wants us to stay there. It's a three-bedroom apartment. When she ships all her furniture, which will be soon, the kids will get their own rooms, and Nestor and I will have the apartment to ourselves. We're looking forward to that."

"Weren't you traveling this weekend to get the kids?"

"Something came up. Nestor postponed it until next week. Don't you dare plan anything before I return," Ismenia warned. "Remember, I'm the maid of honor. What are your wedding plans?" Ismenia asked.

"Orlando wants to have a civil ceremony. When we spoke late last night, he told me Eva is coming to New York in three or four weeks. She needs to take care of some things before traveling. Once she gives us the arrival day, we'll decide when we'll go to City Hall."

"That's why you're not moving in. You're getting married right away." Ismenia was thrilled. "No church ceremony?"

"Not right now." Yasmin was happy they were getting married right away and was looking forward to their new life.

"You should have both," Ani suggested. "Take your time planning it."

"I agree with Mom," Ismenia nodded, grinning. "I'm sure Maria and Luisa will be thrilled."

"They were outraged." Yasmin realized how astute her mother had been. Carmen had ensured they wouldn't spread lies and innuendos. She forced them to reflect seriously on any comments they might make.

"Imagine how they would feel if they saw you walking down the aisle dressed in white?" Ismenia burst into laughter.

"I'm not saying you should have both ceremonies to spite Maria and Luisa," Ani clarified. "They're unimportant. Your wedding is to celebrate your union and love, to allow the Lord to bless the two hearts He united."

"You're right, Ani." She and Orlando had not discussed having a church ceremony.

"Do it," Ismenia urged. "Make sure the first invitations are for Luisa and Maria."

"Don't listen to her," Ani said. "The Lord doesn't want us to repay those who harm us in the same way. You need to forgive and pray for them."

"I will," Yasmin promised, deciding to be obedient. "And although it makes me sad that Raul refuses to participate, now we can visit Mami anytime. Most important, she'll be at my wedding. Did she call you, Ani?"

"We spoke this morning," Ani smiled. "There will be a dinner with just family and close friends to celebrate your engagement. It's a great idea. We'll plan the menu and decorations and set a date when Eva arrives."

"In your father's absence, Raul should give you away," Ismenia said.

"Orlando asked Mario to be the best man," Yasmin said.

"Good for him. Raul is stubborn and obnoxious. He'll never change."

"Leave it to the Lord," Ani said. "All that anger, resentment, and criticism are unnecessary, Ismenia. They don't affect Raul, but they destroy you. You've been with Nestor five years now. Forgive, and move on."

"There's nothing to let go," Ismenia said defensively.

"Sometimes we still care for someone and don't realize it."

Yasmin and Ismenia looked at each other and then faced Ani.

"Why are you surprised?" Ani seemed amused by their reaction. "I knew Ismenia and Raul were in a relationship before she rushed to move in with Nestor."

"How did you find out, Ani?" Yasmin asked, though Ismenia appeared not to care that Ani knew.

"She was going out all the time and coming home late." Ani spoke directly to Ismenia and then glanced at Yasmin. "I left work early one day and followed her. I saw them together."

"That's why you imposed that ridiculous curfew and wanted me to stay home all the time," Ismenia grinned. "I sneaked out to see him."

"Unfortunately, I was working many hours and didn't have time to enforce my curfew. You took advantage of that. Yasmin did too."

Yasmin felt her cheeks redden. "At least I had a good reason."

"Did you?" Ismenia scoffed. "Hiding from Manuel? Does Orlando realize the change he's caused in you?"

"The Lord brought Orlando into Yasmin's life and united them," Ani declared. "He answered my prayers." She lifted her arms up. "Hallelujah."

"I will plan a church wedding," Yasmin said. "I want the Lord to bless our union."

"Amen," Ani said happily. "As for you," she pointed to Ismenia, "I hope you know that some things from the past can't be put aside that easily. You think I haven't noticed that Ismael looks just like Raul?"

Ismenia's face became white as paper, and her eyes widened.

"I never said a word," Yasmin defended herself.

"Isn't Ismael Raul's middle name?" Ani asked.

"Raul Ismael Arias," Yasmin said. "Ismael was our grandfather's name."

"He's *my* son," Ismenia said.

"Does Nestor know?" Ani asked.

Ismenia picked up her cell phone from the table. "Nestor?" She listened and responded. "I'll be right down." Taking her purse, she stood up. "Ismael is mine. Nestor is his father."

"Remember that eventually the truth will become known," Ani commented as Ismenia kissed her cheek.

"Wow! Raul has a son," Yasmin marveled as Ismenia exited the apartment. "I doubt he'd make a good father."

"Our words can uplift or destroy. It's best not to be so critical, Yasmin. Continue to pray for Raul."

"Thanks, Ani," Yasmin said. "Whenever I stray from His path, you guide me back with your wise words and advice."

Ani took a deep breath. "You weren't the only one with a secret, Yasmin. Yours has been brought to light. Ismenia's remains in the dark."

* * *

"Let's talk." Raul swept past Orlando into the apartment and stopped near the table and waited.

"Beer?" Orlando asked, following Raul into the living room.

"Not a social visit," Raul grumbled. "Let's get this over with."

"You called me," Orlando reminded him. Raul had contacted him that morning and insisted they meet. They agreed to meet at Orlando's place. Orlando wanted to change from his office attire into something more casual before picking up Yasmin, dropping by Clara's, and then going to the restaurant.

Although initially Orlando thought meeting with Raul wouldn't alter his agenda for the evening, it did. Clara insisted on preparing dinner, and he had to cancel the reservations he'd made at the restaurant. He hoped Yasmin wouldn't mind the change.

"What's so urgent?" Orlando asked. It had been one day since the gathering with Carmen.

"Why is Manuel looking for Yasmin?" Raul asked.

"I don't know what his intentions are, but I have my theories."

"Based on what?"

Orlando studied Raul's demeanor. His detached stance was that of an acquaintance. "Want to know the truth?"

"What is that supposed to mean?" Raul demanded, tilting his face slightly and glaring at Orlando from the corner of his eye.

"There's what really happened," Orlando said, debating how much he should reveal, "and what you want to hear."

"Now that you're with my sister, you know more than I do. Do you feel good rubbing that in my face?"

"You know me better than that."

"As Ma said, you think you know somebody, but you don't."

"Appearances can deceive." Orlando looked directly at Raul. "You can't rely solely on vision to make conclusions about certain situations."

A smirk formed on Raul's lips. "I made the wrong *conclusion*," he said the word slowly to emphasize it, "when I found you at Yasmin's place."

Orlando nodded. "Roberto did too when he walked in on her and her ex."

Raul's eyes shone dangerously. "Your point is?"

"Whatever Roberto saw, Yasmin was not a willing participant." He noticed how Raul curled his hands into fists.

"She's lying," Raul stated with certainty.

"For what purpose? To convince who?" Orlando asked. "That's why I asked if you wanted to know the truth. Obviously not. There's nothing more to discuss." He pointed toward the door.

Raul remained where he was. "I'm going to pretend what you're saying is true. If that's what happened, why would Manuel be looking for her?"

"Because he was dumb enough to believe she'd stay after his attempt. He expected her to live with him at his mother's place, even though he was married and had a kid. Yasmin heard them arguing, her ex demanding that his mother allow her to stay. She sneaked out during their shouting match and went to Ani's."

"You trust Yasmin and believe all the lies she tells you?"

"I'm not trying to convince you. I don't really care if you believe it or not." Orlando intended on keeping his promise to Yasmin. He would allow the Lord to handle any conflict that arose about her ex. He knew that Raul sought vengeance and was there seeking information, trying to confirm if there was anything he hadn't mentioned the night before so Yasmin and Carmen weren't aware of his intentions.

"I'll find out for myself why he's looking for her. You'd better make sure nothing happens to Yasmin, or you'll answer to me personally."

Orlando smiled. "The Lord will protect her, me, us."

"Now you're religious?" Raul laughed hysterically. "Okay, Mr. Righteous. Going to church all the time, Bible in hand, praying and pretending to be holy—a God-fearing fool," Raul sneered. "Let's see how long your act lasts."

"Prepare yourself to wait indefinitely. I have no shame in admitting the Lord is the center of my life, of my marriage with Yaz, and of everything I do. He's changed me."

Raul laughed rumbustiously.

Orlando waited for him to quiet down. He was undisturbed by Raul's contempt, disbelief, and sarcastic mirth.

"Right," Raul said, grinning, "all your sins forgiven. The dirt you did forgotten. I pretended I accepted the Lord," he said, "that I was religious. I started attending church just to get with some girl. It was a waste of time. You'll feel the same way soon."

Orlando shrugged. "I don't want to be rude, but I have plans with my fiancée."

"You're lucky Ma intervened," Raul said, eyeing him up and down with antipathy. Turning abruptly, he rushed out, slamming the door shut.

Epilogue

"I would have gladly brought you here on our wedding day if we had planned it ahead of time." Taking the key out of the ignition, he reached for her hand and squeezed it gently.

Yasmin smiled, "It was a last-minute thought, totally irrational. It would have ruined our agenda for the day."

"Had you mentioned it before, we could have gone to City Hall early and gone to the cemetery after the ceremony." He regretted not complying with her wish, but it had been unrealistic and impromptu. "On a Friday afternoon, we would have been stuck in traffic going and returning."

"I agree," she said. "We're here now. That's what's important. It seems traffic is always an issue. It's Saturday, and it took almost two hours to get here." They had left the apartment at 9:00 that morning and headed toward the George Washington Bridge to New Jersey. Cars were lined up and moving like snails. It was almost 11:00, and they had just arrived. She expected traffic to be lighter on the weekend. "We made the right decision."

"You looked too beautiful to be sitting in a car for hours instead of being in my arms." He winked at her.

She'd looked exquisite in the long satin gown with a crisscrossed bodice, V-neck, and off-the-shoulder silhouette. It was flattering to her slim, hourglass figure. She wore her hair loose as he preferred. The teardrop diamond necklace and earring set Orlando had purchased as a wedding gift sparkled as brightly as her eyes. Carmen, Ani, and Eva had insisted he couldn't see the bride until the ceremony began. He agreed reluctantly and waited in the lobby until the judge called them to initiate the ceremony. Orlando was mesmerized when Yasmin entered the room and approached him with Mario. She looked sophisticated and elegant. During the ceremony and throughout the celebration, he admired her as she flowed about in her gown with a radiant smile.

"I would have gladly brought you here the day after the ceremony, but I had made reservations for the weekend," Orlando told her.

"Our honeymoon," she said, grinning. She anticipated a night in a luxurious hotel in downtown Manhattan. Instead, they went to a couples resort in the Poconos. The honeymoon suite had a pool, a heart-shaped bed, and a whirlpool. A champagne bottle with two wine glasses, a box of chocolates, and a bouquet of red roses decorated the night table. That was an added perk to the enthralling décor. Bedspread, curtains, furniture, towels, bathrobes—all matched in red and white with Mr. and Mrs. monograms. Her smile widened. That was Orlando, her husband, a meticulous planner. His attention to detail continued to astonish her.

They had breakfast in bed both mornings. Shortly after waking up, a cart was placed by the door. A soft knock indicated that their meal was ready. Orlando rolled the cart into the room, and their day began. There were plenty of activities if they chose to leave the room, including horseback riding, miniature golf, nature hikes, basketball, a game room, and more. In the evening, they dressed up to join the other couples for dinner and entertainment. There was live music, comedians, and singers cooing love songs.

"That was just a weekend getaway, Yaz. When we can take a week off for vacation, we'll go on our honeymoon."

"That's what we just had," she insisted, certain he was already planning their next escapade. "Our wedding was spectacular. Ani did a superb job with my dress." She had felt like a princess. Orlando rarely left her side, and when he did, she felt his loving gaze follow her. "The ceremony, celebration, and cake—all were just the way I wanted them." The Lord had blessed her beyond expectations. The thrill and immense happiness of her wedding day still lingered. "Mami, Ani, and Eva did a fabulous job with the decorations and food."

"If they'd allowed me to order from the restaurant instead of working so hard, they could have enjoyed celebrating without all the fuss," Orlando said. "They spent days planning and preparing the food, and then they had to set up everything, serve, and clean up afterward."

"They loved every minute of it," Yasmin said. The three of them beamed with happiness and pride as they scurried about making sure everything was exquisite. "Mami doesn't like eating out, and Ani doesn't mind going to a restaurant on occasion, but she prefers to cook. Eva vetoed your idea, along with Mami and Ani, so I got the impression she prefers home cooking too."

Orlando nodded. "The food was delicious. They outdid themselves," he marveled, recalling the huge buffet with an array of cuisine and desserts in addition to the wedding cake. The scrumptious feast reminded him of Christmas and New Year's Day. Leftovers were still packed in their fridge a week later, and he doubted they could finish them all before they spoiled. Orlando wished they would have listened to him, worked less, and enjoyed the festivities more. Orlando decided that for their church ceremony, a wedding planner might be a good idea. "They cooked for an army, and it was just family."

"That's always the case," Yasmin said. "Mami always says it's best to cook more just in case someone visits."

"Mom says the same thing," he laughed. He exited the car and walked around to open her door. "This was the first place we came together."

Yasmin stood and slipped on her coat. "It seems like an eternity, though it's just been months," she marveled, aware of how the Lord had transformed her life in such a short time. "I never imagined we'd return as husband and wife."

Orlando embraced her. She tilted her head back and looked up at him. "I watched you stand near the edge of the grave and feared you might jump in."

"I slipped," she assured him, "and suddenly I was in your arms." She laughed, recalling her erratic thoughts. "I worried that with my horrid reputation you'd think I was leading you on."

"Yaz," he shook his head, frowning. "Thank God that mentality changed. All I wanted to do was comfort you and ease your pain."

"Now I know," Yasmin said. "Although it seemed as if we wouldn't overcome all the obstacles and would end up apart, here we are." She hugged him tightly. "It's hard to believe this is where it all began. Dad's death brought us together."

"No, this is where it continued."

She moved back and gazed up at him.

"It started when Roberto walked into the bedroom that day," he said, "and stopped your ex from hurting you." He chose his words carefully and studied her face to make sure she wasn't upset that he'd reminded her of the horrid experience. She was smiling. Her face lit up with joy as it had since their wedding day.

"I never thought about it that way." She rested her head on his shoulder again. Orlando's perception of what occurred made her aware that she focused on the dark side of the situation. She'd never considered her father's arrival as a blessing or a sign that the Lord was protecting her. Her tears changed to joy. The Lord used Orlando to pull her out of the dark pit in which she was trapped. God forgave her despite her failures, loved her despite all her flaws and doubts, and blessed her with a companion who loved, respected, and nurtured her. As if that wasn't enough, the Lord provided a new life where she could have joy, peace, and tranquility.

"Don't forget the flowers." Orlando took the posy bouquet from the back seat of the car and handed it to her.

She examined it. The bouquet was round with white roses and adorned with white pearls and glitter. The arrangement had been in a vase with water all week. She feared the flowers would shrivel or get dry, but they looked fresh, just as they had on their wedding day. Even that small blessing wasn't overlooked.

Orlando placed his arm over her shoulder, and they walked to the plot. Kneeling before the grave, Yasmin placed the bouquet on the dirt.

"A gift from my wedding," she spoke aloud. "Thank you for showing up when you did, Dad." She cleared her throat and blinked. "I love you. I forgave myself, and I forgive you. All the anger, resentment, fear, and pain are all gone. I'm finally . . . at peace."

She took a handkerchief from Orlando and felt him gently squeeze her shoulder.

"I wish you could have been at my wedding," she said through tears.

"Yaz?" Orlando studied her face as she stood. Tears were rolling down her cheeks. "Are you all right?"

"I'm fine." She smiled and gazed at the grave. "Dad, I want to tell you that I'm married. You know my husband. He's Orlando, Raul's best friend."

She touched the white roses on the bouquet with the tips of her fingers and imagined herself standing next to Orlando before the judge during the ceremony, her father beside her, smiling. She felt an indescribable sense of peace. The vision filled her with joy.

She gazed up at Orlando. "It's incredible. We're here—married."

"The Lord united us." Orlando combed her hair back gently. "Our union, our marriage, was the path He chose for us."

Yasmin laughed, placed her arms around his neck, and kissed him.

"Ready to go?" he asked. "We'll stop at the diner and get something to eat."

"That's where you started calling me Yaz."

Nodding, he winked at her.

"I'll have more than coffee this time," she promised. "I'm hungry."

"Glad to hear that."

As they walked away hand in hand, she glanced back at the grave. "We'll come back to visit you another day. I love you, Dad."

Acknowledgments

A special acknowledgment to my nephew Javier James Cruz who worked diligently with me on this venture when we revisited the never-ending story after it was on pause for several years. We had such fun! We put a lot of energy and enthusiasm into this labor of love. This version went through many changes. Living in and with Christ requires a new mindset, a different way to live, and a new view of the world. Thanks for all your support, suggestions, and ideas that contributed to what is now a final product. I'm deeply grateful that you were part of this wonderful venture. I love you and acknowledge you. Thanks.

I would also like to acknowledge and give a special thanks to Kenia Andujar, Yassiel Santos, and Julissa Imbert for previewing the book.

Special Thanks

I'd like to thank my husband, Pedro; my sons, George and Jose; and my daughter, Yesenia, for their encouragement, love, and high regard that my dream would become a reality. All the hours, years, perseverance, and dedication to accomplish this dream led to this moment. To my grandkids, Georgy, Allen, Aleina, Jazmine, Christian, and Brandon; and to my great-granddaughters, Leah and Riley, may you be inspired by this accomplishment and realize that you can also achieve your dreams. God's promise for all of us is in Matthew 19:26: "Jesus looked at them and said, 'With man this is impossible, but with God all things are possible.'"

To the rest of the family, "the never-ending story" has come to its completion. Hallelujah! Glory to the Lord.

It is with gratitude, great admiration, and esteem that I give thanks to . . .

My pastors Cynthia Solis and Mayra Baez whose spiritual leadership provides wisdom, discernment, and guidance to the women's network of our church.

Margarita Bautista and Kenia Amparo for their loyalty, support, devotion, guidance, and prayers in leading and supervising our women's life group.

My partners Rosanna Cabral and Mercedes Martinez who are leaders with me in our weakly women's life group. Also to Ivelisse Ulerio and Melania Garcia. Our friendship and bond have been a blessing as we serve our heavenly Father to extend His kingdom.

Dorothea Martiz, Zenia Rodriguez, and Carmen Lopez for sharing my joy over this victory the Lord granted me. Special, special thanks to Dorothea for allowing the Lord and the Holy Spirit to guide her, me—us—in the selection of the cover.

The Intercession Team of our church. The Lord asks us to pray incessantly, and that's precisely what we do. Pray, pray, pray for everything—including my book!

Thanks to *all* of you for your prayers that the Lord take control, oversee, and lead the publishing process of this book that was written to glorify Him. Thanks for sharing this victory with me, for sharing the exhilaration and joy of an accomplished dream. Thanks for sharing with me "the word" the Lord put in your hearts—His vision, purpose, and plans for this book.

About the Author

Rosanna Almonte worked more than 30 years in education, teaching in early childhood and elementary schools and serving as a staff developer and coach. She is now retired and loves writing, music, and travel. She is a member of a Christian church where she is actively involved in a women's network, the Intercession Team, and as a co-leader of a women's life group. She was born in the Dominican Republic and lives with her family in New York City.

You can contact Rosanna at divineheartdesires@gmail.com or through her website www.divineheartdesires.com.